The moment was here. Ha    Jacey mingled her blood with Hannah's and then looked at Glory, who bit at her bottom lip and stuck her bleeding finger out to them. Standing hand over hand, the sisters looked in turn around their circle. Then, Jacey and Glory settled on Hannah to say the words.

Taking a deep breath, and feeling the weighty presence of her murdered parents in the room, perhaps with their hands atop those of their daughters, Hannah spoke. "We, the Lawless women, swear by this blood oath that we will avenge the deaths of J. C. and Catherine Lawless. And Peter Anglin. We swear we will seek out those who are guilty, no matter where they might be, no matter how long it may take. We swear we will not rest until the guilty ones are dead, and our parents' and Old Pete's spirits are avenged and they may finally rest in peace. We swear it. And so be it."

Jacey and Glory echoed Hannah's words. "We swear it. And so be it."

# Hannah's Promise

## CHERYL ANNE PORTER

St. Martin's Paperbacks

HANNAH'S PROMISE

Copyright © 1997 by Cheryl Anne Porter.

ISBN: 0-312-96170-7

Printed in the United States of America

St. Martin's Paperbacks edition/May 1997

St. Martin's Paperbacks are published by St. Martin's Press, 175 Fifth Avenue, New York, NY 10010.

10  9  8  7  6  5  4  3  2

The *Lawless Women* trilogy is dedicated to the memory of Jimmie H. Deal, Sr., my beloved father who passed away on December 24, 1995.

# PROLOGUE

———

*Something's wrong.* Dread gripped Hannah, jerking her out of her dozing reverie. Her heart tom-tomming like a war drum, she straightened up on the buckboard seat and clutched at her woolen shawl. She looked over at Jacey. "Did you say something?"

"No. Why?" Threading the team's reins through her fingers, Jacey spared her a black-eyed glance.

"I thought I heard or felt—Never mind." Frowning, Hannah turned to the wagon's second seat. Their heads together, Glory and Biddy gossiped and giggled. Facing forward again, still spooked, Hannah searched the low hills that stretched to the horizon. No raised dust to warn of riders. No birds suddenly taking wing. Just the prairie's silence. Just the yellowing buffalo grass, the occasional scrub oak, and the bright reds and deep purples of September's wildflowers.

Everything looked normal, even the lowering sun's pink and yellow rays. But the feeling persisted, increasing Hannah's anxiousness. She turned again to her younger sister and clutched her coat sleeve. "Jacey, stop the team. Something's wrong."

Jacey frowned at Hannah as she pulled her arm free. "What's wrong? Are you sick?"

Hannah shook her head. "I'm fine. It's not me. It's . . . home."

From under her old slouch hat, Jacey eyed Hannah. "Home? How do you know? We've been gone overnight."

"Please, Jacey. Don't get stubborn on me now. Just rein the team in so I can look around."

The roans continued their plodding pace while Jacey stared at Hannah as if she'd just grown a second nose. "I mean it, Jacey. Stop them *now*. Or I will."

Jacey grimaced as she began hauling back on the reins. "Fine. I'll stop 'em." Her abrupt motions startled the horses into a sidestepping dance. Their grunts lifted in the air, mingling with the startled squawks and cries coming from Glory and Biddy.

From behind Hannah came Glory's angry words. "Jacey, you came near to throwing me and Biddy to the floorboards. What's gotten into you?"

Jacey spun to face the youngest Lawless sister. "Hannah's the one with a burr up her skirt, so ask her. She says something's wrong—"

"What's this, Hannah? What in thunder could be wrong?" Biddy Jensen fussed. She looked like a plump old settin' hen as she pursed her lips and resettled the ruffled feathers of her clothing.

"That's what I aim to find out," Hannah told her, standing to peer into the dusky distance. A mocking breeze pulled and tugged at her skirt. But she focused on the next rise, to the just-visible roof of their ranch home. She needed to see more. "Jacey, move the team up some. Just enough so I can see the house."

Fussing under her breath, Jacey nevertheless obeyed. She called out to the horses, slapping the reins against their rumps. The team jumped forward with a lurching motion and then stopped just as jarringly.

Hannah pitched back onto the hard seat, clutched at its edges, and shot Jacey a look. "I swear, Jacey Catherine Lawless, if you're not every bit as contrary as Papa, then I don't know who is." With that, she stood again and studied what should have been a welcoming sight. But wasn't somehow.

Smoke came out of the chimney. Wind ruffled the leaves on the black willow next to the house. But not one living thing moved about. The calm, deathlike quiet was exactly what was wrong. A shuddering shiver slipped over Hannah's skin, making her clutch at her fringed shawl.

Then, a sense of urgency seized her. They should hightail it for the house. Overriding her rash inclinations were Papa's words, his careful training of his three daughters. Hannah fancied she could hear him now, preaching caution. Don't rush into danger. Put your nose to the wind, like a coyote or a prairie dog. Heed your instincts—that's why the Almighty gave them to you.

Doing just that, Hannah made a slow sweep of the property. Then, her gaze riveted on the one detail that screamed trouble. A knee-weakening flush lanced through Hannah. No light shone from inside. Mama always lit the kerosene lamps the minute the shadows got long. She hated the dark.

A hand gripped Hannah's shoulder, spooking her into crying out and jerking around. Glory shrank back and clutched at Biddy's ample arm. Relief mingled with exasperation in Hannah's voice. "Glory, you scared the life out of me."

A pout only enhanced Glory's china-doll beauty. "Well, that's what you get for your talk of something being wrong. Everything looks fine from here. Why, the place just looks empty because Smiley and the men aren't back from taking the cattle to Kansas."

Hannah tried to keep the nagging fear out of her voice. Glory might be nineteen, four years younger than herself, but she was still the baby. "You're probably right. But I don't see Old Pete or his animals. Do you? And there're no lights on inside the house."

Frowning now, Glory stood up. "No lights? Mama hates the dark." She peered into the distance. Then she turned to Hannah, speaking as if just saying the words would make them true. "Old Pete probably did his chores early and went to the bunkhouse. And maybe Mama and Papa are visiting the Jessups."

"When they knew we'd be home this evening?"

Biddy made an abrupt noise to capture Hannah's attention. The expression on her plump, lined face held a warning. "Now, have a care, lest you frighten the young'un further. 'Tis all quiet b'cause 'tis suppertime."

"I hope you're right, Biddy. But just to be sure, I'll go in first."

"No, Hannah." Glory put her fingers to her mouth, as if she meant to bite her fingernails. "We've just been gone the one night. What could go wrong between yesterday and today?"

Now Jacey stood up and faced Glory. "Mama has babied

you to death. Look around you, Glory. We live in No Man's Land. You see any towns full of civilized folk? Hell, no. Just us, the prairie, and all the Indians you'd ever want to face right over that ridge. And if that ain't enough, every two-bit gunman alive wants to make his reputation by shooting Papa. You—a daughter of J. C. Lawless—have to ask what could go wrong?''

When Glory sucked in a ragged breath and abruptly sat down, Biddy turned faded-blue, pleading eyes on Jacey and Hannah. ''Do you see the fuss you're stirrin'? Like as not, you'll have us all squawlin' like Miz Hatfield's baby.''

Jacey stiffened. ''The day I set to bawlin' like a calf for its mama's teat is the day I hang up my guns.''

In the ensuing silence, Hannah looked from one to the other of the solemn women. If they hadn't been scared before, they were now. Even Jacey was, for all her blustering. But the time for caution was past. Hannah stooped to reach for the Winchester under the seat. ''Wait here.''

Jacey's hand on her arm stopped her as she turned to step over the side of the wagon. Hannah looked back questioningly, noting the set of Jacey's jaw. ''If one goes, we all go.''

She pried Jacey's hand off her arm. ''If I go in on foot and alone, I won't make as much noise as the wagon or be as big a target. You wait here. I'll wave to you if everything's fine. But if you hear shooting, come running.''

Glory and Biddy set up an instant protest, but Jacey waved them to silence. Putting her hands to her waist, she faced Hannah. ''Like hell we're waiting here. If one goes, we all go. And *those* are Papa's words. We stick together. That's the Lawless way.''

Hannah took a silent poll of her family. Their solemn nods affirmed their agreement with Jacey. Relieved more than she'd admit, Hannah resettled herself on the wood seat and molded her hands around the Winchester she balanced on her lap. ''All right. We'll all go.''

Hannah wished they hadn't come at all. Not to the bloody, nightmarish sight that began inside the ranch gates and continued into the ranch house itself, where Papa's body slumped over Mama's in the great room. Hearing again the hoarse cries that had torn from her and her sisters' and Biddy's throats at the sight, Hannah wished they could've stayed at Cora Nettleson's place, laughing and celebrating her engagement forever and ever.

Looking down at herself, she saw the blood that stained her skirt. Mama's blood. Papa's blood. Standing on the verandah, she wrapped an arm around one of the overhanging roof's support posts. Laying her cheek against the rough wood, ignoring its splintery feel, she stared blankly at the moonlit wagon yard in front of the house.

Only when her other hand fisted, closing around the charred wisp of stationery that she'd pulled from the fireplace, did she rouse herself. Willing herself to be strong, Hannah stepped back from the post and positioned herself in the moon's light. She looked again at the fragile scrap. She hadn't been wrong. The embossed letterhead was definitely that of the Wilton-Humeses. Mama's family. She fought past her anguish and forced herself to face the one inescapable question that begged an answer. It pounded at her, forcing her hand to her temple.

Why, after all the years of no correspondence between her mother and her family, would Wilton-Humes stationery show up today? And who was Slade Garrett? The man's name, scrawled at the paper's edge, was all that remained of its text. Obviously, he was in cahoots with Mama's family. Hannah would bet the ranch that they hadn't fired the actual bullets, but they sure as shooting were capable of pulling the strings all the way from Boston.

Hannah fingered the stationery as she recalled Mama telling her daughters how she met Papa. He was an outlaw. She was a debutante, making her grand tour of the West with a friend and her family. In Tucson, Papa and his gang kidnapped her for ransom. But she and Papa fell in love and married. Papa even sent the ransom money back. His gang was fit to be tied, but Mama's family was outraged that she married an outlaw. So, the Wilton-Humeses disowned her, declaring her dead to them.

And now she really was dead, along with Papa. On the same day Wilton-Humes writing paper showed up in their house. This was no coincidence. Hannah's heart throbbed painfully as her father's outlaw blood battled with her mother's gentle spirit. Papa said you've got your proof, go after the guilty ones. But Mama said not to rush to judgment, no matter the seeming evidence. Hannah nodded, as if she could really hear her parents talking to her. She would find the truth, she vowed. And then? The guilty ones would pay.

With that promise driving her, Hannah decided to keep the paper's existence a secret for now. Later, when emotions weren't so raw, she'd reveal her evidence. She looked at it again, hating it as she did the Wilton-Humeses. *They're guilty, all right.* Her emotion curled her features into a snarl. *And they'll pay, Mama, Papa. I swear it to you.*

Glory's sudden keening cry jerked Hannah around to face the front door. Strangely unaffected, she listened a moment, hearing Biddy offering comfort. Hannah turned to face the yard. Numb with grief, chilled by the night's crisp air, she stood there, staring into the darkness. Then, without warning, a silent wail tore through her. *Oh, Mama, Papa—why?* Her chin quivered as anguish crashed over her in a hot wave. She put a hand over her mouth. *No, please, God, no more tears. Help me to be strong.*

Hannah stood rigidly still . . . and waited, waited for God to hear her prayer. And to answer it. Within moments, she realized that the rigidity was indeed leaving her. In its place was a warm calm. Hannah straightened up, feeling the heavy mantle of responsibility settle on her shoulders. Not for her the luxury of forgetting or of running away. She was the oldest Lawless daughter. And she would be strong. For her sisters. For her parents' memories.

Accepting that, Hannah catalogued what she knew of tonight's foul deeds. Mama and Papa and Old Pete and his animals were cut down without mercy or warning. She also knew that the murders had occurred right before she, her sisters, and Biddy arrived home this evening. Because there was a fire still glowing in the grate. But where were the murderers now? Were they out there watching her, and waiting?

Jerking in fear, Hannah spun this way and that. But no shadows separated themselves from the night to threaten her. And Hannah reasoned why. Had the murderers wanted to kill her and her sisters, they would have waited for them to come home. It was that simple. That bloodcurdling.

With aching weariness robbing her of emotion, Hannah turned again to the front door. She couldn't put it off any longer. She had to go back inside. To the blood. *Blood splat-*

*tered everywhere. Mama's and Papa's.* She swallowed convulsively, swiping angrily at her gathering tears. Crying wouldn't bring Mama and Papa or Old Pete and his animals back. And neither would vengeance. But the stark emotion grew in her heart, hardening her.

Something soft inside her died. Something hard took seed in its place and grew with each passing moment. It exploded through Hannah, transforming her. Until finally, it was an avenging angel who took a deep breath and turned back to go inside. The murderers would pay. It was a promise to herself, her parents, and to her sisters. And she'd see to it as soon as she buried her dead.

A week later, the last wagon rolled off Lawless land following the burial of J. C. and Catherine Lawless and Peter Anglin late in the afternoon of September 21, 1873. Inside the ranch house, Hannah awaited her sisters in the formal keeping room. Mama's favorite place. It was Hannah's too, what with its delicate furniture and tasseled lamps and lacy curtains.

She fancied she could see Mama in here. This was where she'd run her family and had seen to the girls' educations. When she wasn't instructing them in their studies or their piano lessons, she'd help them practice the gentle arts of being a lady. Many mock-formal teas had taken place in this room, many exaggerated curtsies, many pretend fancy-dress balls.

"We're here now. What is it you wanted, Hannah?"

Hannah jerked around at the sound of Jacey's voice. She hadn't even heard their footsteps. Jacey and Glory filed into the room. They sat down next to each other on the pink brocade circular sofa. At twenty-one and nineteen, only two and four years younger than herself, today they seemed more like lost children than the young women they were.

Hannah's gaze rested first on Jacey. Looking at her was to see Papa. Even her name was a play on his—Jacey for J.C. But tonight, above the high collar of her jet-adorned blouse, Jacey's fine-boned face looked ladylike, for once. But it was also ashen under her tan. Or maybe she appeared pale because her eyes and hair were as lustrously black as her outfit.

Hannah shifted her attention to Glory. She was dressed in black, too, but looked as delicate as a butterfly's wing, so petite, so beautiful, her dark brown hair shining in the smoky lamplight, seeming to turn from copper to auburn to chestnut with each motion of her head. Her grass-green eyes, normally startling in their brightness, tonight appeared almost opaque. As if her tears had washed away their vibrant color.

As for herself, Hannah imagined she must be a difficult sight for her sisters right now, since everyone always said she—

"You look just like Mama, Hannah. Especially there by her piano. You're tall and slender like her. And you carry yourself like her—like you're gliding instead of walking."

A fleeting smile was all Hannah could manage for Glory. She knew that her blue-green eyes and chocolate-brown hair, thick as molasses and curly like a pig's tail, made her Mama's spittin' image. And just might stop a guilty heart or two in Boston. Which was what she wanted to tell her sisters. She was leaving.

But how to tell them? Since finding their parents murdered, they hadn't let her out of their sight. Hannah took a deep breath. She couldn't waffle with her decision now. So, putting her hand in her satiny skirt's pocket, she fingered the charred scrap of stationery. Days ago, hoping to preserve it somewhat against her touch, she'd wrapped it in a lace hanky and tied a ribbon around it. She pulled it out now, unwrapping her hand-iwork and laying it open in her palm as she would a rose's petals.

"Well, here you girls are. I should've known." Glory and Jacey jerked around, and Hannah looked up. Biddy filled the open doorway. "What's that you have there, Hannah?"

Hannah motioned her inside. "Come in. You need to hear this, too."

"Hear what, child? I'd think most things can wait until to-morrow, today being what it is." Still, Biddy Jensen entered the room and took a seat on an upholstered wing chair. She reached over to solemnly pat Jacey's and Glory's hands in turn. Then, all three turned their attention back to Hannah.

"I suppose the only way to do this is just to say it." She held up her secret. "I have a piece of evidence that points to the people responsible for Mama's and Papa's . . . deaths."

A moment of silence followed Hannah's words. She looked from one to the other of her sisters and Biddy. Then, as if they were of one mind, all three sprang to their feet and gathered around Hannah, exclaiming and questioning as they peered down at the bit of lace in her palm. "What is it, Hannah?" Jacey finally asked for them all.

Hannah held it up. "A scrap of Wilton-Humes letterhead. With a name on it. It'd been thrown into the fireplace, but it didn't completely burn."

Now Glory chimed in. "Wilton-Humes? I don't understand. Why would there be—?" The answer came to her, contorting her face in horror. "Oh, it's too awful to even think it. Mama's *family*?" She put a hand to her mouth and stared at Hannah.

The following silence was so deep that Hannah fancied she could hear her own blood rushing through her veins. Looking from one to the other of them, she said the words. "You know what I have to do, don't you?"

"Do? What d'ya mean 'do,' child? Yer just a girl. Nothin' more." With gray wisps of hair sticking out around her face at odd angles, and with her cherubic face drained of all color, Biddy frowned up at Hannah.

But it was Jacey who answered. "We're women now, Biddy. Lawless women." She stared levelly at Hannah. "We'll do what Papa would do, if he were here. We'll go to Boston. And we'll kill Mama's filthy family."

Biddy's response was to stare pop-eyed and then wilt into a faint. Glory shrieked and ran to aid their nanny, who'd fallen harmlessly back onto the wing chair behind her. But Hannah, rooted to the spot, stared at her other sister. Jacey was as hotheaded as Papa'd ever been. "Jacey, there's no 'we' to it. You're staying here with Glory and Biddy. I'm the oldest. It's my responsibility to set things right."

Just as Hannah knew she would, Jacey stiffened and glared out her challenge. "Like hell it is. I'm going, too, Hannah."

Here it was. The first challenge to her being the Lawless in charge. "No, Jacey. You're staying here with Glory and Biddy." When Jacey's bottom lip poked out in defiance, Hannah rushed on. "I need you here, Jacey. Look at them." She pointed to Biddy and Glory and gave Jacey time to absorb the helpless scene they presented. When Jacey looked again at Hannah, her chin was quivering. Hannah spoke more gently to her sister. "Honey, you're the best shot on the spread and the bravest one here. Please. I can't fight you and worry about them and try to . . . set things right all at the same time."

Jacey stared in that hard, direct way of hers. But then her shoulders slumped. "All right, Hannah. We'll do this your way. But before Biddy comes to, we need to make a blood oath."

Hannah flinched. Jacey was giving in, but not without a test. She knew how her sisters hated this ritual, how they recoiled from Jacey's insistence on formalizing every promise between themselves. But if this was what it took, then so be it. Hannah rose to the challenge. "Glory, leave Biddy be a moment and come here." When Glory joined them, Hannah held a hand out to Jacey. "Give me your knife."

Glory moaned, but Jacey didn't hesitate. She matter-of-factly lifted her skirt, exposing the Cherokee beadwork sheath fastened like a garter around her thigh. She pulled out a thin-bladed knife with a bone handle and handed it to Hannah. Something in her sister's black eyes told Hannah that Jacey had just ceded authority for the family over to her.

Taking the knife, Hannah held Jacey's gaze. "Blood oath." She then pricked her finger and handed the knife back to her sister. Grimacing, Hannah pushed on the wounded pad with her thumb, forcing the red bead to a thin flow.

Jacey swiftly nicked herself and held the knife out to Glory. When she hesitated, Jacey fairly hissed at her. "Do it—now. Are you a Lawless or not?"

Watching Glory swipe at her tears, Hannah felt sorry for her baby sister. Jacey always intimidated her into doing things she didn't want to do. But this time, she was on Jacey's side. She held her bleeding finger and glanced back at Biddy, whose eyelids were fluttering. "Hurry, Glory. It's just a prick. If Biddy wakes up and sees this, we'll be burying her next."

Glory took the knife, but she handled it as if it were a hot poker. She bravely stuck her own finger out and gave a yelp when she pricked it. With wide green eyes, she watched her own blood flow. She didn't even blink. Not even when Jacey snatched the knife back from her and, with one-handed, practiced motions, resheathed it under her skirt.

The moment was here. Hannah held her hand out. Jacey mingled her blood with Hannah's and then looked at Glory, who bit at her bottom lip and stuck her bleeding finger out to them. Standing hand over hand, the sisters looked in turn around their circle. Then, Jacey and Glory settled on Hannah to say the words.

Taking a deep breath, and feeling the weighty presence of her murdered parents in the room, perhaps with their hands atop those of their daughters, Hannah spoke. "We, the Lawless women, swear by this blood oath that we will avenge the deaths of J. C. and Catherine Lawless. And Peter Anglin. We swear we will seek out those who are guilty, no matter where they may be, no matter how long it may take. We swear we will not rest until the guilty ones are dead, and our parents' and Old Pete's spirits are avenged and they may finally rest in peace. We swear it. And so be it."

Jacey and Glory echoed Hannah's words. "We swear it. And so be it."

# CHAPTER ONE

---

Hannah's resolve faltered. Not even Mama's stories about the size and bustle of Boston could have prepared her for the reality of the seaport town. Wide-eyed and rumpled from her countless days and nights of traveling, she stood on the covered depot platform, amid the jumbled fortress of her trunks and bags, trying to decide her next move.

All around her, pushing, hurrying people swirled and eddied, each one intent on his own particular business. As if caught in a whirlpool, Hannah steadied herself by leaning against a wooden post. The last time she'd seen this many bodies so packed together and agitated, they were cattle wearing the Lawless brand. And they'd been in a desperate stampede to a gully running with water. Now, *that* she knew how to handle.

With anxious knots kneading her stomach, Hannah threaded her gaze through the human stewpot, seeking the forest of tall buildings beyond the platform's edge. She'd never seen the like, not even in the cities which had passed as blurs outside her compartment window. Assaulted now on all sides by Boston's up-close, jarring noises and noxious smells, she knew a moment of real terror. How far did civilization stretch? And how would she ever find Cloister Point, the Wilton-Humes estate, in this jumble?

Stretching out in all directions were narrow, twisting streets, each of them jammed with traffic, foot and carriage. Rough wagons driven by shouting tradesmen vied with fancy carriages and omnibuses for space. Boys hawked newspapers. Women clutched at children's hands and hurried them along.

A fishmonger sang out, touting the day's catch. Weary travelers hugged loved ones. And heightened Hannah's awareness of how alone she was.

Talk of vengeance and of blood oaths seemed well and good when in the bosom of her family. But here—on a dark, early-October afternoon as a cold, gray rain began suddenly to slant down? Her self-imposed mission now seemed ill-conceived, if not downright dangerous.

Hannah pushed away from the post to squeeze her coin purse. She eyed the train she'd just deboarded. Not thirty feet away, it hunkered, snorting and steaming like a bull pawing the ground. She swallowed hard, thinking of her sum of money. She had more than enough for a ticket home. She could say she couldn't find the Wilton-Humeses. Or she could say she'd confronted them and found they weren't guilty.

A tiny voice in her head wailed in protest. She could also say, it accused, that her father's outlaw blood did not flow in her veins. That her mother's fierce love for her girls meant nothing. That the murderers could live out their days unpunished. That her blood oath with her sisters meant nothing.

Her conscience's mocking words of cowardice shamed Hannah. And then steeled her spine. She focused on thoughts of Jacey and Glory having to shoulder responsibility for the ranch in her absence. Hannah shook her head. No, she wouldn't let them down. She, unlike them, was surrounded by civilized folks, thousands of miles away from where the murders had occurred.

She was also close to the unsuspecting Wilton-Humeses. Who were probably dry and warm, all nestled in at the family estate at this very moment. Narrowing her eyes, giving herself over to the jolt of courage that raced her blood through her veins, Hannah vowed anew that she'd find them, that she'd—

Someone tapped her on the shoulder. "May I be of some assistance?"

Hannah jerked around, her gloved hands flying to her chest, as if seeking reassurance that her heart still beat. The handsome, well-dressed man doffing his hat to her loomed bigger than some of the hills back home. Tall herself, she didn't usually have to look up to meet a man's gaze. But it was either that or talk to the silken scarf knotted at his throat.

"You startled me." Hannah frowned up at him. And realized she couldn't look away from his dark eyes.

Set in a clean-shaven face of wide mouth and hawkish nose, those piercing black eyes twinkled down at her. His smile intensified Hannah's feelings of awkwardness. "I apologize. I simply meant to offer you my protection."

"Your protection?" Like a shadow, belated wariness stole over her, reminding her of her particular circumstance—a young woman alone in a strange city. She took his measure in one sweeping glance. Broad and powerful. Moneyed and self-assured. Used to giving orders and having them carried out. "Why would you do that for the likes of me?"

A black-winged eyebrow beneath his gray top hat arched. "I suspect I'll soon be asking myself that very same question. But you have only to look around you to see your danger."

No one had to tell her of danger. She was looking at it. Hannah blinked, trying her hardest to turn away from his compelling eyes. She felt trapped. He was fascinating. *Like a snake,* a sudden intuition warned.

Jarred by that image, she backed up, wrenching her gaze from his to focus on individual faces in the crowd. Some ferret-faced creatures immediately looked away and melted into the crowd when she sighted on them. A glaze of fear thumped her heart. The gentleman was right. She had attracted the attention of the sort who pounced on weak or unwary prey.

She faced the man in front of her. He appeared straightforward and open, but did she dare trust his offer of protection? To her, his fancy clothes and manners were no guarantees of honorable intentions, despite his words. "You should know I have a gun."

His burst of laughter startled her. "Perhaps I should inform you that I have one, also."

Hannah reflexively cut her gaze down to his hip, where out West a gunbelt would be strapped. But his chesterfield overcoat hid any telltale sign of a weapon.

"Do you see anything down there to your liking?"

When his meaning soaked in, Hannah drew herself up to her full height, which put the top of her head at his chin, and met his bold stare. She pretended she couldn't feel the hot flush on her otherwise cold cheeks, and dismissed him. "I thank you for your concern, mister, but I can make my own way."

A slow grin stole over his mouth, revealing white, even teeth. "Just as I feared. There's no one coming to meet you, is there?"

Heart-fluttering male or not, just who did this Jasper think he was? "I got myself this far. I think I can go a few more miles without getting myself killed."

Apparently—judging by his fit of chuckling—every word that came out of her mouth tickled this tall Easterner. "I believe you. However, just to appease my gentleman's heart, may I see you safely to a cab and on your way? I'd never forgive myself if tomorrow's headline in the *Daily Advertiser* reported the discovery of your dead body in the harbor."

Hannah raised an eyebrow. "You don't believe in pulling any words, do you?"

"No. Especially not when it would be reported that you were last seen alive in *my* company." With that, he gestured over his shoulder, as if to signal someone to come to him. Hannah frowned, trying to peer around him. She hadn't realized he wasn't alone. Sure enough, he wasn't. Four burly men leached from the crowd and stepped forward. Dressed in first-quality but unobtrusive clothing, the big men eyed her dispassionately while silently awaiting their orders. "Take the lady's belongings to a reputable cab and then proceed on to Woodbridge Pond. I can handle this."

Before Hannah could protest, her trunks and bags were whisked away. In much the same manner, so was she when the tall stranger stepped up and took her elbow. Not used to being handled by any man, Hannah stopped just short of an overt flinch when his large, gloved hand closed over her arm. But his warm, steady pressure—not too tight—reassured her somewhat.

Wordlessly, he carried her along with him, his long-legged stride forcing her to skip along beside him, or risk being dragged. Hannah figured she was crazy for letting this stranger take her away from the safety of the crowded station. But would anyone help her if she balked? She doubted it, watching the way the folks who'd buffeted her only moments ago now parted for him. Most folks took one look their way, did a double take, and then moved aside. A few men doffed their hats and mumbled greetings, which he returned with only a nod of his head.

Hannah risked a quick glance up at her escort. "From the way these folks are acting, you must be the biggest toad in the puddle. But I don't believe I caught your name."

Without slowing, without looking away from the line of waiting cabs and omnibuses at the curb, he finally deigned to say, "You didn't catch my name because I didn't throw it."

His response lit the fuse on her Lawless temper. Hannah stopped in her tracks. "Look, mister, the way I see it, you've pushed yourself into my business. You've caused my belongings to be carried off. And I believe that's your hand on my elbow. Now, I'd say all that entitles me to the courtesy of an introduction."

His expression, as he listened to her, changed from displeasure to bemusement. It was a good thing for him that her mother had raised her to be a lady, or she'd have to kick his arrogant-Easterner shin. "What about me is so funny? Don't people hereabouts speak their minds?"

"Yes, *people hereabouts* speak their minds. But not to call me a big toad." Still, he released her elbow and stepped back, sketching a fancy bow in front of her. "Nevertheless, allow me to introduce myself. Mr. Slade Garrett, at your service and pleased to make your acquaintance."

His name staggered her, sent her reeling back a step. *Slade Garrett?* The very name on the charred scrap of letterhead! Helplessly she stared at him. She'd stepped off the train and right into the enemy's hands.

Either God was punishing her for seeking revenge, or the very devil himself was helping her enemies. Even though she hadn't known who he was when she boarded the train in Kansas, the newspapers she'd read along the way were glutted with this man's name. He was the recent heir to his father's railroad stock—a huge share of stock. A controlling share of stock. And she'd ridden here on his trains.

Shock and fear and hateful anger constricted Hannah's chest, making it impossible for her to drag air into her lungs. Clutching at her skirt, she realized, to her horror, that she was going to faint. For even now her vision darkened, narrowing tunnellike until it encompassed only Slade Garrett's handsome, dark, and now diabolical face.

Unable to move, her limbs like pudding, she watched as he sobered and straightened up, reaching for her. The last thing she heard was his voice. "Are you feeling ill, miss? You look pale. Here, let me—"

The matched bays' hooves clip-clopped over the cobbled streets. The steady patter of cold rain spiked against the elegant brougham's roof as it pulled away from the depot. Inside, and seated in an uncomfortable cramp, Slade Garrett glared down at the unconscious girl in his arms and draped across his thighs. Grimacing, he shifted her weight as best he could. What the deuce had he been thinking to even approach her? Now look at this turn of events.

Twitching his nose and mouth around an irritating frill on the girl's hat, Slade considered her green traveling costume. While stylish, it still announced her as not one of the first sort. Perhaps not even one of the second sort. His deprecating snort coalesced into a vaporish cloud. So now he was a Good Samaritan, rescuing lower-class girls. Totally unnecessary. The depot employed an adequate force to aid distressed or put-upon travelers. He'd seen to that detail himself.

So what was he doing here with her in his lap? He'd never done this sort of thing before. Well, what was he supposed to do when the girl fainted in his arms—leave her lying there in the pouring rain? He could already see tomorrow's headlines, had he done such a despicable thing. And all he'd meant to do was see her to a carriage and on her way, just as he'd said. Damn his momentary chivalric outburst!

His thoughts darkening his humor further, Slade again hefted her weight on his lap. And stopped short, his grip on her tightening with the realization that she was well padded in all the right places. And resting on him in all the right places. Feeling his male urges stir, Slade raked his gaze over her form again, this time with the heated awareness of a healthy male. And liked what he saw. Too bad she was too provincial and outspoken to be to his liking, because he—

*What the deuce?* Slade scowled at the carriage's opposite seat. *To his liking?* When he thought of a little country mouse in *those* terms, it was time to visit Francine at Madame Chenault's. How long had it been? His answer was a sharp, burning cramp down his arm. Grimacing, telling himself he deserved this, he angled the girl up some so he could work out the knot.

Confound it, how long before she'd come to her senses?

His conscience posed the same question of him. Slade returned his gaze to the girl and admitted what about her had caught his attention the moment he'd stepped out of the depot office. *Lust. Pure and simple.* No. Would that it were simple lust. But the truth was . . . the girl had captivated him as no woman ever had before. All he'd done was glance in her direction and then glance away. Only to have his attention dart right back to her.

But why? Why her? Holding her close now, he again concentrated on the warmth of her curves against his chest and lap. He stared into her face, right now so still and pale. It wasn't any one feature, not her high forehead, her rich, dark and curling hair, her pert nose, or very kissable mouth, or even the fetching combination of them all that intrigued him. But intrigued he was. Much too intrigued for his—or her—good. Slade shook his head in disgust. Boston's mothers were correct. Young ladies needed protection from him.

As if heeding his silent warning, his burden began to moan and flail about in his arms. When she cried out in waking confusion, Slade gladly slid her off his lap and sat her next to him on the narrow seat. He turned to face her, his hands on her arms, steadying her until she was fully awake.

But then his breath caught. Despite her disheveled clothing, her little black hat being askew atop her ruined chignon, and even with that blinking, unfocused expression on her face, she was in truth a most engaging woman. But, something more about her nagged at him. Something he couldn't quite—

A blinding flash tore through him, leaving him open-mouthed, as if words he couldn't form needed to be said. When he almost had it, could almost name it . . . just as suddenly, it was gone, leaving him reaching out to her on a level not physical. Frowning, Slade shook his head and drew back, staring at her.

She chose that moment to turn her head toward him. The dilated pupils of her otherwise light eyes made them appear almost black in the carriage's dim interior. "Where am I? What happened?"

"You went into a faint as we approached the cabs. Do you remember that?" Then, testing her awareness, he asked, "And do you perhaps remember your name?"

She stared blankly at him, then frowned to the point of

screwing up her features. Slade's eyebrows rose. Here came the tears. But instead, she closed her eyes and put a hand to her forehead, rubbing it tiredly. "Yes. It's Hannah."

A good, working-class name. It suited her clothing, but not her delicate bone structure and well-modulated voice, despite her quaint speech. More intrigued by the moment, Slade heard himself repeating—stupidly enough, in his own opinion— "Hannah. That's a nice name."

Ignoring him, she leaned her head back against the padded wall and closed her eyes. Slade watched her, taking in the curve of her cheek, the set of her slender jaw, and her swanlike neck. Such a feminine ideal. A sudden prick of awareness— not like the first one, but more a sense of having seen this very profile before—stabbed at him. But that was impossible. Because if he'd seen her before, he never would've forgotten her.

When she opened her eyes and lowered her head, she turned to him. And turned on him. "You're Slade Garrett."

She made of his name a filthy slur. Momentarily taken aback, Slade could only frown. At that moment, the brougham jounced heavily, its careening motion sending them into each other's arms. She clung reflexively to him for the barest second, but then pushed herself away. Every rigid line in her body shouted that his touch was repugnant to her.

Then, so be it. Slade crouched over to the opposite seat. Sitting with his shoulders firmly against the padded backing, his legs spread and his arms folded over his chest, he looked her up and down. Why had he thought her desirable? She was nothing more than a common girl. And an ungrateful one at that. Damning his earlier moment of male weakness that put him in her company, he spoke up. "You say my name with a lot of vinegar. Have I perhaps done you some great harm at one time or another?"

His words hung in the air between them, suspended by the brittle October air and her completely unexplainable look of hateful contempt. "That, sir, is something I intend to find out."

*Just who did this little country mouse think she was?* "Find out what? Ahh, I see. You think I took certain liberties. I thought about it, but I assure you, I did not. I take my pleasure from the willing. And the conscious."

Her eyes widened. She looked down in horror at her mussed bodice and her skirt twisted about her legs. Hastily setting herself to rights, she met his gaze with a naked but fleeting look of the purest vulnerability and injured innocence that he'd ever seen. It was gone within a second, replaced by an icy stare of insult taken.

Wondering if he'd imagined that first look, and feeling like a cad for purposely giving her the impression that she'd been mistreated, Slade nevertheless frowned right back at her. Only the brougham lurching to a stop broke the unwavering stare between them. With studied nonchalance, he turned to pull aside the leather curtain. They'd arrived at his brownstone.

He turned to Hannah. "You have no need for concern. Your purity is intact . . . I assume. And don't be alarmed, but we've arrived at my residence. Since you were in a faint, my choices were either to leave you at the depot or bring you here until you were able to continue on."

He paused, assessing her, wanting to rage at her for again looking so helpless, so injured. And for making him feel responsible. "I'm late for my afternoon appointment. A cab follows with your belongings. Perhaps I could hire the driver to take you on to . . . wherever it is you're going?"

"No, you've done enough. Probably too much." She gave another tug to her fitted bodice as if to underscore her meaning. "I can hire him myself." With that, she gathered up her handbag and scooted forward on the seat, preparatory to getting out.

Slade surprised himself by putting his hand over hers on the door's latch. "Wait." She eyed him in a questioning but direct way that Boston's finest young ladies never employed. Disconcerted, Slade realized he had no idea what he'd been about to say. He just knew that he didn't want her to leave. "Rigby will get the door."

Which he did at that exact moment, wrenching it open with a suddenness that flung the occupants together. The girl squawked and Slade cursed. Then he met her blue-green eyes, only inches from his. That shock of awareness coursed through him again. And she felt it, too. Why else did she draw in her breath and remain in his arms?

"Beg pardon, Mr. Garrett." Ribgy's shocked apology broke the moment. Slade pushed back, helping Hannah to regain her seat. Mustering a modicum of dignity, he turned to his open-mouthed young coachman and spoke in a voice laden with denial that anything was out of the ordinary. "Well, don't just stand there, Rigby. See the lady out."

"Yessir." The coachman, in a rain-soaked slicker and with a nose reddened from the cold, bobbed his head and held out his gloved hand to the lady. Slade watched her take Rigby's hand and begin her descent. As he helped her out, Rigby again turned to him. "Will the lady be staying on, sir?"

Before Slade could even blink, the lady took matters into her own hands. "No, Rigby. *The lady* will be on her way." Like a queen exiting her royal carriage, the country mouse named Hannah alit. Then, standing out in the slashing rain, she turned to peer back into the brougham. "Thank you for your help. I owe you that much."

Slade eyed her silently, feeling an inexplicable sense of loss steal over him. Still, he managed to keep all emotion off his face as he tipped his hat to her. "The pleasure was all mine . . . by all accounts."

*There it is. Cloister Point.* Filling Hannah's vision, the vast Wilton-Humes estate nestled on a point of land in a privileged, outlying area of Boston. Staring out the hired cab's window, she gathered her courage. The awful weather and foul traffic and rutted roads had all conspired to make of the journey a slogging, inching trek. But now, it was worth it. She supposed.

The white stone mansion, stately as a tall cake and big as a fort, sat back from the curving road and capped a low hillock. An iron fence girded the immaculate grounds. Barely taking a breath, refusing even to think, Hannah stared at her mother's childhood home until her vision blurred. She sniffed, reaching up to wipe away a tear. Inside were her grandparents. And they hated her because she was her father's child.

Defeated, she sat back from the window, slumping against the seat. Even though she no longer looked at the mansion, it burned in her vision as she stared straight ahead. The estate was beautiful, lavish even, but it struck her more as . . . indifferent in its very inaccessibility. She bit at her bottom lip. It wasn't too late. She could still turn around and leave.

Hearing herself, and cursing her nagging fears, Hannah sat up straighter and raised her chin. She would not, could not go back on her promise to Mama and Papa or on her blood oath with Jacey and Glory. No more waffling. In only a few moments, she would face her kin for the first time. And they would know the wrath of a Lawless.

The cabriolet rocked under her. Caught unawares, Hannah clutched at the seat. Then she relaxed, realizing the motion was no more than the driver climbing off his box. Sure enough, the door opened, and the coachman's bulbous-nosed face poked inside. Shoulders hunched against the wet cold, he informed her, "There don't appear to be no one about, miss. D'ya want me to go an' see before we get yer things down?"

With a sinking feeling, Hannah looked from him to the mansion, this time seeking particular details. Shuttered windows. No light shining from within. Had she come all this way for nothing? A flutter rippling through her belly, she refocused on the little man in front of her. "If you would, please."

He bobbed his head and closed the door. Just as suddenly, he opened it again. "And who shall I say is calling? These Brahmins don't take kindly to . . . visitors they ain't expect-in'."

Hannah locked gazes with the man. Clearly he didn't think she was worthy of gaining entrance through anything but the kitchen door. For the first time in her life, she uttered her middle name with a sense of using it to put someone in his place. "Tell them Miss Hannah . . . *Wilton* Lawless has arrived."

The driver's expression changed, became more deferential. He even dragged his cap off, leaving his balding head exposed to the elements. "*Wilton*"—he swallowed on the word— "Lawless? Sorry, miss. I'll be gone only a moment." With that, he swiped a hand over his wet scalp and quickly resettled his cap. One darting movement later, he rounded the cab and disappeared from sight.

Her heart thumping like a scared rabbit's, Hannah waited, her gloved hand holding back the leather curtain over the window. The coachman reappeared almost immediately as he padded up the curving drive and then rounded a corner of the mansion, obviously going to a side door. With nothing to do but wait, Hannah steeled herself with a review of her plan.

She had to admit, it wasn't much of one. Beyond getting

herself here and insinuating herself into the Wilton-Humeses' lives, she didn't have structured intentions. But she did know she couldn't blurt out her accusations and expect to get the truth. No, she would have to reside here, under false pretenses, in order to gather any evidence of their guilt or innocence.

And if they were responsible? What would she do then— go to the authorities? What could they do about two murders that occurred out in No Man's Land—a territory bounded by no law agency's jurisdiction? Would Boston officials investigate her accusations of Wilton-Humes treachery? She looked again at the mansion, and knew on whose side the law would fall—the Brahmins'. The coachman hadn't confused her with that term. She'd often heard her mother refer to her family as Brahmins, a term bordering on affectionate sarcasm that identified those members of Boston's highest social caste.

Seeing what and who she was up against, Hannah accepted that she would have no help in this town. She could not afford to trust anyone, and she would have to exact vengeance herself. But what form it would take, she had no idea. Could she kill someone in cold blood? She rubbed at her throat when the very idea constricted it. What had she gotten herself into?

Her attention quickened when she saw the coachman round the same corner again and, holding on to his cap, retrace his steps back to his cab. Gasping, out of breath, he told her, "Sorry . . . miss. Place is . . . locked up tight. I couldn't raise a . . . soul." His rapid exhalations puffed white in the cold air.

Hannah'd never considered that they simply wouldn't be home. What now? What if they had several homes? They could be anywhere. How could she find out? Who would know? A strong, mocking face with piercing black eyes popped into her head. Aha. He'd know. She had evidence of that in her handbag. The letterhead with his name on it.

But did she dare face him again? She'd escaped him once with him knowing only her first name, one common enough not to arouse undue suspicion. Could she be so lucky a second time? It occurred to her that he could quietly have her killed, and no one in Boston would be the wiser. An ugly picture of her body floating in Boston Harbor—his own words—assailed her overworked imagination.

"Beg pardon, miss, but it's a long drive back to Boston proper, and I've got a family to get home to. It's gettin' darker, and it ain't gettin' no drier, nor no warmer out here.''

Hannah's vision cleared as she focused on the poor man in front of her. He shifted his weight from one foot to the other. ''I'm sorry. But please, just another moment.'' Fraught with doubts, she kneaded the folds of her handbag, until her fingers traced the reassuring outline of her pistol. She suddenly wished she were back home, where Western justice was fast and simple. But she wasn't home. And she'd have to play the hand she was dealt.

Forced into a corner by circumstances, Hannah came out fighting. She would be bold. She would take chances. The moment was here to engage the enemy, to stride right into his camp. To show Slade Garrett what it meant to have Lawless blood flowing through one's veins. Hannah turned to the shivering driver. ''Take me back to Mr. Garrett's brownstone.''

# CHAPTER TWO

—

"Dudley Ames, does the current financial panic mean nothing to you? One look at this portfolio tells me that your years at Harvard were seriously misspent, my friend. Just as your dear mother feared." Enjoying an after-dinner cigar, a brandy, and his friend's company, all in the snug comfort of his study, Slade sorted through the sheaf of papers in his lap.

When a knock sounded on the closed door, he shot a sly grin at the senator's son seated across from him. "That must be Hammonds."

Dudley groaned, collapsing his large-boned body into his leather wing chair. "Not again, I beg you. Leave off with the man, Garrett. If dueling weren't outlawed, I believe your poor butler would call you out. Still, should he, I intend to offer him—and not you—my services as his second."

"You wound me mortally, my inconstant friend." He then bellowed out, "Yes? What is it?"

The door opened and in stepped Hammonds.

A bemused grin claimed Slade's mouth when his butler wrinkled his nose at the smoky air. Slade laid Dudley's papers aside, uncrossed his legs, and sat forward, flicking a long ash into a crystal vase not meant for such a purpose. Another groan issued from the red-haired Dudley.

But from the thin-nostriled servant came a sniff of censure. It never ceased to amuse Slade that Hammonds, in his employ for the five years since he'd inherited this brownstone, still behaved as if Slade were a callous, messy intrusion into the neat and orderly world of his own domestics.

"Well, Hammonds, what is it? Are you lonely for our company?'' He pretended to reach for a book. ''If so, allow me to read you a passage Mr. Ames and I found particularly amusing in Aldrich's *The Story of a Bad Boy.* I borrowed it from Jacko and Edgar.''

The very idea, him borrowing a children's book from his newly hired housekeeper's sons. But his words had the desired result, for Hammonds's face was turning a satisfying red. ''Perhaps later, sir. At the present, a . . . young lady at the door insists on seeing you. What shall I tell her?''

''A young lady?'' A wrench of emotion tore through Slade's chest, squelching his humor. No, it couldn't be her.

''How's that? A young lady? Here? Now?'' Dudley snapped to attention, his hands gripping the chair's arms. He furrowed his brow to match that of his frowning host. ''I'm not sure I can name a proper young lady in all of Boston who would be at your door at this hour. Or any hour—without her mama and several armed men in escort.''

''My thoughts exactly. So, this can only mean, my friend, that our luck has changed—and she's *not* a proper young lady.'' Slade snuffed out the cigar in the already maligned vase, rose to his feet, and swept his hand in a grand gesture at his butler. ''By all means, show her in, Hammonds.''

''Yes, Hammonds, by all means,'' Dudley seconded, rubbing his overly large hands together in glee.

Staring straight ahead, and pinching his features into alarming primness, Hammonds didn't move. He clearly had no intention of doing any such foolish thing.

First exchanging a pointed look with Dudley, Slade then exhaled loudly as he turned to his butler and crossed his arms over his white-shirted chest. ''All right, what's wrong with her?''

Hammonds cut his gaze over to his employer and then refocused on the portrait over the fireplace. Following suit, Slade and Dudley shifted their attention to the same painting. What was it about the long-dead Garrett ancestor pictured there, they often wondered aloud, that so captivated Hammonds? ''I'm sure there's nothing . . . wrong with her, sir. She's just not . . . uh, how shall I say it?''

Staring at his ancestor, just as Hammonds was, Slade asked the family likeness, ''One of us, you mean?''

"Quite, sir," Hammonds agreed with the man in the oil painting.

"But that's exactly what we're hoping." Slade headed for the room's open door, calling out to Dudley over his shoulder, "Will you excuse me?"

"Not on your life." Unabashed and eager, Dudley charged after him.

Knowing from long experience that he'd never dissuade his friend, Slade strode down the narrow hall. Dudley's booted steps marched in regimental cadence behind his. Past the darkened dining room and the parlor on their left, and then past the stairs on the right and into the tiled foyer.

There, sighting their quarry, they stopped short, staring. Slade ignored the soaring bird that was his heart and forced himself into an attitude of nonchalance. Putting his hands to his waist, he turned to eye Dudley, and then pivoted to his unlikely visitor—the bedraggled Not-one-of-us, surrounded by her various luggage. "Somehow, I just knew it."

The girl Slade knew only as Hannah held her dripping self erect with dignity. But the uncertain light in her eyes as she looked from him to Dudley and then back to him gave her away. "Knew what?"

Slade almost smiled at her tone of voice. She managed to make it seem that he was the interloper here. *Must have been coached by Hammonds.* "I knew it would be you."

When she didn't answer, he took the moment to note that her gloved hands were twisting her handbag's strings into knots. And that she was shaking all over. His abrupt manner in danger of dissolving, he resettled his attention on her face, waiting for her to explain her presence.

She again darted her gaze from him to Dudley to him. "I'm sorry. I'm intruding, I know. I wanted only to ask you some questions, but the coachman . . . he put me out." She bit at her bottom lip and frowned. "I shouldn't have come here." She jerked around, grabbing for the heavy doorknob.

Two long strides saw Slade beside her and stretching out his arm to hold the door closed. He looked down into her upturned face. Purplish smudges underlined her blue-green eyes. A red chafing, no doubt from exposure to the cold wind, claimed her nose and cheeks. Dark tendrils of hair hung limply from under her ruined bonnet.

"Stop pretending you have anywhere else to be. Because if you did, you wouldn't have come back here. And yet you did—which says a mouthful. And which makes you my problem . . . at least for tonight."

She stared up at him momentarily . . . and then burst into tears, covering her face with both hands. Slade went wide-eyed and made a helpless gesture at Dudley, who just as silently gestured back for him to take her in his arms. Slade frowned hugely, shaking his head. Dudley renewed his efforts, managing only to look like a redheaded dancing bear.

Slade quirked up his face in reluctance and looked back at Hannah. Her slender shoulders shook convulsively. Then cursing himself for a cad—wasn't the girl undone enough without him attacking her?—he muttered a curse and wrenched her into his arms. He glared at Dudley, to see if he was happy now. Dudley silently applauded. Slade mouthed an especially descriptive curse at his oldest friend. Dudley made tsk-tsking noises. He then pantomimed getting his hat and coat and exiting out the back door. Slade nodded.

Alone with her now, Slade concentrated on the cold, wet body pressed against his warm, dry self. Smelling her wet hair, breathing in cold rain and dark night, he took himself to task over this most unusual behavior of his. He wasn't in the habit of sheltering pathetic waifs who landed on his doorstep. He patted the girl's back awkwardly. Then, why this one?

A slight movement in the hallway caught his attention. "Ah, Hammonds, there you are. Have Mrs. Stanley open a bedroom and draw a bath. And see that the room is heated. Get her boys to move these trunks aside. Then have her put together a dinner tray." He looked down at Hannah and then back up at his man. "I believe the lady is staying."

Her hair pinned atop her head, Hannah sat in the first plumbed tub she'd ever seen. Such luxury. And it was in a private bath attached to the bedroom Mrs. Stanley'd shown her to. To Hannah's further wonderment, the entire brownstone was heated by a coal furnace and lit with gaslights. She'd never seen the like of such conveniences. She'd heard of these things, had read about them, but she'd never expected to experience them.

And especially not in Slade Garrett's home. She soaped her arm and then dragged the fragrant bar over her chest. She then leaned forward, waggling her bobbing breasts through the water to rinse them. Sitting up, she sluiced water over her shoulders as her unguarded thoughts wandered to the feel of Slade Garrett's arms around her. She hadn't liked the warm, solid feel of him, the bay rum scent of him. *Yes you did.* She plopped the soap into the water, sending a splash over the side. *No she didn't.*

Her glare crumpled. Yes she did. She covered her face with her dripping hands, gulping back a sick lump in her throat. *God help me.* To even think of the man like that was as good as a slap in the face to Mama's and Papa's memories. But as long as she was being harsh on herself, she admitted that at the depot and then downstairs, she'd felt something for him that she'd never felt before. She could forgive herself for what occurred at the depot because she hadn't known who he was. But now she knew. And the feeling was stronger.

Hannah straightened up, staring at the painted wall in front of her. Her hands curved over the rolled edges of the tub's sides. She had to get out of here. Just leave this house. She couldn't stay here—not even for one night. But then she slumped. Just as he'd pointed out, she had nowhere else to go.

Then, so be it. Giving in to this circumstance of her own making, and reaffirming that being here was part of her plan, she resolved that tonight was the only night she would stay. Tomorrow she would be stronger. She could locate her hated kin, or rent a room in a respectable boardinghouse until she did. A boardinghouse. Of course. Why hadn't she thought of that first, instead of racing here? *Because you wanted to see him again.*

No. Hannah abruptly stood up in the tub and pulled the plug out of the drain. She watched the soapy water sluice out in a rapid tide and then, when almost empty, in a noisy whirlpool down the thirsty drain. *Just like her brilliant plans.*

She quirked a grin at her own bungling thus far. Relieved that she could still laugh at herself, she reached for the thick towel on the washstand and vigorously dried herself. Then, laying the towel aside, she inched open the bathroom's door to peer into the bedroom. Her gaze swept the room, furnished in highly polished mahogany. Good. She was alone. Mrs. Stanley'd seemed surprised that she hadn't wanted her to stay to help with her toilette.

A chuckling snort escaped Hannah. She'd been doing for herself since she was a little thing. Yes, Biddy and Mama'd raised three young ladies, but she and her sisters were young ladies who could see to their own needs.

Feeling better for the memory, Hannah opened the door and skittered to the high bed, where her waiting bedgown lay. Spooking herself with the vision of the door bursting open to reveal Slade Garrett, she made a girlish noise and grabbed up the linen garment. Only to realize that she hadn't unpacked the one cloth bag she'd brought upstairs with her. Then, who had? She clutched the gown's familiar folds to her chest and stared blankly at the heavy draperies covering the window. Mrs. Stanley? Of course.

Thus reassured, Hannah pulled the gown over her head, grateful for its simple rounded neck, long sleeves, and feeling of security. Her nakedness now modestly covered, she eyed the high, narrow bed with yearning, wanting nothing more than to melt into it and sleep for an eternity. But Mrs. Stanley should knock at any moment with the promised supper tray.

Still, she couldn't resist. She reached out a hand to test the overstuffed mattress, giving it a firm downward press. A feather mattress, thick and soft. She gave in to a delicious shiver. A real bed. After endless nights of sleeping sitting up on the train, it would feel wonderful. That stopped her short, putting a frown on her face. She wasn't a welcome guest here. This house was the enemy camp. She must remain alert, for she was merely assuming her host didn't know her identity. But if he did, he could even now be loading a gun. Or could be right outside her door, readying to choke the life out of her—

A light knock sounded on the door, spinning Hannah around. Startled and fearful, she covered her mouth with both hands. For a long second, she stared at the door, as if it had snarled. Then, sanity returned. Such a silly girl she was. Envisioning the nice housekeeper on the other side, Hannah relaxed. To prove to herself that she was recovered, she moved her hands to her hair, unpinning the heavy curls as she called out, "Come in, Mrs. Stanley."

The door slowly opened, and the tray appeared first. Hannah quirked a bemused grin. The housekeeper was being awfully cautious. Then, just as Hannah released her hair to swing in a cascade down her back, the door fully opened, revealing not Mrs. Stanley at all, but Slade Garrett. Shock turned Hannah to stone.

Garrett stared at her for the longest time before clearing his throat. "I sent my housekeeper on to bed. She has her children to see to." He hefted the tray. "I brought your supper. You said earlier you had some questions to ask me. I thought . . . we can talk while you eat."

Rooted to the thick carpet under her bare feet, Hannah made not a sound. But her very soul screamed from her toenails to the roots of her hair. Questions? Talk? There was no doubt that her family name would come up. And all of a sudden, asking him how to find her kin here in Boston and if he'd had a hand in her parents' deaths, especially if he was in cahoots with Mama's family, was not something she wanted to explore over a meal in this house. Wondering how she could get out of this, she finally noticed that his expression had changed. Had the man never seen a woman in her bedgown?

Her bedgown? Lord above! With maidenly shock animating her, Hannah grabbed for the only thing she could find—the bed's counterpane. Desperately, she yanked and tugged on it, finally freeing enough of it to cover herself. By twisting around in it, she fashioned a cumbersome toga, the ends of which still graced the bed's sheets. Keeping her back to him, she clutched the coverlet to her bosom. "I thought you were Mrs. Stanley."

After another moment of silence, he remarked, "What with my wearing an apron and having my hair in a bun, we're often confused for one another."

A chuckling guffaw erupted from Hannah, which she promptly bit off. No good could come of warming up to this man. She forced herself to concentrate instead on her rather precarious situation. With fumbling fingers, she worked at covering more of herself. "Why are you lingering in here, Mr. Garrett? I appreciate your kindness, but anything I have to ask you can wait until I'm not in my unmentionables." She thought a moment about what she'd just said, and amended, "Of course, I mean when I'm fully clothed—not just *out* of my unmentionables."

There it was—that deep, masculine chuckle. Anger took hold of her heart and raised her voice. "Is it a particular habit of yours to see to the physical needs of unmarried young women in their bedchambers?''

"Every chance I get, my dear Hannah. Every chance I get.''

His twisting of her innocent words was shocking enough, but it was his accompanying bellow of laughter that finally spun her around. And spin she did, tangled as she was in her twisted toga. But that didn't disconcert her as much as did the sight of him nudging the door closed behind him with a booted foot.

He meant to kill her. Or worse. Her eyes widened more with each step he took farther into the room. She nearly fainted in relief when all he did was set the tray down on a low table by the bed. Then, lean, square hands to his trim waist, he turned to her, his black-eyed gaze raking over her, much as if she were on *his* supper tray. "That's quite a fetching costume you're wearing.''

Trying not to notice the prominent veins in his powerful forearms, or the light sprinkling of dark hair covering them, visible with his sleeves rolled up nearly to his elbows, Hannah raised her chin, determined to be as plucky as the moment called for. "A girl learns to make do with what's available.''

Eyebrows quirked in obvious amusement, he smiled like Satan. "And are you available, Hannah?''

Gasping in displeasure, Hannah took an outraged step backward, only to bounce her bottom against the stuffed mattress behind her. The buoyant recoil sent her staggering forward two coverlet-tangled steps. Right into his arms.

"I like your way of answering.'' He pulled her to him and smiled down into her eyes.

Hannah froze at the feel of his strong, warm hands claiming her arms. Her titillated senses besieged her with the clean, musky scent of full-grown male. With the faint aroma of cigar and brandy that coiled like an aura about him. With his full, parted lips only inches from hers, and slanting ever downward.

In a detached moment, Hannah realized she was straining toward him, parting her own lips. She recognized that she wanted nothing more than to press herself against the muscled length of him, to run her hands over the expanse of his chest, to feel Slade Garrett's kiss on her lips.

*Slade Garrett's kiss?* What was she doing? Shocked at her own behavior, but more terrified of her yearnings, she jerked her head sideways. His kiss lit on the point of her jaw, just under her ear. And staggered her. A cry escaped her, seeming only to have the effect of urging him on. His questing mouth, as it tasted of her neck and then her collarbone, sent shock wave after shock wave of desire rippling through her. In only moments, all would be lost.

Hannah dragged in a mind-clearing breath and twisted in Slade Garrett's arms. She loosed her grip on the counterpane, allowing it to sag between their close-pressed bodies, and pushed against his chest. ''No!''

She'd meant for the word to signal her intense displeasure, but it came out as a strangled cry that echoed in the otherwise tomblike quiet of the bedroom. But perhaps the emotional sob was just as well.

Because Garrett immediately stilled, and then straightened up, looking down at her as if he'd just realized what he was doing. ''My God, Hannah, I'm sorry.'' With that, he released her and stepped back.

The ends of the counterpane dropped like a weight to tangle around her ankles. Hannah clutched at the bed's steadying bulk beside her, all the while watching her enemy, whose kiss still dewed the skin of her neck. He held his hands up and out in a momentary gesture of helplessness, and then ran them through his longish hair. A black-winged cascade fell across his brow, only deepening his dark sensuality. Hannah dragged in a breath through her pinched nostrils, and stared numbly when he spoke.

''I'll see myself out. Despite what just happened here, you can sleep soundly. I'm not in the habit of forcing myself on my guests.'' Here, he paused, searching her face. Was he looking for forgiveness? He frowned away a look of confusion and turned on his heel.

Hannah watched him stalk to the door, unavoidably noting his broad shoulders under his white shirt, his muscled buttocks and long, tapering legs under the close fit of his dark brown pants. When he reached the closed door, he gripped the knob and turned back to face her. Hannah met his steady gaze. And knew what he would say before he ever uttered the words.

''Just who the hell *are* you?''

\*     \*     \*

Slade chuckled. She hadn't answered his question last night before ordering him out of her room. It didn't matter. He'd find her. This morning's long and dreary railroad board meeting had only delayed his searching her out by a few hours. Home now for his luncheon, he stood just inside the guest bedroom, empty now of the dark-haired woman who'd set his senses aflame.

*Dark-haired woman.* Slade relived the moment when, ladened with her tray, he'd come in here last night. The sight she made. Waist-length hair flowing loosely around her. Her white gown. The lamp backlighting her, showing him every curve beneath the thin fabric. He thought he could see her here now.

He wanted again to apologize for kissing her against her will. He wanted to apologize for his harsh words to her in front of Dudley. For letting her think he'd mishandled her during her faint. For startling her at the depot before that. For everything since the first moment he saw her. Slade ran a hand through his hair. What had gotten into him? His circle of friends, sworn bachelors all, would laugh at his besotted state. And they'd be within their rights, for here he stood, mooning over a female of no consequence. Ridiculous behavior. Then his heart thumped achingly. *Dammit. She's gone. Who is she? Where did she go?* Certainly, she'd made her point that she had no desire to be involved with him. Then, fine. So be it. He eyed the stripped bed, the only evidence she'd ever been here. A particularly harsh curse escaped Slade, echoing in the room's stillness. Hating this agony of loss, he turned to leave.

A bit of white under the bed stopped him. He stared at it with enough intensity to prove that force of will could not affect matter. For if it could, the thing would have scooted across the carpet to him. Apparently, Mrs. Stanley's cleaning had missed this. His curiosity piqued, and telling himself he wasn't hoping for some link that would help him find Hannah, Slade stalked to the bed and bent over, going down on one knee to reach under it.

His fingers closed over a lady's folded, ribbon-tied hanky. Which crinkled when he grasped it. Crinkled? Frowning at that, he stood up and lifted the delicate fabric to his nose, hoping to capture Hannah's scent. And thought he did. But her faint legend was overpowered by a subtle burned odor that made him pull back.

Intrigued now, and holding the fabric in his cupped palm as he would a baby bird, Slade untied the ribbon and lifted the carefully folded edges to lay bare the contents. He could only stare at what he saw. First his eyebrows shot up, but then they lowered when he frowned. Not able to make sense of what he was seeing, he muttered, "What the deuce?"

"Did you say something, Mr. Garrett?"

He looked up. Mrs. Stanley stood in the doorway, her arms full of folded linens. With his mind still working on what he held in his hand, Slade took a moment to refold the curious piece. He slipped it and the ribbon into his pocket. Then, he asked, in a deliberately offhand manner, "Did . . . the lady say where she was going?"

"No, sir." She then nodded, causing the thick bun atop her head to bobble. "Hammonds did as you asked, though. He requested she stay here until you came home. But Miss Lawless would have none of it."

The name struck him like lightning. "Did you say . . . Lawless?" *Lawless.* It hadn't been uttered by his family since his father cursed it one last time when he lay dying five years ago.

"Yes, sir. Your guest last night—Miss Lawless. Unusual name. Same as that outlaw out West. I used to be quite taken by his exploits when I was a girl. Such a romantic, dashing figure." Her voice breathless with curiosity, Mrs. Stanley wondered, "Could she be related to him?"

"Closely, no doubt." A crushing weight on his chest made breathing difficult. No wonder she'd kept her identity secret from him. "Did she volunteer her name to you?"

"No, sir. Hammonds told me. A coachman stopped by this morning after you left. He had a piece of baggage, saying it belonged to the young lady he'd dropped off here last night, and that he'd overlooked it in the dark. He asked if we would make his apologies to Miss Lawless."

"I see." A dark cloak of a mood settled over Slade. "What happened next?"

Mrs. Stanley frowned, apparently at a loss with his curious line of questioning. "Hammonds gave me her bag, I carried it to her—she was having her breakfast. I addressed her as Miss Lawless. When I did, she jumped up and lit out of here. She even spilled her handbag in her haste. We barely had time to gather up her things before she and her trunks were gone in a cab.''

Which explained her missing the little item now in his pocket. He thought of the care with which it was folded. And of the ribbon that secured its contents. Her care with the scrap of letterhead showed the value with which she endowed it. And his name was written on it. Intriguing.

''Sir?''

Slade forced his attention back to the housekeeper. ''What is it?''

She hefted the linens she carried. ''May I make the bed in here now?''

Slade shook his head. ''No. Give me a moment, Mrs. Stanley, would you?'' He stared pointedly at her, until she finally nodded and then stepped out of the room. Her footsteps echoed down the hallway.

Alone again, Slade walked to the room's window, leaning his shoulder against the casing and bending a knee. With his arms crossed over his chest, he looked down upon Public Garden. But the familiar landscape couldn't hold his attention. In fact, the world outside looked strange to him. He felt unconnected to it. *He'd sheltered a Lawless whelp in his home.*

And held her in his arms. And kissed her. With one vicious swipe, he scrubbed his fingers over his lips, as if he could wipe away the deed. What a fool he'd been. Those helpless tears, the wide-eyed looks. But at least now he knew why the girl struck such a familiar chord in his memory. She looked just like her mother. He'd never met Catherine Jane Wilton-Humes. But he knew her. Slade saw himself as a boy gazing up at Catherine's smiling face in the portrait Ardis Wilton-Humes kept in her suite at Cloister Point.

But it wasn't only from his visits with his grandmother Isabel that he knew of Catherine Lawless. If only that were all. Hadn't he, like his mother, been forced to live with her image all his life? In truth, Catherine's specter had killed his delicate mother and followed his father to his grave.

Dwelling on that, feeding his steadily darkening mood, Slade recalled yesterday's events. Two things immediately stood out. One, Hannah Lawless had fainted when he said his name. So, she knew the name—probably from its being scribbled on the Wilton-Humes letterhead—but hadn't known the face. And two, once he'd identified himself, she'd reacted with venom and no small amount of wariness. Slade quirked up his mouth. He'd do well to reserve for himself some wariness toward her.

Because she'd sought him out last night—in his home, even knowing full well who he was. What then was her game? Catching his hazy reflection in the windowpane, Slade looked his ghostly self in the eye and wondered how it was that he didn't feel the depth of anger and, yes, hatred that he should feel for her. Instead, all he felt was a disappointing sense of loss. Of what? Or whom?

Slade shifted his stance and searched his soul. Yes, he harbored strong feelings of family fidelity, a righteous sense of old wrongs that needed righting. But not the hateful rage he'd always expected he'd feel if chance or fate were to put him face-to-face with a Lawless. Was that because this Lawless was a mere girl? A soft and pretty young thing?

Slade dismissed that notion. Mother'd been both of those things when her life was ruined by Catherine Wilton-Humes. With that thought came the surge of anger, the mistrust of anything Lawless. In the window's pane, Slade watched his mouth straighten into a grim line and found himself swearing to his mother's memory that he would finish what Hannah's mother'd begun more than twenty-five years ago with his father. He also swore that he'd finish what he himself had started with her last night.

With that thought came a revelation. Slade straightened up, focusing on a far steeple that rose above the other rooftops. By God, now he knew her game, why a Lawless dared come to Boston—and right at this particular time. A slanting grin split his face.

He'd give her a game of cat and mouse she wouldn't soon forget. He admired her courage, but too bad her efforts would be for naught. Slade laughed out loud, wondering how long it would take her to realize that she was now the mouse to his cat. Fingering the scrap of Wilton-Humes stationery in his pocket, he grinned. Thanks to her guilty haste, he knew exactly where to find her. As he strode across the room, intent on his mission, his parting hope was that she would survive her foray into Cloister Point long enough for him to get there and exact his pound of flesh from her.

He called out, "Mrs. Stanley. You may make the bed now."

# CHAPTER THREE

——

Clad in her best visiting dress of bronze satin, her hands folded demurely in her lap, Hannah sat in the drawing room at Cloister Point while her great-aunt poured tea. An outward picture of calm, inside Hannah was a mishmash of raw nerves. She sent up a prayer of thanks to Mama for her repeated instruction on a lady's deportment during a formal call. Because not for anything would she give these rigid Easterners, blood kin or not, any reason to fault her upbringing, and thereby Mama.

Eyeing her great-aunt and great-uncle, two long-nosed, white-haired specimens, Hannah also counted herself grateful for the deferential silence in the room. She was supposed to be absorbing her grief and shock over just finding out her grandparents were no longer amongst the living. But she felt nothing for people she'd never known, people who'd declared their daughter dead just because they didn't approve of the man she loved.

Instead, Hannah spent the moment fearing that any grief or shock she'd experience would come later at the hands of Slade Garrett. For certainly the man now knew she was a Lawless. Coupled with that terror was her discovery, on the way here, that her ribbon-tied hanky was missing from her handbag. Heaped onto that was her certainty that there was only one place it could be. And hence, she was left with the fatalistic acceptance that once it was discovered, she herself would no longer be amongst the living.

"You're awfully pale. Are you quite all right?"

Hannah jerked her attention back to the moment, starting

when she realized Cyrus was now standing over her, offering her a cup of tea. "I apologize, Uncle. It's, um, just the shock of learning my grandparents have passed on." She took the cup and saucer, merely holding them for the moment.

"So sorry to have to give you the news. It's still a bit raw to us, too. Poor Hamilton and Evelyn. Only three months ago in a carriage accident. It doesn't seem possible that my older brother is gone. And yet you say you heard nothing about it? Pity. We did send word. But wait. Your . . . mother sent you to us when? Perhaps you were already on your way here when she received word?"

"That could be. I've only just arrived in Boston." She hoped he didn't notice that hers was no real answer. Perched on the edge of a bird's-eye-maple chair covered in blue damask, Hannah fingered the delicate china cup, bringing it to her lips. But as soon as her great-uncle turned away, she promptly set it down, unsampled, on a gold-inlaid table next to her chair.

So, her grandparents died two months before Mama and Papa had. Well, that didn't change the facts or her evidence of Wilton-Humes involvement. It merely cast her suspicions onto Uncle Cyrus and his wife, Patience. Therefore, she'd taste her tea only after they drank theirs. Lord knows what they might be capable of.

Hannah darted a glance at her great-aunt. Seated on a medallion-backed sofa, the only large piece of furniture in the room other than Hannah's chair, this sharp-eyed woman frightened her more than her uncle did. Because this imperious lady remained intimidatingly silent as she stared a hole through Hannah. Her chalky expression assured Hannah that she hadn't missed her not tasting the tea. With every action a pointed one, the older woman picked up and sipped at her tea.

Just then, Uncle Cyrus cleared his throat. Hannah gladly gave him her attention, finding he now stood positioned beside the hearth and under portraits he'd said earlier were of her late grandparents. Looking up at them now, she saw only a cold man and a haughty woman who were complete strangers to her. How had these two produced a daughter as warm and loving as Mama?

"Quite the handsome couple, are they not?" Cyrus crooked an elbow up on the mantel, and went on as if he hadn't asked her a question. "Still, it's a shame your mother couldn't have seen fit to allow you to visit while your grandparents were still alive. I think they would have found your striking resemblance to her quite . . . unsettling.''

Unsettling? Just as she'd hoped. Hannah feigned a dramatic sigh. ''Yes. It is a shame. But then again, my mother was dead''—gasps from her aunt and uncle gave Hannah more satisfaction than was probably good for her—''to them all these years, since she married my father.''

''Quite. All those years ago.'' Cyrus recovered beautifully, in Hannah's estimation. ''Your mother's . . . defection was all the scandal. None of us ever recovered.''

''Oh, I'm sure it was awful for you, but you don't appear to have done so *poorly*.'' Hannah raised an eyebrow at the man and then did a slow sweep of the regal room. Just the furnishings alone—though surprisingly few in number—were probably worth more than the entire Lawless spread.

''Young lady?''

Hannah jumped. This was the first time Aunt Patience'd spoken since she'd entered the room. ''Yes, ma'am?''

''Perhaps you'd best tell us exactly what your point is in coming here. Yours is a most unusual presentation. I find it quite odd that you would arrive within minutes of our own return from Nahant. And I don't believe for a moment that Catherine sent you here. She detested us all. So, come, out with it.''

Hannah stared at the sharp old bird. Time for the lies. ''You're right as all outdoors, Aunt Patience. I do apologize for inconveniencing you with my presence.'' Hannah paused, making a dramatic dismissive gesture at her own expense. ''Oh, I never should have tried lying. I'm no good at it. But, you see, it is true that I came here hoping to confr—'' A sharp thrill chased through her at her near slipup. ''Uh, meet my grandparents. And now you tell me they're both . . . gone. It's all too sad.''

She looked down at her lap, twisting her fingers together and collecting her scattered thoughts. Taking a deep breath, she raised her head and pushed on. ''I . . . well, I've had a falling-out with my parents. Life out West is just not for me. We had a terrible fight, and I left, telling them I intended to come here. I stopped along the way to visit with friends, so it's taken me a while to arrive unannounced on your doorstep.'' She peered intently at them. *They were breathing, weren't they?*

With no encouragement or murmurs of sympathy from them, Hannah plowed another row of pure corn. "When my parents and I had our set-to, I up and told them that the Wilton-Humes family—every last one of them—could not be as cold and as hateful as they tried to make me believe you were. But Papa said you'd never accept me. And then he told me never to come back, should I darken Cloister Point's doorway.''

She managed a long-suffering sigh here, turning purposely widened doe-eyes their way. "So you see, I made my choice. And now I'm at your mercy.''

Not one blasted peep did Uncle Cyrus or Aunt Patience make. Hannah wriggled in her chair when a trickle of sweat rolled slowly down her back. *Had they turned to stone?* Feeling a need to jog a reaction from these two, Hannah blurted out, "Oh, please don't tell me he was right, that you're greedy and grasping and back-stabbing and despica—''

"We take your point, young lady.'' Aunt Patience then exchanged a look with Uncle Cyrus. "A rebellious child. How interesting, Cyrus. And she comes to us. I find that life's ironies can be quite . . . satisfying.''

"Yes, quite, Patience dear.''

Hannah watched this bit of byplay between the two, assessing their reactions. They were falling into her trap. So, beyond the whoppers she'd already told, she figured now was the time to keep quiet. Either she'd get invited to stay or she'd be tossed out the door.

But apparently Aunt Patience wasn't ready to welcome her into the fold just yet. "How unfortunate that your . . . *set-to* with your parents didn't come sooner. As it is, we're forced to be the ones who must heap more bad news onto your head. Your great-grandmother, Ardis McAllister Wilton-Humes, passed away six weeks ago.''

"Oh, no, don't tell me that.'' Hannah brought a hand to her mouth in genuine shock and sorrow. If Mama had loved that grand old lady, as Biddy'd told her and her sisters countless times, then Hannah held that same love in her own heart. And here she'd missed meeting her by six weeks. Realizing they were staring at her, waiting for her to say something, Hannah forced herself to speak up. "I'm reeling from all these deaths, as you must be. How did it happen—her death, I mean?"

Aunt Patience's beady little blue eyes stared at her. "As you can figure, Grandmother Ardis was quite old. She didn't see very well. On that awful night, she got up from bed, wandered into the hall, and fell down the stairs. Cracked open her skull. It was quite a gruesome . . . accident."

Hannah clutched spasmodically at her own skirt. A coldness traveled up the back of her throat, closing it. She shook her head, feeling a terrible sickness invade her soul. *These people are monsters. None of the deaths were accidents. They had Mama and Papa killed.* She was suddenly sure of it, blindingly sure. And she'd just thrown herself on their "mercy"?

Aunt Patience added, "We're still in mourning."

"I see." But she didn't—not really. Because not one stitch of black clothing, not one wreath, or even an armband, adorned anyone or anything here. In mourning, were they?

Cyrus clapped his hands together suddenly. Hannah jumped as if he'd fired a gun at her. "Well then, with all the unpleasantness behind us, you must tell us how your dear mother is."

That was twice he'd asked how Mama was. Could it be that they weren't certain that their murderous plot had been carried out? Of course, she was acting on the premise that they indeed were guilty. Better to assume that and guard herself accordingly, than to be caught unawares and empty-handed. But Uncle Cyrus's pointed questioning did confirm her belief that the only thing that could keep her alive was making them believe she thought everyone at home was alive and well. Hopefully, if they believed she didn't suspect them of treachery, they'd feel no need to kill her. Especially if they thought her estranged from her parents and unlikely to contact them.

When she could see through the angry red haze that clouded her vision, Hannah answered her great-uncle. "My *dear mother* is not a topic I like to discuss—given my circumstances. I hope you don't think me rude for saying so."

"Quite the contrary, my *dear* niece. Forgive me for bringing her up. I assure you, we don't spend an inordinate amount of time discussing her here." He then exchanged a nod with his wife before turning back to Hannah. "Which means, I'm happy to say, you'll find you won't be discomfited while you stay here . . . for as long as you like." With that, he came to attention, snapped his heels together, and bowed slightly to her.

Victory. It tied Hannah's nerves in knots. She'd won her way in. Now to keep her body and soul together under this roof. She'd have to guard herself night and day against some "gruesome accident." If her predicament weren't so dire, it might almost be funny, for she was now truly the spider that got caught in its own web, only to put itself in danger of being eaten by bigger spiders. Rousing herself, she smiled in feigned delight. "Oh, thank you so much. You have no idea what this means to me." And she meant that.

"Or to us." Aunt Patience sized her up, looking like she was considering tasting her great-niece's flesh.

Hannah's insides roiled. The currents in this room threatened to pull her under. No one, including her, was saying what he or she meant. If she weren't careful, she'd become just like them. But wasn't she already?

Smoothing her expression, she jumped up and fluttered to each of them. She forced herself to clasp her aunt's and uncle's hands in turn. She even managed to plant a dutiful-niece peck on their cheeks. To her surprise, their skin was warm and dry. Unlike hers at that moment.

That accomplished, and wanting with all her soul to be out of their presence, even if only for a few hours, she minced to the middle of the nearly bare, spacious room, clasped her hands together at her bosom, and chirruped, "I can hardly wait to see my room. I just know it will be as lovely as the rest of Cloister Point."

Aunt Patience smiled. "Yes. Your room. I've just the one for you, my dear. You should feel quite comfortable there. Your mother occupied it . . . while she lived here."

Her mother's room. *Wasn't Aunt Patience just the most thoughtful thing?* With the drapes drawn against the day's light, Hannah lay atop the Louis XV bed. Disrobed down to her chemise, she held a damp cloth over her eyes. Not one ounce of strength or bravado remained in her body after waiting for the room to be opened and then overseeing her own unpacking.

Legs flung carelessly wide, she groaned out her success in gaining entry at Cloister Point. If every encounter with her aunt and uncle proved as draining as today's, she'd be a gray-haired, wizened old hag inside of a week.

Being manipulative and underhanded was hard work, she mused, for someone who hasn't honed those . . . talents. Nagging at her too was the tiny doubt that she could be completely wrong. What if the burned scrap of letterhead was simply what remained of the letter Uncle Cyrus'd said he sent to notify Mama of the family deaths?

Hannah groaned. What if none of these people were guilty? What if Slade Garrett was just as he seemed—something of a rake, but a gentleman, nevertheless? And what about her aunt and uncle? What if they were just as they seemed—haughty but honest, truly suffering through wrenching accidental losses, and taking her in out of the kindness of their hearts and their shared bloodlines?

*Lovely.* She plucked the cloth off her eyes, rolled onto her side, and plopped the rag onto the rosewood nightstand beside her. Sweeping her hair to one side, she resettled herself on her back and laced her fingers over her abdomen. Staring into the gray thickness of the darkened room, she reminded herself that doubts and sudden attacks of timidity would be her downfall.

And somehow she didn't see Jacey being so afflicted. Lucky for Cyrus and Patience that her younger sister hadn't made this trip with her. Because Jacey would come in shooting and ask questions later. Picturing Jacey bursting into the refined drawing room, her six-shooter blazing, brought a smile to Hannah's face. What she wouldn't give for an ounce of Jacey's spirit and grit.

Then, her eyelids drooped. Hannah rubbed at them. No wonder she was exhausted. She hadn't slept well since she'd left home. The nights on the train were a numbing blur. Then last night at Slade Garrett's, worrying if he would return to her room, was a nightmare. But now? And here? How was it that she could feel comfortable enough in this house to doze off? Especially not knowing if she was safe.

No, she'd better get up, better remain alert. But lying there in the quiet made her lethargic. She turned on her side, nestling her hands under her cheek. *Get up, Hannah.* Her eyelids drooping again, she fussed that she would in a moment. Surely a little nap wouldn't kill her.

Maybe only moments elapsed. Maybe hours. She had no

way of knowing which when she first realized she was awake. The why of that brought a frown to her face. What had awakened her? She blinked, trying to adjust to the dimness. A shadow moved at the foot of the bed. Hannah caught her breath and clutched at the quilted counterpane under her. Slowly exhaling, she asked, ''Who are you? What do you want?''

The shadow's answer was to grab her ankles and wrench her roughly to the side of the bed. Shocked into breathlessness, Hannah tried but couldn't scream. Time slowed to a nightmarish, molasseslike sludge. Still clutching frantically at the bedcovers under her, fighting for her life, she twisted and jerked her legs. But to no avail. Her assailant's grip tightened. The covers obligingly slid right along with her.

When her ankles were abruptly released, causing her legs to flop limply over the side of the high bed, Hannah tried again to twist away. But she was immediately gripped about the waist and hauled up hard against a warm granite wall—a man's chest. Pushing against him, a yelp of terror escaped her. *Did they mean to kill her so soon?*

As if answering her terrified thought, he flexed his arm, tightening his iron grip about her back. The air whooshed out of Hannah's lungs. Her feet barely touched the carpeted floor. She couldn't move, couldn't breathe. Her next scream died as a hollow echo inside her head. The man's other hand closed tightly over her mouth. Dragging in precious, shallow breaths through her nose, she fought the paralyzing fear that seeped through her limbs.

''Make one sound, and I'll snap your neck. Do you understand me?''

The rough, whispering voice, warm against her ear, chilled her to the bone. Reflexively gripping the man's shirt with fisted hands, she managed to nod her understanding. But even through the thick haze of terror, she recognized the voice. *Slade Garrett.*

''Good. I'm going to let you go. And you're going to sit right there on the bed while I let in the light. And you're not going to move. Understand?''

She nodded again, half afraid she'd lose consciousness before he released her. For an interminable second, he didn't respond. He just held her. Hannah could only blink and wait, and try not to smell the acrid scent of her own fear . . . and his ruthlessness.

"Make sure you understand, *Hannah Lawless.*"

His voice was no more than a growl when he said her name—her full name. Hannah stiffened, became even more still in his arms. But it was only when she finally slumped against him, defeated, that he released her, loosing her with no more regard than a child showed for a broken, unwanted toy.

She fell in a heap onto the bed's softness. Unhurt but momentarily stunned, she didn't move. Then, a sound caught her attention. As wary as any prairie dog peeking out of its burrow, she raised her head, pricking the dark with her need to hear. There. Again. Footsteps. His. Moving away from her. Toward the window.

Realizing this was her chance, reduced to whimpering yelps of relief, she finally thought to scrabble and scramble across the bed's length. On her hands and knees now, she prayed for just one more moment of darkness to reach the nightstand. She'd put her pistol in the drawer before lying down—just in case something like this happened. If she could just get to it.

Desperation, as much as having to grope blindly, made her clumsy, robbed her of coordination. Her searching, fumbling fingers knocked a china knickknack to the floor, but finally her hand closed around the knob on the—

Light flooded the room, washing away her element of surprise. With a cry, Hannah jerked around, half sitting, half lying across the bed. Through the tangle of her hair, she saw him standing at the window. He faced her, his tall, muscular outline filling the narrow opening.

"Hannah, you disappoint me. You said you wouldn't move." Hands to his waist, his feet apart, and with sunlight filtering in behind him, his face remained in shadows. But not so dark that she couldn't see the glitter of his eyes.

Hannah'd seen wolves with similar expressions . . . as they closed in for the kill. She knew better than to show fear to a wolf. "I guess I lied."

He laughed, but there was no humor in the sound. "I guess you did." He then paused, as if allowing for a change in subject. "You should never have come to Boston."

When he started toward her, when he steadily advanced

with a measured tread, slowly closing the gap between them, Hannah's heart lodged in her throat. *He's not going to let me leave this room alive.* Having no more than thought it, she sat up straighter. That simple revelation had the amazing effect of calming her. She had nothing left to lose then, did she?

He stopped beside the bed, running his gaze over her as if her death were already a done deed. She looked up into his black eyes. "Are you going to kill me?"

"I should." He then reached out, capturing a lock of her hair. Hannah flinched at the contact, turning her head away from his steely gaze. "But I've decided not to. You should know one thing, though—if I wanted you dead, you'd already be dead."

Hannah's heart leapt at his words. She didn't doubt him for a moment. *The bastard.* Hating him for making her feel helpless, she raised her chin and forced herself to meet his unnerving stare. "Your . . . mercy just might prove to be your first mistake, Garrett."

He quirked up a corner of his mouth. "We'll see, won't we?"

Hannah abruptly reached up to slide her curl out of his grasp. She watched him watch it slip through his fingers. Only when he raised his head and settled his gaze on her did she question him. "Did you ride all this way just to tell me you're not going to kill me?"

"Are you daring me to try, Hannah?" Sounding threatening and incredulous all at once, he leaned over her, forcing her back . . . back . . . back onto the bed until she was lying prone under him, her hands clasped at her bosom, her legs trapped between his. He rested his big fists to either side of her shoulders.

Looming above her, pinning her in place, he raised the ante with an ice-cold stare. She tried to match his unblinking expression, but fear penetrated to her very soul. Her resolve crumbling, she jerked her head to the side, closing her eyes.

The increasing pressure on the bed told her he was leaning ever closer to her. Indeed, when he spoke—in a slow, drawling threat—his breath brushed over her temple. "Know this— I don't make mistakes. So consider this a social call. You're still alive, Hannah Lawless, because that serves my purpose. You're no good to me dead. No, I want you to live a good, long time . . . so you can regret—every day of your life—having ever crossed my path.''

Chills of dread claimed every inch of her skin. He wanted her alive? Why? But no sooner were his words a memory than the bed shifted under her again. He gripped her chin, forcing her to turn her head back to him. ''Open your eyes and look at me.''

Hannah opened her eyes, only to see him running his gaze over her prone figure, as if he hadn't noticed until this moment that she was practically naked. And lying under him. For a moment, he settled his gaze on her nearly exposed breasts. Hannah was sure her heart would pound right out of her chest. But then he swung his gaze back to her face. ''I'm going to let you play out your little game with your kin, Hannah. But you play it, sweetheart, knowing that I know why you're here, thanks to that little lace hanky of yours.''

''No!'' She raised her fisted hands to him. But he was quicker. He grabbed her wrists and forced her arms to the bed, where he held them pinioned above her head.

''I'm watching you. And I can get to you whenever I want—just like this. There's nowhere you can run. And no one who'll help you.''

A ragged sob tore from Hannah. Tears blurred her vision. Thinking of her parents' senseless deaths, and this man's part in them, she cried, ''Why are you doing this? Why?''

''Because you're a Lawless. Catherine's child. For me, that's reason enough.'' He punctuated his words with a glare. But then, slowly, the angry light in his eyes dimmed . . . and then died. A new emotion, a new expression claimed his features and rendered his voice hoarse. ''A Lawless. God*damn* you. Since I first saw you, I've felt things I—'' After drawing in a tortured breath, he went on. ''I will *never* forgive you for making me feel them. Never. I should want you dead. But you know what, sweet Hannah? I can't think of a more perfect revenge than making you a Garrett. Only then can you know what hell is.''

With that, he pushed himself up and away from the bed. He stared down at her for another agonizing moment and then turned away from her. When he skirted the bed, she lost sight of him, but heard his retreating footfalls, muffled by the carpet. She heard the door open and then close . . . softly.

Struck dumb, as much by his words as by his attack, Hannah lay still as a stone and stared up at the ceiling. Unthinking, unfeeling. For a long time.

Two days later, late on a bright and windy afternoon, Cloister Point's first floor stood in polished readiness. In the warm kitchen, a wealth of foods that hadn't been seen here in countless months were being joyfully prepared. Soups and sauces simmered. Fish and fowl roasted. Breads baked, and fruits and cakes were glazed invitingly. Tonight's event, a formal dinner and entertainment to welcome Miss Hannah Wilton Lawless to Boston promised a fabulous feast, tantalizing conversation, and polite entertainments.

Maybe for the ranks of the Brahmin, but not for the guest of honor.

She was supposed to be resting in anticipation of the long night ahead. But Slade Garrett's . . . social call two days ago during that one nap of hers had cured her of that particular pastime. Napping all afternoon. She shook her head. The wealthy sure were a peculiar lot. What she couldn't figure was—with everyone lying about, how'd they ever get anything done? Well, let them waste the best part of the day. Not her. So, more bored than tired, more driven than cautious, Hannah took advantage of the quiet for a stealthy mission.

In her stocking feet, she slipped out of her room and tiptoed past closed doors, aiming for the upper hallway's far end. As she passed her great-grandmother's portrait about halfway down, she transferred a kiss from her fingers to Ardis McAllister Wilton-Humes's face. With tears misting her eyes as she stood there taking in the kind, strong face and black velvet dress of the only Wilton-Humes her mother had loved, Hannah let out a sigh and hurried along with her task.

Two days of peeking in doors had revealed that all the bedrooms were empty. And she didn't just mean of people. She meant of furniture. Except for hers and—she assumed, since she hadn't been in them—for Uncle Cyrus's and Aunt Patience's. Another peculiarity of the rich, she supposed, giving the thought a dismissive shrug.

No time to ponder on it now. Using great care, and stealing glances all around her, she opened the unpretentious door that hid the servants' stairwell. Narrow and dim, the shaftlike descent also proved deserted. She figured the odds of that were good, seeing as how there were curiously few servants ever around, for a spread this big.

Biting at her bottom lip, she gripped the handrail and cautiously padded down to the first floor. Her other hand clutched her blue wool skirt's pocket. Under her fingers, her first letter back home to Jacey and Glory formed a thick packet. Hannah couldn't say why, but seeing the original, full-sized portrait of Ardis yesterday in her snoopings had triggered a memory that had grown into a suspicion, which had caused her to write home.

Perhaps it was nothing, or perhaps it was everything, but where was the miniature of that exact portrait now? It was the one thing Mama'd kept from her life at Cloister Point. Her most treasured memento, meant for Jacey after her death. She knew Jacey wouldn't move it from Mama's room without saying something. And now that she thought about it, Hannah certainly didn't remember seeing it after . . . well, afterward. So, in her letter she asked her sisters to look for it. Because the tiny oil likeness kept calling to her, kept hounding her thoughts. It had to mean something. And, if it was missing, who had it? And why? What could it possibly mean to anyone outside their family?

With her thoughts carrying her to the first-floor landing, Hannah looked both ways down the long stretch of hallway. To her left, she heard noises—pots and pans banging, people laughing, dishes clattering. She paused a moment to sniff the air, so mouthwatering with the mingling aromas of tonight's supper, and hoped the portions were bigger than what she'd been served here so far. But maybe with all the lying around everyone did, they didn't need to eat much.

Crouching furtively, she looked to her right. No one. Good. She'd just have to take her chances in the main rooms. Her mind made up, she immediately went in search of Olivia. The chattery little downstairs maid, whom Hannah had embarrassingly encountered during yesterday's snooping mission, had at least smiled at her and cheerfully explained the layout of the rooms. Today, Hannah was hoping she could find her and ask her to post her letter. Hopefully, the girl was dusting or polishing something. And was alone.

Treading lightly, Hannah silently approached and then

opened the first door on her right. Cautiously peering inside, she recognized it as Uncle Cyrus's office. One glance told her there was no Olivia. But happily, there was no Uncle Cyrus, either. Just thinking the man's name drew her attention to his high-backed leather chair. Hannah poked her tongue out at it and then noiselessly closed the door, edging down the hall to the next room. The solarium. Hannah peeked in. *Aunt Patience*. She promptly drew back around the corner, her muscles tense, every nerve ending alive.

But all remained quiet in the bright, fern-bedecked room. Hannah risked another glance inside. Sitting in profile to the door, and with a tray of tea and cakes at her side, the older woman was innocently absorbed in writing in some sort of journal she balanced on her lap.

Hannah retreated around the corner again and leaned back against the wall. She must be trapped in an insane asylum. For why else would her aunt and uncle go about the most ordinary of ways, as if nothing were afoot? And include Hannah in every activity? They took their meals with her. They invited her on their rounds of social calls to all the best homes. They chatted amiably enough with her in the evenings. They even included her in their plans for future outings. All as if theirs was one happy family.

Which it most certainly was not. Hannah absently nibbled at her lower lip as she sought an explanation for their behavior. Well, there was only one—the Wilton-Humeses were evil monsters posing as harmless old folk until she lowered her defenses. All right, then, she wouldn't lower them. But how was Slade Garrett involved in all this? And *why* was he? What did he stand to gain?

An ample dose of angry reaction raced over her nerves at the memory of his . . . visit to her room. How dare he speak of her mother and then accost her and threaten her with . . . marriage? How, and for what, would making her marry him figure as revenge? Well, if his barging into her room was his proposal, then he'd never see his revenge. Never.

Leaning her head back against the wall, feeling the weight of her commitment to her family, Hannah made a promise to herself. If she got out of this alive, never again would she take for granted the virtue of honesty, and never again would she think lightly of trust. Because there was not one soul in all of

Boston she could trust to be telling her the truth.

*And there's not one soul in all of Boston you're telling the truth to.* Stung by her own conscience, Hannah grimaced. She hated the polite restraint, the superficial courtesy, and the mild demeanor forced upon her by her own charade. Instead, she yearned to scream and publicly accuse them all and shout and pound her fists, and demand answers and—

*That was it!* They were all waiting for *her* to make a move. What was it that despicable Garrett said . . . play *your* little game? She stared at the formal drawing room across from her. Wouldn't she just love to play her own little game tonight? For the benefit of Boston's finest. A shrug of guilty glee brought Hannah's hands to her grinning mouth.

Did she dare? Think of the scandal. *But wait* . . . if her suspicions and accusations were public knowledge, wouldn't that assure her own well-being? Wide-eyed, she straightened up. Yes, it would. A public accusation would render her untouchable. But how could she accuse them without evidence? That hateful Garrett now possessed the charred letterhead.

Then she had to find other evidence. As her mind raced with possibilities, she forgot about finding Olivia to post her letter. This was more important. Perhaps a document of some sort, she mused—a record of payment to the actual murderers? She slumped her shoulders. Would they be stupid enough to actually keep a written record of their foul deeds? Into her head popped the vision of their stationery she'd found lying in the fireplace embers at home. Yes, they just might be.

Now, where to find this evidence? Hannah turned her head, catching sight of Uncle Cyrus's office door. If other evidence existed, it would be in that room. A grin born of pure calculation stole over her features. Before she could lose her nerve, she skittered back down the hall, sliding to a silent, shoeless stop as she grabbed for the doorknob. Darting a quick look to her left and right, and seeing no one, she inched the door open and slipped inside.

Turning her back to the room, which smelled of stale tobacco smoke and stuffy volumes, she soundlessly edged the door closed. Letting out her held breath, she turned around to face the office. Her gaze immediately lit on the desk that dominated the middle of the room. Quickly she went to it and began opening drawer after drawer, filtering through each one's contents as she searched for . . . something, anything she could use against Uncle Cyrus and Aunt Patien—

The door opened. Hannah jerked upright, staring. "Aunt Patience!"

# CHAPTER FOUR

—

"Hannah!"

That one word was all she said. But it was enough, Hannah judged. She watched her aunt standing across the room from her, one blue-veined hand on the doorknob, her other to her chest as her darting gaze slipped from Hannah's face to the open desk drawers and back to Hannah's face.

When the accusing silence descended like a pall, Hannah blurted out, "I'm looking for . . . for some writing material."

"Oh?" With that, Aunt Patience pointed to the letterhead stationery and pen-and-ink stand clearly visible on the desktop. "Were these not satisfactory?"

Hannah stared at the blasted items and felt a guilty flush creeping up her neck and cheeks. She shifted her gaze to Aunt Patience's face and made a self-deprecating gesture as she forced a smile, hoping it wasn't as sickly as she felt. "Why, silly me. I completely overlooked them. What was I thinking?"

Aunt Patience didn't even blink. "I'd like to know that myself. But, tell me, Hannah dear, to whom are you going to write? Not your parents?"

Hannah's eyes widened as she suddenly recalled her own story of being estranged from her family. "No. No, of course not. I wish to write my . . ."—her gaze darted about as she thought desperately—"my friend. Yes, that's it. My friend. I'm going to write my friend."

"Your friend. I see. Well, take the materials with you, but perhaps tomorrow would be a better time to write. It's nearly time to dress for tonight's event. Which is in your honor, if you recall. Your uncle and I have gone to tremendous trouble and expense to make you feel welcome here. I hope our confidence in you isn't misplaced."

Hannah was certain she could feel herself shrinking in stature. "I assure you, Aunt Patience, it's not."

The blueblood Brahmin nodded her head slowly. "Good. Then we'll not speak of this incident to your uncle. It would only distress him terribly. And I know you wouldn't want to do that. Would you?"

"No, Aunt Patience." Hannah forced herself to hold her aunt's steady gaze. The threats implicit in Patience's words were not lost on her. But the room's sudden stuffiness seemed to make Hannah's heart beat thunderously, and brought her near to begging. "May I be excused now? As you said, I need to dress for this evening."

Aunt Patience let go of the knob, stepping aside. "Certainly. And I do believe you'll find a surprise waiting for you in your room. So, go. Certainly, no one is forcing you to be in here against your will."

Another wrench of guilt lowered Hannah's gaze to her stocking feet. Taking a deep breath for courage, she raised her head and put one foot in front of the other. When she drew even with Aunt Patience, the older woman snaked her hand out and grasped Hannah's arm in a surprisingly strong grip. Despite her best effort not to, Hannah gasped. Staring down at the small woman who frightened her so, peering into her birdlike, sharp eyes, Hannah could only wait for her to speak.

"You forgot what you came in here for, dear."

A frown marred Hannah's features. "I beg your pardon?"

"The writing materials. Surely you still want to write your friend?"

Hannah dashed back up the stairs, this time using the elegant central stairway. She no longer had the stomach for stealth. In her hands were the pen, ink, and paper that she had no use for, since she already had the same things in her room. They'd been thoughtfully placed in the small secretary there. And of course, as her hostess, Aunt Patience would know that.

With each unladylike leap up the stairs, Hannah berated herself soundly. What could possibly be more humiliating and damaging than the scene she'd just created? Now she'd raised

Aunt Patience's suspicions and, worse, now she would have to produce a letter tomorrow for posting to some imaginary friend. Too bad she couldn't just hand over the one she'd written Jacey and Glory. But she didn't dare, not knowing if it would be read by prying eyes here and never sent. Hannah huffed out a frustrated noise as she gained the second-floor landing. *How in the world could things get any worse than they were right now?*

Her answer awaited her on the other side of her bedroom door, which she opened with the sense of gaining a haven. But the feeling left her in a whoosh of breath as she stopped suddenly, clutched the writing materials to her bosom, and surveyed the scene before her. *This was Aunt Patience's surprise?* She stepped inside and closed the door behind her. Moving with stiff, mechanical motions brought on by her mounting confusion and disbelief, she took in the open doors of her now-empty armoire and the open drawers of her equally empty chest of drawers.

What was going on? But she thought she knew, as she approached her bed. Or tried to. Her way was blocked by box after piled-high box after spilled-over box. Hatboxes. Dress boxes. Shoe boxes. Boxes overflowing with thin tissue paper and dainty unmentionables.

*Who? What?* Without taking her eyes off her bed, Hannah dropped the pen, ink, and paper on the secretary. Then, she just stood there, as suspicious as she was mesmerized. Surely, Aunt Patience and Uncle Cyrus hadn't—No. Hannah refused to believe that. Because if they'd done this, if they'd gifted her with a completely new wardrobe, then they just had to be innocent of the deeds she thought them capable of. Why would they go to the tremendous trouble and expense of providing all these clothes, if they meant to kill her? So, if indeed they had done this, that made her a despicable person and a dastardly niece.

Spying a card on her pillow, Hannah stared at it as if it might come alive and spring at her with bared teeth. But finally, curiosity got the better of her, and she stepped over and around the stacks and piles until she laid her hand on the card. Opening it, she read, *For you, my little country mouse. Slade Garrett.* Stunned, Hannah looked up at nothing in particular, even as her arm dropped to her side. Slade Garrett did this?

And he thought of her as a country mouse? The man's gall was not to be believed.

But still, she wondered what his taste was like. Flipping the card back onto the bed, Hannah reached for a closed box. But just as quickly pulled back. She couldn't. It would be wrong. So very wrong. Biting at her bottom lip, she looked all around her. She was all alone. So what would be the harm? One tiny peek wouldn't hurt anything.

Within moments, Hannah's one tiny peek became a fire-storm of openings and unwrappings and oohs and aahs of delight. Seated amongst and surrounded by elegant female frippery and petticoats and stockings and shoes and day dresses and traveling costumes and unmentionables and silk evening dresses and satin opera dresses and—oh, an entire wardrobe, for heaven's sake—Hannah tore through each one, eagerly opening them all.

*Well,* she assuaged her screaming conscience, *it isn't as if I can return any of these things. All my old clothes are gone.*

A fresh fit of wonder assailed her as she lifted a particularly fetching aquamarine gown out of its box and stood to hold it up to herself. The gown was exquisite—lavish material, simple lines. She looked for the card in the box. All the other boxes had cards from *him* in them, so why shouldn't this one?

Spying it, she lifted it out and pushed aside the fabric mountain on her bed, making space for herself. Acknowledging a sense of shy hesitancy in her actions, she bit at her bottom lip and sat down to read his words. He wrote that the gown was like her eyes, that the fabric too changed color with every movement, every emotion. He asked her to wear it that night. She reread the card, sitting very still now and staring at Slade Garrett's handwriting. The man was clearly trying to seduce her.

Hannah took a deep breath. Then, draping the gown over her arm, she ran a finger over his words, noting their formation and forcing her mind on to practical considerations. His was a firm hand, straightforward lettering, no fancy scrolls. And it wasn't the same as the handwriting on the Wilton-Humes letterhead she'd found in the grate at home.

Feeling her throat close around that truth, and refusing to name it relief, Hannah carefully replaced the card in the empty box. What in the world was she going to do about Slade Garrett? Her posture slumped. What *could* she do about him? Could she beat him at his own game . . . whatever it was?

Her thoughts contorting her lips into twisting peaks and valleys, Hannah looked down to see her hand smoothing the gown's folds. Feminine curiosity got the better of her. Leaping up, the gown in her arms, she flew to the cheval glass. Holding the gown to her waist and with a hand flaring out the skirt, she posed for the mirror, turning this way and that, until she decided he was right. The gown did do nice things for her eyes.

Without thinking, she began humming a tune and took a mincing dance step or two. It was only when she caught sight of her dreamy expression in the mirror, and realized she was fantasizing about dancing with *him,* that she pulled up short and let go of the dress as if it were hot. The dress puffed out and slowly pooled in folds around her ankles.

"Here now, miss. Have you no manners? That's no way to treat such a lovely gown."

Hannah whipped around. Holding a smallish rectangular black box and what looked to be a notecard, Mrs. Wells was just coming back into the room. Hannah pronounced the lady's maid a snotty old ass.

Making an awful face at the woman's back when she turned to the bedside table, Hannah nevertheless bent over and picked up the *lovely gown,* walking with it to her bed. She carelessly flopped it on top of the expensive pile. "My manners are not in question here. Mr. Garrett's are. What type of man has a lady's wardrobe discarded and then replaces her belongings with this?" She plucked a scandalously sheer bedgown out of a box and held it up.

*Ha, that got her.* Mrs. Wells pinched up her unpleasingly plump face. "Mr. Garrett is the best of gentlemen, young lady. And he's done you a tremendous honor in purchasing these costumes for you. Why, he had to've spent an entire day at the shops. And you're that ungrateful. He merely means to avoid having you be an embarrassment to the Wilton-Humeses."

"Embarrassment?" Feeling the rising heat in her veins that surely colored her warming face, Hannah rounded on the servant who'd done nothing, from day one, but make openly rude statements about her shortcomings. "I've plenty of clothes that are good enough. Or I would have, if they hadn't all vanished.''

Mrs. Wells plopped the box and the notecard on the bedside table. ''Are you accusing me of stealing, Miss Lawless?''

''You?'' Hannah gave the hateful hag her best imperious look—down the end of her nose, and hopefully in a fair imitation of the way Aunt Patience looked at everyone. ''Despite the evidence of your snooping through my belongings, I hardly think you'd risk your station here by taking any of my *inferior* clothing. Let's just say, I know you do nothing on your own. You obey orders and report what you find.''

Mrs. Wells's mouth worked furiously. ''If you'd been in your room earlier, as you were supposed to be, young lady, you'd have seen nothing so damning as me performing my duties. I merely gathered up your things and took them downstairs to the laundry for a proper washing.''

''A *proper* washing? Is that what you said?'' Hannah smiled, hoping it conveyed even one tenth of the contempt she felt for this mean-spirited woman. First Slade Garrett's impertinences, and now this woman's. Too bad for the maid that she was someone Hannah could do something about.

''I'm going to count to five, Mrs. Wells. One.'' She walked over to the nightstand and opened the drawer. Reaching in, she pulled out her pocket revolver, a Smith & Wesson .32. ''Two.'' She turned back around and leveled it on the astonished lady's maid. ''Three. And if you're not out of this room by the time I reach five—''

The woman fled. Hannah smiled at the empty space where the maid's bulk had been. She lowered her arm and stared at her weapon, smiling. Shrugging, she replaced it in the drawer and turned to look at the mess in her room. Putting her hands to her waist, she told the room at large, ''It appears I need a new lady's maid.''

One who had the run of the place, someone with more freedom to come and go than she had. Someone she could trust. Hannah stepped up to the bed and felt the letter to her sisters in her pocket. Of course—Olivia. Now she remembered. This gave her the perfect excuse to ask for the girl. She walked to the bellpull and gave it a tug, wondering who would show up. It sure as shooting wouldn't be Mrs. Wells.

While she waited, and in high humor now, Hannah turned

her attention to the black velvet box and the notecard on the nightstand. Opening the envelope first, she inhaled sharply when she recognized the handwriting. Slade Garrett's again. What now? Hannah flipped open the card. Two words. *"For you."* And then his signature. *"Slade."*

Tapping the card absently against her jaw, she stared at the velvet box, narrowing her eyes as if it were a scorpion in her path. Then, calling herself silly—it was just a box—she laid the card down and snatched up his latest gift. She opened it, gasped, and almost dropped it.

"I take it that means you like them?"

She whipped around, sending the sparkling jewels flying about the room. *Slade Garrett.* A hand to her floundering heart, she gave vent to her startlement. "Do you *live* here? You seem to just . . . pop up at the oddest moments."

"Some would say in a puff of smoke, no doubt. But no, I most certainly do not live here. And believe it or not, I gained entrance in the most conventional of ways—I knocked on the front door." With that, he entered her bedroom and immediately set about searching for the far-flung jewels. Bending over with athletic grace to retrieve a huge emerald set in heavy gold whenever he encountered one, he finally held them all. Looking from them to her, he asked, "Are these not suitable?"

"No. I mean yes. They're beautiful. But I—" Flustered, Hannah sent the empty box sailing onto the bed. Calling upon her Lawless temper, she raised her chin and put her fisted hands to her hips. "I have no use for your gifts."

She nearly ate those words when, in three long strides, he stood in front of her. His mouth a grim line, he unceremoniously grasped her wrist, forcing her arm out and her palm up. Into it he dropped the oval earrings, bracelet, and matching necklace. By their sheer weight, Hannah was forced to cup both hands around them.

Garrett cupped his long-fingered hands around hers. Hannah tried to wrench her hands from his grip, only to have him tighten his hold until the jewels poked hard against her flesh. Hannah glared up at him. To no avail. He grinned like a wolf. "Perhaps you would have preferred opals?"

Then he slid his hands off hers and stepped back. Hannah blinked, lowering her gaze to the fortune in gems that spilled through her fingers. She ought to throw them at him. But admitted she didn't have the courage. So, she stood there, lost in indecision as to what her next move should be. Maybe he'd think she was suddenly fascinated with the jewels' sparkle.

But in truth, she was making mental connections. The clothes. The jewelry. His constant attention. Her aunt and uncle. The proper people of Boston. Even the answers she needed. This one man appeared to possess all those. And now, he sought to possess her. For revenge.

Feeling him awaiting her reply, Hannah hefted the emeralds again, running a finger over their facets. *Then, so be it.* Perhaps she'd allow him to possess her. To a point. He meant to use her, and he made no secret of that. Well, two could play this game. She'd use him for her own ends, but unlike him, she'd do it secretly. And just like him, she wouldn't involve her heart.

A slow smile marched across her features, putting the cap on her decision. Lifting her head, she adjusted her smile to one of maidenly appreciation. "I apologize for my silence. I find I'm simply overwhelmed, Mr. Garrett—"

"Slade."

She simpered prettily. "Slade, then. I feel complimented that a man like you would notice me. What have I done to deserve such attention?"

Looking askance at her, he backed up another space and shifted his weight as he crossed his arms over his chest. He stared at her in dark contemplation for a moment or two. Then, an amused light twinkled in his eyes, even as his eyebrows arched. "Hannah Lawless, I expected better than that from you."

Hannah fought to maintain her pretty smile. She batted her eyelashes at him . . . until it became painful to continue. Forced to relax her facial muscles, or risk developing a tic, she frowned up at him. "Whatever do you mean?"

He burst out laughing. No one had to tell her that his hilarity was at her expense. Yet, when he was in better control of himself, he apparently felt compelled to do just that. He wiped at his eyes and insulted her. "You're not very good at that, are you?"

"At what? I have no idea what you mean."

"The devil you don't. Flirting and affecting pretty pouts. That awful face. I thought some flux had seized you."

Beyond mortified but affecting outrage, Hannah leaned toward him. "You are the most insulting and ornery man I have ever met."

"I am all that and much worse. But I think I'm also the *only* man you've ever met." He paused, considering her. "Perhaps that's it." His expression softened, became openly sensual. "Or at least the only man you've allowed this close to you. Am I right?"

Suddenly weak-kneed and wilting under that hot stare of his, Hannah looked down as she fought for control. He probably looked at all women this way, the cad. Steeling herself with such thoughts, she raised her head to stare boldly into his black eyes. "I have not *allowed* you any closeness. I think you'll find you have *taken* your liberties with me."

Twisting his mouth into a wry expression, he dipped his head to her. "Touché, my sweet. But you've enjoyed every moment of it, haven't you?"

*Why, the high-handed, conceited—!* Hannah grabbed up the velvet box, plopped the jewels into it, snapped it shut, and slapped it down on the nightstand. Stepping up to him, she pointed a finger at his chin. "I am not—nor will I *ever* be— your sweet. You play at seducing me with your kisses and your baubles, but we both know what you're doing. You've even said what you're about. You mean to use me to satisfy some . . . some *imagined* insult—"

His face like a thundercloud, Slade grabbed her wrists and yanked her against him. "Nothing was imagined. And it was no mere insult. The name Lawless is—"

A timid knocking on the room's open door cut off his next words. With him, Hannah jerked her head in the direction of the sound. Olivia stood there, wide-eyed, fearful.

The downstairs maid started to say something, but Slade loosed Hannah and turned to the thin, brown-haired girl. "Begone. Your mistress will be with you in a moment."

She bobbed a curtsy. "Yes, Mr. Garrett. I didn't mean—"

"No." Hannah slipped around Slade and put a hand out to the maid. The poor child froze in place, looking close to tears. "Please stay, Olivia. Mr. Garrett was just leaving." She turned to glare pointedly at him.

His black eyes shot daggers at her. "As you wish, *my sweet.*" He eyed the open boxes scattered about the room. "I trust everything is to your liking? I guessed at your exact measurements, of course. But then again, I had a fair idea as to your contours, having held you in my arms more than once. Until tonight, then?''

Stunned at his insulting forwardness, Hannah regarded him with an icy stare. Slade turned on his heel and strode to the door, causing Olivia to flatten herself against the wall when he drew even with her. And then, with a turn to his right, he was gone.

Hannah slumped, a marionette whose strings were suddenly loosened. So much for her grand scheme to seduce him. He'd seen right through that. She put her fingers to her pounding temples and sat heavily on the bed, not caring if she crushed anything delicate under her.

''Miss? Are you all right?''

Hannah looked up, realizing she'd forgotten Olivia. The maid's thin hands crunched and recrunched her starched apron. Hannah waved her in. ''I'm fine. Please come in.''

Watching Olivia step into the room, Hannah realized something. Slade Garrett had almost blurted out his reason for hating the Lawless name. And he would have, too, had Olivia's knocking not cut him off. Interesting. So, he could be goaded into showing his hand. Perhaps that should be her tack—instead of seducing him, she should concentrate instead on that quick temper of his. Liking that idea, and smiling more to herself than to the maid, Hannah nevertheless focused on the girl. ''Close the door, please.''

''Yes, miss.'' She did as ordered and then stood quietly, her hands folded in front of her, her expression hesitant.

Hannah tried to reassure her. ''I'm surprised, but glad, that it's you who answered my bell, Olivia.''

''No more surprised than I am, miss. I was polishing the silver when you rang for Mrs. Wells. But she ordered me up, saying it would be a warm January day in Boston before she'd come back in here.''

Hannah grinned, liking this girl more and more. ''I feel the same way by her. Olivia, would *you* like to be my lady's maid?''

The straighter she stood, the more Olivia's eyes widened. ''Me, miss? Are you sure? I've never been—I thought Mrs. Wells—''

"Not anymore. Not unless there *are* warm January days in Boston, which I doubt." Hannah paused. May as well see what she was made of. "And not since I pulled a gun and threatened to shoot her."

Olivia fought hard not to giggle, but finally it got away from her. "I heard as much, miss. We all did. Belowstairs, that is."

Hannah bit down on the inside of her cheek until she no longer felt like giggling herself. She looked down at her sleeves and tugged on them. "Did you, now? And what do you think about that?"

"I was hoping you'd prove to be a good shot, miss."

Hannah looked up, nearly choking on the laughter in her throat. She'd judged this girl correctly. Finally, someone in Boston she could come to trust. Genuinely happy for the first time since she'd stepped off the train four days ago, Hannah folded her hands together in her lap. "Before you decide, I think you should know that things could get . . . up-and-downish. You should also know I'll be the one causing the ups and downs. Now, having said that, do you want the position? Oh, and I promise not to shoot you—either way you decide."

"I appreciate that, miss. But don't worry about a few ups and downs along the way. My life . . . and working here, I'm used to it." She looked down at her hands twisted together in front of her and then looked up, now projecting a sincere attitude. "Even though you didn't ask . . . I *can* keep a secret. I think you're going to need someone who can." Then, taking a deep breath, she plunged ahead. "I've never been a lady's maid, but I'll try my best."

A sudden warmth flooding her, Hannah stood and clapped her hands together. "Well, I can't ask for more than that, Olivia. And thank you. I'll arrange it all with my aunt later. Oh, before I forget, tomorrow I need you to post a letter for me—without anyone knowing about it. But, right now, I need help getting dressed for this evening. Are you up to the task?"

Olivia's eyes lit with glee. "Oh, yes, miss. This is so exciting. I just know you'll be the most beautiful lady in the room tonight."

*    *    *

"Good God, man, surely you're not serious. That drowned little mouse of a sobbing waif from the other night? You intend to *marry* her?"

Slade looked from his formally attired reflection in his cheval glass to Dudley Ames, who was similarly dressed for the evening's entertainment at Cloister Point. "As it turns out, that drowned and sobbing little waif is none other than Miss Hannah . . . *Wilton* . . . *Lawless*."

Slade watched in amusement as Dudley sucked in a huge breath that appeared to be inflating his eyes. Slade turned back to the mirror, making an adjustment to his gray neckcloth. "Her name does have the effect of a stomach punch, does it not?"

Dudley performed an ungainly flop onto the nearest unfortunate chair. "And here I thought your disdain for the services of a valet capped the climax." He shook his large head and stared at his polished shoes. Then he bolted forward in the dwarfed chair. "Wilton and Lawless together can only mean one thing, Garrett."

"Nothing slips past you, does it, my friend?" Slade drawled.

Waving off the insult, Dudley jumped to his feet, pacing the room and questioning Slade, as if he were on trial. "Does she know who you are—I mean, *really* know who you are—to her?"

Slade gave a final tug to his silk waistcoat as he recalled Hannah's fainting reaction upon first learning his name. He turned to Dudley. "I have reason to think so."

"Then, why is she here?"

Slade put his hands to his waist. "There's only one reason why she'd show up in Boston at this particular time. You know what it is, as well as I do."

Dudley gave that due and frowning consideration. "True. But you'd think the mother would come for her inheritance and not the daughter."

Slade stared in silence at Dudley. But then he gave a careless shrug. "Perhaps the mother . . . wasn't able."

Dudley nodded. "And so she sent her daughter in her stead. Yes, that could be. But do you know if Hannah knows you know why she's here?"

Slade stared at his pacing friend's back, trying to decipher

the you-knows and she-knows. When he felt sure of the re-
lationship, he called out his answer. "Yes."

Dudley whipped around, pointing a finger at him. "And
you've actually ventured over to Cloister Point *alone* and *unarmed*? And *she's* even residing there?" He shook his head.
"Unbelievable. And neither one of you is dead yet?"

"Dudley, my mutton-chopped friend, I know you hate to
hear it—because becoming one would please your mother too
much—but you'd make an imposing lawyer. Rest assured,
Learned Counselor, that the lady was alive when I left her a
mere hour ago. And here I stand. So, obviously neither one
of us is dead."

"Hold on right there, Garrett. Something's just occurred to
me. Not about Mother, but about you." The red-haired senator's son put his thick finger to his wide lips and frowned in
concentration. A moment later, he wagged that same finger at
Slade. "You're telling me that, in no more than"—he counted
them out on his other hand—"four days, you've come to care
enough about this girl to marry her? You can just throw aside
all the years of hating J. C. Lawless?"

Slade laughed and shook his head at the openly suspicious
Dudley. "Care about her? Hardly. Nor do I intend to. But I
do mean to see that she falls desperately in love with me. And
that, my serious friend, is the beauty of my plan. Trust me,
I've not forgotten or forgiven J. C. Lawless."

Dudley approached Slade, laying a hamlike hand on his
shoulder. "I see your game now. You can't do this. It'll destroy you, as surely as it did your mother. And hurting this
innocent girl won't change anything. It won't bring your parents back. And it won't change the truth of their lives. Or
yours."

A cold shadow fell over Slade, turning him to emotional
stone. He wrenched away from Dudley's touch. "You go too
far. Don't presume on our friendship, lifelong though it is."

Black eyes bored into brown. Then, slumping in defeat,
Dudley stepped back and let out a labored breath. He paced a
step or two and ran a hand through his short-cropped hair.

Finally, he spoke softly as he turned to Slade. "You have
my apology. But as your 'lifelong friend,' no one is more
qualified than me to say these things to you. What you're

doing is wrong. And you know it.'' He thinned his lips in judgment.

When Slade remained unyielding, he heaved out his breath. ''All right. I'll not bring it up again.'' In the ensuing silence between them, Dudley appeared to regroup. He gave a so-be-it nod of his head and shot Slade a playful look. ''This ruse of yours could be the season's amusement. Especially if you lose your heart to this girl. Frown if you like, but it is possible, Fate being the jokester she is.'' Dudley then grinned. ''Who knows? I may even prove useful to you somehow. Wouldn't that surprise Mother?''

''Surprise her? It would put her in her grave.'' The balance restored, Slade moved to his étagére, plucked his top hat off it, plopped it on his head at a jaunty angle, and turned to Dudley. ''Let's see. Do I have everything?'' He patted himself down, stopping his hands at his chest. ''Hold on—what's this? No heart there. Well then, how can I lose it? Come, Dudley, let's go engage the enemy.''

Hannah clamped her jaws shut to keep from saying the pretty words. She'd rather die first. Especially galling was having to admit that the blasted man seated conveniently next to her as her dinner companion was correct. She looked around her at the glittering ladies. Seeing them proved that her own gowns would have been woefully inadequate for this company.

Slade Garrett leaned over to her, speaking softly. ''Oh, come now, Hannah, my sweet. Admit it—in one of your own gowns, you would have stuck out like a laying hen among songbirds. Thanking me for caring enough to save you from being a laughingstock won't kill you.'' He straightened up, sipping at his wine and keeping his amused gaze on her.

''Are you enjoying your *game*, Mr. Garrett?'' Hannah spoke loudly, purposely drawing the attention of the diners closest to them. Smiling for them, but glaring rigidly at him, she amended, ''Of course, I mean this wonderful game *hen*.'' She stabbed her fork into the headless, plucked, gutted, and baked bird on her plate. ''Exquisite, isn't it?''

Slade dipped his head in acknowledgment that the battle was begun. With a smile resembling the curved slash of a scythe, he very deliberately set his wine glass on the white linen tablecloth. Then, revealing only to her the dangerous black lights dancing in his eyes, he otherwise became the perfect gentleman. "I'm sure the . . . little brown bird is exquisite. Normally I would devour such a *hen*. But I find, my dear, that in your presence I've lost my appetite."

After allowing for an insulting space of time to elapse, he added, "For anything but you, that is. Could my affected state be because of your lovely new gown? I see that I was right about this dress. I thought when I purchased it for you that it, just like your eyes, changed color with every motion you make."

Hannah sat openmouthed at his public and damning confession. Around her, a few of the younger men raised their glasses to her in a hearty and concurring toast. But older heads joined the feminine heads in bending together, repeating Slade's words. Their whispers telegraphed the length of the table. Tipsy gentlemen rapped on the table with their knuckles, repeating a jolly "Hear, hear."

Not everyone was amused by Slade's forward words. To her left, Aunt Patience gasped. Hannah turned to her. The older woman was pale and clearly incensed at her niece's part in this public scene. Biting at her lip, Hannah started to turn back to her hated dinner companion, but instead her attention was caught by the man across the table from her. Dudley Ames. He persisted in aiming a sappy, besotted grin her way, just as he'd been doing from the moment she'd been properly introduced to him tonight.

The huge man was sitting forward in his chair, his elbow propped on the table, his chin resting in his huge hand. With his other hand, he jabbed his finger to her right, as if pointing out to her who her enemy was. But Hannah knew. She turned her head. Slade Garrett's attention remained riveted on her.

Hannah raised her chin a notch. He was wooing her publicly, staking his claim. And doing so boldly, insinuating he already enjoyed the lady's favors. Thus, he insured that no other man would approach her. Or help her.

Her heart picked up its beating pace as a hush settled over the gathering of avid Brahmin. She knew without looking away from her adversary that all heads were now turned her way. An extended silken rustle told her the titillated diners were actually leaning in over the table, the better to hear her reply.

Under cover of the tablecloth, Hannah twisted her linen napkin into knots, and wished it were instead his neck in her hands. "Imagine my . . . delight, Mr. Garrett, over your very *public* appreciation of my gown. I'm afraid I must disappoint you, however. You see, I—for one—don't particularly like this creation. I'm wearing it only because I am *forced* to, as you well know. And thanks to your meddling in my bedroom, I have nothing else to wear."

# CHAPTER FIVE

—

*Good Lord.* She hadn't meant to blurt out her last words. They weren't what she meant—at least, not the way they sounded. Her hand covering her mouth, she stared wide-eyed at Slade. She'd just confirmed his innuendo.

A drawn-out silence first met her words, but then a determined clattering of silverware and a rash of loud conversations broke out. Servants appeared from nowhere to retrieve the decidedly fowl course. On their heels came others, these serving each diner the vegetable dish, asparagus in a cream sauce.

Well, no one could say she hadn't gotten in the last word. Even if she had, to put it mildly, lost this round. Hannah picked up her fork and despondently cut her asparagus. Peeking to her right, she saw Slade mimicking her actions. Did he have to sit so close? Would she never have respite from his stinking bay rum scent and hatefully handsome face?

As if he'd heard her thoughts, he leaned over to her. "I'm still waiting for you to thank me."

Gritting her teeth to keep from screaming and stabbing him with her fork, Hannah gritted out, "You've already humiliated me. I'll not repay you by thanking you for having my own clothing spirited away, leaving me with nothing to wear but your charity."

"Charity? You've a king's ransom around your pretty neck alone." He put his fork down and fingered the emerald necklace at her throat. He made deliberately sure—in her opinion— that his fingers caressed her bare skin.

Hannah raised her chin and leveled a cool stare in his direction. He withdrew his hand. But only to rest it on the back of her chair. For a moment, black eyes blazed into blue-green eyes. With his face only inches from hers, and his voice no more than a gritty rattle, he whispered, "Have I made you angry?"

*Damn him.* Her breathing constricted by the tight bodice, she gathered as much air into her lungs as she could. Slade's gaze went immediately to the exposed swell of her bosom. Hannah redirected his gaze to her face by clutching her knotted napkin to her chest and all but whispering, "Have it your way, then. Anything to get you to leave me alone." She inclined her head regally. "I thank you, Mr. Garrett. I am eternally grateful." She snapped her head up, hoping her eyes reflected the blaze of fury in her heart. "There. Are you happy?"

"No." Moving his hand from her chair, he ran his knuckles up the column of her neck and leaned over her, whispering into her ear. "I'll not be happy until your name is Garrett and you're . . . *mine.*"

With his warm breath feathering over the sensitive shell of her ear, a sudden light-headed feeling swept over Hannah, washing away her fighting spirit. She gripped the table's edges and whispered, "Stop this. I beg you. You're making of me a public spectacle. And I don't appreciate it."

He put his warm hand on her bare shoulder and squeezed gently. But the smile on his mouth didn't quite reach his riveting black eyes. "The daughter of J. C. Lawless—such a famous outlaw—afraid for her reputation? I would think you'd be used to being a public spectacle, if not the curiosity these Brahmins find you."

Hannah's anger bubbled up. She fought it, knowing he was deliberately provoking her. She couldn't care less what these people thought of her. But how *dare* this murdering snake even *speak* of her father?

Feeling cold inside, unable to move or to look away, she didn't even flinch when he reached up to smooth back an escaped ringlet of hair at her temple. "This little game we're playing, Hannah . . . I hope you're good at it. Because I sure as hell am. And there can only be one winner."

*A game?* He thought of his actions as a game? Feeling suddenly disconnected from this room, from her body, Hannah stared at Slade Garrett. She wondered how he could be so handsome and so evil. And for four days, he'd been pushing her, baiting her, taunting her.

During that same time—even in the space of the same day, he'd do a complete turnaround and hold her and comfort her and lavish gifts on her. She knew why he did all that—his revenge. She could fight that. But what she couldn't fight was his exciting her, his awakening in her the feelings and desires she did *not* want to feel. Not for him. One look, one touch . . . and she was lost.

Slade suddenly pulled back from her, raising his eyebrows. "Such a face, Hannah. So forlorn. Don't tell me I've already won. If so, I'm disappointed. I expected more of a fight from the daughter of J. C. Lawless."

That was twice he'd said her father's name. *So it was a fight he wanted? Then a fight he would get.* Hannah exploded. Lost to reason, she jumped up, knocking her chair over backward and startling everyone in the room into stunned attention. She slammed her hands onto the table, rattling china and crystal stemware. Her wine overturned, spilling a crimson puddle across the white tablecloth.

The sight, so reminiscent of blood, incited her further. Screwing her face up into a tortured mask of hatred, she glared at a wide-eyed Slade Garrett. "You . . . murdering . . . *bastard.* This is *not* a game. Not to me. Can you not understand that? My parents are *dead.*"

She curled a hand into a fist and slammed it down onto the table. "*Dead.* My sisters and I returned home to find your handiwork"—she stabbed her finger at him—"and yours"— she pointed in turn at her aunt and uncle, seated at opposite ends of the table. "Mama and Papa. Their murdered bodies. Their blood everywhere. Was that a *game* to you?"

Hot, salty tears rolled unheeded down her face. She dragged in a labored breath, noting the disbelieving expression on Slade's face. Into the crushing silence, she spoke softly, wrenchingly. "How could you? *Why* did you? What could it matter now?"

Then, she straightened up, reveling in the sneer forming on her face as she gazed at her aunt and uncle. A part of her brain registered their expressions for her. Pale, hating, blank masks. But they no longer scared her. Hannah shook her head, not even recognizing the hoarse, unholy voice that issued from her. She pronounced each word with deadly emphasis. "Did you think"—she swallowed hard—"we wouldn't know who killed them? Did you think . . . we wouldn't care?"

Knowing she'd get no more of an answer from them than she'd gotten from Slade Garrett, she nevertheless turned back to him. And saw him, with deadly calm motions, put his napkin on the table, push his chair back, and slowly rise to his feet. Hannah followed his movements with her gaze and her words. "What made you think . . . we wouldn't come after you?"

Towering over her now, Slade took hold of her arm. "That's quite enough, Hannah. Don't say another word."

She jerked her arm, meaning to break his hold, but his strength was too much for her. "You take your hand off me, you murderer."

"I murdered *no one*!" His bellowing response caused everyone to jump and gasp. For her part, Hannah shrank down nearly into a crouch. But still he didn't release her, not even when he pounded his other fisted hand on the blameless table, sending a tall flower arrangement to its death. "I had *nothing* to do with your parents' deaths. Nothing! And I will *not* sit here and be accused of such treachery."

He glared at her until she looked down. When Slade moved, turning more to his right, Hannah looked up at him. And jerked in a ragged breath. The enraged glare he focused on the other end of the table would make Satan tuck in his pointed tail and run. Hannah's gaze followed his, sighting on Cyrus Wilton-Humes.

Following their lead, the Wilton-Humeses' dinner guests, mere innocents trapped in this remarkable tableau, also focused on their host. Cyrus, his face no more than a death mask, gripped the table with both hands. But he said nothing. Neither did anyone else. They all waited. For Slade Garrett.

And he didn't disappoint them. "I had nothing to do with these murders. And I *will* prove it. But I don't for one minute doubt that you and your lovely wife had everything to do with Catherine's death. And we know why, don't we?"

Hannah jerked upright. He *knew* why? How? And if he knew, but wasn't involved, as he'd just said, why hadn't he done anything to stop them? What sort of man did that make him? She put her free hand to her heart, even though the questions beat painfully at her temples.

After a tense silence, Cyrus became the third person to rise from the table. ''How dare you! *You*—of all people. You have more reason than we do to hate what she stands for.'' He made a sweeping gesture toward the room's wide entrance. ''Leave, both of you. This is my home. Mine. I will not listen to such outrageous lies, especially from''—he now pointed an accusing finger at Hannah—''you—an *outlaw's bastard.* You came to us seeking shelter—all lies! You're no better than your mother. We never wanted you here to begin with. You weren't invited. And now? You're not welcome. Leave!''

Hannah jerked against Slade's hold on her, wanting to be free to scratch her great-uncle's eyes out. By God, she'd not listen to this man's name-calling! But Slade wrenched her back to him, forcing her to meet his eyes. ''No, Hannah. You've said enough.''

She opened her mouth to protest, but her words withered into silence when she realized there was a pleading, almost fearful glint in his so-black eyes. Not expecting either emotion from him, and now more confused than ever, Hannah stilled in his arms.

Registering her compliance with only the barest of nods, Slade turned his sober attention once again on his hostile host. ''We're going, Wilton-Humes. But this isn't over. Not by a long shot. My man will be along tomorrow for her belongings. See that they're ready. But you be warned—she's under my protection now. And I will be seeing personally to her well-being.''

He paused, letting that sink in. His final words, as much to Hannah as to Cyrus, were, ''We'll get to the bottom of this, I promise you.''

Hannah stared up at him in surprise. The man was more of an enigma than ever. Watching his every movement, forced by his hold on her arm to turn with him, she saw him make a slight gesture at Dudley Ames across the table from them. Needing no further prompting, that large, ruddy-complected man pushed himself up out of his chair, slapping his napkin onto the table.

Slade once again turned to the numbed gathering, bowing slightly. ''Ladies. Gentlemen. We'll say good-night now. I trust the evening's entertainment from this point forward will prove more . . . mundane.''

Then, with the room's charged silence as background, and still gripping Hannah's arm, Slade kicked his chair and hers back against the wall, clearing a walking space for them. Her heart pounding, her limbs weak, she gathered up her skirt. Slade finally released her arm, but only to put his hand at the small of her back. With Dudley joining them as they reached his side of the table, Hannah marched out of the room, followed closely by her entourage.

With renewed murmurings and the clatter and tinkling of resumed activity at their backs, down the wide hallway the threesome strode, past portraits of generations of Hannah's disapproving ancestors. She ignored them, focusing instead on the men's footfalls. Their heavy tread sounded a certain finality on the polished wood floor.

Deposited between the two men, and pushed along by Slade's hand at her back, Hannah spoke as rapidly as she walked. ''I do not intend to place myself under your protection, Mr. Garrett. I'd be a fool. Because, by your own words, and by the evidence I brought with me, I have more than enough reason to doubt your sincerity when you say you'll get to the bottom of this. My fear is that the bottom you refer to will be the harbor. And I'll be in it—dead.''

''What the devil? Dead?'' That came from Dudley, but Hannah ignored his outburst.

As did Slade. ''I've said it before, Hannah—if I wanted you dead, you'd be dead. I *will* tell you this—in this house, you're already as good as buried in the ground. That much is certain.''

She shot him a look. ''I never said I intend to stay here after this. I can take care of myself. After all, I'm still alive, aren't I?''

He never looked down at her. ''By the grace of God and my continued presence here over the past four days.''

Hannah snapped her gaze up to him. A muscle twitched in his jaw. He stared straight ahead. Her steps faltered. He pushed her along. But Hannah couldn't believe her ears. ''Your presence? Do you expect me to believe that you've been protecting me?''

''I do. You serve my purpose, remember?''

"Ahh. Your revenge. So you've said. But tell me, revenge for what?"

"Now's not the time. Not in this house."

Hannah stopped abruptly, forcing the two men to do likewise. "I'll know this minute."

Over her head, Slade exchanged a look with Dudley, one she couldn't interpret. A quick glance at Dudley revealed he stared hard right back at his friend. Hannah turned again to Slade. And waited.

Finally, he refocused on her. "With no more evidence than my name scrawled on a piece of paper, you show up in Boston and publicly accuse me of murdering your parents. By doing so, you've slandered my name and my reputation. And that of my family. We are now—all of us—in danger, and in line to be the next victims.

"Therefore, Miss Lawless, you'll make no demands on me for explanations. And know this, I'll answer no questions until I'm ready. Nor will I be subjected to your protests. My personal plans for you aside, I now intend to keep you close to me—the better to draw out the Wilton-Humeses. Nothing more. You're a pawn. A means to an end. But you *will* consider yourself under my protection."

It was a good thing for him that he finished right then, because Hannah was close to exploding again and couldn't wait to get her words out. "Protection? Ha! You mean to have me close by so you can have your revenge."

In sudden angry and ugly reaction, he grabbed her arms and jerked her to him. From behind her, she heard Dudley Ames say, "Easy now, Garrett." But as before, he was ignored.

Hannah had eyes only for the rigid emotion shaping Slade Garrett's features into planes and angles, and making his voice a low growl. "I am *not* the one you need to fear. The Wilton-Humeses are as much my enemies as they are yours. You have no idea, Hannah, of who and what you're up against. But I do. Whether you trust me or not, it doesn't matter. You involved me. So now, you have to deal with me. And like it or not, you have to trust someone. And it will have to be me."

In the following silence, with his black eyes boring into hers, Hannah digested his words. And realized the futility in making her situation worse. "I see." When his grip on her eased the slightest bit, she forced a calm control to her features and asked, "Where are you taking me now?"

"That's better, Hannah. Much smarter." He looked deep and hard into her eyes, as if trying to gauge her meek acceptance against what he knew of her defiant spirit. Hannah remained absolutely still. Then, a frown flitted over his strong features, creasing his forehead. Abruptly he released her arms. But made no apology for his rough treatment as he straightened up and put his hand to the small of her back, once again directing her steps. "I'm taking you to my grandmother's estate. You'll be safe there. Isabel is the one person in the world the Wilton-Humeses fear."

Hannah glanced up at him. This was his first mention of family. Somehow, she'd never thought of him as connected to loved ones. He seemed so unattached to other people. With the possible exception of Dudley Ames. "And will you be staying there, too?"

"Afraid so." He eyed her briefly and then cut his gaze to Dudley.

Lost in the deepening heat on her face, Hannah chewed on her bottom lip. She hadn't meant it as it sounded, as if she wanted to him to stay there, for heaven's sake. Would she never win with words tonight?

Mercifully, they rounded into the foyer just then. Hannah stood quietly as Slade signaled to three servants. In a voice that reeked of authority, he barked out, "You there, Mr. Ames and I desire our hats and coats. And you, have my brougham brought around. That leaves you to send word upstairs that Miss Lawless will need her cloak—the lined one with the hood."

The first two men bowed, departing immediately to carry out their orders. The third nodded, began his bow, but then pulled up short when Hannah added, "I also need Olivia." She stubbornly looked from Slade to Dudley and back to Slade. "My lady's maid—Olivia O'Toole. I won't leave her in this house."

Slade took a deep breath and thinned his mouth. But finally said, "As you wish." He turned to the waiting man. "And the girl. That will be all."

"No it won't." Feeling Slade and Dudley slide their attention back to her, Hannah ignored them, speaking instead to the liveried servant. "Tell Olivia to gather up for herself what she'll need for tonight. Also tell her to bring me my handbag, a *decent* bedgown . . . and the gun in the nightstand drawer."

The servant, as unknown to Hannah as the bevy of others in attendance tonight, dropped his starchy pose to stare open-mouthed at her. He recovered somewhat, bowed again, and then turned around, practically running to the grand sweep of the central stairway.

"Did she say 'gun in the nightstand drawer'?" That was Dudley. Hannah looked up to her left at the big man and then turned to her right when Slade answered. The men carried on the conversation, literally over her head and as if she weren't present.

"I believe she did, my friend."

"I say, Garrett, I don't believe the lady trusts you."

"I believe the lady has reason not to trust me, Mr. Ames."

"That's true. But you'd think after your masterful performance just now that the lady would realize you mean to help her."

Slade raised his eyebrows at his friend and then sighted on Hannah while answering him. "Hardly. The lady understands that I am helping myself."

Hannah raised her chin a notch, refusing to have further words with him. But as she stood there waiting, her prideful stance relaxed, weakened. Suddenly drained of all emotion and overwrought from her tirade, an inutterable tiredness overtook her. She longed for nothing more than a bed.

She cut her gaze to Slade Garrett and amended her thought—her *own* bed. A big, fat, soft one. With lots of covers. And lots of quiet. Blinking rapidly to stave off a case of drooping eyelids, Hannah hoped that Grandmother Isabel's estate wasn't too far away.

The sleek brougham turned smoothly into the wide drive. Hannah peeked out the window. *Something's wrong.* Wrapped in her cloak, wedged warmly against Slade, she turned to him. "If this is your idea of a joke, then I—"

"I promise you I'm in no mood for jests. This *is* my grandmother's estate—Woodbridge Pond."

"He's telling the truth." Sitting across from her and Slade, Dudley nodded good-naturedly, perhaps desperately, at her and then down at Olivia, all but lost next to him on the narrow seat. "He is."

Wide-eyed, the young girl nodded back at him. "Yes, sir. I know."

Hannah stared in disbelief at them all. "But we've only just left Cloister Point." She then looked up at Slade. "That would make your family estate—"

"The next one over from there. As luck would have it."

She swiveled her shoulders until she bodily faced Slade. He sat spread-legged, his arms crossed over his chest. Even in the brougham's dim interior, she could see he was grinning at Dudley. She tugged on his sleeve to gain his attention. " 'As luck would have it'?"

Sobering, he looked from his friend to her. "What would you have me say, Hannah? The Garretts and Wilton-Humeses have a long history together. I assumed your mother would have talked about home. Even under her particular set of circumstances."

Hannah noted the sudden thick quality to the air at the mention of her mother. "She did. But apparently she left out a few details—such as who the neighbors were. It's not that I doubt you. It's just that—well, I don't see how I'm any safer here, with only a fence separating the two properties."

To her surprise, Slade reached over to take her hand and tug it over to rest on his thigh. Smiling down into her face, and ignoring Dudley's laughter from across the way, he confided, "Trust me, my dear Miss Lawless. There's much more than a fence to separate the Wilton-Humeses from the Garretts. As you're about to see."

"It's good to see you up and around, Pemberton."

"Thank you, sir. A nasty cold, that was. Still, one is feeling very fit, age being what it is." The ancient butler, whose round little head was capped by tufts of whitish hair, peered around Slade to squint his watery blue eyes at the two women with him.

Slade looked at them, too, noting Hannah's bemused uncertainty as she looked from him to Pemberton. He then turned back to the butler. "Amazing, isn't it?"

"Indeed, sir. She's the spitting image of her mother."

Slade ignored Hannah's gasping intake of air to answer the

older man. "I thought so, too. Although I didn't realize it as quickly as you did. I've brought her as a surprise for Isabel."

"I see. One can only hope that she doesn't piddle on the carpet, like the last surprise you and Mr. Ames bestowed on your grandmother."

Laughing out loud, and wisely ignoring the insulted noises from Hannah, Slade shed his overcoat, feeling happy and alive in the high-ceilinged, richly papered foyer. He tossed his heavy garment to the Garrett institution that was Pemberton. "Speaking of Mr. Ames, you've just missed him. I sent him home in my carriage."

"More's the pity for his mother."

"Exactly." Slade then turned to help a visibly miffed Hannah off with her cloak, also giving it and Olivia's thin cape over to the man.

The frail butler, toppling under the garments' combined weight, staggered forward a step. Only Slade's quick hand on his arm saved him from landing on his thin beak of a nose. "Thank you, sir. Herself is in the drawing room with Esmerelda. They're both pretending to nod in front of the fire. But one fears they're actually devising new methods of torment for the unwary."

"Then we're just in the nick of time." Slade turned to Hannah. "Isabel and Esmerelda are quite the rounders. You three should get along famously."

"Oh? Especially if I don't . . . piddle on the carpet?"

"No. Especially if you do." Grinning at her wide-eyed look, Slade nevertheless noted the gray pallor of her tired face. The poor thing was nearly done in. She needed to rest. He turned to Olivia. "Pemberton will direct you to your room. Have him light my room as well. By the way, he likes to order everyone around, but we all ignore him. So you may as well, too. Right, Pemberton?"

"Correct, sir. One fears the shock of being obeyed would put one in one's grave." With that, Pemberton edged in a snail's-pace shuffle toward the coat closet.

Behind him, and gripping the two small bags she'd packed for herself and her lady, Olivia shrugged good-naturedly at Slade and Hannah. Then, shifting the carpetbags to one hand, she put her free hand to the thin old gentleman's elbow, easing his way. "Come along then, Pemberton. We wouldn't want to grow roots, now would we?"

"One wouldn't think so, miss."

His hands at his waist, Slade watched the unlikely pair until they disappeared around a corner. Only then did he look down at Hannah, standing quietly next to him. Her face was still splotched from her recent emotion and her hair was coming all undone. But it didn't matter. She was still beautiful. In spite of himself, Slade felt his heart swell at the nearness of her. "Well, what do you think?"

"I think that little man is older than God."

He chuckled, as much at the expression on her face as at her wry comment. "We've often suspected as much. I'm the third generation of Garretts he's confounded." Then, something new in the way she looked at him caught his attention. His smile faltered. "You're looking at me as if I just grew a tail."

"If you did, it wouldn't surprise me." Her saucy expression then changed to thoughtful. "You're just—You're more like— Oh, I don't know how to put it. It's nothing. Never mind." With that, and accompanied by the silken rustle of her aquamarine gown, she moved with a gliding grace around a centrally placed walnut table. There, she reached out to fondle a delicate figurine.

Slade contented himself with quietly watching her. His brain warned him against her, but his body warmed to her. With her every movement, with every curving, graceful feature of hers he outlined, sharp darts of desire coursed through him.

Perhaps sensing the thickening awareness in the air between them, she stilled and looked up at him. The emeralds at her ears and throat caught the chandelier's light, sparking fire against her dark hair and velvety complexion.

Caught unawares, Slade stood up straighter. The jewels. The gown. They were mere afterthoughts on her. She needed no such adornment. His hands itched to rip the dress off her, to throw her naked onto the table, and to finally make her understand what she did to his control.

Because even without touching her, he could feel her body against his. He could taste her skin. His hands longed to shape themselves to the firmness of her high breasts. Hurting from simply looking at her, Slade fought his own sexual nature. In another moment he'd leap across the space between them, freeing her soft and silky hair from its pins, and take her—

She made an abrupt movement, as if breaking a spell. And indeed, she did. If she only knew it. "You're different here . . . in this house. Somehow. That's what I'm trying to say. And I certainly shouldn't add this next, but this being the night for me to speak my mind . . ." She allowed her sentence to trail off as she looked down and then up again at him. "Your way with Pemberton. Your care with Olivia. And with me. I find I almost like the man I see."

"Almost?" In an agony of lust barely controlled, Slade smirked at his own expense. "You wouldn't like the man I am at all, if you could read my mind just now, Hannah."

She frowned, looking contrite and hesitant. "I don't suppose I blame you for feeling the way you do."

Slade's eyebrows shot up in amusement. "You don't?"

"No. How could I? Not thirty minutes ago I accused you of—"

He held up a hand, feeling desire and humor wilt. "I know what you said. If a man had accused me of those things, he'd be spitting his teeth out. Or lying out in the street. But those words between you and me . . . with everything else there is between us? Mere grist for the mill. Now, come on, I'll take you in to meet the old dragon. And then we'll go on to bed."

When her eyes widened and she clutched at her gown's skirt, Slade thought about his words, and added, "Your own bed. Alone. Now, come on. This way." He held his hand out to her, indicating she should precede him.

After a moment's hesitation, she did as he bade. And made him sorry. A delicately perfumed scent, warmed by her body, wafted to his nostrils when she passed him. He rolled his eyes at his own weakness, but was then completely undone by the sight of her slender, innocent nape as he walked behind her. With her head bent forward the slightest bit, with her hair upswept, exposed along her neckline was a fringe of tiny, down-soft curls. Exposed also was the shadowed cleft of her graceful neck where it met her regal head.

Overwhelmed, undone, and before his better sense could stop him, Slade reached out to her, clasping her by her shoulders. A tiny gasp coupled with her start of surprise. Slade turned her to him. Hazel eyes, so open and yet so injured, and fringed with the blackest of thick lashes, silently questioned him.

Without uttering a word, he dragged her against his chest, encircling her in his embrace. She fit there so perfectly, despite remaining perfectly still and rigid, her arms at her sides. Slade couldn't even detect her breathing.

Forcing his words out, denying the raw wound this new tenderness wrought as it ripped through his soul's armor, Slade righted the one wrong that he could. "Hannah, you've got to believe me. I knew nothing about . . . your mother and your father. Not until you said it tonight—I didn't know. I swear it. I'm no fan of your father's, but I wish to God I could have been there to spare you that sight. Or to prevent it from ever happening."

She stiffened even more. Slade held her fast against him, sensing the building storm. And then, like a young, wind-battered willow, she broke. Slumping against him, she encircled his waist with her arms and clutched at his clawhammer coat. Gasps of agony escaped her, echoing in the foyer. Like a child, she called out for her mama and her papa. She pressed into him, seeking his warmth. And his strength. Through tearful sobs she spoke of blood . . . blood everywhere. She even cried for someone named Old Pete.

A rock-sized lump lodging in his throat, Slade bent his cheek to the top of her head. He brought his hand up from her back to brush aside emotion-dampened tendrils of hair from her brow. His eyes blurred with a moistness he would not acknowledge. And still he held her. And still she cried.

In another moment, approaching footfalls caught his attention. From all directions, the Garrett household was responding. On the stairs were Rowena and Serafina, twin spinster-sister maids, concern etching their wrinkled old brows. Others, all of them just as aged and in various stages of bed dressing, toddled down after them. Even Olivia and Pemberton once again stood in the foyer, holding on to each other.

Not to be left out, from the deepest recesses of the house came the waddling, arthritic cook, Mrs. Edgars, and her entire gray-haired entourage. And off to the right, in the drawing room doorway, Isabel stood, one hand to her matriarchal bosom, her other clutching at Esmerelda's collar. The impossibly huge mastiff wrinkled her brow in apparent concern.

With a nod of his head, Slade sent a silent message to his grandmother. She nodded. Letting go of the dog's collar, she went into action, silently shushing everyone and shooing them back. But Olivia, sighting on the dog and clearly terrified, took up residence at Slade's side. She clutched at his coat's hem and refused to budge. No one else obeyed Isabel, either. Including the calculating Esmerelda, who elected to sit on her haunches beside Olivia and eye her consideringly.

And so it was with such a grand and silent audience that Slade picked Hannah up, cradling her in his arms while she turned her bleak, tearstained face against his lapel.

With Isabel leading the pack, Slade carried Hannah's whimpering form up the stairs. The two old maids scurried ahead of him, shooing all from his ascending path. On the second floor, the sisters let him pass, and then fell in line behind their mistress, the tongue-lolling Esmerelda, the lady's maid Olivia, and joined the ranks of Isabel's gray-haired, concerned domestics.

When he reached the door he wanted, Slade stopped and turned to face it. Several gasps sounded at his choice of rooms, as he knew they would, but Olivia innocently leapt forward to open the door, pushing it inward and then stepping back. Slade crossed the threshold and, without looking back or uttering a word, caught the door with his foot and nudged it shut behind him. Directly in the faces of everyone in the hallway.

Knowing they wouldn't dare interfere—not even Isabel—Slade marched straight to his bed and deposited his droopy-eyed burden on the quilted counterpane. Walking around to the other side, his gaze never leaving the sight she made on his bed, he shrugged out of his jacket, loosened his clothing, and then bent to draw his shoes off. Taking a deep breath, he perched next to Hannah's huddling body. Her back to him, sound asleep, her breaths came in a sob-stilted rhythm.

With practiced hands, Slade unfastened her gown and likewise her corset. He'd never understand why women wore these instruments of torture—torture for the men trying to divest their women of them, that is. There. Now she could most likely breathe. Not daring to undress her further, except for her dainty shoes, he scooted up against the mound of pillows at his back. Then, with great tenderness, he turned Hannah into his arms.

Refusing to think about what it was he was doing, he re-settled them both. And then, crossing his legs at the ankles, he simply held her, content to rest his cheek against her hair. He closed his eyes. His last wakeful thought was *When she wakes up tomorrow, what then?*

# CHAPTER SIX

—

Lying on her stomach, her legs kicked out wide, Hannah greeted the day slowly. Frowning, she realized that her limbs felt weighted. As if she'd slept in one position all night. She bobbed her eyes open and then immediately closed them. Not that there was any bright light to assail her morning vision. There wasn't. It was just that her eyes burned and itched.

She tried to turn over so she could rub them, but something restricted her movement. She lay still, focusing on that something. Then, it came to her. Why, she was fully dressed. Right down to the emeralds poking at her collarbone. She lay momentarily still, frowning.

Then, she flipped over and, after a protracted battle with the tangled yardage of her skirt, sat straight up, her legs out in front of her, her bustle riding up to poke at her back. She braced herself with her hands behind her on the bed's coverings.

Looking down at herself, she saw long, tortured curls of her hair hanging all about her. Which mattered not. No. It was instead the gown's bodice flopped down to her waist and her loosened corset poking out lewdly, as if offering a view of her exposed bosom, which rendered her aghast.

Hannah quickly drew the two up and against her skin. Remaining absolutely motionless for a moment, she took advantage of the thin, gray light filtering through the drawn curtains into the . . . she slowly looked around her . . . large, completely unfamiliar, and very masculine room. At least she was alone. But *where* was she?

As if in answer, the door across the room, in a direct line

with the foot of the bed, opened. Hannah clutched tightly at her ruined bodice. A long shadow fell into the room, bleeding across the carpeted floor and then onto the bed. Hannah blinked, trying to adjust her vision. Then, seeing who stood there, she let out her breath and fell limply back onto the pillows beneath her. Her stiff dimity bustle threw her immediately onto her side in one ungainly motion.

Olivia bustled in, going immediately to work picking up and straightening as she chattered. "Oh, good, miss, you're awake. You had us all quite worried. It's after noon, you know. Allow me to straighten up a bit in here, and then I'll help with your toilette." Casually strolling by on her way to a huge armoire, the lady's maid half turned to Hannah. "By the way, I posted that letter you gave me. And no one's the wiser."

Hannah watched the girl walk by. She heard her words, absorbed them. But found she could do nothing but stare at the maid's back as she continued past. She had a million questions for her, but the words simply wouldn't come.

Olivia didn't seem to notice or to mind the lack of a response. Across the room now, she bent over to retrieve a shirt and then popped up, turning a bright smile on Hannah. "Oh, miss, I do love it here. There's plenty of good food and everyone is most kind. Not like some other place I could name. I was always hungry and cold there. But there's more—Mr. Garrett says I may have Wednesday afternoon and *all* of Sunday off each week . . . if you agree, of course. He's paying me *twice* my wages to stay on with you. Isn't that lovely?"

Then, her face clouded up. "Although I'm not too fond of that Esmerelda." She appeared to mentally consider the reasons why—without enlightening Hannah. And then she changed course again. "Do you know that everyone here at Woodbridge Pond—except for me and you and Mr. Garrett—is anciently old? Why, I suspect they can remember the Great Flood. Probably came here on Noah's Ark, they did."

*Woodbridge Pond! That's it!* Quick on the heels of that revelation came the other images of last evening. The disastrous dinner party, the very short carriage ride. What he'd said about her parents. Her in his arms and crying. And then—she stared, unblinking, at the quilt under her—that was all she remembered.

Suddenly galvanized, Hannah struggled back to a sitting position, held her bodice up, and stared after Olivia, who continued to bustle and chatter. Hannah reaffirmed for herself what the girl had said. She was at Woodbridge Pond, and it was after noon. *After noon!* "Olivia!" she called out, stopping the little maid's happy musings. "Come here."

With discarded clothing bundled in her arms, Olivia immediately skittered to her side. She dropped her burden onto the bed and put a hand on Hannah's arm. "What is it, miss? Are you ill?"

Hannah thought about that. "No. At least, I don't think I am." She focused on the girl, noting that she was completely lost in a clean and starched but oversized gray uniform, topped by an equally large white apron. "Olivia, tell me *exactly* what is going on."

Olivia looked askance at Hannah. "Why, nothing is going on, miss. I'm just gathering the laundry." As if to prove it, she plucked from off the top of her pile a wrinkled shirt and held it up. "See, miss?"

Her gaze riveted to the shirt, Hannah tightened her hands on her gathered bodice. But then, heedless of the resulting exposure, she let go of her gown to snatch at the garment. Quickly she sorted it out, finally holding it up and away from her by the ever-so-broad shoulders. "Where did this come from?"

Acting as if she were humoring a mad woman, Olivia patiently explained, "From off the floor over there, miss. You saw me pick it up. But before that . . . why, off Mr. Garrett's back, I'm sure."

Hannah dropped her arms heavily onto her lap and stared hard at Olivia. "This is *his* room, isn't it?"

"Yes, miss. You were crying and so overcome. He carried you here himself, he did. Closed the door in all our faces, too, I can tell you."

Mortified, Hannah refused to think about who the "all" was. "And then what happened?"

Olivia blinked two or three times. "Well, miss, we all went on to bed. And so did you and Mr. Garrett . . . I suppose."

Hannah's heart plummeted to her belly. "Mr. Garrett slept here? With me?"

Olivia opened her mouth to answer, but the voice was much too masculine to be hers. "Yes. I did."

Olivia's eyes went as wide as Hannah's suspected hers were. The girl whipped around, and Hannah jerked her head up. *Slade Garrett.*

Exhibiting sartorial splendor, he was clean-shaven, dressed in buff riding pants and knee-high black boots, and a freshly starched white shirt under a dark-brown waistcoat. Looking rested and well and confident in his world, he stepped over the same threshold Olivia had trod only moments ago and approached the bed. He spoke first to the little maid. "That will be all for now, Olivia. Miss Lawless will be fine with me. She'll call for you in a moment."

"Yes, Mr. Garrett." She grabbed up the laundry, shot Hannah a quick, reassuring smile, and then fled around Slade, practically loping to the open door.

With Slade's back to her as he turned to watch Olivia's hasty departure, Hannah took in his stance, which emphasized the musculature of his thighs and the slimness of his hips. She credited the heavy thumping of her heart and suddenly moist palms to the inappropriateness of being alone with him. Again. In a bedroom. His bedroom.

When Olivia scurried into the adjoining room and closed the door, Slade turned again to face her. His eyes dipped to her bosom and sudden bemusement etched his features, making him seem almost boyish. He then met her gaze and jerked his thumb at the closed door. "Does Olivia ever walk anywhere? All I've ever seen her do is hurry."

Caught up in his dark, provocative aura, so reminiscent of a wild, barely leashed creature, Hannah mumbled out her words. "I think she's afraid of you."

His slanted gaze caused a black lock of hair to fall across his forehead. "No. *You're* afraid of me. That one isn't afraid of anyone . . . except Esmerelda."

Hannah sat up straighter, and felt a sudden airiness in the vicinity of her breasts. A sneaking glance downward confirmed her worst fear. Beyond mortified, she clutched his shirt to her chest. And froze. *His shirt?* With one hand, she promptly flung it away from her, sending it puffing out and sailing to the floor, right at his booted feet. Clutching the aquamarine bodice with both hands, she held it against herself like armor. "I'm not the least bit afraid of you. And who's Esmerelda?"

"Yes you are." Without so much as a moment of hesitation, he bent over, retrieved his shirt and handed it to her. "Here. Put it on to cover yourself. And yes, I undid your fastenings. I wasn't sure you could breathe otherwise."

He then nonchalantly sat, perching a hip on the mattress, and unabashedly watched her struggle to hold her own garments in place while still trying to don his shirt. "Don't tell me you don't remember Essie? Well, you'll become reacquainted soon enough." And then he smiled at her in a wide, white, dazzling display of male self-assuredness.

Hannah refused to return his good humor. Too much was wrong here. Like this shirt, which smelled so enticingly of his own particular musk. She gamely pulled it on and, with fumbling fingers, buttoned it over her exposed flesh. "Was there something you wished to tell me? Something extremely important—such as the house is on fire—that would give you the right to be in here while I'm still in—"

"My bed? No, there isn't. I just like seeing you in my bed."

Her fingers stilled as a rising heat flamed over her cheeks. "Please don't say things like that."

Black eyes glittering, he shrugged his shoulders goodnaturedly. "As you wish."

Finding she couldn't sustain eye contact with him, Hannah looked down at the buttons and realized she could not fasten more of them over her voluminous skirt. So, abandoning her efforts, she looked everywhere but at him. "I know, Mr. Garrett, that—"

"'Slade. Under the circumstances."

Sparing him a fleeting glance, she immediately looked away again. "Then, Slade . . . I know that I owe you a huge debt for your help. And I do thank you—"

"But?"

"Must you always interrupt me? *But* I find I'm . . . not comfortable here—"

"In my bed? Or my grandmother's home? Would you perhaps be happier in my brownstone? If you think Pemberton is a howl, wait until you meet Hammonds. He thinks I'm a reprobate."

Hannah stared at him. "I can understand why he would.

Now, let me finish. I find I'm not comfortable *here* or anywhere else where I might be putting your family and staff in danger. Aunt Patience and Uncle Cyrus are—''

''Gone.''

''Gone?''

''Gone. They were closing up Cloister Point this morning when I sent for your belongings. No doubt, in light of last night's developments, they've left to lick their wounds and refigure their strategy at their Nahant retreat. I find that appropriate, don't you? Them in retreat?''

Distracted, Hannah nodded her agreement. They were gone. That meant that she was free. In a sense. Free to move around, to leave the confines of a house. Explore. Stretch her legs. Smell fresh air. Breathe easily.

Great good humor suddenly boiled up inside her. Without a warning or an explanation, she slipped her legs over the far side of the bed and, tugging his shirt down at least to her waist, she very nearly skipped to the drapery-covered windows. Ripping aside the heavy damask, she . . . slumped her shoulders in dejection. Rain. Sheets of it. And wind. Gales of it.

She didn't realize that Slade had joined her there until he spoke at her side. ''Disappointing, isn't it? I was dressed for a ride and came to see if you'd care to join me. No sooner did I change than it began to rain. Unfortunately for us, I don't think it'll let up anytime soon.''

Hannah looked up at him, gazing at his strong, handsome profile. He'd wanted her to join him? Her—his pawn? His means to an end? His accuser of foul deeds? One minute he wanted to kill her. Another he wanted to marry her. Then another he held her in his arms while she wept. And the next he said he'd snap her neck. Which one was truly him? Or were they all him?

He looked down at her, catching her staring. She quickly turned her head to focus on the wet and windy sight outdoors.

''I suppose we could saddle Esmerelda and take turns riding her around in this drafty old house. What do you say?''

Hannah snapped her gaze back to him. ''*Saddle* Esmerelda? Then . . . she's not a person?''

''No. But don't tell her that. Or Isabel. They both think she is.''

''But . . . she's not a horse, either?'' Hannah looked askance at him. "You wouldn't keep a horse in the house, would you?"

He chuckled. "No, she's not a horse. Just the size of one." Then, his eyes took on a sparkling, assessing quality as he looked down at her. "You think me capable of most anything, don't you, Hannah?"

Hannah was happy to affirm his suspicion for him. "No, I *know* you to be capable of most anything. Like actually riding this Esmerelda, who's not a person or a horse."

Now he laughed out loud at her. And then completely disarmed her by pulling her to him and planting a friendly, smacking kiss on her forehead. Releasing her just as abruptly, he set her aside and, with her turning to keep him in her sights, he strolled to the same door by which he'd entered.

"I'll send Olivia in. By the way"—he pointed to the closed door—"on the other side of this door is your room. All your things are unpacked, so it's too late to protest. Get dressed and come downstairs. And I was joking about Esmerelda. I'd stand as much chance of saddling her as I would you. Come to the family drawing room—the first one on the right downstairs, where we'll have tea with Isabel. That should cheer you up."

Having said all that, he proceeded across the room to the hallway door, opened it, stepped through, and closed it after himself. Without so much as a glance back at her. Hannah stared blankly at the door. Who in truth was this man, that he would feel the need to cheer her up on a rainy afternoon?

"Well? Is the Lawless girl dead from the shock of waking in a Garrett bed?"

In the staggeringly opulent drawing room downstairs, blazing hot from the roaring fire in the grate, Slade bent over his grandmother to kiss her wrinkled brow. "No. She's alive and well."

Once she'd patted his cheek, Slade moved to the hearth rug, squatted in front of the sleeping Esmerelda, and knowing full well she hated it, rubbed her ears vigorously. Lying on her side, the mastiff lazily opened an eye and shoved him away with one swipe of her mighty paw.

"She's going to bite you in half one day."

Slade snorted his opinion of that as he pushed himself upright. He flopped down in a half-reclining posture on an over-stuffed and tasseled rose brocade sofa. "There's as much chance of Essie doing that as there is of me becoming a fish-monger."

"It's good, honest work. You ought to try it."

"I will—if you'll push the cart. Especially in that red dress." Slade grinned over at his frowning grandmother. Tiny, wizened, ornery, and even with her legs covered by a blanket, she was the most formidable person he'd ever met.

Apparently feeling she'd lost that round, Isabel resorted to her ace in the hole, her favorite subject of late—Slade's un-matrimonied state. "You'd best be careful with these maidens in your bed. In my day, you'd have to marry her for compro-mising her reputation so—even if she is a Lawless."

"Ahh, we're back to my being a bachelor, I see." Propping a shoulder against the well-padded armrest, Slade grinned hugely. "If it makes you feel any better, you'd have to marry her in my day, too."

She waved a hand in irritation. "Not me. You. But you'll never marry. Like as not, the Garrett line will die out for all your rakish carryings-on."

Chuckling at her, Slade contemplated his father's mother. And decided to broach the subject on both their minds. "Tell me, Isabel, what *do* you think about having a Wilton Lawless in our midst?"

Isabel pinned him with a shrewd stare. "Hmph. The walls haven't come tumbling down yet. But I'm more concerned with what you were doing with a Wilton Lawless in your arms last evening—as well as in your bed."

This long pause, Slade knew, was intended as a space for him to comment. He wisely said not a word, offering her only a wide grin and arched brows, completely subject to any in-terpretation she chose to give them.

"Just as I thought. Well then, where is she? It's very nearly mid-afternoon."

Never tiring of baiting her, Slade adopted a serious expres-sion. "No, it isn't. You and Esmerelda napped past mid-afternoon. It's more nearly candle-lighting time."

Isabel pinched her face up into a prune. "It's nowhere near dusk. We haven't even had tea yet. Don't think that because I'm old, I don't know what's what. Now, answer my question, boy. And stop all that infernal grinning at me. Makes you look like a jackass.''

A snorting guffaw erupted from Slade. ''It's a family trait, dear Isabel. But to answer your question, she's upstairs dressing. And should be down presently. I promised her we'd saddle Esmerelda and ride her around the house. Do you want a turn?''

His grandmother stared solemnly at him for a full ten seconds. ''Of course I do.''

''Bully for you. And since this is your house, we'll even let you go first.''

Isabel zeroed in on his words. ''Yes, this is my house. And like everything else I own, it will be yours one day. I just hope I live long enough to see my great-grandchildren—my *legitimate* great-grandchildren.''

''Now, Isabel, you know there are no little Garrett bastards running around. I'm much more careful than that.'' He then sobered, readying to test the waters. ''But what if I told you . . . I intend to marry Hannah Wilton Lawless and give you those great-grandchildren?''

''Pshaw! The devil you say. I don't know which one this family hates more. A Wilton or a Lawless.''

A smile to match his calculating heart stole over his features. ''And she's both. Which makes it perfect.''

''What's perfect about it? That doesn't make any sense.''

''It does. If you'll think about it for a moment.''

''What's there to think about?'' But still, Isabel did just that. Slade knew the exact moment she got his meaning because she sat up rigidly. Her wrinkles even seemed to smooth out as her expression sobered. ''Tell me you're not serious, Slade Franklin Garrett.''

He had her attention now. She only used all three of his names when he was in dire trouble. ''I can't do that because I *am* serious. I mean to marry her. Consider it revenge.''

Isabel's mouth thinned with displeasure. ''Revenge for what?''

''You have to ask?''

Isabel gave him a harsh look. ''You mean your mother? Ha. That woman caused most of her own unhappiness. Now, you listen to me, Slade. Your father was my son, but he was far from perfect. He wasn't a good husband to Mariel, heaven knows. But she wasn't much better, with her continually feigning illnesses to keep him out of her bed. They were both weak people, and they deserved each other. And deserved exactly what they got."

Slade didn't . . . couldn't respond for a moment. He'd never heard Isabel talk like this before about his parents. Angered beyond measure, feeling she was being disloyal to their memories, his voice rose in proportion to his high emotion. "Are you excusing Catherine Wilton-Humes's part in their lives, Grandmother?"

Not to be outdone, Isabel drew herself forward and in turn bellowed out her opinion. "Catherine *had* no part in their lives, Slade. And that was your father's fault. You weren't even born when she left for Tucson. So all you know is the tripe your mother poisoned you with as a child."

Isabel stopped, put a hand to her chest, drew in a long breath, and went on, this time speaking slowly, quietly. "I'm begging you, son, you must let go of this. You are the only worthwhile thing to come of that marriage. And despite your mother and father, you're a good, strong man. You're all I have left. Don't tell me I'll lose you, too."

In a stew of conflicting emotions, Slade tried to brush away her concerns with a laugh. But even to his own ears, the sound was hollow. "You're not going to *lose* me, Grandmother. I know what I'm doing."

She slumped back, seeming to shrink into her chair's very fabric. Then, a great sadness claimed her features, emphasizing her advanced age. "No you don't. Revenge is an acid, Slade. And remember—'Acid does more damage to the vessel in which it's kept, than it does to that on which it's poured.' "

Huffing out his breath, Slade leaned back, extending his arms along the sofa's spine. Disgust marked his words. "An old saying, meaning—I suppose—that I'll hurt myself more than Hannah?"

Isabel nodded sagely. "You'll do more than hurt her. You'll destroy her, most likely. Just like your mother was. Is that what you want?"

Angry, thwarted, Slade jumped to his feet, pointing down at her. "Eureka! Now you see my plan. Because that is *exactly* what I want."

Isabel threw her hands up. "Then, God help us all!"

The sleeping mastiff jumped to her feet. Shaking herself mightily, she swung her accusing gaze from one to the other of the combatants. Isabel clapped her hands together. "Come here, dear girl. Did we awaken you?"

Esmerelda wagged her heavy tail, sweeping everything off a low table behind her. After nosing Slade's hand and getting only a nominal response, she padded over to Isabel, sat on her haunches, and laid her huge, square head on the old woman's frail lap.

"Esmerelda, we silly humans are such an awful breed," Isabel sighed, all the while rubbing the dog's head. "Just look at me and my grandson. All this fussing. It seems we seek to destroy those we love the most."

Staring at the pathetic little figure his grandmother made, and already sorry for their harsh words, Slade mimicked Esmerelda by going to the old woman and squatting beside her chair. The mastiff edged over, making room for him. Taking Isabel's thin hand in his, Slade spoke softly to her. "Isabel, I don't mean to hurt you. But you've got to understand—I mean to have her."

Isabel smiled tenderly at him. But then her eyes widened. "You mean to have her? An interesting choice of words." A slow smile of pure calculation lit her features. The fire's reddish reflection on her face made her seem positively devilish. "Perhaps as interesting as my own only a moment ago to Esmerelda. That's it! All is not lost. I do believe I'll help you."

Slade stood up with a total lack of grace. "Help me what?" He knew real fear when Isabel shifted her weight about in her chair and then put a thin, arthritic finger to her lips, tapping at them as she stared fixedly into the fire. Still rubbing the dog's tan head with her other hand, she nodded several times.

"Isabel, I don't like the looks of this. What are you thinking?"

Isabel broke her reverie to focus on Slade. Narrowing her eyes, she looked him up and down, as if he were a side of beef for sale. She then wagged her finger at him, speaking thoughtfully, as if still hatching a plan even as she spoke. "You're right, you know—it is perfect. It would bring events full circle. And I like that. Yes, this just might work."

Just as he'd feared. A plot. Knowing his goose was cooked,

Slade slumped onto the sofa behind him. "No it won't."

"How do you know it won't? You don't even know what I'm thinking."

"I don't have to know what you're thinking. I know *you*. And I'm about to be sorry I was ever born, aren't I?"

Isabel fairly cackled out her glee. Esmerelda caught her mood and turned her great head, grinning hugely and confirming for him that he was indeed in big trouble now. "My dear boy, I do believe I see a way to—Well, you'll see. This will work because I know you better than you know yourself."

"Impossible," was Slade's one-word condemnation of that idea.

"Ha! I'm willing to bet your inheritance on it."

Slade snorted. "My inheritance from you? Or the one from Ardis Wilton-Humes?"

No sooner were the words out of Slade's mouth than Esmerelda jumped up and whipped around to face the room's arched entry. Her ears pricked. The hair on her back stood up. Then, in silent stealth, she moved away, meandering through the shadowed room's maze of furniture. Slade and Isabel followed the dog's progress for a moment, but then they both spotted her unwitting prey at the same moment.

Looking especially beautiful in a simple dress of soft gray cashmere and garnet velvet, and with her dark, waist-length hair tied back at her nape, Hannah Wilton Lawless stood framed in the entry. Her hands were clasped in front of her, and a hesitant smile lit her delicate features.

Slade tore his gaze from her to exchange a look with Isabel. His grandmother's frowning face seemed to reflect his own guilty thoughts. As distracted as they'd all been, how long had Hannah been standing there before Esmerelda picked up her scent? And how much had she heard?

"Esmerelda! Come here, you bad girl."

Hannah blinked in confusion and looked behind her. No one. Turning again to face her hostess, she confirmed for herself that the lady was indeed looking at her. Had she traded one insane asylum for another?

Seeking reassurance, she sought out Slade's eyes. He immediately looked down. Hannah bit at her lip, wishing she could disappear into thin air. She'd heard the raised voices as she entered the room. They'd been arguing, and she'd interrupted. She suspected she or her relatives were at the root of the fuss. After all, she'd heard Slade say Wilton-Humes-something-or-other. What if Mrs. Garrett didn't want a Wilton in her home?

Then, she'd leave. It was that simple. She stayed nowhere she wasn't wanted. But knowing a hasty, unseen retreat was now out of the question, she settled her gaze on the tiny, white-haired woman just then throwing aside a lap blanket and arising from an overstuffed chair. This could only be Isabel Garrett.

Who was again staring at her, clapping her hands together, and calling her Esmerelda. This instance marked the third time in less than an hour that she'd heard that name—and in more and more curious circumstances. Not knowing quite how to proceed, Hannah nevertheless took the initiative. "Um, Mrs. Garrett . . . I presume? My name's Hannah, not Esmerelda."

Swathed in bright red wool, the spry, amply bosomed robin smiled as she toddled in her direction. "Of course it is, dear. I'm speaking to the dog." She pointed to a man-sized, richly upholstered chair off to Hannah's left.

"The—?" The woman thought the chair was a dog? Completely in a stew now, Hannah glanced to her left. Yes, a normal-enough chair. With four wooden legs. And four huge paws. What could she—?

Hannah froze. Four huge paws? Suddenly wary, she edged backward one step and then over one to her left. Her heart stopped—she gasped to prove it—and then stumbled back, her hands now crossed over her chest. How long had this . . . this horse been sitting there?

"Now, see here, Esmerelda. You and your infernal sneaking up on people are going to be the death of someone." The white-haired woman fussed over to the dog—which even seated was nearly as tall as her—and clutched at its collar. As if that would hold the animal in place. She then grinned at Hannah. "She's perfectly harmless. Come here and let her smell you."

Hannah recovered enough to back up even more. "I'd prefer not to."

The woman laughed at her, waving her over to them. "No,

no. Don't be afraid. Come here. Esmerelda is quite the sweet puppy.''

Hannah stayed firmly in place. ''Puppy? That anim—she's a *puppy*?''

''Why, yes. A mastiff puppy. She'll be quite large one day.'' She turned to Slade. ''How old is she now? Nine or ten months?''

Hannah followed her gaze, looking too at Slade. What the Sam Hill was wrong with him now? He was looking at her as if she'd grown a third eye.

''Ten months, Grandmother,'' he finally said, seeming to shake off his lethargy. Coming to stand beside Hannah, he put a hand to her elbow and smiled down at her. ''Forgive my manners.'' Then he looked up at the red-clad woman opposite them. ''Grandmother, allow me to introduce you to Hannah—''

''I know who she is. Hannah Wilton Lawless.'' Then her gaze swept over Hannah approvingly. ''You may call me Isabel. After all, if you're going to be my granddaughter-in-law, we should—''

''Grandmother!''

''Granddaughter-in-law?''

Isabel released the dog's collar to put her tiny fists to her nonexistent hips. She settled her fractious attention on Slade. ''Did you not say to me, less than five minutes ago, Slade Franklin Garrett, that you would *have* this girl?''

''I did, but I never meant for you to blurt it out like that.''

He'd shared his horrid plotting with his *grandmother*? Hannah was too surprised to do more than stare transfixed at Slade's reddening face, even when his grandmother next spoke.

''Well then, boy, there you have it. Now it's out in the open.''

Hannah watched Slade's face harden into cautionary lines as he stared at the tiny old woman. Speaking in a syrupy, singsong voice, as if he were trying to talk a small child into handing over a loaded gun, Slade entoned, ''I see your game now, Isabel Winifred Garrett. I'm warning you—it won't work.''

Isabel Winifred Garrett, for her part, crowed triumphant. ''Balderdash! You wouldn't be warning me if you didn't think it would work. So, ha! You're caught in your own trap now, grandson mine. Now, quit being such a sore loser and bring the girl over here to meet Esmerelda. We can't have her pouncing on your fiancée every time she enters the room.''

*Pouncing* on his fian—her? Hannah snapped her attention back to the dog. Which eyed her with a certain amount of detached, tongue-lolling disdain. Clearly, the animal was wondering how she would taste. More than a little undone, Hannah backed squarely into Slade, forcing him to steady her with his hands at her shoulders.

But having done so, he set her aside abruptly and rounded on his grandmother. Hands to his hips, his booted feet apart, he struck a defiant pose. And got no further than opening his mouth preparatory to saying something, when a great rattling of dishes out in the hallway announced the imminent approach of someone. Hannah, the dog, and the two Garretts looked in the direction of the noise. Almost immediately, Isabel's face lit up. "Oh, good! Serafina and Rowena bring tea. Won't you have some, dear? We can discuss your wedding."

Hannah stared at the woman. Slade would kill the poor, dotty creature if she persisted in this vein. Even now, just standing next to him, she could actually feel the steam building up in him for an eruption. She had to make Mrs. Garrett understand—before there was violence. "There's not going to be any wedding, Mrs. Garrett. Surely you càn understand why, my name being what it is. Now, I don't know what *he's*"—she jerked her thumb over at Slade—"told you, but I have never agreed to such a . . . such an arrangement."

Isabel Garrett raised her eyebrows and smiled angelically, nodding as if she understood. "I see. Then it is your habit, Miss Lawless, to be carried upstairs by a man *not* your husband—in front of a score of witnesses—and then to follow up that *scandalous* breach with spending the night *in his bed,* all without benefit of clergy? Well, now I understand. We'll speak of it no more."

She blithely turned her back on a slack-jawed Hannah and a red-faced Slade, and headed for her chair in front of the fire.

"Stop right there!" This was the first time in her life that Hannah'd bellowed.

Unfortunately, it had the disastrous result of causing Rowena and Serafina, two wizened old mirror images of each other, to stop right there. They collided, with the silver tea service between them, as they rounded the corner into the room. Hannah and Slade rushed to right the silver and the sugar and the creamer and the cakes and the cups and the maids on the highly polished wood floor before tea was served.

In the midst of this flurry, Hannah looked up to see Isabel Garrett smiling broadly at her as she patted Esmerelda's head. ''I thought as much, my dear. Now, come sit by me and we'll discuss the details of your wedding.''

# CHAPTER SEVEN

---

*Wind and rain be damned.* Hannah tromped down the central stairway and whipped her lined cloak around her shoulders. *Sip tea and discuss me marrying Slade Garrett.* After fastening the cape's frog closure, she pulled the hood up over her hair. *Did no one think she had a mind of her own?*

Because it sure seemed that everyone was trying to run roughshod over her. Why, just to get out of her own bedroom, she'd had to promise Olivia she'd be back in time to dress for supper. Servants and butlers and lady's maids. Telling her when to dress—even *what* to wear. Telling her when to eat—even *how* to eat. And when to rest. Let's not forget those enforced naps. These highfalutin Easterners would never make it out West where a body stayed up and busy all day and saw to her own needs—or they went untended.

Her thoughts having carried her down to the first-floor landing, she turned back sharply to her right and nearly collided with the fragile Pemberton. Stopping short, she met the butler's equally startled gaze. "Why, good afternoon, Pemberton."

"A subject worthy of debate, miss." He began immediately to fall forward. She reached out to steady him, but then realized he was merely executing a respectful bow. She jerked her hands back before he straightened up.

Hannah then frowned at the ancient old gentleman as he oh-so-slowly looked her up and down with his faded-blue eyes. "What is it, Pemberton?"

"Why, I believe it's a cloak, miss."

Hannah swallowed the burst of laughter in her throat. "No, I meant, did you need me for something?"

"One would think so, wouldn't one?" With no further ado, he stepped around her and continued on his way.

Hannah pivoted to look after him until he finally disappeared around the other side of the stairs. Shaking her head, she set off again on her quest for the outdoors. She stalked down the dim hall to the narrow door at its end. The final barrier to her freedom. And exactly where her calculations said it would be. Reduced now to muttering, she fumed about her need for fresh air. Preferably air unbreathed by any Garrett. Or their dog.

Hannah gripped and turned the polished knob. The door opened a fraction and then slammed shut in her face. Yelping out her surprise but refusing to be denied, she renewed her efforts. This time she shoved a shoulder against the door, forcing it open.

The blast of cold air which greeted her, wet with stinging, wind-whipped rain, snatched the door out of her hand and sent it slamming outward against the white stone of the mansion. Hannah gasped, clutching at her flaring cloak as it too took wing. Hastening outside, lest the door take a notion to swing back in her face, she stepped onto the tiny landing, grabbed the resisting door with both hands, pulled on it with all her might, and finally succeeded in flinging it closed behind her.

Triumphant, she turned and skipped down the three steps. The instant her feet touched grass, brown though it was, and not even caring that her hood now trailed down her back with her hair, Hannah flung her arms wide and pirouetted with Mother Nature. She stopped suddenly, sending her cloak swirling around her legs and her ribbon-tied hair over her shoulder to rest against her bosom. It seemed like years since her feet'd touched raw earth. Raw earth, blue sky, rolling hills, tall buffalo grass, wildflowers. A sudden stab of homesickness, so tangible she could almost taste it, assailed her.

In that moment, the rain fell against her face like needles. The cold wind took on a mocking quality. Hannah looked around her, seeing only bordered formal lawns, bare flower beds, precisely cut shrubs, and pruned trees. There was no room here for a spirit to be free. With her thoughts nipping at her heels, Hannah fled down the long gravel path to the far end of the manicured grounds. She didn't slow her pace until she made a right turn past a copse of tall trees, which ran parallel to a vast gray-green and restless pond on her left.

Hannah slowed her steps. Here was what she sought—a bit of untamed nature to restore her soul. She looked up, up, trying to see to the treetops. Overcome, she closed her eyes, the better to listen to the wind whistling through the arching branches, the better to absorb the lapping sound of water against land. When she opened her eyes and looked down at herself, she saw wind-tossed leaves—wet and mottled but still red and gold—clinging to her cape and the path before her.

A smile carried Hannah's skittering feet to her destination— a small cottage, the roof of which she'd spied earlier out her second-floor bedroom window. Her gaze went to the latch on the weathered old door. And her smile faded. *What if it were locked?* Why hadn't she thought of that while still indoors?

She tried the latch handle. Yes! Luck was with her. She quickly entered, whipping around to close the door behind her. She then turned to face the one silent, staring room of the wood-slatted retreat. Only pieces of sheet-covered furniture, a small stone fireplace, a kerosene lamp, and her. Truly alone. A delicious shiver, perhaps fueled somewhat by the frigid, stale air, wiggled her around in her cloak. Crossing her arms, she rubbed at them and looked around her. A one-room cottage with windows on three sides.

Having now thoroughly taken in her surroundings, Hannah laughed out loud at herself. Now what? She sighted on a rick of stacked firewood. And there, on the mantel—a tinderbox and sulphur matches. No, she didn't intend to be out here that long. Nor did she want the smoke to be seen from the mansion, for surely curiosity would bring her a visitor.

A sudden vision of rippling muscles under a white shirt, sculpted thighs encased in close-fitting breeches, and snapping black eyes fringed by dark lashes assailed her. As if retreating from his physical presence, Hannah stepped over to a large window which looked out on the pond. Woodbridge Pond? Fascinated, she watched as the wind whipped the water up into lunging, foamy waves that attacked the rocky shore. Lost in the sights before her, Hannah's unguarded mind again conjured up images of Slade.

So tall and handsome. It seemed the man was always in her

thoughts—even when he wasn't bedeviling her with his presence. She saw him laughing at her. She saw him angered and bellowing. She saw him leaning over her on the bed, threatening her. She saw him protecting her, his hand at her elbow. She saw his gentleness with Pemberton, his kindnesses to Olivia. Then, Hannah saw him kissing her neck, and felt again his arms around her—

The metallic sound of the latch opening, coupled with a blast of cold air as the door flew open, whipped Hannah around. *Slade*. Hannah stilled, barely breathing, her heart pounding. Coatless, rain-dampened from head to toe, his hair wind-tousled, he filled the doorway, quietly holding her gaze. A blowing leaf flew crazily around between them on a puff of wind. The white sheets covering the furniture billowed out, as did her cape.

The moment lingered. Her awareness of him, like an arcing bolt of lightning, dried her mouth, made her womb feel heavy and soft. He stepped into the room, closing the door behind him. All without speaking or breaking the spell. He then just stood there, staring at her. His expression, so open, so naked, struck a responsive chord in Hannah. A frown claimed her features. She had the oddest feeling that she should reach her hand out to him. No. With every ounce of her strength, she resisted the impulse.

Shifting his weight, Slade ran a hand through his black hair and then swiped his sleeve over his rain-soaked face. Hannah drank in his every movement. And realized his presence warmed her like no fire could. Then, he made an abrupt movement, reaching a hand out to her. As if he . . . knew. But knew *what*? Hannah could do nothing more than stare at his hand. Slowly, he lowered it. "What are you doing out here, Hannah? You'll catch your death."

The spell burst, popping into thin air.

"Me? What about you? At least I have on my cloak." Hannah turned her back to him. She stared out at the wheeling gulls above the churning water. Slanting a look back at him, she said, "I came out here for the fresh air. And for the time *alone*."

"I see. Before I interfere any further, are you armed?"

Hannah turned back to the window. "No. I left my pistol in the house."

"Good." His footsteps sounded on the bare floor. He came into her view on her left and then promptly performed an about-face. Bracing his hands on a waist-high table, he effortlessly pulled himself up to sit on it. With his legs spread, his booted feet dangling above the ground, he rested his hands on his thighs. Only mere inches from Hannah now, he faced her as she stared out the window. "You want me to leave?"

Hannah took a deep breath, preparatory to telling him that yes, obviously she wanted him to leave. But instead, his damp, warm, and musky smell assaulted her senses, tightening her stomach muscles. "It's your property. Suit yourself."

"Well then, it suits me to stay—until I'm sure you're all right."

"Why wouldn't I be?" Hannah darted him the barest of glimpses before she resumed her quiet staring out the window. But her gaze was the only thing about her that wasn't focused on him. An invisible thread, stronger than any spider's silken web, seemed to be tugging her toward him. She gritted her teeth, resisting his pull.

"Why wouldn't you be? Well, that was quite an interesting tea we just had, for one thing. And interesting doesn't begin to cover Isabel and her ancient servants. But perhaps you should know I was sent to check on you."

Hannah frowned at him. "Who sent you?"

"Isabel. Pemberton. Rowena and Serafina. Mrs. Edgars—she's our cook. Even Olivia interrupted my reading to let me know—"

"Good Lord, the entire household? Why?"

He shrugged his broad shoulders, rippling his damp and clinging shirt over the hard muscles underneath. "Because Isabel's told them all you're to be the next Mrs. Garrett. So they've taken you to heart. Then, when they saw you come outside, they informed me I was to come see about you."

"And here you are. Do you always do everything they tell you?"

Grinning, he raised an eyebrow at her. "Don't you?"

She thought about it and laughed with him. "I guess I do."

This was amazing. She was actually having a friendly conversation with him. Even though her mutinous eyes insisted on lowering to stare at his crisp and curling black chest hair, just visible through his damp shirt. And darned if she didn't have her mental hands full trying to keep her eyes from roaming lower. When she realized she *was* staring . . . lower, she snapped her head up.

And met the sensuous light in his black eyes. Near to a panic now, she stumbled on. "I don't know what to make of your grandmother. I would think she'd toss me out the door. After all, I'm . . . well, if not an *enemy*, at the least I'm a relative of very bad neighbors."

"At the *very* least." He crossed his arms, giving her a considering stare.

Hannah felt he looked at her as if he were wondering how best to dispose of her body. In the ensuing quiet, sharp needles of rain pelted at the windows. Determined gusts of wind rattled the panes, as if some spirit desperately tried to gain her attention. To warn her? And if so—warn her of what? She blurted out the first distracting thing that came to her mind. "At least you didn't bring Esmerelda."

Slade relaxed into a slouching position. "She has more sense than to come outside on a day like this."

Hannah crossed her arms over her cloak-covered bosom. "Aren't you the one out here without a coat? At least I had sense enough to protect myself against the weather."

Amusement softened the lines and angles of his face. He touched two fingers to his temple in a mocking salute to her. "Point taken. Let's just say my concern for *your* well-being made me forget my own."

Hannah chuckled at his outrageousness. "I hardly think so. We both know better than that, Mr. Garrett."

"Do we?" His smile faltered at the edges, and a look she couldn't interpret flashed over his face. But then just as suddenly it was gone. "Call me Slade. I've asked you to twice already."

Overcome with a sudden shyness, Hannah looked down at her shoes. When she next lifted her head, she stared not at him, but straight ahead at the grayness outside. "I can't. Because it would mean we—I don't—" Frustrated with her own babbling, she took a deep breath and started over. "You've been calling me Hannah since the moment we . . ." Again her voice trailed off.

"Ye-es-s?" Drawing the word out, he leaned over until he'd poked his face into her line of vision.

Fighting a sudden giggle, Hannah stepped back, swatting at him. "Stop that. I don't like it."

He sat up obediently enough, but arched his eyebrows at her. "I think you do, *Hannah*."

A rising heat in her veins dried her humor. She raised her head a regal notch. "I'll thank you not to tell me what I like and don't like."

Slade laughed out loud, startling her into dropping her pose. "Stubborn spitfire to the end, aren't you?"

Heat suffused over her cheeks before she could think up some tart comeback. But instinct warned her not to spar with this man. So Hannah simply changed the subject. Maybe she could distract him from his continued staring at her. Pointing to the window off to her left, she asked, "What are those trees out there? We don't have any like them at home."

It didn't work. He never looked away from her face. "You mean 'What are those trees out there, *Slade*?,' don't you?"

Peevishness quirked her mouth up. The man worried a subject like a bobcat with a field mouse. "All right, then. What are those trees over there . . . *Slade*?"

He grinned hugely, still not looking away from her. "Elms."

Hannah cried foul, poking her finger at him and raising her voice. "You didn't even look."

"I don't have to. They're the only trees out there. And they have been since before I was born."

Bested, Hannah gave up her pique, sobering as she entertained another thought. "Were you born here? Is this where you lived as a boy?"

His expression changed, too, mingling wariness with a subtle withdrawal. "Yes. To both. Why?"

The flatness of his voice told Hannah she'd made a mistake. "No reason. I was just thinking about how beautiful it is around the pond. And the house. Well, all of the estate. It must have been wonderful growing up here."

"Wonderful?" He stared at her for the longest moment. Then he abruptly pushed himself off the table, landing lightly on his feet. His black eyes glinted down at her with a little boy's pain. But his mouth twisted with a man's hated remembrances. "It wasn't wonderful at all. In fact, it was pure hell."

\*    \*    \*

"Damn all the Garretts to hell, I say!" Hands clasped behind him, Cyrus Wilton-Humes stood peering out the closed French doors which overlooked the sun-swept lawn of Cloister Point. "I only hope no one of consequence sees that . . . that *tradesman* leaving our property, Patience."

Outside, a cabriolet pulled away from the front door. Just the sight of it soured Cyrus's mood further. "Why am I betrayed by my family at every turn? Is it not enough that Hannah's public accusations sent us to Nahant for a full week? And now, on our first day home, we're forced to sell more of my inheritance to pay off creditors. What pitiful circumstances Ardis foisted on us."

"As it turns out, she was hardly worth the effort of her accident, was she?"

"Not so." He kept his gaze trained on the departing coach. "I could have cheerfully seen to her demise all over again after the reading of her will. Only a pittance of a trust left to me. And after all our caring for her. What did Catherine ever do for her? Nothing. Or Slade Garrett? And yet she leaves everything to them—ahead of me. I, her own grandson—a distant third to inherit."

He turned to Patience. Seated on the medallion-backed sofa, she was counting the stack of greenbacks spread before her. Only when she finished did she look up and raise a pale eyebrow at her husband. "There's nothing we can do about the will. But there is something we can do about Slade Garrett. He's all that stands between us and Ardis's fortune."

"And that's what worries me. He won't be as easy to dispose of as Catherine. Or even Hamilton and Evelyn."

Patience shook her head. "Poor Hamilton and Evelyn. I do miss them. But your father should've never left Cloister Point to both of you. It proved to be the death of the man. And his wife." Then, with subtle malevolence reflected in her blue eyes, she smiled at Cyrus. "You're such a wonderful husband. I don't know of another man who'd rid himself of his own brother to provide such a lovely home for his wife."

Cyrus glanced at the room's closed doors. Shaking his head, he approached the sofa. "Don't speak so plainly, my dear. Someone could hear you. And then what would happen?"

Patience put a beringed hand to the fine lace covering her emaciated bosom and adopted an innocent expression. "Why,

I suppose the law would come for you, and then they'd hang you for murder. And leave me all alone. With the money.''

A cold fist clutched at Cyrus's stomach. So that was her game. ''I won't go alone, my dear. *You're* in this as deeply as I am.''

Patience pursed her thin lips and looked down, puffing her gray-blue satin skirt out around her before responding. ''This is getting us nowhere, Cyrus. The fact remains that unless we take further steps—and soon—we'll be forced into poverty. As it is, we have few servants left and only the barest of furnishings remain. Why, we're even down to one ancient carriage and team. Where will this end? All these . . . tragic deaths, and we're still not any better off.''

Cyrus went to the sofa and sat down, turning to face her. ''There, there,'' he consoled, patting her shoulder but barely taking his eyes off the money that lay innocently between them. When he could no longer resist, he clutched up the thick wad of United States notes. Holding the dirty stack in one hand, he fanned the paper money with his other thumb. A bubble of greedy glee spread his lips back over his teeth. ''Is it all here?''

''Of course. Do you think I'd let that . . . that *man* leave with my jewelry, if it weren't?''

Detecting the catch in her voice, Cyrus tore his gaze from the money to look at his wife. He reached over to squeeze Patience's clawlike hand. ''Now, don't fret, Patience. I know what a sacrifice you just made, parting with those pieces of Evelyn's jewelry. Just be patient. We'll soon have all the money we want, I promise you—once Slade Garrett is no longer an obstacle.''

''I certainly hope so.'' Withdrawing her hand from his, she pulled herself up from the sofa and paced the room as she spoke. ''If word gets out of our reduced circumstances, we'll be ruined. And I simply won't stand for that, Cyrus. What's worse, our dinner for Hannah—that ungrateful little wretch— drained our resources. And what did we get for our efforts? The damaging gossip among our friends. And, worst of all, not *one* social invitation awaiting us today upon our return. And here it is November—the very height of the season.''

Desperate to avoid her anger, knowing what she was capable of, Cyrus said what he knew would cheer her immensely. "Well, then, my girl, since Hannah involved herself, we'll just take care of her when we solve our problem with Garrett."

Patience stopped and put a hand to her bosom. A feral gleam lit her face. "Oh, do you mean it, Cyrus?"

As always, her innate ruthlessness brought unease to Cyrus's heart. He alone knew how deadly she was. She was like a badger that killed for the pleasure. Whereas he killed only for personal gain. "Why, of course, my pet. We'll have to be careful, though." He put a bony finger to his lips, tapping thoughtfully. "Perhaps we can do something like we did for Catherine. Yes, that might be the way to go. But then again . . . Well, there's no way around it. They'll be more difficult than the others and will take more time."

"But you *will* come up with a plan, *won't* you, Cyrus?"

"Of course, my pet." Cyrus smiled, but his mind was racing. That tone was back in her voice, the one of subtle threat. The one that said if he didn't get her what she wanted, she'd get *him* . . . any way she could. Cyrus's guts churned with his fear of her. "It will be brilliant. And should give you a wonderful entry for your journal of our . . . family deaths. Why don't you tell me where it is, and I'll get it for you, dear?"

Patience's eyes narrowed to slits. "My journal is fine where it is."

*Damn her.* She made sure he knew of the journal's existence, but not its location. He knew in his heart she'd use it against him one day, if he failed her in any way. Cyrus decided to remind her of her own guilt. "As you wish. But you *will* help me—as always?"

Patience looked him up and down. But then she smiled. "Of course. You're my husband, aren't you? I wouldn't want anything to . . . happen to you."

*Patience is quite mad. Why don't you rid yourself of her, too?* Shocked, Cyrus sat upright, just barely stopping himself from turning to see who'd said that. But he knew his own mind had formed the question. Just as he knew his heart was considering it. Cyrus looked down at his lap, making a show of laying the money down. In that moment's space, he searched the darker regions of his soul. Could he actually do it? Could he kill Patience? Slowly, inexorably, the answer made itself known to him.

He raised his head, a changed man. Smiling at his wife, he patted the sofa's cushion, indicating for her to rejoin him. *Poor dear. Forty years of marriage, and it came to this*. Well, he'd be merciful and allow her to die quickly. Then, he'd search her bedroom, where she never allowed him, until he found that damning record. And then he'd destroy it. "Come sit here, and we'll discuss what to do."

Patience obediently sat down, even taking his hands in hers. She was most pliant, most cheerful when plotting murder. "Good. Because I've thought of someone else we need to rid ourselves of. Olivia—that little turncoat of a maid Hannah took with her. Damned girl knows too much about our . . . special problems here. And now, surely she has everyone's ear at Woodbridge Pond. She could be quite damaging to us."

Cyrus pulled back, eyeing his wife. How many deaths would be enough for her? But still, the longer he thought about it, the more he realized she may have a valid point. Her mind was, after all, diabolical. He was going to miss her when she was dead. "Brilliant, Patience. I'd quite forgotten about dear little Olivia. And, as you say, by now she's earned everyone's trust at Woodbridge Pond. No one would question her or suspect her for a moment."

Patience affected a pout. "Suspect her? I thought we were going to—"

Cyrus withdrew a hand from hers to put a finger to his lips. "Shhh. We are. But only *after* we use her for our purposes."

"Our purposes? How do you mean?" But before Cyrus could enlighten her, her beakish features lit up and she raised her hands to stop him from answering. "How stupid of me. I see now. Very good, Cyrus. She'll be our spy. I like it." But then a frown of doubt turned her mouth down. "How are you going to ensure the girl doesn't betray us?"

Cyrus laughed. "That's the easiest part. Surely you remember her condition a year ago when she came to our door seeking employment? And we hired her on when no one else would?"

Patience frowned until it came to her. "I'd completely forgotten."

"Ahh, but I didn't. Because I thought then her plight may prove useful to us one day. And now it has. We know her secret little shame, one that I'd wager she's not divulged to

Hannah or to Slade Garrett—who'd show her the door if he knew the sort she was.''

Cyrus quickly outlined his scheme. "She's got to leave Woodbridge Pond alone at some point. And when she does, I'll be ready. A few well-chosen words with her and she'll cooperate—gladly.''

# CHAPTER EIGHT

—

*Damn them for returning so soon.* Exercising his gelding, Slade reined in at the summer cottage among the elms and dismounted so he could watch the signs of renewed activity at Cloister Point. The breeze on this crisp November day carried to his ears the whinny of a horse and a man's calling out to someone else. Just then, a trade carriage pulled away from Cloister Point. *Interesting. Was Cloister Point a little barer for that visit?*

Slade frowned. *Damn you, Ardis, why didn't you just give Cyrus the money?* Huffing out a disgusted breath, Slade thought of the danger the rascal next door posed to them all, but especially to Hannah. Just thinking her name conjured up a vision of that blue-green-eyed girl letting her dark hair down that rainy night at his brownstone. And this was all the provocation his pent-up, frustrated male energy needed. He was next treated to the feel of her in his arms that night he held her all night. Just held her. Again he felt her softness and her warm weight against his side. Slade ran a finger around his collar and shifted uncomfortably in his suddenly too-tight pants.

"Mr. Garrett, where are you? Go, Esmerelda. Find him."

Slade turned toward the sound. Olivia. Leading Champion, he took to the path, quickly approaching the break in the hedges that allowed for the gravel walkway. But before he could call out or step into view, Esmerelda bounded around the turn, coming to a skidding stop when she saw him. Immediately she circled him and the gelding and set up a horrific baying. Startled, Champion bucked and plunged.

Cursing the dog, calming the horse, Slade settled Champion and turned on Esmerelda, shouting, "Enough, Essie." Essie obediently sat down, her tongue lolling out of her grinning, slobbering mouth. Slade then rounded the corner to see the lady's maid running full-out toward him. Her white apron flapped crazily against the outline of her thin legs under her gray wool uniform. She came to a sudden stop with a wild windmilling of arms and legs.

Slade held up a cautionary hand. "Whoa, Olivia! What is it?"

Olivia, red-faced and out of breath, braced her hands on her knees. "Sor-sorry, Mister . . . Garrett, sir. I was . . . I was—"

"Running. I know. Take your time."

"Can't. Some . . . something's wrong . . . at home."

"At home?" Slade looked to the white-stone mansion behind the girl. "Here. Hold on to Champion." He already had his hand out, offering her the reins. His muscles bunched for action.

But instead of taking the reins from him, Olivia grabbed at his sleeve. She shook her head, further loosening her coronet of braids. "Not . . . your home. *My* . . . home."

Slade stared at her heaving form. He'd never thought about the private lives of his domestics. "Your home? Don't you live here?"

Olivia let go of him and straightened up, brushing away wisps of hair from her damp face. "Yes, sir. Most of the time. But . . . I got a . . . message." She plunged a hand into her pocket and came up with a crumpled note, which she held out to him.

Suddenly Slade had an image of another note, one held in the folds of a lace handkerchief and tied with ribbon. He made a mental note to get it out of the safe at his brownstone and give it back to Hannah. He'd forgotten all about it. Funny. She hadn't mentioned it, either.

Coming back to the present moment, Slade took the offered note and smoothed its edges so he could read it. The crude lettering told of the sickness of someone named Colette. He looked up. "Is this Colette your mother?"

Olivia shook her head no as she took the note back from him. Strange—even though she hadn't moved a step, she seemed to have withdrawn. Suddenly alerted by her closed-mouth attitude, so unlike her, Slade offered, "Is there anything I can do to help?"

Fat tears gathered in the girl's light brown eyes. For a moment she seemed on the verge of accepting, but then she said, "No. May I go, sir?"

Wary now, wondering what was behind her hesitance, Slade looked her up and down. But the girl's heart was in her eyes, and she wanted to be away. He waved his hand. "Of course. Go. Have Rigby take you home."

Again she shook her head no. "He's still out with Mrs. Garrett and Miss Lawless at the shops. But I can make my own way. I'm just sorry to be ducking out on my duties like this."

Not liking the feel of this one bit, Slade spoke a trifle abruptly. "It can't be helped. Take as long as you need. And don't worry about your position here. It's secure."

Olivia looked at him with gratitude-widened eyes. "Thank you for your kindness, sir. You're a rare man." She grabbed up her skirt and apron. Esmerelda, unusually docile for the past moments, came to her feet and padded over to Olivia's side.

Slade stared levelly at the maid. "Hardly rare. Now, go on with you." He waved his hand in a dismissive gesture and watched as she and Esmerelda ran back the way they'd come and then disappeared into the house.

Contemplating the gravel path at his feet, Slade's thoughts brought a frown to his face. Then, his mind made up, he turned, leading Champion at a fast walk. When he neared the neat red stable, he spied one of the young stablehands and bellowed out, "Jonathan! Come take Champion. And have Rigby come to my study the minute he gets back with the ladies."

Hannah, escorted by her new shadow, Esmerelda, approached the closed door to the study. She'd only just doffed her lined cloak, hat, gloves, and fitted jacket bodice after arriving home from her outing with Isabel. But the news of Olivia's departure sent her downstairs in search of an explanation. "Well, here goes, Esmerelda." She rapped sharply on the door.

From the other side, male voices cut off their conversation. Hannah absently rubbed at the mastiff's head and took a deep breath for courage. "Like confronting an old bear in its cave, heh, girl?"

Esmerelda whuffed out her agreement and added a tail-wagging.

"What is it?" bellowed the old bear.

Affronted by his outburst, Hannah put her hands to her waist and bellowed right back. "I won't shout my business through the door. Can you spare me a moment?"

A moment's silence from the other side was followed by the sound of bootsteps on wood floor. Readying for the sight of Slade's commanding height, Hannah stood up straighter, only to have the door open to reveal Rigby at her eye level. The likable young man ducked his head respectfully to her and smiled. "Pardon, miss. I was just leaving."

Surprised and suddenly suspicious—was he reporting her day's business to his employer?—Hannah's hand went to her bosom. "Rigby, I'm sorry. I wasn't expecting you. Don't let me interrupt—"

"Come in, Hannah." Slade's voice boomed out impatiently from deep inside the room. "We've concluded our business. Now, what is it you want? I've several matters to attend to yet this afternoon."

That was twice he'd bellowed at her in as many moments. Hannah raised an eyebrow as she stared at Rigby's smiling face. She spoke purposely loud enough for the lord and master to hear her. "Well, Rigby, I see he didn't bite any chunks out of your hide. Let's hope I fare as well with the old bear."

"What the—? Old bear?" A chair scraped on the polished floor, as if pushed back suddenly.

Rigby's eyes widened. He started to look behind him, but apparently thought better of that and settled for stepping aside, allowing her and her escort to enter. As they swept by him, he leaned in toward her and whispered, "Careful, miss. He hasn't had his ration of raw meat yet today."

Hannah acknowledged the friendly warning with "Neither has Esmerelda."

Rigby grinned and slipped past her, exiting the room and noiselessly closing the door behind him.

Left facing the old bear on her own now, the joke wasn't quite so funny. With him eyeing her from behind his desk, in his own home, and with her at his mercy for the very food she ate and the clothes she wore, Hannah found she didn't quite know how to proceed. She remained in place as she waited for him to wave her over. Or at least to finish staring at her.

Finally, he raised an eyebrow. "You've brought Essie. I thought you were afraid of her."

Hannah looked down at the mastiff and then back up at Slade. "I was at first, but now we're fast friends. I like having her around. Except when she thinks she can sleep with me." Her words hit the air with the impact of a slap across the face. Hannah's mouth dried as Slade straightened up.

"I know. I hear you fussing at her. Every night. Through the door."

"I . . . hear you, too, getting ready for bed . . . I suppose." Hannah's hand went to the cameo brooch at her throat. "I hope I don't keep you awake."

A smile fraught with seductive promise played with the corners of his mouth. "You do."

She didn't need to be a woman of the world to know exactly what he meant. But still, did he have to continue to stare at her as if he could see through her clothes? Slightly disconcerted, Hannah half raised a hand to her upswept hair. "You're staring at me. Is something wrong with my appearance?"

"Well, let's see." With studied casualness, Slade stepped around his solid desk to perch a hip on its corner and cross his arms over the expanse of his chest. He casually swung his foot as he looked her up and down, making her feel certain she'd come in without a stitch on. "Not from here there isn't. And I do like that particular blouse."

"My blouse?" Her hand went to her bosom. She fingered the delicate material and glanced down at herself, relieved to see she indeed had a blouse on. Feeling her face warming, she looked up again at him. And saw Esmerelda padding over to him to lay her great head on his thigh.

Even though Slade kept his gaze on her, he rubbed the mastiff's ears. Esmerelda shook her head at this indignity and turned away, going to flop in the center of a sunbeam that warmed the floor. Hannah watched Slade watch the dog until the animal'd laid herself down. Only then did he turn back to her. "I trust you enjoyed your outing with Isabel?"

A sudden memory of the bits and pieces that Isabel had divulged about Slade's childhood, and why he might refer to it as pure hell, deepened the heat on Hannah's cheeks. "Of course. She's delightful."

He nodded. "And . . . informative, perhaps?"

Hannah never missed a beat. "Yes. She told me all about Boston. About the fire last year. About the annexation of Charlestown. We drove by Faneuil Hall and then to that wonderful museum—"

"I'm sure you saw it all."

Hannah took a deep breath. "Actually, I came about Olivia. I just saw Serafina upstairs, and she said Olivia ran out of the house in tears earlier after getting some message. I was hoping you knew what happened."

Slade shrugged his shoulders. "I don't know much more than that. She showed me a note. It said that someone named Colette was sick. She wouldn't say who that was, but I told her to go see about her and to take as much time as she needed. I was sure you wouldn't begrudge her absence."

"No, of course not." Hannah walked over to the leather chairs facing his desk, sweeping her cashmere skirt by Slade's dangling foot. She sat down in the one closest to him and studiously ignored the play of shifting muscles in his thigh as he swung his foot lazily back and forth. To keep her hands from reaching out on their own to touch him, she tightly laced them together in her lap. "I find this strange, Slade. You know how much Olivia talks. Well, she's never said a word about family, or having anyone to care for."

Slade squinted down at her with a sudden critical stare, putting Hannah on the alert as her heart beat faster. She sat up straighter. "What?"

"I think we've just crossed some line, Hannah. We've been residing under the same roof for the past week, seeing each other daily as we go about our lives and our routines. But that's the first time you've called me Slade without my prompting you."

Hannah slid her gaze down to her lap. She didn't even remember saying his name. Was he becoming that familiar, that comfortable to her? She finally managed to raise her head to look him in the eye. "Is it?"

His answer was a very warm smile. But what he said was,

"It is. But back to Olivia. I see it didn't take you long to become a Brahmin, like the rest of us."

"A Brahmin? How do you mean?"

His smile changed from intimate to mocking. "It's in the blood. We Brahmins have no clue regarding our domestics' private lives. Neither do we care enough to ask."

Stung, Hannah jumped up. "You speak for yourself because I most certainly *do* care. But where I come from, we don't pry into other folks's lives. You live a lot longer that way."

Slade came to his feet and towered over her. "Lucky for you, I've seen fit to pry into a lot of *folks's* lives lately—and on *your* behalf. Otherwise, you wouldn't live much longer, if at all."

Hannah stared into the gleaming jet of his eyes and swallowed the sudden lump in her throat. With apprehension robbing her of spine, she flopped limply into her chair. "What do you mean? What's happened?"

Slade perched again on the desk. He laced his fingers together, resting them at the juncture of his thighs. "While you and Isabel were out on the town, your beloved great-aunt and -uncle arrived home. You'll have to be more cautious now in your comings and goings."

Hannah's heart leapt at that news. "I keep a gun with me at all times. And I already have armed men practically escorting me to dinner. How much more careful can I be?"

Slade looked at her as if she were a naughty child. "Hannah, you'd do well to have a healthy fear of Cyrus and Patience. They're dangerous people with a long reach. And they're becoming more desperate with each passing day."

Hannah huffed out her exasperation. "Are they now? And just how should I know? You keep me squirreled away here and practically hog-tied, making it all but impossible for me to learn anything for myself. So, *you* tell me about Cyrus and Patience's desperation."

The very air in the room seemed to be holding its breath with her as she watched the flicker of emotion over his face and the hand he reached up to rub over his jaw. "All right, I will. First of all, you're right about the Wilton-Humeses. I don't have any proof, but—"

"But you do—that scrap of their own letterhead! You do still have it?"

"Yes. It's safe at my brownstone. Do you want it back? No? Then I'll leave it there for now. But all it proves is that they *wrote* your mother."

"After twenty-five years, they just wrote her? Hardly. I found that paper burning in the fireplace at home on the same night we . . . found Mama and Papa. . . ." She turned her head as her voice trailed off on a sobbing catch.

"And my name's on it. No wonder you thought I was involved with them." His voice, mixing compassion with irony, brought her attention back to him. "We'll save that mystery for later. Right now, I need to tell you—Well, this next part's harder. Are you up to it?"

She raised her chin. "I came a long way for answers."

"So you did." He thinned his lips into a grim line and then plunged ahead. "Your mother was killed for no other reason than your great-grandmother's will. Except for sizable trusts left to each of her sons—both of which Cyrus now has since Hamilton's death—Ardis left her entire estate to your mother."

A fist clutched at Hannah's heart. She gripped the chair's padded armrests. "Mama's own kin had her killed because of . . . because of *money*? Not because she married Papa?"

Horrified, she put a hand to her mouth, removing it only when her next words spilled out of her. "Poor Papa. He died protecting Mama." She lowered her gaze and stared blankly at the floor. "He was lying across her body."

Slade leaned forward to cup her chin and raise her head. "I'm so sorry, Hannah. I should've seen it coming, but I didn't."

Hannah brushed away his hand. "Why should *you* have seen it coming? At Cloister Point, you said something similar—something about *knowing* they were responsible. You could *know* only if you're as guilty as they are. Only if you're involved."

She'd just accused him—again—of murder. The first time she'd done so, he'd reacted violently, causing her enough doubt to place herself under his protection. But this time, he didn't jump up and bellow out his innocence. Instead, without blinking, without breaking eye contact, Slade confessed, "I am involved. But I'm not guilty."

Hannah's grip on the armrests tightened. "How can that be?"

Slade ran a hand over his jaw. "I'll start at the beginning. Ardis left your mother a *tremendous* fortune, Hannah. In the millions. Cyrus and Hamilton believed it would be left to them when their mother died."

Shaking her head, staggered by the sum, Hannah sagged back into the chair. "I never realized. . . ." She looked up at Slade. "Why did Ardis leave her sons trusts?"

Slade huffed out a breath. "The trusts are big enough to sustain them through their lives. But it galls Cyrus to have his money doled out to him by Ardis's solicitors and to have to give them an accounting of his expenses. He's a lavish spender, way beyond his means. But as to why, I know only what Isabel tells me. She says Ardis never forgave Hamilton for disowning your mother. And Ardis knew what Cyrus is like. She never trusted him. So, who's to say why she did it? Maybe she was trying to right the wrong done your mother. Isabel says Ardis loved your mother very much."

"I know. Biddy told me." The numbness seeped slowly from her bones, leaving in its place a clammy sickness that kept Hannah in a slump.

"Who's Biddy? And what did she tell you?"

Hannah frowned at the sharp note in his voice. "Biddy's . . . well, she's everything to us. She was Mama's lady's maid when she had need of one. And then she was our nanny. But now she's like a grandmother to us. She told us stories of Boston and how Ardis loved my mother. That's all."

"I see. She . . . never mentioned my family?"

Hannah stared hard at him. "Maybe in passing, but I was nothing more than a girl when I last heard stories of Mama's life here. We didn't talk very much about Boston. Remember—I didn't even know your estate was next to Cloister Point."

"That's true." Seemingly satisfied with that, he relaxed again.

Storing away that reaction, Hannah went on. "Mama never would've taken the money. She said being rich like her family chained a person's soul. She probably would've given it right back to Cyrus. He didn't have to kill her."

Slade again surprised her by hesitating, by scrubbing his

hands over his face. When he lowered them, she could describe his expression only as tortured. "She couldn't have given it back to him."

"Why not?" Wariness crept over Hannah's flesh when Slade didn't answer, but just stared at her. Her heart set up a pounding tempo that seemed to make her palms feel slick. She clutched at the folds of her woolen skirt as she noted every detail of his chiseled face. The high cheekbones, the square, stubborn jaw, the black eyes, the shadow of a beard. Although they caught at Hannah's heart, they gave nothing away.

When he finally spoke, he made a simple statement of fact that sounded as if he were reading from a will. "In the event your mother didn't want the money or was already dead, Ardis named me as her heir."

"You." She should have been afraid for herself. She should have jumped up and gotten away while she could. She should have been crying for everything she felt for him in her heart. But instead, she stayed where she was. And felt nothing. Hearing only a loud ringing in her ears, she sat very still, so still she feared she was becoming one with her chair. And repeated the only word she seemed capable of uttering. "You."

He said nothing, offered no explanation as to why her great-grandmother would leave *him* the Wilton-Humes fortune.

Unblinking, Hannah turned her head toward the window. Dust motes danced in the pooled sunbeam that shone on the sleeping mastiff. Whimsical though the sight was, it couldn't penetrate Hannah's armor. She saw instead that piece of writing paper—with his name on it. Heartsick, hating him, hating herself, she nevertheless turned back to him. "You *are* in this with them."

He never moved a muscle. His voice, when he spoke, was as flat as hers. "No, Hannah. If I were, you wouldn't have lived past your first day in Boston. I'm on *your* side. You've got to believe me."

"Why should I believe you, when I have every reason not to?" She clenched her so-cold hands together in her lap.

"You have every reason to believe me, if you'll just think about it." With his black eyes focused squarely on her, he enumerated the reasons for her. "Once I knew who you were and *where* you were, I became a constant presence at Cloister Point."

Hannah made a scoffing noise. "Are you still saying you were there to protect me? We both know you came to scare me and threaten me."

"Yes, I did. But that has nothing to do with this. I've kept a cautious eye cast over the fence since the reading of Ardis's will. Three suspicious deaths occurred in that house right after that. Knowing that, I didn't want you dead before I had my chance at you. So, the night of the ill-fated dinner party, I seized my chance to get you away."

Hannah pinched her features up into what she hoped was as much a sarcastic retort as were her words. "And such a *selfless* act, as it turns out. I should've known you wouldn't risk your neck for someone bearing both the Wilton-Humes and the Lawless names."

He surprised her by glancing down and away for a moment. When he looked back at her, a stark emotion shone in his eyes and in the set of his mouth. She had the distinct impression he started to say one thing, but then settled for another. "Think what you will. But for the past week I've had my men asking questions, talking around. And the news is not good."

His words forced a fatalistic chuckle out of Hannah. "There hasn't been any good news since I stepped off one of your trains here in Boston."

He swept his gaze over her face, as if weighing her mood change. "True. And I don't have any for you now, either. I'm sure you suspect that your grandparents and great-grandmother also were killed by Cyrus and Patience?"

Numb already, beyond emotion, she simply nodded. "I have all along. I just didn't know *why*. Now I do. Money." She rubbed at her temples as she added, "I wish to God that Ardis had just left the money to her sons. Maybe then the only one who'd be dead would be the survivor of their own treacheries."

Slade surprised her by leaning over to squeeze her hand. "That would have been best, I agree. But there's still more, Hannah. From living there, I guess you know that Cyrus and Patience are quietly selling off Cloister Point's furnishings and family jewelry to keep up appearances."

Images collided with one another in Hannah's mind. Lack of food. Lack of furniture. Lack of servants. She nodded in agreement with him. "I realize now that's what I was seeing.

But looking around Cloister Point . . . well, the little they still have is so much more than anything I've ever had that I didn't realize the problems. It's such a grand place."

He nodded. "Yes, it is. And the upkeep alone takes a king's ransom—and half the combined trusts. Which only makes Cyrus more desperate for Ardis's money. He'd be ruined socially if the barest hint of even any belt-tightening got out, much less if they lived in reduced circumstances. Appearances, Hannah, appearances. Money affords social acceptance—and *that's* their lifeblood. And you stole it from them when you made your public accusations."

Hannah paused, biting thoughtfully at her lower lip. "So I guess they'll come after me next?"

"I'm sure of it. They'll come after me, too—and not just because I took your side."

Hannah stared at him as she searched her heart. Could she believe him and trust him? She wanted to. But could she trust her own heart any more than she could trust his words? She had no proof of what he told her. Dispirited now, she leaned back in her chair and gazed up to where the wall joined with the ceiling. "What could they gain by coming after you? The money's yours now."

"No it isn't. It too is in a trust—until I marry and father a child. If I don't, only then does Cyrus *finally* inherit."

Hannah lowered her head with a suddenness that made her dizzy. "What did you just say?"

He shook his head and chuckled. "You heard me. That damned Ardis. The old girl was as much a caution as Isabel is. Those two were lifelong friends, so she put that rider in her will for Isabel—who as you know wants great-grandchildren in the worst way." Having said that, he turned grim. "When I was notified that I had to attend the reading of Ardis's will, I was not pleased. I've made a lifelong habit of staying out of Wilton-Humes affairs. But then, when the terms were read, I was as stunned as Cyrus.

"Ardis'd left her fortune to Catherine—a name not spoken at Cloister Point for twenty-five years. I got a good laugh at Cyrus's greedy expense and considered the matter closed. But then you showed up and . . . enlightened us all. It was only then that I knew I stood squarely in Cyrus's path."

He grinned again and crossed his arms. "You saved my life

by coming here. With me totally unaware of my status being elevated to first heir, I'd probably already be dead. And now you've ruined Cyrus's element of surprise for me. I'm certain he won't forgive you.''

Hannah stared wide-eyed at him, realizing that she had indeed saved his life. She looked down at her lap. Her desire for revenge had saved a life. *His* life. With those tossing and tumbling emotions causing her to frown, she cocked her head in question. "Why didn't Ardis simply leave the money to me and my sisters in the event of Mother's death?''

Slade shrugged. "I'm sure she would've, if she'd known of your existence. But it wasn't up to Ardis to name your mother's heirs.''

"That makes sense." Now things began to click in Hannah's mind. She sat up straighter and pointed at him. "But of course Mother was killed before she could take possession of her inheritance.''

Slade nodded. "Exactly. So it reverted to me. And, the will being what it is, the quickest path for Cyrus to get his hands on the money is to kill me before I marry and produce an heir.''

Hannah stared steadily into the blackest eyes she'd ever seen and felt a sudden coldness creeping over her soul. "That explains Cyrus. But not you. It doesn't explain you.''

He frowned, tilting his head questioningly. "I just told you—''

"No. You haven't told me anything about *you.* All I still know is why you need to watch your back around my great-uncle. But there's more going on here—between you and me. Because you didn't give a hoot that I had Wilton-Humes blood." She watched him tense up, watched his eyes narrow to slits. And knew she was right. "It's the Lawless blood in me that sets your blood boiling. Why is that?''

"I owe you no explanations." His voice was as flat as the prairie.

Hannah sat rigidly still and glared up at him. "The hell you don't. And I'm betting it has nothing to do with your needing to marry someone in a hurry to get your hands on that blood money.''

Slade eyed her down the end of his blueblood's hawkish

nose. "I neither want nor need Ardis's money, Hannah. And I never asked to be involved."

Even though his voice warned her to tread easy, Hannah ignored it. "So you say. But what else can I believe? You marry me—a Wilton-Humes—and get the best of my uncle. Use one Wilton-Humes to keep the money from another one. That's revenge. And isn't that the game you're playing?"

"Game?" Slade came abruptly to his feet. Broad gestures put the emphasis to his words. "It's *your* family being killed off by your great-uncle, Hannah. Not mine. But now I'm next on his list. That is my sole interest here on that score. Beyond that, if I wanted to marry simply to produce an heir, it wouldn't have to be you. I could marry *tomorrow* any woman I chose. But if I do marry you, then I could see the money *finally* in the right hands—yours. You are, after all, your mother's heir."

Hannah jumped to her feet and pointed her finger at his chin. "It's too late for such noble words from you. You're in this up to your ears—in some other way than the one you're telling me. Let me tell you something, Garrett—I don't want one cent of that blood money. Not one. All I want is to see the guilty people pay. With their lives. And if you're one of them . . . you'll be first on *my* list."

Breathing hard with rage, Hannah finished him off with, "And that is what it means to cross a Lawless."

Fury suffused a dusky red over his features, contorting his face into a horrific mask. He grabbed her by her arms, pulling her to him. His voice was no more than a low growl. "Don't you throw that name in my face, girl. Not if you want my help. Just remember one thing. *Five* people in your family are dead. Make no mistake here—if my ass wasn't on the line, too, I wouldn't give a good goddamn what happens next. But my life is on the line. So is yours. So are two others you obviously haven't thought of. And every one of us is as good as dead if you and I can't work together to stop Cyrus and Patience."

Toe to toe with him, she pushed against his chest. "Now there're *four* more? Where'd you come up with four? There's only me and you."

"That's where you're wrong, Hannah. There're your sisters—Jacey and Glory."

# CHAPTER NINE

---

Hannah stiffened in shock and then wrenched herself out of Slade's grip. Backing up a few paces, unable to absorb or respond, she turned her back on him. She walked over to the window, skirting Esmerelda. She stared outside at nothing in particular. In the stillness, she heard a clock chime the five o'clock hour. Like a death toll.

At that moment, Esmerelda snored loudly and snorted. Hannah turned enough to spare the dog a glance. The mastiff's legs worked as if she were running. Wishing she could run away too, Hannah turned back to Slade. He hadn't moved that she could tell. She centered on him, as if she were sighting down the long barrel of a Winchester. "How do you know my sisters' names?"

His face set in lines of weary disgust. "I'm not guilty of anything, Hannah. I told you—I've been doing some checking. My men tracked down a man who'd bragged in a saloon here that he'd earned some easy money following an outlaw's daughter to Boston. This tracker said he'd been following you since you left home." He pierced her with his black-eyed stare. "But he won't anymore."

"Following me? And you had him killed?" A cold heaviness spread over Hannah, locking her muscles into a stiff stance. "My sisters. Are they being followed?"

He nodded grimly. "Yes."

"Who did this?"

"The man . . . died refusing to say. The obvious guess is Cyrus. But your father had a lot of enemies of his own, Hannah. It could be anybody."

Images of Jacey and of Glory essentially alone on the ranch—and both of them unaware, just as she'd been—besieged Hannah's heart. She shook her head, feeling the panic building. "I never saw anyone watching me. I never even noticed. Neither will they. I can't reach them. Not in time. It may be too late already. Oh, my God, my sisters—!"

Slade took long strides over to her, stepping over the mastiff to grab her arms. He held her tightly, steadying her. "Listen to me, Hannah. Listen. I don't think these men have orders yet to kill you and your sisters. If they did, they would've just waited at the ranch for you to come home and killed you then. Or they could've done so at any moment after that. Even while you were on the train. But that didn't happen. You're fine, so there's every reason to believe your sisters are, too."

Hannah watched his mouth move. She tried to listen to and absorb his words. But a surge of hatred, darker than the bowels of hell, claimed her. With deliberate movements, she pried his hands off her arms and pushed him back. She then slipped a hand into her skirt, pulling out her Smith & Wesson pistol.

Slade jerked in a breath. "What the hell! What do you think you're going to do with that?"

"I'm going over to Cloister Point and rid the world of two monsters. You and I both know they're responsible for me and my sisters being followed." She pivoted on her heel, but was immediately jerked back around and held onto.

"You're not going any-damn-where, Hannah."

She unfeelingly poked the gun's barrel square up against his abdomen. "I say I am. And I'm the one with the loaded gun. Now, let me go. Or say your last words in this life, Garrett."

He held on to her and said his last words. "If you kill Cyrus and Patience, and they *are* the ones paying the trackers, they'll kill your sisters for sure."

Hannah narrowed her eyes. "You just said their orders weren't to kill us."

"I said *not yet.* And I'm only guessing. They could have orders to kill if they should check in and there're no follow-up instructions. Or money. That's the type of men we're dealing with. I don't know yet who's paying them. Hell, I don't even know *why* you were being followed. Until I find all that out, I just have suspicions. And no way to call them off, if Cyrus and Patience die.''

It made sense. But Hannah wasn't ready to trust him. Or to lower her gun. ''Just how do I know I can trust you? Just how do I know that everything you've told me, from the first minute I met you, isn't a load of so much cattle crap?''

He blinked in surprise as he let go of her and stepped back. ''Cattle crap? That's quaint, Hannah. All my efforts come down to so much cattle crap. Fine. I don't give a damn if you believe me or not. It doesn't change the fact that my life is in as much danger as yours over Ardis's money—maybe more.''

Hannah narrowed her eyes and kept her gun poked against his gut. ''I don't want the damned money. You keep it.''

Enraged to the point of stuttering, he bellowed, ''It's . . . goddammit, it's not mine to keep! If you don't want it, then . . . your sisters might. Now put that *damned* peashooter away and come here.''

Then, with complete disregard for her weapon, he turned his back and went around his desk. He sat down, pulled out a bank ledger, and inked his pen. ''If you can't trust me after everything I've already done for you, after all the information I've shared with you''—he began writing—''after everything I've just told you, when I didn't have to, then to hell with you. You want to be on your own? You want to find your own answers with no help from me? Fine. That can be arranged.'' He finished writing and then looked up at her.

Hannah remained in place. Her gun was still pointed at the empty space where his belly had been. She watched him with eyes narrowed—and mind slowly opening. If he only knew it.

He capped the ink and inserted the pen back in its hole. Then he tore the draft out, holding it out to her. ''Take this draft. I'll also make my town house in Boston and a brougham available to you, as well as my employees there. You can take everything I've already given you, too. That way, you won't be *hog-tied* by my presence or by my interference. And you can then learn for yourself the truth. And match it against what I've told you. Fair enough?''

He looked from her to the draft in his hand and then back at her. ''Well? Don't you want it? If it's a matter of pride, consider it a loan against your inheritance.''

Hannah was through watching him. Up to now, except for

bringing her here, he'd pretty much been a man of words. But now he'd just become a man of action. That she understood. When a man put his own money where his mouth was, you could bet yours that he was telling the truth, Papa'd always said.

Hannah lowered her gun, slipped it back in her pocket, and walked slowly up to the desk. She looked him in the eye, saw naked challenge mirrored there, and took the draft from him. She looked down at it and swallowed. She'd never seen a number that big before. Too bad she wasn't going to keep it. Looking him in the eye again, she tore the bank draft into tiny pieces and tossed them onto the desk between them. "I don't want your money, Slade. I want you."

His eyes widened, but he quickly recovered and narrowed them. He then slouched back in his chair, his legs wide, his elbows on the armrests. He put a finger to his bottom lip and rubbed it thoughtfully as he looked her up and down. "What are you saying, Hannah?"

"I'm saying . . . I believe you. I'm saying I want to stay here with you. But most of all, I'm saying I want you to pretend to marry me and let Cyrus think we're hard at work producing you an heir."

Slade catapulted to a stand, leaning stiff-armed over the desk with his fingers tented on its surface. "What the hell do you have up your sleeve, besides another gun?"

The very air crackled with his shouting voice. Esmerelda jerked to a sitting position, woofing out her displeasure at being awakened so rudely. Hannah turned with Slade to the source of the woof. Esmerelda, seeing she had their attention, frowned in judgment and then flopped back down on her side.

Hannah exchanged a look with Slade and then perched her hip on the desk's corner, dangling her foot and mimicking his posture from when she'd first entered. "I'll explain, but first you have to sit down." She waited . . . and waited.

He finally sat, but gingerly, as if he thought the chair under him would explode. Crossing an ankle over his opposite knee, he spread his hands wide as he leaned back. "Go ahead. I'm listening."

Hannah raised her chin. If only her fluttering stomach had as much bravado as her words did. She ticked off her points on her fingers. "Isabel's already planning a real wedding. Let her. It'll make everything seem that much more believable.''

Slade eyed her without blinking. His look said he was seeing her in a new light—a very unfavorable one. "I see. We use and deceive my grandmother. Go on.''

"Don't look at me like that, Garrett. And don't judge me. Go ahead—tell her. Tell her it's not a real wedding. Or a real marriage. See how convincing she is then. Just remember—your life's at stake here, too.''

"Of course. My mistake.'' Gripping the armrests now, he swiveled the chair slowly, slowly, side to side, in place. "For the first time, I'm beginning to see evidence of Wilton-Humes blood in you. Or maybe it's that famous Lawless blood. Or the mix of them both.''

Stung, ashamed of herself but seeing no other way, Hannah narrowed her eyes at him. "You got a better idea?''

He raised an eyebrow. "Yes, I do, as a matter of fact. And you already know what it is.''

Hannah fairly squinted at him now. "Marry you for real? And give you that damned revenge you're always spouting off about? That's not going to happen. Ever.''

His changing expression, like a fast-moving storm racing across the plains, framed his struggle for control. But in the end, all he did was grin. Like a snake would, if it could. "Not ever. That's a long time. But do go on.''

Hannah's heart lurched. What was he thinking? Forced into a corner of her own making, she valiantly plunged ahead. "All right. We stage this mock-wedding here in the next couple of weeks or so, and we—''

He held up a hand. "I won't involve tremendous expense in this scheme. Nor will I break Isabel's heart by lying to her. Let's rethink this lavish wedding. The more people we involve, the more chance there is of the truth coming out. I suggest we appear to elope. Dudley Ames will pretend to be our witness. That will lend credibility to this farce. Our story will be that we were swept away with love and desire. That should be a huge scandal and produce a tremendous amount of publicity. And satisfy even you.''

"Don't act as if I'm enjoying any of this. I'm not. No one has to satisfy me . . . least of all you.''

He shot forward with lightning quickness and grabbed a fistful of her blouse, pulling her slowly toward him, until the tip of her nose was touching the tip of his. "If I don't *satisfy* you—or appear to—we'll never convince Cyrus we're working on that little heir we need. And isn't that what all this is about?"

Hannah didn't dare breathe or blink. When would she remember how dangerous this man was? Finally, she managed the barest of nods.

"Good girl." His voice was warmed-over death. "Now, Cyrus isn't stupid enough to storm over here on the day we announce our elopement and try to kill us. Not with every Brahmin dropping by to belatedly congratulate us and laugh behind their hands. No, he'll let the furor die down. Then he'll make his move. So, you see, we have time. A lot of time. We'll have to be . . . *convincing*."

Hannah swallowed and nodded again. This wasn't going as she planned. But at least he was agreeing. After a fashion. As for that making-an-heir part, she'd worry about that when the time came. She'd handled him so far, hadn't she? Yeah, that's why she was hauled up against him with his fist at her throat. Stung, Hannah gritted out, "Take your hands off me, Garrett."

He held on to her for another second or two. His grip even tightened the least bit. Then he released her as if she'd bitten him. Pulling back from her, he straightened up. His expression right then would scare small children. "When this is all over, Hannah, you get the hell out of Boston. And don't you ever let me see your face again."

Near to tears, Hannah fumblingly righted her clothes and snarled right back at him. "Don't worry, Garrett. That was always my plan. Did you think I was staying here forever? Ha. I want to get this over with as much as you do. Maybe more so because my life, my family, are out West. But I'm here now, and I refuse to wait around for my great-uncle to order my death. So, the way I see it, I've got to make Cyrus make a move."

Slade contemplated her. "You don't have to convince me, Hannah. I think you're absolutely right. But tell me, what do you plan to do when he makes his move? What do you get out of this?"

Just thinking about what she'd get, Hannah concentrated on all the hate coalescing around her heart. "I get to kill the man responsible for murdering my folks, that's what."

\* \* \*

"Good Lord, Slade, you were serious." Dudley Ames, a Scotch in one hand and a fat cigar in the other, shot forward like an arrow to the edge of his well-padded and comfortably worn leather chair. He looked around at the censuring stares of his fellow members at the Sommersby Club and promptly lowered his voice to a hiss. "You're serious? You're going to marry Hannah Lawless?"

Slade raised his drink. "I am. May I have your blessing, my friend?"

Dudley sat back just as abruptly as he'd slid forward. "Hardly. I wouldn't sanction something that will damn my own soul for just *knowing* about it. You're determined to dishonor yourself and destroy this girl, aren't you?"

Slade grinned and took a sip of his whiskey. "Not really. Besides, it's her idea . . . after a fashion."

Dudley slid forward again in a wreath of hazy smoke and jerked his cigar out of his mouth. "Now I've seen the elephant. Her idea? Since when?"

"Since two days ago. She begged me to marry her and get her with my child."

Dudley flung himself back into his chair. "What a load of horse apples. You think me a fool—of course, Mother would agree—but I wasn't born yesterday. Tell me why she would do that. Hannah, I mean. Not Mother. I *know* why she thinks I'm a fool."

Slade shrugged, enjoying this banter with Dudley. It felt good to be with men again and not in the company of ancient servants, his crafty little grandmother, and the about-to-be-very-surprised, yet still irresistible Hannah. "Simple. She's found herself totally in love with me and must have me."

"Bullsh—" Dudley cut off his epithet at the gasps and shocked stares of the older members. "Pardon," he excused himself to them. He turned back to Slade, whispering. "She's not the first young lady to profess those sentiments to you, if she did at all. And no one leads you around by your—um, nose. So it's the other way around, isn't it, you old sock?"

Slade leaned forward, also whispering. "I admit to nothing. Let's just say I see the sense in her plan. With my own added twist, of course."

His cigar held between his fingers, Dudley slammed his

hamlike hand down onto the soft leather of the armrest. "Then, bully for you! And for her!" Again, he was forced to turn to the richly paneled room's aghast company. "Once more, I beg pardon." Turning back to Slade, he eagerly sipped at his drink and then clenched his cigar between his big teeth as he grinned in open curiosity. "Well?"

"Well what?"

"What's this *plan* of hers? And when did this all happen? But first, I almost forgot—you've been notably absent from society for the past weeks. Which has been duly remarked upon, I must add, by more than one brokenhearted young lady. Respectable and otherwise."

"Give them all my sincere apologies. Especially the otherwise ones. And tell them I regret that I won't be back in their arms—er, their society—anytime soon. If at all." Slade grinned at his friend's rapidly changing expression.

"If at all? Now, dammit, Garrett, this is serious. Something's afoot, and you're going to tell me what it is. No hedging, now—I've always been able to best you with my fists."

Slade remembered anew why he liked this senator's son. Such bravado for someone who made a good-natured mess of everything he attempted. "First of all, Dudley, you're about to spill your ash down the front of your shirt. And second, her plan is to seduce me. That will gain for me an heir. And for herself—her great-grandmother's money and the chance to kill her great-uncle and then leave for home on the next train out of town, once all that is accomplished."

Slack-jawed, cigar tipping out precariously from between his lips, Dudley stared blankly at him.

Slade arched an eyebrow. "That particular expression of yours is my favorite, Ames. It speaks so well of your intelligence."

Dudley clamped his jaws shut and bit clean through the butt end of his cigar, sending it tumbling down his front to land lit-end on his crotch. He didn't seem to notice—not for several . . . long . . . moments.

But Slade couldn't take his eyes off the smoldering tobacco. "Dudley, you might want to—"

A screech tore out of Dudley. "Great jumping Jehoshaphat!" He jerked up and out of the chair in a flurry of arms and legs, sent his drink flying, and—amid the shouted protests

of the other members—began to dance around in a circle and
beat at himself. In the process, he managed also to crush the
errant cigar into the thick maroon carpet. Finally, he stopped
his stampeding about to look down at himself. "I nearly
burned the damned thing off before I ever got to put it to
legitimate use."

He thrust his hips forward obscenely, took hold of his pants,
and then fanned the general area. Finally, he turned an ap-
palled expression on Slade, who simply stared at him, one
corner of his mouth quirked up. Dudley, hands to his waist as
his pants smoked and smelled up the room, burst out laughing.

Within moments, Slade found himself out on Beacon Street
with Dudley, who was gainfully occupied in buttoning his
chesterfield over his ruined attire. Slade held on to his friend's
shoulder for support as he bellowed out his laughter. "Dudley,
old man, this is a new record for us. In and out in less than
an hour."

"I've been thrown out of better," Dudley fumed. But then
his face lit up. "Now there's an idea—let's try our luck at my
dear father's country club." He then slipped a hand under the
overlapping fold of his coat to unabashedly fumble around and
once again assure himself of his member's well-being. "I
could've gelded myself."

"What, and deprive your mother of the pleasure?" Slade
turned to signal to Rigby to follow them with the brougham
as they walked in the crisp autumn air of late afternoon. He
turned back to Dudley. "You are such an ungrateful son."

Dudley grinned at Slade. "Oh, you've been visiting Mother,
have you?"

"No. Actually, she was visiting Isabel and Hannah when I
left."

Dudley feigned horror. "She's been loosed on the unsuspecting population? What a nightmare for your household."

"More for her, I'd say. Esmerelda dragged in a dead rat
and deposited it at your mother's very proper feet."

Dudley's broad-boned face lit up with beatific glee. "God
love that huge horse of a dog. I knew we were doing the right
thing when we imported her from jolly old England." His
expression then sobered some. "Now, back to this Hannah
thing. As I understand it, she's simply going to become the

next Mrs. Garrett, obligingly supply you with an heir, and then promptly *leave*?''

Slade nodded. ''That's the public version, yes.''

''The public version. I see. Now, we're talking about a year's time, at the least, for all this to occur—given Mother Nature's requirements for the actual conceiving and producing of a born child, whether it be an heir or not. And we're assuming that the virile husband can get her with child on, say, the first outing. Here now. Wait a moment. If your lady is in such a tear to leave your company, then why would she get herself . . . ?'' With his hand, he indicated a very rounded belly. Then he went on, happily considering all the details.

''First of all, I don't see the law looking the other way— your wife or not—if she succeeds in cold-bloodedly killing the very deserving Cyrus. But, that problem aside, neither do I see a mother leaving her infant child behind, never to see it again. Nor do I see you allowing her to return to that savage-plagued prairie with your heir in tow.''

Slade clapped Dudley on his impressively wide back. ''Ames, if only you could order your own affairs as neatly as you do mine. Let me assure you, none of your concerns are going to transpire.''

Dudley stopped in the middle of the street. ''The devil you say.''

''I do. Hannah's going nowhere. She's not going to kill anyone, but she will marry me in a scandalously short time and produce my heir. But neither she nor my child is leaving here. Ever.''

Dudley shoved at Slade's shoulder. ''Go on with you. Does she know any of this?''

''Of course . . . not. Not really. No, not like she thinks. Oh, the hell with it—it's a surprise.'' Slade stopped short when Dudley did. ''Stow it, Ames, I swear it. Now listen, I've just had a brilliant idea.''

Dudley's face outdid his voice for drollness as he clapped his hand over his heart. ''God save us all.''

Slade grinned. ''Are you game for a little adventure?''

''No. The last two times you asked me that and I agreed, I found myself rowing the tiniest little craft as an oarsman for Harvard—and promptly swamped the damned thing. Then, the next time, I was your victim on the tennis courts. But wait—

there was a third. And a fourth. Suffice it to say I like neither guns nor archery as a result.''

''Are you quite done?''

Dudley feigned giving Slade's question deep thought. Then, he nodded. ''I believe I am.''

''Good. So, are you game for a little adventure?''

''Of course,'' Dudley pronounced cheerfully. ''What are we about?''

Slade put his arm around Dudley's shoulder. ''My friend, we're about to get rip-roaring drunk. And then we're about to get me married.''

''You're not serious!''

''I am. Til-death-do-us-part serious, my friend.''

''See? Right there. By next April, we'll have the most beautiful lilacs where that bare patch is—Oh, for evermore, Esmerelda! Get out of that flower bed and go bury your rat elsewhere! You've already scared everyone you can with it. Poor Mrs. Ames lay on the fainting couch for thirty minutes. And it's all your fault. You ought to be ashamed, you great cow of a dog.'' Done with upbraiding the bounding-about mastiff, she turned to Hannah, a delighted smile lighting her tiny features. ''She's not the least bit sorry, you know.''

''I believe you're right.'' Hannah smiled, more at Isabel's unflappability than at the mastiff's far-off antics in the afternoon's freshness. ''I can picture them now, Isabel—the lilacs, I mean.''

''Wait until you can smell them, come next spring. They're quite fragrant.''

Next spring? She wouldn't be here then. A pang lanced through her as Isabel slipped a child-sized hand under Hannah's elbow. Then, the little bird of a woman at her side peeked back over her shoulder. Hannah grinned. Isabel loved to bedevil their guard. The square, dour man shadowed their every move outside the manor, so she knew without looking what Isabel would see.

Isabel finally turned her highly rouged face up to Hannah and whispered, ''That Jones is still back there. Slade's always said I need a keeper.'' Her black and twinkling eyes attested to her opinion of that. Then, right out of the blue, she raised her voice and changed the subject. "Are you enjoying your stay here, Hannah?"

"Certainly," Hannah rushed to assure her hostess. "I feel very welcome at Woodbridge Pond. I think I could come to love it."

"Good. That's good."

Hannah glanced down at Isabel's softly smiling face as that one kept a watchful eye on Esmerelda. Hiding both a frown and a smile, Hannah reminded herself that—make no mistake—a sharp and calculating mind lurked inside that head. And missed nothing.

With her free hand, Hannah pulled her shawl around her shoulders. Walking quietly beside Isabel, enjoying the cool, windless day, she cast her gaze over the winter-readied formal gardens through which they walked. The sculpted greenery stretched from the mansion itself and ran to the high hedges this side of the pond. Was she already coming to love this place?

"You're awfully quiet, Hannah. Are you worried about your little Olivia?"

Glad Isabel hadn't divined her true thoughts, Hannah nodded. "Yes. Very much. Not one word from her, and tomorrow will be three days. I miss her chattering, cheerful presence. If I knew where she was, I'd go get her myself."

"Oh, I don't imagine that great, frowning man back there— or my great, frowning grandson—would like that."

Hannah huffed out a scoffing noise at that notion. "I don't care what either of them likes. I do as I please."

Isabel cackled and patted Hannah's shoulder. "You're quite his match, you know. You two should make very lovely children. The Good Lord knows we need the healing sounds of laughing and running children through this house." She pulled back, the better to eye Hannah. "And I just can't believe it's you—a Wilton-Humes *and* a Lawless."

Hannah clamped her teeth together and managed a smile. She'd almost blurted out that there would be no children . . . not really. Slade was right—her charade was going to break Isabel's heart. She was completely convinced that a marriage between the two children, as she called them, was exactly what they both wanted and needed. And she felt it was her God-given duty to bring them together. Why, she'd even told Dudley's mother to expect an announcement.

Her conscience roiling now as much as her stomach, Hannah changed the subject. "Isabel, tell me about Slade's childhood. I'm sorry to say, but from what little bit I know, it doesn't sound like a very happy one. What I mean is, I understand his strong feelings regarding the Wilton-Humeses, but not regarding my father."

"Ahh. I suppose I brought that up, didn't I? Well, obviously your mother never told you."

Hannah stopped, looking down pointedly at Isabel. There it was again—that sense of some mystery that only she knew nothing of. "Told me what?"

Isabel raised a brown-spotted, thin-veined hand to her brow, using it to shade her eyes from the sun as she squinted up at Hannah. "That many years ago our families were to have been so much more than mere neighbors."

Hannah's heart thumped, warning of bad news yet to come. "How do you mean?"

Isabel considered Hannah a moment and then tugged on her arm. "Come, we'd best sit down. There's a nice bench by the pond where we can visit and keep an eye on Esmerelda, lest she dig up the summer cottage itself."

With Isabel directing, they walked in silence to the other side of the tall shrubs. Hannah helped the winded grandmother to settle herself and then sat down beside her. The continued crunching of the gravel behind them told of the guard's approach. Jones came into view, making his presence conspicuous on the other side of the walk from them. He remained unobtrusively silent.

Sighing at the need for such measures, Hannah then looked around until she spied Esmerelda careening joyfully around the pond's perimeter, the dead rat's fat and nasty, long-tailed body still clutched in her jaws. A purely feminine shudder rippled over her.

Isabel drew Hannah's attention back to her when she spoke. "Esmerelda is quite the handful. Just like Slade."

Hannah laughed with her. "Yes, I've noticed—on both scores." Her laugh subsided to a smile and then gentled into an open, neutral expression as she looked out over the calm water. And waited for Isabel's explanations.

"Quite simply," Isabel began abruptly, bringing Hannah's gaze to her face, "your mother was supposed to marry my son, John."

The air left Hannah's lungs as if lightning had flashed out of the clear, blue sky and struck her. She put a hand to her heart, not certain that it still beat. Or that her blood hadn't congealed in her veins. "Your son—Slade's father—and my mother were to marry? *My* mother?"

Isabel nodded, looking far off, over the pond's waters. "Yes, they were. Ironic, isn't it?" She turned now to Hannah. "I've always prayed for healing in my family, Hannah. And perhaps now, with you and Slade, that healing can begin." She stopped, putting a knobby-knuckled hand to her lined cheek. "But what am I saying? Neither you nor Slade would have been born, if events had turned out differently. And I suppose I'd be sitting here by myself."

Staggered, Hannah could only frown and make a helpless gesture. "Mother never said anything. Why didn't they marry, Isabel? What happened?"

"It's all so sad." Isabel shook her head, as if a great burden weighed her soul down. Sighing, she surprised Hannah by reaching for her hand, holding on to it as she spoke. "You look so much like your mother that I . . . Well, it doesn't matter. I believe your mother saw a bad something in my John that none of us did for a number of years. A weakness. Or a coldness or cruelty. Something like that."

When Isabel didn't say anything else, Hannah stroked the older woman's fragile-boned hand and broke into her thoughts. "Your hand is awfully cold. Do you want to go back inside?"

Isabel shook her head. "No. It's the memories, not the weather." She was silent another moment, but then launched into her story. "John and Catherine were childhood playmates. Then, they became betrothed after your mother's coming-out season. The happy date was set for the following year."

She turned now to look at Hannah. "We were quite good friends back then with your family. But it wasn't to be. You see—Catherine never would say why—but she very suddenly just broke it off. And, I'm sorry to say, John didn't take it so well. He began drinking and raging about. Nothing Herbert—my late husband—and I said or did seemed to help him. Or to stop him. Especially on . . . that night."

# CHAPTER TEN

—

A clammy coldness seized Hannah. "What night, Isabel? And stop him from what?"

"That slipped out. I wasn't going to tell you, but perhaps it's time someone knew. Promise me you won't tell Slade. It's so shameful, and it happened before he was born, so I never told him. Do you promise, Hannah?"

Hannah looked into the old woman's anguished face. "I promise."

Isabel let out her breath and withdrew her hand. "Thank you. Late one terrible night, John apparently worked himself up into a particularly drunken rage. Herbert and I'd already retired for the night, so we knew nothing of what was afoot. But John's brooding turned violent. He tore out of the house, fought his way through the hedges, ran to a rear door, and stormed up the servants' stairs ... to your mother's room and—" Isabel stopped on a ragged breath. "I'm sorry. Give me a moment." She lowered her head to look at her lap.

Hannah's heart pounded faster. Her poor, sweet mother. "Did he—?"

Isabel jerked her head up. Tears stood in her eyes as she shook her head. "No, but very nearly. Your grandfather heard her screams and came running to trounce John good and send him packing, as Hamilton had every right to do. The next day ... that very fence there began going up."

Hannah turned to stare with Isabel at the fence. When the grand old lady again took up her story, she spoke with a briskness that suggested she wished to be done with the topic. "Servants talked, the word spread quickly, and an awful scandal followed. Within mere days, Catherine was sent away with her lady's maid. They left with the Foster girl and her family on an extended grand tour through the West. We never saw her again.''

Hands gnarled together in her lap, like the twisted roots of an ancient oak, Isabel stared quietly at them. After a moment, a ragged sniff shuddered out of her. ''Hannah, I'm so sorry.''

Hurting for her mother, for herself, and for Isabel, hurting for Slade and for the tortured man who was his father, Hannah gathered Isabel's frail body close and kissed her forehead. ''I'm so sorry for you. It must have been awful.''

''It *was* awful. Still is, I'm afraid. My family—or yours—never quite recovered. I wish I could've been a better mother to John.''

''Don't say that, Isabel.'' Hannah rested her cheek against Isabel's soft, white hair. ''You can't blame yourself. It sounds to me like your John loved my mother very much, and did something stupid when he was drunk. He suffered terribly, I'm sure, for loving her so much, and for not having her return it.''

Hannah blinked, hearing her own words. Why was she making excuses for John Garrett? She should be reviling him. What he'd done then was still playing hell with peoples' lives twenty-five years later—through his son. Thus conjured, the darkly handsome face of Slade Garrett smiled mockingly at her. Hannah stiffened, and welcomed Isabel's distracting words.

''You're very generous to say that. But still, I've never understood how a son of mine could. . . .'' She let her voice trail off and then gently tugged herself out of Hannah's embrace. ''I'm fine, dear. Thank you.''

Hannah thought the subject was done, but apparently there was more, because Isabel continued on. ''After Catherine left, we thought John would die from regret and his broken heart. He continued drinking and behaving irrationally. But right away, a shy girl he'd never paid the least bit of attention to— Mariel Whittington was her name. Her family's since moved to New York—stepped forward to comfort him. John married her within a month. And nine months to the day later, Slade was born. Their only child.''

Hannah smiled. ''There. You see? A lovely ending, Isabel.''

"No." She shook her head. "John never, ever got over Catherine. He made Mariel miserable, belittling her, comparing her unfavorably to your mother. No matter how the poor girl tried, she couldn't be Catherine. She came to hate your mother's memory, and John finally drove her to hate him and to take to her bed with feigned illnesses. She died of a broken heart when Slade was ten. He was devastated, but John barely noticed she was gone."

Isabel fiddled with her skirt a moment. "John was a failure as a husband and a father, but he had a brilliant head for business. When my Herbert died shortly after Mariel did, John threw himself into managing the Garrett affairs. And was tremendously successful. But all his life—and Slade's—he cursed J. C. Lawless, laying on your father's head all his own failures. He especially hated him for possessing the one love he could never have."

Now tears stood in Hannah's eyes for the sad, lonely little boy that had been Slade Garrett. She dabbed at the wetness with her shawl's ends. "I understand so many things now, Isabel. Thank you for telling me."

"You've every right to know, dear. I raised him, seeing what his parents were like. I just hope I've succeeded with him where I failed with John."

Hannah clutched Isabel's hands in hers, gripping them with no small amount of emotion. Her heart ached for this woman. "You did a wonderful job with him, Isabel. He's a good, strong man, worthy of being admired."

"Thank you." Isabel smiled tremulously and freed a hand to pat Hannah's shoulder. "He's also worthy of being loved. That's all I want before I die—to know that Slade is happy and loved. Do you love him, Hannah?"

Later that evening, Hannah sat alone in her delicately furnished bedroom. She faced the oval mirror mounted in the cherry vanity, but paid not the least bit of attention to her own reflection. Dressed for bed in white cambric, and deep in thought, she absently brushed her unbound hair. She focused on a chocolate-brown curl when it wrapped itself around her fingers.

Did she love Slade Garrett? Her sigh rent the silent air. Isabel was correct—he did deserve that much. Hannah set her hands in motion again, brushing and brushing, but a moment later, her hands stilled yet again. This whole affair was her own fault. *Pretend* to marry? *Pretend* to be happy and . . . going about the business of producing a baby?

Producing a baby. She was a grown woman with normal desires and yearnings, and she lived on a ranch. Yes. And had . . . seen things, with the cattle and horses and all. So she knew the . . . baser particulars of producing a new life. But was it really that violent and . . . and that messy for humans? Hannah grimaced, telling herself she certainly hoped not.

But then, unbidden came her mother's words to her and her sisters about love and marriage. She'd said it was sacred, beautiful, that she wished for each of her daughters a strong, loving husband. Mama'd said there was nothing more beautiful between a man and woman than the physical side of their love. So maybe it was different for humans.

Well, all she knew of it was how Slade Garrett made her feel. And not just in her heart. Gasping at these racy thoughts, and still clutching her silver-backed brush, Hannah jumped up. Possessed of a restlessness she couldn't name, she began to pace, tapping the brush against the palm of her other hand.

She couldn't go through with her own plan. To make it work, she and Slade would have to sleep together. No! They would *pretend* to sleep together. Merciful heavens, what made her think she could get Slade Garrett to pretend to anything? Well, he had agreed to her plan. Yes, but why? She saw the way he looked at her. Those dark eyes of his had already possessed her. The rest was a mere formality. Did she really believe she could get him to play parlor games with her at bedtime?

Hannah stopped her pacing and put a hand to her mouth. Such deception she was practicing. She saw Isabel's hopeful face, asking her if she loved Slade. Slade was right—she'd be more hurt than anyone when she found out they weren't really married. Or in love.

In love. She'd been spared answering the bald question when Esmerelda'd presented herself with an uprooted shrub in her mouth, which they'd had to pry out of her jaws and replant. But love . . . how could she know? Who could she ask? She'd never been in love before.

She knew only what she felt in her womanly places when

he was near, when he touched her. But was that love—or the same thing the cattle and horses felt? Hannah gripped her brush harder, wanting to throw it against the wall. This was unbearable. She needed a distraction.

A sudden scratching and whining at the closed door that connected her room to Slade's jerked Hannah around and swirled her wrapper's folds about her legs. Her first thought was of Slade. But then she realized what she was hearing. Esmerelda. Her heart pounding out its tremendous relief, she crossed to the closed door and began talking as she opened it. "You want out. You want in. You've got me completely trained, haven't—

"You," she completed. Esmerelda was not alone. With her was a disheveled, madly grinning duo. Slade Garrett and Dudley Ames. They reeked of spirits and each had an arm around the other's shoulders. Behind them stood a young, sober-appearing, bespectacled man of the cloth.

Hannah couldn't seem to settle her gaze on any one of the three men. Was this their elopement charade? Were Slade and Dudley really drunk? Was the preacher a real one? Not sure of anything anymore, except that she was eternally grateful that they hadn't awakened the ancient household, Hannah whispered, "What are you doing?"

"We're gettin' mar-married," Slade slurred out. Without releasing Dudley or even looking behind himself, he reached his other hand back and unerringly snagged the poor preacher by his already crumpled lapel. As one, the threesome stumbled into the room, forcing Esmerelda through the door ahead of them and Hannah backward several steps.

Dudley belched airily and announced, "Yeah, we're ... gettin' married. Not me an' S-S-Slade."

That struck the two drunks as tremendously funny. They clutched the poor preacher between them and hung all over him as they bellowed out their hilarity. Nearly buckling under the combined weight of the two much larger men and their eyebrow-singeing breath, the middle man's spectacles fogged. He made a horrible face, looking as if he might promptly be ill on the carpet.

Hannah sympathized completely, breathing as she did the same air he was. She wrinkled her nose and stepped back. Well, that answered one question—they were really drunk.

Hannah knew she should stop this madness, but how? She'd never dealt with a liquored-up man before. Perhaps the preacher could. . . . She eyed the suffering young man. No, he wasn't much bigger than she. He'd prove no help. In an agony of indecision, she put a hand to her mouth and remained frozen in place—even when Slade shoved the holy man forward a step.

"Look, Hannah—we brought a rev—A rev-rer—A preacher." Then, making a supreme, serious-faced effort, he pushed himself off Dudley and tried his best to straighten up and smooth his own clothes some. Dudley followed his cue. The two succeeded only in mincing and staggering around and pulling out things that needed tucking in.

"Please, miss," the heretofore silent preacher begged. "Can we just do this so they'll let me go?"

Hannah finally uncovered her mouth, lowering her hand to her heart. "You do know I'm not *really* marrying him? He told you that, right?"

Clutching his Bible to his chest, the poor preacher swallowed hard and made a face, as if his own saliva tasted bitter. "Yes, miss. He told me you'd say that. I understand."

Relief nearly buckled Hannah's knees. This *was* the charade, the pretend ceremony with Dudley as a witness. She'd no more than let out her breath than Slade recaptured her attention with "Well? We're . . . we're ready."

Hannah and the holy man stared at the dangerously bobbing and weaving twosome, who swayed like two saplings in a stiff breeze. She exchanged a look with the silently pleading, desperately hopeful preacher. And then she looked down at herself. Beyond horrified at what she saw, she clutched at a handful of white cambric, holding it out as proof. "But I'm not dressed and—"

"Iss white, ain't it?" Dudley waved a hand erratically in her direction. "You look gor-gor-jis-ness." He frowned mightily. "I mean beaut—beaut-fidul." Slade slapped him hard on the back. "You look pretty." Supremely proud to have gotten it out, the senator's son grinned and emitted a ferocious hiccup, forceful enough to stagger him.

Hannah cut her gaze over to the preacher. He shifted his Bible, holding it against his skinny chest. He then raised his joined hands prayerfully to her. "Please, miss. I beg you. They pulled me out of bed and . . . and—You don't know the places I've been tonight, before they remembered what they were about and where you were. I've seen things and been forced to—''

Hannah held up her hand. "Say no more. Get it over with. Come on, before they wake the dead."

"The dead? I'm afraid it's too late. You see, we've already been to the cemetery. We went there after the . . . after the—pardon me, miss—the den of iniquity." The preacher spoke as if he knew his soul was forfeit.

"Sweet Jesus." Hannah shook her head and stepped forward to place herself between the two totally despicable men. Looping an arm through each of theirs, she made a face to match her disgust and said levelly, "Say the words, so we can all go to bed."

To her right, Slade straightened up and reached around in front of her to poke Dudley in the chest. "See, my drunken frien'? I tol' you she wanted me."

Slade jerked awake to the sound of loud snoring. On both sides of him. He blinked against the dry scratchiness of his eyeballs. As the fog began lifting from his brain, his body told him he was lying on his stomach—on a narrow bed but mashed in a hot, sweating heap between two other bodies. His face was pressed against the softness of a damp pillow, and his mouth was slacked open.

Slade blinked again, marking that the room was blanketed with the thick grayness of an ungodly hour. He then made the mistake of smacking his mouth open and closed as he worked his tongue. His breath burned his nostrils and forced a grimace on him. "Gee-sus," he croaked. "What the hell is going on?"

Having invoked both heaven and hades, he attempted to roll onto his back. But the only thing that rolled was his stomach. He groaned and flopped back to his original position. Someone who lay up against his back sounded a hellacious snarking snore. Slade felt his head swell. Groaning, he stretched his face muscles into an unnatural contortion.

Then the door from the hallway burst open and swung back to hit the wall behind it. Slade and his dark-shrouded bedmates all popped their heads up off the pillows. Haloed in bright light was the cheerfully smiling, happily striding Hannah.

Fully dressed, she crossed the room and came to stand at the bedside. ''Good morning,'' she chirped—in an unnecessarily loud voice. ''And how are we this morning?''

The other two succumbed, flopping limply back onto the pillows. Slade spared them not even a glance as he braced himself on an elbow, narrowed his eyes—at the light, at the noise, at her—and told her in very vulgar and no uncertain terms how ''we'' were this morning.

Hannah shook her perfectly coiffed head. ''Such language on the first day of our marriage.''

Slade wondered if she'd always been this obnoxious. ''Whose marriage? What the hell are you talking about?''

''Ours,'' she chirped brightly, gushing out her words. ''Mine and yours. Now, don't tell me you don't remember our *beautiful* ceremony and our two *lovely* attendants?''

Slade didn't move a muscle, but he did repeat himself. ''What the hell are you talking about?''

She cocked her head at a coquettish angle and put her hands to her narrow waist. ''You don't remember?'' Her smile suddenly became an angry snarl and her eyes glittered. ''Well, then, my dear *husband*, allow me to refresh your memory.''

Belatedly recognizing her cheerfulness as the ruse of a towering temper, Slade watched her stomp around the bed and head for the draperies. He stretched out his arm—marked that he still had on his coat—and sucked in a huge breath. ''I swear to God, Hannah! Don't!''

Too late. She yanked the draperies open, revealing the full and bright glory of God's most magnificent creation—the yellow, golden, blazing . . . sun. Its burst of light instantly illuminated the room's remaining shadows and sent Slade, eyes closed tightly, into a sickening thump back onto his stomach. He made a noise like a dying animal and buried his face in the pillow. Around him, his mystery bedmates made similar noises.

''Oh, no you don't,'' the angry woman said. ''We need to talk, mister.''

''Idon'twannatalk,'' Slade garbled directly into the pillow.

He next felt the bedcovers being ripped back. Without moving his head, he made a grab for them, but came up with air. That was quickly followed by him and his bedmates being pummeled repeatedly with a pillow by the angrily grunting woman. "Get up! I want you wide awake when I kill you. Get up!"

Fine. He was as close to death without actually going over as he'd ever been, so why fight back? Defeated, Slade joined his companions in rolling over onto their backs. If he could just grab that pillow from her, all would be right with the world. He raised a hand in supplication. Next to him he heard a groggy groan that begged for mercy. On his other side, a lazy woof. Woof?

Slade popped up to a sitting position, his fully clothed legs and still-booted feet spread out before him. The pillow pummeling stopped. Next to him, Dudley—*Dudley!*—snapped to, his red hair spiked up at odd angles. He turned his slack-jawed head to stare at Slade.

Slade grimaced. "Geez, man, do you know what you look like? Like warmed-over sh—"

"Then we came out of the same chamber pot. What are you doing here?"

Slade thought about that. "I live here." He sought corroboration from Hannah. Frowning like a demon, she stood at the foot of the bed with the pillow raised over her head. "Don't I?"

"Oh, yes. You live here. You're going to die here, too."

Slade blinked at her and then turned to Dudley. "See? I live here. You're the one who's displaced."

"Do tell. Then I find my presence here somewhat odd." Dudley hung his red head limply forward and stared at his lap. He fingered the burned hole in the crotch of his pants. And then pointed to it. "What's this?"

"The same thing it's always been. That's your—"

"Gentlemen!" The angry woman spoke very loudly. "There's a lady present."

Slade joined Dudley in turning their painful attention back to her. Grimacing, he and his boon companion each held an arm up and out, as if collectively they could block out the sun's dazzling brightness. Slade spoke for them. "We see you, Hannah. And I'll give you a thousand dollars to quit shouting and close those draperies."

"Keep your money, Garrett. But thanks to you, it's mine now, anyway. Besides, I'm not the lady I referred to. Look to your right."

Slade exchanged a look with Dudley. Then, as if performing a carefully choreographed sequence, they obediently complied, gawked wide-eyed, and jumped off the bed as if shot out of a sling.

Dudley whipped around and pointed accusingly at the body in question. "That's a—that's a dog! Esmerelda's in our bed."

Hannah thumped the reclining dog with her pillow. The mastiff stretched mightily and raised her head. She blinked twice at Hannah and lay back down. "No, Mr. Ames, Esmerelda's in *my* bed. Ask me why."

"I can't—I feel ill." He doubled over and went in a headlong search for the wall. Reaching it first with his outstretched hand, he held on to it and slid down to a knees-drawn-up, sitting heap.

Slade made his own headlong, stumbling dash for the connecting bathroom door. "When I come out, if any of you three is in here, I'll shoot all of you."

Hannah paced in the music room. It was too late. There was nothing she could do about it. She was married to Slade Franklin Garrett. Legally. Lock, stock, and barrel. Oh, no, that was no *pretend* ceremony last night. Oh, no, it was as real as Slade's and Dudley's drunken stupor. The whole thing—it was real.

Including the real and terrified preacher who'd been fed a story of Hannah's "mental incompetence" to convince him of the need for the unusual time and place of the ceremony. Hannah snorted—apparently marrying crazy but rich heiresses to ambitious suitors was nothing new among these Brahmin. She'd even signed that real and legal document the red-eyed preacher'd presented for her signature this morning at first light, thinking it was part of the charade.

Then, seeing that Slade had already signed it, she'd asked the preacher when he'd done that. Only then had he divulged the truth, talking to her as if she were a simple-minded harridan. Well, certainly no amount of yelling and screaming from her at that point had convinced the man of her mental competence before he fled the premises, coattails flapping.

That damned Slade had even purchased her ring before the fact. Hannah looked at her finger. A real and hugely glittering diamond. If she could get the tight-fitting thing off, she'd heave it into the pond.

She glanced at the tall clock's face on her next pass around the room. Three hours. Dudley, his tail tucked between his legs, had left an hour ago. Would Slade never come down? She'd awakened the lout three hours ago. What was he doing? Hannah reached into her brown cashmere skirt's pocket and pulled out her pistol. She checked the chambers for the tenth time. It was loaded. All she needed was a target.

Where was he? Hannah stomped to the room's sliding-panel doors and yanked them open, startling the passing Serafina, cloak in hand, into standing stock-still, somewhat like a surprised deer. The thousand-year-old maid hunched her shoulders, clutched the thick garment to her pouter-pigeon chest, and squinted fearfully at Hannah. "I was being quiet, miss. Missus. I swear it."

Hannah huffed out a laden breath. "I'm not going to harm you. And tell everyone to quit tiptoeing about. Haven't they ever heard a body yell before?"

"Yes, missus. I mean—no, missus. Not for three solid hours, missus."

"For God's sake, call me Hannah. I'm not anybody's *missus*."

"Yes, Mrs. Garrett, ma'am."

Hannah eyed the maid, screamed out her rage, and wrenched the paneled doors closed again. Death was too good for him!

Turning, Hannah eyed the room, hating everything in sight. Then, she settled on her revenge. Storming across the highly polished wood floor, nearly losing her slippered footing twice, she stepped onto the thick, rose-patterned square of carpet that set off the room's centerpiece like a river's island. The grand piano.

Flinging herself down on the piano bench, Hannah banged out her frustration on the ivory keys of the delicately wrought and finely tuned instrument. She played no tune known to man. Instead, her original rendition was simply noise. It was violent-sounding. Therefore, it was good.

Just as she built to a heart-stopping crescendo of a finish, a large male hand, attached to a muscled male arm, reached around her and grabbed her raised hand. Her proposed grand finale ended up nothing more than an anticlimactic, petering-out, one-handed, sickly plinking of the keys.

In the ensuing and blessed silence, the owner of the hand and arm, close enough behind her to be touching her back with his legs, said, "I'll double my earlier offer of a thousand dollars, if you'll cease and desist torturing this fine instrument, our ears, and my grandmother's entire household staff. All of whom have wisely retreated to the summer cottage. The general feeling is I created this beast, so it's my job to tame it."

Vowing he didn't yet know the meaning of the word "beast," Hannah frowned up her mouth and narrowed her eyes at the big hand holding clawlike onto hers. She tried to wrench her hand free, but succeeded only in feeling his grip tighten. That did it. Snarling like a badger, she turned as best she could to stare up into his ... shockingly pale, sickly frowning, squint-eyed face. At least he was restored to his sartorial splendor and smelled of better things than the bottom of an ashtray, a whiskey bottle, and a brothel.

Even though surprise at his state widened her eyes momentarily, sympathy for him died an easy death in her heart. "Take your hand off me."

"Not until you give me your pistol."

"So you admit I have good reason to want to use it."

"The best. Now give it to me."

"Never."

"Hannah, I'm not in the mood for games."

"Games? I assure you I'm not playing any game."

"Then you actually intend to shoot me?"

"Yes."

Slade's face darkened into a storm cloud. "Just give me the damned peashooter so I can talk with you without dodging bullets."

"You want to talk? It's a little late for that. We're *married*."

"Right you are. Much to Isabel's tremendous delight. And Dudley's laughing sarcasm. And apparently your anger."

"Oh? My anger's only apparent? Well, what can I do to make it more obvious? Hmm, let me think." She raised her free other hand—the one bearing his wedding ring—high above the ivory keys and curved her fingers, preparatory to attacking the piano again. Positioned as it was, stray sunbeams caught her hand, splintering rainbowed light off the gem's facets, sparkling her and Slade.

"Oh, no you don't." He grabbed her by the waist and lifted her bodily off the stool.

Hannah kicked and screamed, sending the bench and its seatload of music scattering about, like so many thrown playing cards.

"Scream all you want," Slade breathed into her ear as he fought to gain control of her scratching hands. "We're—ouch, dammit—totally alone, *Mrs. Garrett.* And as you so rightly pointed out, it's too late for talking."

Hannah stilled instantly, absorbing his words—and their veiled meaning. She then renewed her efforts with vigor, kicking back at his shins, wrenching in his arms and calling him every cuss word and foul name she could remember hearing the cowboys use back home. When the raw verbiage ran together into a blue streak, she smirked malevolently. Until she realized he was hauling her over to the narrow fainting sofa that reposed against a near wall.

"Impressive, my sweet. But words will do you no good. You're—dammit, Hannah!—mine now. Under my control— if you bite me, I swear I'll bite you back!—with the full sanction of the—give me that!—law and the church on my side. I can do with you—that hurt!—as I please."

Slade abruptly turned her to face him and then flung them both down onto the sofa. Every bit of air whumphed out of Hannah's lungs when his weight landed squarely on top of her. She made shallow gasping noises, like a fish out of water, as she tried to haul air back into her lungs.

Red-faced from their brief skirmish, Slade edged his knee between hers, forced her skirt-tangled legs apart, looked into her eyes . . . and leered. "Why, Mrs. Garrett, I do believe you're under me now."

Hannah stiffened and then began to fight in earnest. For more than ten minutes she struggled uselessly underneath her equally determined husband. Finally, close to tears and wrung-out emotionally and physically, she stilled. And stared up at Slade's dark and handsome face. He grinned and oh-so-nicely asked, "Are you through, my sweet?"

That did it. "Get"—teeth gritted, the word hanging in the air, she again grappled with him, but he caught her wrists, clasped them in one hand, and held them over her head—"off me, you rotten, snake-bellied, dung-covered—"

"Son of a sway-backed mule. You've already used that one."

Breathing hard, resigned to his weight, and too tired to be angry, she nearly grinned at his drollness, even as she promised, "I've got more."

His eyebrows rose. "Really? I'd love to hear every dirty one of them—especially while I'm making you my wife."

Hannah frowned up at him. "What did you say?"

"I said I'd love to hear every dirty—"

"Not that. About making me your wife. I signed a paper three hours ago that says I am. And I have on a gold band with a diamond as big as a calf's head that says I am. So . . . aren't I already?"

"You did sign the document? Interesting." He ran his gaze over her face and settled himself more fully in between her parted legs. Eyebrows raised over glittering black eyes, he informed her, "You are already. But in name only."

Grinning like a satyr, he lay atop her, watching her intently. Hannah met his gaze, raised her Lawless chin a notch and narrowed her eyes. *In name only? What was his meaning?* Then, it came to her. Her eyes flew open wide and her mouth became a perfect O. "Never!"

He nodded fatalistically. "It will be much more frequently than never. Much more, my sweet." With that, he lowered his head at a slant and, catching Hannah by surprise, claimed her mouth.

As his firm and practiced lips moved seductively over hers, as his tongue forced her lips apart, Hannah closed her eyes and tried to resist him. She really did. For a moment. But where the spirit defied, the flesh was all too willing. After all, the man was her husband. A whimper, a mewl of defeat, sounded low in her throat. She wanted this. Wanted him. With every part of her being.

She was too honest with herself to pretend this was against her wishes. For if it were, her soft womb wouldn't already be responding to the hard pressure of him against it. Her mouth wouldn't be opening to allow his tongue inside to explore. Her arms wouldn't be going around his neck the instant he let go of her wrists. Her heart wouldn't be responding to the rapid beat of his, or her hips to the rhythmic thrust of his. She wanted him, yes. But she couldn't let him. Because if she did, she'd be lost forever.

When he broke their kiss, Hannah breathed out. "Oh, God, Slade. If you do this, I'll hate you forever."

A gleam backlit his eyes as he hungrily ran his gaze over her face and jaw and neck. "You already do, remember? You just tell me when to stop. And I'll stop, baby."

He waited, staring at her. A slow heat roiled low in her belly. Her breath caught in her throat. He'd never been more darkly handsome. His seductively lowered eyelids, the dusky redness of his face, the moistness of his full lips all inflamed Hannah's senses. Her pulse racing, she gave in. Defeated. Lost. In love. "Slade, I never—This is—I don't know how . . . to love you."

A look of great tenderness, and perhaps relief, claimed his features. His eyes also reflected his naked desire, his towering need for her. Then he nodded slowly. "I'll show you."

With that, he once again claimed her lips, reconquering virginal territory, heightening Hannah's desire to fever pitch. When she was sure she couldn't feel anything more, when she was sure the raging flood inside her would break and drown her . . . he broke off the kiss and pulled himself up and off her.

The rush of air between their bodies fluttered Hannah's eyes open. Confused, dazed, she pulled herself to a half-sitting position and looked around. *He was gone. Dear God, he was gone. Had it been a dream?* Then, the room darkened ominously. Hannah swung her legs off the sofa, jerking around.

*Slade.* He was closing the curtains. Hannah slumped back onto the sofa, flinging an arm over her eyes. For a moment, she'd thought she was losing her mind. Then she realized what she was feeling under her other hand. Exposed undergarments. Eyes widened by shock, she jerked again to a sitting position. Why, her blouse was completely undone. When had that happened?

She looked from her chest to Slade as he swaggered confidently, like the full-grown, healthy male that he was, back to her. Hannah jerked her blouse closed over her exposed camisole.

Slade seemed to know immediately what was wrong. He smiled tenderly and lowered himself to a squat in front of her.

He pulled her hands from her blouse and held them lightly in his, resting them on her thighs. Then, he reached up to brush back a wisp of hair from her face. "I won't hurt you, Hannah." His voice was low and throaty and alluring. "But we can't do this with our clothes on, sweetheart."

When he moved as if to pull himself up, Hannah grabbed at his shirt. "Slade!" He stilled, waiting for her to speak. "Will you . . . tell me what's happening when . . . it's happening, so I won't. . . ." Again she looked down at her other hand clutching his so tightly.

Slade reached out his free hand and cupped her chin, raising her head until she met his eyes. "Your eyes are so blue right now, they outdo the sky. Yes, sweetheart, I'll talk you through it. Don't be afraid." He gently ran his thumb over her jaw. "Are you ready?"

Her gaze still on him, her mouth dry, Hannah swallowed and nodded. Chuckling, he stood up with all the natural grace of a mountain lion, and held his hand out to her.

Hannah looked into his eyes and then lowered her gaze to his hand. Square-palmed. Long-fingered. In perfect symmetry with the rest of his body. It was the hand of a man of the world, a man who commanded respect. A man of power and charisma. A man of flesh and blood, and wants and needs. And right now, he wanted her.

When she took his hand, there'd be no going back. Hannah tugged at her bottom lip with her teeth. Here was her last chance. Who was she kidding? There'd never been any question. She reached out her diamond-bedecked hand, placing it— as well as her heart and her life—into his keeping.

He exhaled softly, again as if relieved, and then gently, firmly closed his fingers over hers, making her feel adored, protected, needed. Perhaps loved.

# CHAPTER ELEVEN

—

When Hannah stood, her hand in his, she allowed Slade to tug her forward as he walked backward with sure and measured steps, stopping only when they were once again on the rose-patterned carpet. Sheets of music crunched under his boots. "You're so beautiful, Hannah."

Overcome with shyness, Hannah dropped her gaze to the sight of her hand held in his against his chest. Feeling she was supposed to say something back, she said, "So are you."

Chuckling, he tipped her head up with his finger under her chin. "I am?"

She nodded, certain that the beating wings of the butterflies in her stomach were creating the heat on her cheeks. "I've always thought so."

"So have I—that *you're* beautiful, I mean. Not me."

Hannah was so grateful for his softly teasing, romantic manner that she could have wrapped her arms around his neck and kissed him fully. *Why don't you? He is your husband.* No, she couldn't. She didn't dare. *He is your husband.* Half terrified he'd laugh at her or frown in scorn, Hannah blurted out, "I want to kiss you."

A grin lit his face. "Then why don't you? I am your husband."

Shocked to hear him repeat her thoughts, Hannah's eyes widened as she freed her hand from his and backed up a step.

Slade put out his hand, but didn't touch her. "It's more than all right for you to want me, Hannah. You don't have to be ashamed of your feelings." He grinned teasingly at her. "Did your mama tell you that only bad girls like it?"

Hannah shook her head, watching his expression sober as he heard his own words, his mention of her mother. "No. Mama told me that it was beautiful between a man and a woman"—she looked down—"when they love each other." She looked up at Slade and suspected that he, like her, was thinking of his father and mother. And of her father and mother. "Mama told me never to be ashamed of my desires and to give myself fully to the man I love. She said nothing else in life matters . . . if you don't have love."

Slade eyed her quietly for a moment. "Words to live by. Sounds to me like your mother was a . . . a smart woman."

"Yes, she was." Hannah stepped up to him and flung her arms around his neck, claiming his mouth with all the hunger she held inside. Slade's arms encircled her back, his mouth responded to hers. Relieved, Hannah melted against him. He could just as easily have walked away, what with her mother's memory popping up like that. But he didn't. And that spoke volumes.

With Slade returning her ardor, Hannah thought no more of problems between them. She instead gave herself up to the sensations that were uniquely Slade. He tasted as good as he smelled, like soap and leather and warm sunshine and bay rum and cool breezes and musky male. Breathing deeply of him, Hannah tried to press herself more fully against him, wanting his delicious length from lips to toes imprinted with her desire. And with her claim on him.

When she broke her kiss and pulled back, resting her hands on his so-broad shoulders, and looked up into his eyes, she saw herself mirrored in their black depths. And knew she loved him. Now and forever. But before she could say what was in her heart, before she could decide if she would or could say the words, Slade spoke first.

"Hannah, my sweet, I want to see you as God made you."

She swallowed her words of love in a gulp. "What if you don't like how He made me?"

Laughing, Slade pulled her to him, placing a smooching kiss on her forehead. "I'll love how He made you. I swear it."

"You will?" Her words were as breathless as her emotions. She then looked around them. "Are we—are we going to . . . do it here?"

He nodded lazily, moving his hands to her hair and loosening the combs. "A bed in a darkened room is but one place for making love." As her long curls fell, he lay her hairpins and ornaments on the piano and then ran his fingers through the dark tresses.

They were making love. Hannah watched Slade enjoying her hair. Her scalp tingled with the warm pressure of his touch. *Making* love. She liked that—the notion that two people could meet and make a love that hadn't existed before. Did he mean all that when he said it? Hannah ran her gaze over his handsome face. His features seemed to be lit with a wondrous something deep inside him. Was it love?

She suspended thought when Slade stepped back and ran his gaze over her, as if assessing how she looked with her hair down. Speaking in a soft, husky drawl, and touching her nowhere, his voice alone inflamed her senses. "The first time I saw you—at the depot—I couldn't take my eyes off you. You looked so afraid, so innocent. Right then I wanted to take you in my arms and love you."

Thrilling to his impressions of her, Hannah mutely watched the play of emotions over his face as he told her more about herself. But even more about himself . . . if he only knew it.

"You're so elegant, Hannah. Your face, the way you walk, the way you sit. Even your smile. You're like that harp over there, all slender lines and graceful form. A pleasure simply to stand back and behold. And yet"—his expression changed to quizzical—"you draw me to you. How do you do that?"

"I don't. . . ." The words dried up as she shook her head and kept her eyes on his mouth.

A soft chuckle greeted her befuddlement. "It doesn't matter. But looking at you will never be enough for me. I have to touch you. Like playing that harp, I want my body wrapped around yours, I want you to be one with me. I want to coax from you a harmony that only you and I in all the world can create."

Breathing shallowly now, Hannah knew she was undone. Her hair, her blouse, her desire. With a seeming will of their own, her eyes closed and her mouth opened slightly. His feather-soft touch, so unexpected, on her arms, her face, her neck, nearly sent Hannah to the floor. He continued to caress her with his whispers of her beauty and to remove her clothing, even helping her out of her thin slippers.

Not once, not until the only thing covering her nakedness was her chemise, did he touch her with anything but his trailing fingers. Until finally, through the thin fabric, she felt a hot moistness close over her nipple. A jolt of needle-sharp desire jerked her body. She opened her eyes to see Slade down on one knee in front of her. He released her nipple to lay his head between her breasts and to wrap his arms around her hips. "You are exquisite, my love."

Hannah's knees crumpled. Slade shifted his weight, drawing her down to him, down amongst the ivory sheets of scattered music. He brushed some away, but a few sheets remained, like petals from a huge flower. Hannah watched Slade drink his fill of her as he tugged his shirttail out of his pants. She pulled herself up on an elbow and reached out a hand, stopping his movements. "Let me. You said we'd undress each other."

Slade smiled down at her and let go of his shirt. "You're right. But hurry."

Frowning, cutting her gaze to the closed panel doors, Hannah quickly sat up and began trying to wrench his shirt over his head.

Slade laughed and stopped her hands. "No one will come in. I just meant you—" The first look of uncertainty she'd ever seen on his face clouded across his brow and at the edges of his mouth. "Well, here—to put a fine point on it—I'll show you." With no further ado, he took her hand and placed it against the hard length encased in his breeches.

In a blazing agony of maidenly embarrassment, Hannah froze, her eyes widening. She stared at his hand holding her hand over . . . him. Wetting her lips with the tip of her tongue, she looked up to his face. Slade smiled and slowly raised her hand to his mouth. He kissed her fingers, her palm, the inside of her wrist. Delicate little tendrils of desire danced up her arm. "I'll hurry," she breathed.

Slade raised his head, letting her tug her hand out of his. "Good."

Hannah hurried. Slade helped her. In a flash, his white ruffle-fronted shirt was unlaced halfway down his chest. Hannah caught her breath when he crossed his arms at his waist and drew the shirt over his head. The finely toned, powerful muscles rippling over his large-boned frame, the crisp black hair on his chest, his tautly stretched skin, his dark brown, flat nipples. She was right—he was beautiful, only she hadn't known until now just how beautiful.

When he threw the shirt aside and sat on the carpet to tug his boots off, Hannah grabbed for the toe and heel and pulled with all her might. The boot came off more readily than she expected, setting her hard on her bottom and promptly onto her back. Lying there, clutching Slade's boot to her chest, she laughed with him when he crawled up to her and drew her to a sitting position.

"I appreciate your enthusiasm, but I'll get the other one." And he did. With blinding speed. So, bootless, sockless, and shirtless now, he stood. Staring down at Hannah, holding her gaze, he began unfastening his pants.

Hannah dropped her gaze from his smoldering black eyes to his busy hands and . . . hard length. Wonder filled her that she could produce this . . . grand effect on him. Slade's hands stilled at the last button. Hannah snapped her gaze up at his face. He smiled, kept his pants on, and lowered himself to sit facing her, his legs stretched out alongside her. "Sweet Hannah."

He reached out to cup her nape in his hand and draw her to him for a kiss. With practiced motions and soft caresses, Slade inflamed her desire again. Hannah heard soft moans, knew they were hers, suddenly realized she was lying full-out on the carpet, and Slade's muscled warmness was beside her and yet hovering over her. He put an arm under her head, cascading her hair over it and the carpet, and then cradled her to him.

Leaning into her, covering her legs with his muscled thigh, he edged her even nearer with his calf and foot. His other hand found her breast, cupped it, swirled the tender nipple, and then went exploring down her quivering belly. With each new sensation, Hannah gasped, making low guttural sounds she'd never made before. Slade moved his leg off her so he could trail his hand down her thigh to gather up her chemise's hem and draw it up, up ahead of his smoothing hand, over her thighs and belly. Only there did he stop.

At the same time he claimed her mouth, his hand urged her thighs apart and then claimed her womanhood. Hannah jerked, breathing in equal doses of shock and shooting stars when his fingers found her bud and stroked it softly. The heel of his hand gently kneaded her woman's mound, until a moment later when his fingers splayed the folds of her innermost self. Hannah stiffened, dragged her mouth from his, turned her head. ''No. I can't.''

Slade kissed her jaw, nipped at her earlobe, moved his hand up onto her belly. ''You're just scared. I won't do anything until you tell me to. But don't tell me with words. Tell me with your body.''

Hannah opened her eyes, blinked, looked up at him. Saw his gentle smile. And saw the desire-inflamed edge to that smile. She wanted him so desperately. ''But how will I know?''

His wide, white grin turned into a chuckle as he tilted his head back and shook it. ''Ahh, virgins.'' With a lock of black hair falling across his forehead, he looked back down at her. ''You'll know by touching me.''

Hannah narrowed her eyes and looked askance at him.

Slade laughed again. ''You believe nothing I tell you, do you? Here, give me your hand. No, not there again—I promise. See? Now, with your hand on my heart, I swear to you that you will know . . . by touching me.'' He then pressed her palm to his heart and held it there.

Smitten now with the warm, hard-yet-yielding feel of him, Hannah raised her wondering eyes to his face. ''I can feel your heart beating.'' Impulsively she laid her ear to his chest and listened. As she did, its pace quickened. She pulled back and looked into his eyes.

The devil grinned like one. ''I told you so.'' Then with maudlin emotion, he clutched at her hand, gushing, ''My heart beats for you, Hannah. Only you. For all of eternity.''

Giggling, Hannah wrenched her hand out from under his and smacked at his powerful chest. ''Now, you're making fun of me.''

''I'm mortally wounded.'' He pantomimed being shot in the heart and fell over backward, lying still, eyes closed, head lolling, arms and legs flung out.

Screeching in humor, Hannah scrambled up and flopped on top of him, whooshing more than a little air out of him. He jerked his head and knees up reflexively, catching Hannah in the middle of him. With one deft roll, he was again lying on top of her, supported by his elbows, and grinning down at her. "That backfired, didn't it, miss?"

Still playing, Hannah bucked her hips against his. And knew instantly the teasing game was over. She sobered right along with him and felt her expression changing, warming . . . right along with his. With tentative motions, knowing he watched her, she reached up, smoothing her hands over his powerful arms, up across his shoulders, down around his chest, and then under and around to his back. Her fingers curled into loving claws and scratched lightly over his skin.

Slade's muscles quivered under her touch. And no small degree of holding back. Hannah knew that. Even in her inexperience, she knew that. When he lowered his head, resting his forehead against her shoulder, Hannah lifted her hips again, grinding them in a slow circle. Slade raised his head, breathing shallowly, raggedly. He sucked in a breath through his flared nostrils and stared down at her, a question in his passion-glittered eyes.

Suddenly, Hannah knew the terrible responsibility of being a woman. She'd brought this powerful and feared man, this handsome and virile male to the brink. And she'd done it with no more than a look, a touch, a kiss. She held his heart, everything he was or ever could be, in her hands. She could uplift him. Or she could destroy him. And by marrying her, he'd given her that power. Only her. In all the world.

Blinking back sudden tears, her chin trembling for all that she felt, for all that she now owned, Hannah moved her hand from his back and slipped it around to cup his cheek. Her voice no more than a whisper, she confessed, "I love you, Slade. I give myself to you."

Slade stared at her for an eternal second and then, as if he'd lost control, grabbed her to him and held her so tightly she feared she'd break. No longer so carefully tender, his hands moved over her in a fevered state of smoothing and kneading. He left no inch of her untouched. Hannah's heart beat faster, passion intermingling with a little fear. What had she unleashed? But it was a fleeting thought as Slade swept her along on their time-hazed, sensual journey.

Hannah slowly became aware that she was out of her chemise and that her bare skin was touching Slade's bare skin. All of it. When—? She hadn't felt or . . . seen a thing. But it

didn't matter. Because Slade was now ensconced in the saddle
of her hips and pushing gently against her maidenhead while
he stoked her passion with kiss after kiss. He reared back
enough to rake his hand down her belly and stroke her bud to
the point of madness.

Hannah tossed her head from side to side, overcome,
breached, wanting . . . something. She couldn't name it,
couldn't convey it. She pulled passionately, impatiently at his
shoulders, wanting him to . . . do something.

And Slade did. He slipped down her length until he could
capture her nipple. Hannah cried out, arching her back. Thus
encouraged, Slade gripped her about her waist and suckled the
bud to an aroused peak. Grimacing, gasping, Hannah clutched
handfuls of his hair and called out his name.

Slade answered her in gruff syllables, speaking in a loving
language of rough words. He kissed and mouthed his way over
to her other breast, giving it the same attention. Hannah's legs
jerked in response. She could barely stand the swirling, rippling spasms in her womb. She wanted them to stop. And to
go on forever. "Slade, please!"

The cry rang out in the room's silence. Slade immediately
pulled himself up and over her again, holding his weight off
her with his elbows. Capturing her tossing head in his hands,
he forced her to look at him. "This will hurt, Hannah. Not
because I want it to, but because it's your first time. It will
only hurt a moment. And then it will never hurt again."

Why was the man talking? She didn't want words. She
wanted *him*. Then, suddenly she knew—she wanted him *inside*
her. "Please," she begged again, completely worn out with
desire.

Slade kissed her gently, briefly. "All right, my love." And
then lowered himself onto her. He helped her get her legs
positioned right, wrapping them around his hips. He then began edging into her. Hannah stilled for a moment, staring
wide-eyed at Slade. He kissed the tip of her nose and pushed
in a little farther. Hannah instinctively thrust into his push,
surprised at the wonderful feel of him slipping smoothly along
her slickness.

"Easy. Let me this time, okay?"

Hannah nodded, feeling his muscles tense and gather, readying. Slade claimed her mouth in a dizzying kiss. Hannah

forgot about what was going on at her hips . . . until Slade thrust fully into her. A searing tear stilled her, stopped her breathing. Slade stilled, too, whispering into her ear, "I'll wait for you, Hannah. Tell me when you're ready. Tell me with your body."

Gooseflesh raced over her naked skin. His voice was the most sensual thing about him. He lay ensheathed, arching over her, kissing her cheek, her jaw, her forehead. He smoothed her hair out of her face. And waited. Hannah loved him all the more for his care of her. She concentrated on the pulsing hardness inside her and shifted the slightest bit under him. Slade's breath caught, exhaled on a ragged cry. Hannah frowned in curiosity . . . and did it again.

Slade jerked, clutching at her. "You're killing me, Hannah."

Hannah grinned. This . . . loving between them was what she wanted. All along, *this* was what she wanted. Happy tears welled and then spilled down her face. She grabbed Slade around his muscled neck and locked her ankles around his hips. And thrust her hips up and into him. It didn't hurt. It didn't hurt at all.

And that was all the notice Slade needed. He gently rocked her with him until they found their pace, until they put their own rhythm to their sensual dance.

If Hannah thought this act would relieve the coiled tension in her belly that his lips and hands had wrought, then she now knew she was mistaken. His thrusting into her only wound the band tighter, only rubbed her bud to an agonizingly tender, stingingly hot pitch.

The harder Slade drove into her, the harder she wanted him to. The more fevered his thrusts, the more she scratched at his back, clutched at his shoulders and arms and called out his name. Suddenly, she could take no more. She'd beg him to quit—

The dam exploded. The pent-up, sizzling heat rushed in rippling waves out from her core to freeze her in place, to lock her muscles as she desperately held on to him. Her toes curled, the back of her mouth felt dry, her head and back arched up off the carpet, and she breathed in gasping cries.

When she feared she would faint from the pleasure, Slade tensed over her, held himself rigid as he thrust to the hilt into her. The muscles in his neck corded. His eyelids fluttered as he grimaced and then cried out. Her name. He cried out her name. And remained poised over her. Then, he collapsed on top of her.

Slick with loving sweat, breathing in gasps, weak of limb, Hannah lay spread-eagled under him, completely satiated. She stared up at the vaulted ceiling, blinked, focused . . . and frowned. She hadn't noticed before now that there was a fresco of heavenly cherubs up there. Well, neither had she lain on her back in this room before.

Slade brought her attention back to the floor when he lifted himself and rolled off her. With the rush of cool air over her nakedness came the awkwardness. What did she do now? Dress? Lie there like a hussy?

Slade answered her by pulling her to him. He lay on his side, raised up on his elbow. She lay next to him on her back, her knees bent. He then surprised her by reaching around him to produce his shirt and hand it to her. "Here. You'll need to clean yourself up."

Hannah took the shirt, looking in confusion at him.

"There's blood the first time, Hannah. There's some on the carpet there, too. We'll have to get that up next."

Hannah jerked on her side, putting her back to him. There, on the ivory-colored fibers, was a bloodstain. Why couldn't it have been on one of the rose petals in the pattern? Mortified, she bit at her lip and tugged his shirt down between her legs and wiped away more evidence. It was awful being a woman.

Slade moved behind her, kissing her arm and pulling her over on her back. He caressed her belly, and then very casually took his shirt from her and tossed it away from them. He smiled tenderly down at her. "Are you all right?"

Belatedly self-conscious, Hannah covered her breasts with her hands, crossed her legs, and focused on her dangling foot. "I was until you asked me that." Then, wagging her chin up a notch, she looked up at him. "Are you?"

Slade gawked wide-eyed at her and then flipped over on his back, laughing heartily, lying nakedly glorious and spread-eagled, half under the piano. "Hell, I've never been better. But then, I'm not the one who just lost my virginity."

Hannah, still on her back, uncrossed her legs so she could

kick at his leg with her bare toes. "You're a smug devil now, aren't you?"

Slade rolled back to her and playfully smacked her thigh. "Come on. We need to get dressed. Isabel and the rest will be frozen to death out in the cabin by now." He gripped the piano's edge and pulled himself up, already looking around him for his clothes.

But Hannah lay there, stunned, her mouth open. She grabbed at his ankle, capturing his attention. He raised his eyebrows in question. Hannah blinked two or three times, having now her first bald view, and a snail's-eye view it was, of his . . . maleness. Forcing her attention back to his now clearly amused expression, she ignored the suffusing heat on her cheeks and used her embarrassment to fuel her disbelief. "The cabin, Slade? *The cabin?* That little one out back? You mean to tell me that Isabel and Pemberton and Sera—"

He cut her off. "Serafina and Rowena and all the other chambermaids and Mrs. Edgars and her kitchen help are out in the cabin. I told you, you scared them. They fled the house, refusing to come back inside until I calmed you down."

Hannah jerked to a sitting position, bracing her hands behind her on the carpet. "But I thought you were just . . . just exaggerating! Oh, the poor dears! They'll catch their deaths." She rounded on Slade, smacking his calf—hard. "How could you?"

"How could *I*? I'm not the one who—"

"Don't say it! And help me up." Hannah raised her hand to him. The diamond flashed in the late afternoon light.

They both stared at it for a moment, as if the reality and the finality of their act was just then coming home to roost. Hannah's gaze met Slade's at the exact moment he looked at her. An unspoken truth passed between them—what was done, was done. Their lives were now inextricably entwined. From here on out, they'd have to find their way together.

As if confirming that, Slade took her hand and effortlessly pulled her to her feet. "I'll scrub out the stain with my shirt and go get a clean one. You get dressed. Just leave your hair down—I like it better that way, anyway. And put on only what you need—forget that bustle and corset. You don't need them."

Hannah nodded, silently storing away his compliments and noting how he liked to see her. Going in search of her chemise, she turned away from him, but took only two steps before he burst out laughing. She jerked back around in time to see him sit down abruptly on the piano's ivory keys, his buttocks striking very discordant notes. One arm was wrapped around his lean and muscular middle, but his other hand was pointed directly at her.

All of Hannah's insecurities burst to the fore. Had what happened here between them been one big joke on her? Or did he find her God-given body funny after all? More than a little hurt, Hannah froze. "What is so funny?"

He wagged his pointing hand at her, laughing and crying out, "Come here, my sweet."

"I will not." Hannah raised her Lawless chin and drew her hair around her, over her nakedness.

Slade tried to sober up, but he took another look at her, and wilted into a belly laugh again.

That did it. Decorum be damned. Hannah stalked over to him and shook a finger threateningly at him. "If you don't tell me *this instant*—"

Slade jerked her around and ripped something from off her buttocks. Hannah squealed out at the stinging bite, put a hand to the offended area, and twisted in his grip. "What is that?"

Slade relaxed his jaw and stretched his face muscles, trying to focus around his happy tears. "Let's see. Why, it's a piece of sheet music." Grinning like a Cheshire cat, he handed it to her. "Look at our song."

Half afraid to, Hannah nevertheless snatched the paper from him and looked at the title. And wanted to die when she read "Nobody Knows the Trouble I've Seen."

Samuel Rigby ducked into the narrow alley next to the West End tenement. The young driver-turned-spy stepped gingerly over the noxious debris in his way. Kicking aside a broken chair, he took up his place against the wall and out of the sunlight. He then reached into his coat pocket and pulled out a pad of paper and a bit of pencil. Leaning toward the daylight, he turned to a clean page, flipping past his notes from the past four days of following Olivia.

Around the corner, a door closed with a bang. Rigby's head

came up. Sounded like the first floor—where Olivia's mother's apartment was. If the two rooms could be called an apartment. Pocketing his notepad and pencil, he sidled up to the front corner of the weathered-wood building. He peeked around the corner and jerked back, flattening himself against the wall. Olivia was walking down the two sagging steps of the landing. In her arms was her blanket-wrapped baby.

She was coming this way. Rigby stepped back farther into the shadows, accidentally kicking a stray cat. The tabby jumped straight up, shrieking in outrage. Rigby heard Olivia gasp. He mouthed a curse as the mangy creature flew like an arrow out of the alley and across the buckled walkway right in front of Olivia. Rigby held his breath. If she looked in the alley, all would be lost.

"Stupid cat!" Olivia called after it. Then her voice lowered, became soothing when the baby coughed hoarsely and fussed. "Shh now, Colette. Mama's right here. It was just a cat. No need to fret. There's my big girl."

Rigby heard her words accompanying her feet right past where he hid. He slumped in relief. But in a way, he wished she had seen him, because he'd like to confront her and maybe convince her to let him help her. He missed her chattering and smiles and airy ways about the old place. But he'd no sooner thought it than he frowned and shook his head. When would he ever learn? She was a lady's maid. Much too good for the likes of him.

Sighing, he pulled out his notes again as he peeked around the building's corner, checked to be sure she'd walked on, and then stepped into the daylight. Flipping through the pad, he found the blank page and made his new entry. He then looked up to Olivia's retreating back. If she turned right at that next corner, then she was taking the little one to the doctor's office in the next block.

Then, that meant that her old mother was alone. Rigby'd been dogging Olivia long enough to determine that, mother though she was, she was wife to no one. And apparently her father was dead or just gone, either way leaving her and her mother alone. A shudder seized him when he thought about the crippled old woman alone with the baby on the days when Olivia worked.

Rigby scratched thoughtfully at his neck, wondering what

Mr. Garrett would say if he knew about Olivia being mother to the little babe, her not being married and all. You couldn't tell with these Brahmin—who may boot you out for daring to have a care outside of their whims. No, Mr. Garrett wasn't that sort. Hadn't he allowed her to come with no threat to her position? True. But too, Himself'd charged him with following Olivia to see if the reason she asked off so suddenly was because she had suspicious doings with her former employer. Rigby now knew nothing could be further from the truth.

He watched Olivia turn right at the next corner. Ah, the doctor's. He wrote that in his pad and then pocketed it. Having added protector to his assigned role as spy, Rigby made up his mind. He'd speak right now with Himself regarding Olivia's troubles. Mr. Garrett was a fair man. And the new missus seemed to care about Olivia. Hadn't she as much as spirited the maid away with her when she left Cloister Point?

That settled it. He was right to speak up. The sweet girl needed help. And he would get it for her. Maybe then she'd look kindly on him. A smile wreathed Rigby's Irish good looks as he sprinted across the narrow street. For two blocks, he dodged carriages and pedestrians to where he'd hitched his horse. Then, his feet slowed. Damn the lad! The roan and the street urchin to whom he'd given a coin to look after it were nowhere in sight.

Turning right at the corner, stepping around the other people crowding the walkway with her, Olivia walked briskly, frowning in worry as she tuned her mother's ear to Colette's coughing. Rattling carriages and yelling children made it hard to hear, but she believed Colette sounded better.

Olivia reassured herself by recalling the cheerful Dr. Rowe. Such a good man to hold a free clinic two afternoons a week here in the West End. He'd reassured her that Colette had a common chest congestion of the sort to afflict babies at this time of year. But still, Olivia couldn't help but be scared. Mum and Colette were all she had. And Mum was on her last leg.

Olivia bit at her lip, trying not to worry. One thing at a time. With her new wages—she sent up a prayer for Mr. Garrett and his generosity—she ought to be able to move Mum and Colette into something a little more respectable. But to get her wages, she'd have to go back to Woodbridge Pond.

Which meant leaving Mum with a nine-month-old to care for, and her with her crippled-up legs.

Almost beset with tears, Olivia forced a cheerfulness on herself as she shifted her daughter's weight in her arms and bounced her playfully. "There, now, sweetling. Perhaps we can give Dr. Rowe a good report this afternoon." She hugged the brown-eyed, chubby child to her breast. "We'll get through this, Colette. I swear we will."

Just then, someone bumped her from behind. She clutched reflexively at Colette as she stumbled forward a step. Regaining her footing, Olivia spun around, already sounding her protest. "Here now, watch yourself. Can't you see I have—?"

The words died in her throat as a jet of fear lanced through her and held her immobile. Jostling people brushed by, cursing her for being in the way. But she had wide, unblinking eyes only for the hated man she faced.

"Were you going to say . . . you have a baby? But then, I already knew that, didn't I?" He reached out to stroke the babe's cheek. "And a lovely girl she is. May I hold her? I promise to give her right back."

Mutely, Olivia shook her head and backed up a step. She'd die before she'd hand Colette over to Mr. Wilton-Humes.

# CHAPTER TWELVE

———

*The Garretts must chew locoweed*, was Hannah's exasperated thought. She laid her soup spoon down, dabbed at her lips with her linen napkin, and turned to her left. "Isabel, we never should have told you my real reason for being here. My kin are my problem. Not yours. I won't allow you to put yourself at risk. There can be no party. It's insane."

Isabel waved her hand in the air. "Oh, pooh. I can take care of myself. You two cheated me out of the wedding I was planning. And then the way you carried on in the music room this afternoon, I may already have a great-grandchild on the way. Right, Esmerelda?"

Hearing her name, the mastiff cocked her ears up and scooted closer to Isabel for a head-rubbing. For Hannah's part, a burst of heat flared over her cheeks as she stared in numbed shock at her grandmother-in-law.

Isabel mumbled to her pet, "That piano never will be the same." She looked beyond Hannah. "Will it, Rowena?"

Hannah whipped around in her chair. There stood the ancient maid at the sideboard, her back to the table as she lifted a lid on a silver tureen. She didn't turn around, but she did shake her head in agreement. Or maybe it was just her palsy. Hannah jerked back around and shot her so-far-silent husband The Look.

Slade picked up his cue. "Isabel, you're shocking Hannah. She's not yet been a wife for an entire day, so she doesn't need the added worry of being a mother."

Flames of embarrassment licked at Hannah's cheeks. She was hardly used to the idea that she had a . . . love life, and much less ready to hear it discussed publicly. She made a show of smoothing her napkin across her lap before she spoke up. "Slade, I may never have the chance to be a . . . a mother if you allow Isabel to persist in her dash to get us all killed."

He leaned forward over the table. "If I *allow* her? My sweet, the entire Garrett family will erect a huge sculpture in your honor if *you* can stop her where we have all failed." He made a sweeping gesture toward Isabel. "Have at it."

Hannah frowned as she turned her gaze from her husband to her grandmother-in-law. *Why was everyone so afraid of Isabel? She was just one tiny little woman.* Isabel grinned satanically at her. *Wasn't she?* Somewhat daunted, Hannah nevertheless chided the elder Mrs. Garrett for her breach in front of a servant. "Isabel, where is your sense of decorum? That you would say such a bold thing about our private married life in front of . . . in front of—"

"Who—Rowena? Oh, pooh. She changed Slade's nappies. It's not like I placed an announcement of your musical consummation in the *Advertiser.* However, an announcement of your elopement will appear in tomorrow's editions of all the newspapers. Prepare to be swamped with callers and gifts." She then turned to her grandson. "I believe she'll out-Brahmin *us* with all that twaddle about decorum, don't you?"

Piqued at being brushed off, Hannah turned to Slade, but that one nodded at his grandmother and then winked at his wife. Hannah raised her chin and showed him a cool façade. When that elicited a chuckle from him, she was pleased to turn back to Isabel when that outrageous lady next spoke.

"Enough about your lovemaking. You two didn't invent it, and you're not the only ones engaging in it. What's more important, young lady, is you're daft if you think I'll sit around here like some silly old helpless ninny and allow a Garrett—any Garrett!—to be threatened by the likes of Cyrus and Patience."

Hannah pushed her shallow soup bowl away from her and leaned an elbow on the table. "No one thinks you're a silly old helpless ninny. Least of all me. And you should know that, Isabel. Especially after our talk about our families in the garden—"

Across from her, a hand smacked down on the tabletop. "What talk?"

Hannah's gasp echoed Isabel's. They stared at each other and then both turned to Slade. Protecting the secrets Isabel'd shared, Hannah lied. "It was nothing. Just a walk through the gardens."

"I heard that. I asked you, what talk?"

God love Rowena. The antique maid chose that moment to shuffle over from tending the sideboard and reach around Hannah toward her soup bowl. "That I did, Miss Hannah—change his nappies. Slade was quite the big baby. Nearly tore his mother in two, he did, when she brought him into the world."

Leaving Hannah openmouthed with that terrifying image, she picked up the flower-patterned dish, narrowly missing the hem of Hannah's green satin skirt when her slight tremor upset the bowl's contents.

Isabel chuckled, further sidetracking her grandson. "Look at her face, Slade Franklin. Young girls think they can't get with child their first time with a man. But they can. I did." With that, she smiled gleefully and began feeding hunks of bread to the patiently slobbering Esmerelda.

"Enough, Isabel. You and Rowena are terrifying Hannah."

Hannah glanced across the table at her new husband. He was quick to take her side. A bud of tenderness opened in her heart, but quickly wilted as she absorbed his posture. He slouched in his chair with an elbow propped on the armrest, his thumb and index fingers supporting his jaw and chin. He stared unblinking at her, and then made as if to speak.

Fearful of his topic, Hannah desperately turned to Isabel. "Isabel, dear, we haven't resolved anything. I still say you cannot hold a dinner ball for the sole purpose of drawing out Cyrus and Patience. What makes you think they'd even show up?"

Isabel tore off another hunk of her dinner roll and fed it to the eager-eyed mastiff. "They'd come, all right. You heard Mrs. Ames say—before Esmerelda gave her the dead rat and made her faint—that Cyrus and Patience aren't being received. That's worse than death to them. So, if we have a little party and invite them, it'll seem as if we forgive them, won't it?"

Hannah was forced to nod in agreement, but jumped when Slade snorted in amusement. "She's got you there. Didn't Pemberton warn you on your first night here about her plottings?"

Isabel chunked a wad of bread at Slade. "I'm not plotting. I'm merely trying to bring this situation to a head. I want nothing whatsoever to do with those people. So the sooner this convoluted mess of Ardis's will is over and done, the sooner we'll be rid of all the despicable Wilton-Humeses." Isabel stopped, apparently hearing her own words. Unrepentant, she looked directly at Hannah. "You'll be glad to know I don't consider you one of their ilk."

Hannah grinned, her respect for Isabel's legendary toughness rising by the moment. "Thank you. Neither do I. But I am a Lawless through and through. I hope that's not a problem for you."

Isabel's face sharpened with a sly look tinged with humor. "Too late if it is, eh, *Mrs. Garrett*? No matter. We'll just temper all that outlaw blood with some good Garrett stock. But don't be so quick to deny your McAllister blood. You get some of that backbone and sass of yours from your great-grandmother Ardis. She and your mother were the best of the lot, I'll warrant. Wouldn't give you a cat's behind for the rest of them."

Slade captured Hannah's and Isabel's attention when he applauded. "Bravo, Isabel. Wonderful recovery."

"Show some respect, young man," Isabel huffed as she shifted toward Hannah. "Now, say Patience and Cyrus are here. What's your plan?"

Hannah didn't even hesitate. "It's simple. I plan on shooting them. But other developments tie my hands right now." Thinking of the men tracking her sisters, Hannah sought Slade's eyes. He shook his head no. Hannah took his meaning, not to speak of it with Isabel, and turned back to her. "It's just that it's too soon to confront Cyrus and Patience. We have no proof yet. And I certainly don't want another scene like the one I caused at Cloister Point."

Isabel laughed gleefully. "I heard all about that one, missy. I knew right then what kind of a girl you were. Damned proud of you, I am."

Hannah narrowed her eyes in mock-slyness. "I see your game, Isabel, and it won't work. Pretty words to me won't change my mind about being a party to . . . your party."

Isabel shrugged. "I'm not trying to change your mind. You're trying to change mine, remember?" She then shoved

at Esmerelda, who stood with her massive paws on the arm
of her chair. "Get down. Next thing you know, you'll want
your own chair at the table. I swear, I don't know who spoils
you so."

Esmerelda got down, but she wasn't happy. She tucked her
haunches under her as she sat and stared accusingly at Hannah.

Ignoring the beast, and thinking of her sisters' well-being
over her own, Hannah issued her ultimatum. "You've forced
me into a corner, Isabel. If you won't stop with your fancy
ball, then I'll move out. And I won't come to the party."

"The hell you say!"

Like Isabel and Esmerelda and Rowena, Hannah jumped at
the harsh words directed at her from across the table. A hand
to her throat, she turned to Slade. His black eyes glittered.
"You'll go no farther away from me than I can smell you."

Hannah swallowed, again feeling the heat on her cheeks.
He hadn't moved at all, but she felt he was at her throat. She
didn't like that feeling. "Don't think that your ring on my
finger makes me your property. If I choose to leave this room,
this house, or this town—I *will* go."

"Just where do you think you'll go?" His voice was low
and threatening.

Hannah could take only shallow breaths against the tight-
ness in her chest. Still, she raised her chin and glared back at
him. "Your brownstone. You offered it to me not so long ago.
So, now I'll take it. There. I've said it. If plans for this or any
confrontation go forward—before *I'm* ready for it, I'll leave
Woodbridge Pond."

Slade's eyelids drooped dangerously low. He leaned over
the table, like a panther in a crouch. "How far do you think
you'll get being tied to my bed?"

Up to those last words of his, Hannah'd only been half-
serious about leaving. No more. In the deadly quiet that followed his threat, she felt her Lawless blood boiling. "You
wouldn't dare."

Slade dipped his head, catching light and shadow in the
planes and hollows of his face, intensifying his pantherlike
pose. "Try me."

Isabel shoved back in her chair and flittered from one to the
other of them, patting a shoulder here, a hand there, and cau-
tioning, "Now, let's not quarrel so. Forget the stupid party.

What do I know? I'm just a silly old woman.''

But Hannah ignored her in equal measures with Slade as they shot daggers at each other. The first one to speak or look away . . . lost. Papa'd taught his girls that—and he should know. J. C. Lawless'd survived more than a hundred battles of guns and wills. Even as fear pounded at Hannah's heart, her stubborn Lawless streak demanded she rise to his dare. And she would, if only she could first remember how to rise from her chair.

An image of Jacey and her bravado came to Hannah's aid. She placed her napkin beside her plate. Slade did likewise. *No man threatened a Lawless, be he husband or not.* She wasn't unequal to his black-eyed glare, and she *would* leave this room. Hannah put her palms flat on the table and began pulling herself to a stand. So did Slade. They could've been two gun-slingers at high noon on a dusty Western street as they stood straight and tall, never looking away from each other.

Except momentarily when the door from the kitchen opened. A tremendous rattling of dishes heralded the entrance of the ever-shuffling Pemberton, followed by the quick-stepping Serafina, who balanced in her hands and against her paunchy little stomach a silver tray laden with covered plates. ''Make way!'' she bellowed irritably to the ancient butler.

He did. She made for the table, crashing her load down with a sigh. Apparently oblivious to the tension in the room, she went smiling and humming about her job, placing a steaming dish at each setting. And placing herself in great danger between the two combatants, who again glared at each other.

Exhibiting a death wish of his own, Pemberton came to stand by Serafina, overseeing her efforts. Equally oblivious to the sight of Hannah and Slade standing, and to the sight of Rowena and Isabel Garrett backed up against a wall, each gripping the cowering Esmerelda's collar, the butler waited.

When Serafina stepped back, happy with her efforts, he then placed himself in the line of fire at the table's head. Staring dramatically at the far wall, he announced, ''The main course . . . is now being served.''

No one moved. No one spoke. Hannah's peripheral vision noted that Pemberton cut his gaze from her to Slade and back to her. ''Oh, I say.'' And then he stepped back one giant step before repeating, ''The main course . . . is now being served.''

After a second's hesitation, he stepped back again and added, "To the survivors, at any rate." No one moved. No one spoke. He took another step back. "Providing there are any."

The silence glared on for another moment before Isabel came crashing back to the table, noisily drawing her chair out and sitting down. "Oh, for heaven's sake, I'm hungry. You two can kill each other on a full stomach as well as you can an empty one. Now, this is my house, and I say sit down and eat."

Esmerelda padded up to the table. She seconded her mistress's sentiments by barking loud enough to startle angels in heaven. And to rouse Hannah and Slade. By mutual and tacit agreement, the newlyweds blinked and sat down as well.

Shaking with angry emotion, Hannah quietly ate her meal, keeping her head down and her gaze on her plate. She had no idea if Slade ate or didn't eat. She had no idea if he stared at her or kept his head down, too. And furthermore, she didn't care. Nor did she have any idea what she ate as she went through the motions from habit.

It wasn't until she stabbed her last bite of—she focused on what dangled from her fork—roast beef that she became aware of the conversation going on around her. She looked up, staring in disbelief. Isabel was detailing the fabulous menu she wanted served at her dinner ball.

"You miss Olivia's help, don't you?" Slade spoke softly, but immediately his voice changed, became testy. "Dammit, Hannah, I don't know why you bother with this infernal contraption."

In only her unmentionables, hands to her waist, her back to her husband as he unlaced her corset, Hannah ignored his outburst. And the gooseflesh bumping her skin as his warm touch traveled down her back. "I miss *her* more than her help. She's been gone four days. Are you sure she didn't say where she was going?"

His hands stilled as he finished. "Yes, I'm sure. But I'll look into it tomorrow, if it'll make you feel better." He slipped the long laces free of the garment and pulled its hard ribs aside. A gasp preceded his outburst. "Look at your back. It's all red and gouged by this damned thing. How do you breathe, much less eat?''

Without warning, he grabbed a side of the corset and whirled her in a complete circle as he divested her of the object of his anger. He turned with it in hand and stalked over to the hallway door of his room.

Her arms crisscrossed over her breasts, Hannah's mouth opened in proportion with her eyes. ''What are you doing? Come back here with that, Slade Franklin Garrett.''

''Don't you call me that. Makes you sound like Isabel. And that's not an image I want in my bedroom.'' He commenced muttering to himself. ''Never should have bought the damned thing to begin with. But that magpie of a dressmaker was so scandalized that I wasn't buying one . . .'' His mumblings carried him to the door, which he opened long enough to toss the corset out onto the hallway floor.

Hannah's hand covered her mouth, just thinking of her corset being found by an unsuspecting Garrett domestic. Quickly, she tugged on her bedgown and sent up a prayer that the discovery wouldn't send the poor unfortunate to an early grave. In her head, she pictured the ancient domestics. Well, a grave, at any rate.

But obviously her errant husband had no such qualms. Closing the door with a solid thump, he started across the room, dusting his palms together as if rubbing dirt off them. ''There. Never have liked those damned things on my women—'' Halfway across the room from her, his feet stopped and his eyes widened. A sickly, new-husband-who-just-forgot-himself grin lit his features.

Fighting her own grin at his expression, Hannah crooked a knee and folded her arms. With her head cocked at an angle, she teased, ''Your *women*?''

His eyebrows shot up. Darn him, he saw she was trying not to grin. But still he stayed in place and lied. ''No. I said 'woman.' I don't like those damned things on my *woman*. That's you. Are you hard of hearing, my sweet?''

''I am not your sweet, and no, I'm not hard of hearing. But *you* will be—once I box your ears.''

Now his mouth opened. ''Hannah, are you jealous?''

Awareness that she actually was tore through her, spinning her around to face his bed. She spoke over her shoulder at the big oaf. "No, of course not. I just won't allow you to make a fool of me by being seen in the company of—"

He grabbed her arms, spun her around and pulled her flat against his chest. He grinned in triumph just before planting a big, wet kiss on her mouth.

Hannah suffered through his passion. All the way to her curled toes and thrumming womb. But the moment he broke their kiss, she picked up, a mite breathlessly, where she'd left off. "Fast women or ladies of the night."

His mouth wet with her kiss, his black hair slanting over his high forehead, Slade ran his hungry gaze over her face as he informed her, "Same thing."

Lost in his black-lashed eyes, his high cheekbones, and sensual mouth, she stared up him. "I know."

His gaze sobered as he looked down at her. "Are you sore?"

A scoffing noise escaped her. "At you? Always. I could take my pick of topics. There's that remark you just made about your women. There's the dinner party you won't discourage Isabel from planning. There's your high-handedness with me at supper, daring me to leave and saying you'll tie me up if I try. And—"

"Not that." He gripped her tighter, wrenching her to him again. Hannah sucked in a breath as her nipples grazed his stiff shirtfront. "What I meant was"—he chuckled and shook his head—"are you sore from this afternoon . . . in the music room?"

"Oh." Hannah exploded in a molten flush. Embarrassed tears sprang to her eyes. She bobbed her head as she bit at her bottom lip. She was sore *and* swollen, even following a thirty-minute soak in a warm bath earlier. A single tear escaped to roll down her cheek.

"Sweet Hannah." Slade's grip turned affectionate as he leaned down to touch his forehead to hers. "Sweet, sweet Hannah." A rippling shudder shook him. He exhaled a warm, brandy-tinged breath and settled nipping kisses on her cheek, neck, and shoulder.

The heavy heat between them was almost unbearable. Near to buckling to the floor, Hannah closed her eyes in surrender, only to have Slade release her and turn away abruptly. He took several steps away from her, stopped, and stood with his back to her, a knee bent, his hands to his waist. His head hung forward, and he took deep, deep breaths.

Biting at her bottom lip, Hannah curled her toes into the thick carpet and clutched at her gown, wadding it unmercifully. What was wrong with him? As if in answer, he straightened up to his full height and tilted his head back. A sudden cry, more like a growl, escaped him. Hannah blinked and stiffened. When he looked back at her, his expression trapped her breath in her lungs.

She'd seen this look once before. On the faces of a wolf pack which was rebuffed by an enraged mother buffalo defending her calf. The wolves' faces and cries, just like Slade's, served notice that the reprieve was temporary. The wolves then howled out against being denied. Hannah suspected something similar was wrong with her husband. But still, she was too new at this sexual game to be sure. She decided it couldn't hurt to ask. "Are you sore, too?"

"Am I—?" Slade looked at her as if she'd just spoken in an unintelligible language. He then ran his fingers down his chin, jaw, and neck.

Hannah's pulse picked up guiltily. Maybe it hurt men, too, and you weren't supposed to ask because it made them feel . . . less manly. Feeling awful, she shook her head and quirked her mouth up regretfully. "I'm sorry if I hurt you . . . in your music room. I didn't mean to."

Slade stared at her and then exploded into laughter. He bent over, hands on his knees, and guffawed like a jackass, in Hannah's insulted opinion. She crossed her arms, hoping to high heaven that she had hurt him. And if she hadn't, she may yet. But not in the way he wanted.

Lucky for him, he recovered quickly, straightening up by walking his hands up his thighs. Standing tall again, he wiped at his eyes and chuckled. "You didn't hurt me in my . . . music room. But you're killing me there now."

*Well, what did that mean? They were nowhere near the music room.* Hannah poked out her bottom lip threateningly. And sucked it in when he advanced on her.

When he reached her, he spun her around and smacked her bottom, giving her a push toward her own bedroom door. "Go now, while I'm strong. It's off to our own chaste beds for tonight."

Hannah stopped exactly where her momentum from his push played out. She turned back to him and caught him watching her with frank yearning in his eyes. Still uncomprehending, she looked down, watching herself pick at her fingernails as she spoke. "I thought . . . Well, my parents always slept in the same bed. I thought we would, too."

Hearing his forcefully exhaled breath, she looked up. His expression was now one of naked hunger, which he tried to scrub away by running a hand over his jaw and mouth and then both hands through his hair. "Dammit, Hannah. You're standing there sore and half-naked. If you're in this room at the end of ten more seconds, you'll be naked by then—and one hell of a lot more sore tomorrow morning. In fact, you may not even be able to walk. Because we won't be doing any sleeping, baby. Not if we're in the same bed."

"Oh." It was more of a yelp than a word. "Uhm, good night, Slade."

"Good night, Hannah. One. Two. Three. Four—"

Four was the last number Hannah heard as she turned tail and ran for the door that connected her room to his. Jerking it open, she flung herself into the unlit room and slammed the door behind her. Breathing rapidly, feeling the least bit silly for her girlish flight, she leaned her back and her head against the wooden barrier that was the door.

"Lock it, Hannah."

She screeched and whipped around. His voice came from just the other side of the door. In the room's total darkness, she fumbled for the key, found it, and turned it in the lock.

Slade's chuckling laughter accompanied her skittering feet and groping hands all the way to her bed, which she scrambled onto with no thought to dignity or decorum. No sooner was she atop it, on her knees and yanking at the protective covers, trying desperately to pull them down—than the door from the hallway opened. Hannah jerked around with a cry and fell on her back, freezing in place atop her bed.

There stood Slade, his tall, heavily muscled self framed in the rectangular opening. Hannah's heart lurched as she pulled herself up onto her elbows and bent her knees, sending her bedgown up around her hips. She peered at him through the vee her exposed legs made. Watching him, seeing him, wanting him as she did, a sudden pride in his rampant masculinity seized her heart. This man owned his ground, as surely as did any half-naked Cheyenne warrior standing atop a jagged cliff.

The filtered light from the hallway sconces behind him cast him in deep shadows, playing over him like cloud-cloaked moonlight. He leaned a shoulder against the jamb, bent one knee, and crossed his arms over his powerful chest. But Hannah wasn't fooled by his studied pose. She didn't even have to see his eyes to know the wolves were back on the scent.

After a mouth-drying, heart-pounding moment, he finally spoke, his deep, resonant voice sparking a purely delightful shudder over Hannah's nerves. "Eight. Nine. Ten." Done counting, he straightened up, stepped into the room, and closed the door. The room plunged again into absolute darkness. "I owe you an apology, my sweet."

"For what?" She bit at her bottom lip, cursing herself for sounding like a bleating sheep. He didn't answer. Hannah raised her head, straining her hearing, listening for any sound he might make. There was none. Darned carpet. Not knowing his whereabouts in the room raised the hair on the back of her neck.

He was coming for her. She knew that, as surely as she knew she was a woman. He was coming for her. Closer and closer. Like a scared deer, she didn't move. But she knew he'd find her. Like a wild predator, he could sense her. He didn't need light. He didn't need touch. He only needed her scent.

With no warning, with no darker-than-black shadow extricating itself from the surrounding thick velvet, a large, warm hand settled unerringly on her knee. Hannah gasped. It slid slowly down the inside of her thigh. Hannah gasped again, lying back in white-hot need.

"An apology for what? For not warning you to lock that other door."

Hannah rose stiffly from her bath's tepid water, watching the rivulets sluice down her. Slade was right when he said she'd barely be able to walk today if he was in her bed last night. He was in her bed last night. And she could barely walk today.

She stepped out of the tub and reached for her towel. A sudden sensation, as if Slade still touched her, brought lurid images to her mind's eye. She'd never known a man could . . . kiss a woman . . . down there. Almost spasmodically, as if the motion could erase from her memory the feel of his mouth on her, Hannah reached up to shove an errant curl under the satin ribbon that secured her upswept hair. She winced with the effort. Last night, she'd used muscles she'd never known she had.

That stilled her hand. She was certainly quick to give up girlish pruderies for womanly pleasures. She began a vigorous drying of her body. Well, what choice did she have, given the lusty male she'd married? Married. Hannah went limp, allowing the thick towel to hang from her fingers.

After she'd exacted her family's revenge on Cyrus, what then? Would she still be married? Well, of course she would. She looked around the elegantly appointed bathroom. She couldn't stay in Boston. She was needed at home. She'd promised her sisters to return. But how could she leave Slade? She loved him. Defeat tugged at her heart. Not one word had passed between them about that coming day.

Sighing over the depth of her problems—revenge was certainly convoluted—Hannah decided she'd write another letter to Glory and Jacey once she was dressed. Things were happening so quickly that each day saw a whole new situation arising. What in the world would her sisters think when she wrote she was married to Slade Garrett? And possibly carrying his child?

Hannah stiffened, clutching at the towel, remembering his words about needing an heir. She splayed her hand over her belly. Never. He'd have to kill her to separate her from her baby. If there was one. Hannah brought the towel up to her mouth and closed her eyes. She loved him. A Garrett. The son of the man who'd tried to force himself on her mother. The son of the man who'd changed her mother's life forever. Hannah took a sighing breath. For the better, though. He'd changed it for the better.

Mama and Papa never would have met, if not for John Garrett's rash and drunken behavior. Slade and his poor mother suffered so much more at John's hands than her mother ever did. Hannah opened her eyes. What a coil this was. Fearing she'd give herself a headache if she kept on in this vein, she finished drying, laid the towel over the tub's rim, and reached for her white cambric wrapper, which hung from a peg on the back of the bathroom door.

A knock sounded against the same door, startling Hannah and momentarily stalling her hand in midair. Then she shook her head at her own silliness. Slade had her jumpy about doors. "One moment."

No one called back, but Hannah thought nothing of it as she hastily donned the garment and closed enough of the hook-and-eye fastenings to render herself decent. Well, it couldn't be Slade. He wouldn't knock. Or wait.

Besides that, about an hour ago, she'd shoved him bodily out of her bedroom, telling him to go take care of his business in Boston. Or go see Dudley. Or ride Champion. Or toast their marriage at his club. Anything to give her some peace. Chuckling again at his petulant expression as he'd left, she sang out, "Is that you with my breakfast, Serafina? I'll be right out."

"No, miss. It's not Serafina. It's . . . it's me—Olivia."

# CHAPTER THIRTEEN

---

Hannah jerked the door open, hugging the girl to her. "Olivia! I've missed you so much. I've been worried sick." She drew back and held the girl at arm's length. "How's . . . um— Colette, wasn't it? Is she better now? Oh, I'm so glad to see you. Slade is impossible as a lady's maid. Did you even know we're married? You couldn't have picked a better day to return. I'll need your help right away—Isabel says we're to expect hordes of callers."

When the girl's eyes brimmed with tears and her chin dimpled, Hannah's expression wilted into a mask of sympathy. "Olivia, what's wrong?"

She put her arm around the silent girl and led her to a grouping of delicate chairs around the fireplace. Hannah sat on the edge of her chair, soberly noting several things at once. If it were possible, the girl was even thinner. Her brown hair hung in strands around her face. There was no color in her cheeks. Neither was she in uniform. She wore a faded blue, very worn wool skirt and basque, and scuffed boots. Hannah looked deeper. The child's face was . . . careworn, drawn. And she kept her gaze centered on her lap.

A tenderness piercing her heart, Hannah reached over and clasped Olivia's thin, cold hands. "Olivia, look at me." When she did, it was with more of a skittering, sliding glance than a direct stare. "Whatever it is, Olivia, we'll help you. I mean that."

Olivia finally settled her gaze on Hannah. Who nearly gasped at the flatness that pervaded the little maid's brown eyes. "There's nothing wrong, miss. I'm just tired, is all. And

. . . and glad to be back.'' She looked down at her lap again.

Hannah sat back in her chair. The girl obviously didn't want to talk. Hannah knew she could make her, being her employer, but she wasn't the heartless sort. Perhaps some cheeriness and pampering from the Garrett domestics would bring her around. Maybe Olivia'd talk to one of them. ''I'm glad you're back, too. I've missed having you to talk to. Remember, you're one of the few people I can trust.''

Olivia flinched visibly and looked up, shaking her head vigorously. ''No, miss—I mean, madam. I don't think you should talk to me. Or tell me things. It ain't fittin' for—for your new station.'' She stood up. ''If that's all, I'd like to go to my room and get into my uniform. And then I'll come back and help you dress.''

Smarting more than a little bit from Olivia's chastisement of her, Hannah spoke quietly. ''All right, Olivia. Thank you.'' The girl remained silent. Hannah sighed deeply. ''That will be all, then.''

Olivia nodded and made as if to leave, but then she hesitated and shot Hannah a glance. She looked on the verge of saying something, but then she paled and dipped into a curtsy—the first one Hannah'd ever seen her execute.

Hannah dipped her head in acknowledgment and watched Olivia walk out of the room. The girl's shoulders sagged with the weight of the world. Once Olivia closed the door behind her, Hannah turned back in her chair and stared at the empty fireplace. Thinking back over the past few minutes, she realized that Olivia hadn't answered a single one of her questions.

That brought her to the edge of her seat. Clapping her hands on her knees, she turned to stare at her rumpled bed. A smile came to her face. Maybe Olivia hadn't answered her, but she knew someone who had promised to get her those answers.

*Never should have left her alone.* His heart in his throat over Hannah's cryptic message, Slade yanked the carriage door open, left Dudley in his wake, and bounded up the wide steps of Woodbridge Pond's front entrance—almost before Rigby could bring the brougham's team to a halt in the circular drive. ''Send Jonathan to the club to get Champion for me,'' he called over his shoulder to his bruised driver.

Slade grabbed the door's handle, depressing the latch as he

threw his weight and momentum into expecting it to open. It didn't. He slammed into the unforgiving wood, very nearly dislocating his shoulder. He bellowed out as he clutched at his numbed arm and danced around in agony.

"I say, that looks painful. Teach you to be in such a hurry that you won't allow Rigby to drive around to the porte cochere."

Slade glared at the cheerful Dudley, who stood next to and dwarfed a huge flower urn on the ornamental landing. The senator's son nonchalantly removed his gloves, slapping them against his other palm while he considered Slade with an arched auburn brow.

"You're enjoying this, aren't you, Ames?" Slade neither expected nor got a response from his gloating friend. The guttersnipe loved catching him in a mishmash of emotions over a woman. Still, Slade was in no mood for his friend's taunting attitude. "Don't help me. Just stand there like the bastard you are."

Dudley chuckled out loud. "As you wish." And remained standing there, like the bastard he was. He whistled a jaunty tune and reached up to remove his top hat, so he could scratch at his scalp. The sun's rays glinted off his unruly thatch of kinky-curly, carrot-red hair, creating the effect of his head being aflame. Suddenly he turned to Slade, wearing a mock-injured expression. "By the bye, I am telling Mother what you said about me being a bastard. That doesn't speak well of her morals."

"Tell her. I still say it would explain a lot. And put your hat on before a passing fire brigade throws water on you." With that, and still holding his stinging, tingling arm hard against his side, Slade stalked back to the door and kicked out a knocking tattoo with his booted foot.

The retaliation against the door seemed to ease his pain. But not to bring Pemberton. However, following his kicking with a substantial amount of voluble cursing, coupled with banging on the door with his one viable fist, finally brought the old man around. The sounds of the lock being worked from the inside . . . and worked and worked . . . caused Slade to exchange glances with Dudley. His own, fatalistic. Dudley's, amused. The door at long last opened.

Pemberton, all starch and polish, and with a gravy-stained

napkin tucked into the too-big collar of his shirt, squinted into the bright sunlight and looked down his long, thin nose at the interlopers. "I'm sorry, sirs. But the Garretts are not receiving guests at the moment. They've had quite a full morning and are now taking their luncheon."

Muscles bunched to barge in, but stopped by this bit of unexpectedness, and by twenty-five years of minding Pemberton, Slade stood rooted to the landing of his family's estate. He shot Dudley another look. Then, working the last vestiges of numbness out of his arm, Slade turned to the butler, who effectively blocked the entry with all ninety pounds of himself. "Pemberton, you old caution, it's me—Slade Franklin Garrett."

Pemberton blinked, lowered his head, and shaded his watery blue eyes with a brown-spotted hand. He frowned as much as he peered at the face before him. In a moment, his face lit with recognition. "I say, sir. You're absolutely right. You are the young Mr. Garrett." He then immediately reverted back to his butler pose, formally intoning, "One would therefore think you'd be aware of the visiting hours. The family is having luncheon. You'll have to come back later." He started to close the door.

Slade wedged his foot in the jamb and nearly got it smashed for his efforts. "Ouch. Dammit, man, I live here. Now move aside." Slade wedged a shoulder around the old man and carefully pushed by him, stalking across the black-and-white marble-tiled entryway. "Where's Mrs. Garrett, Pemberton?"

"Which one, sir? And who shall I say is calling?"

Slade stopped in his tracks and turned around—again to stare in disbelief at Dudley. That reprobate grinned a big-toothed smile and encouraged, "Well, don't just stand there, Garrett. Tell him who's calling. Can't you see the man is trying to have his luncheon?"

Slade got no further than poking his index finger at his friend before feminine steps, accompanied by the one voice in all the world that could make his heart skip and stutter, echoed behind him.

"Pemberton, what is all the fuss? Is that Mr. Garrett at long last?"

Slade pivoted. And caught his breath at the sight of her. How could he have ever thought he'd simply marry her and ignore her? The Lawlesses had the last laugh again on the Garretts. For if she ever knew how gut-wrenching her effect on him was, he was doomed to a life of dancing attendance on her and being very foolish with his time and money. Somewhat like now.

But not allowing one trace of lovesickness to shade his manner, he affected a stiff posture and an instant scowl. "At long last, is it? I came as soon as I received your note, madam. And all the fuss, as you say, is due to me rushing home from the club, thinking you're injured or dead, only to find ·you happily engaged in luncheon."

"Happily engaged? I've been receiving callers all morning who've all wanted 'all the details,' as they put it, and I've been dealing with a fortune in arriving gifts. And where have you been, sir? Gone, that's where, leaving me to fend for myself—all while being exhausted from a sleepless night last night—" Her eyes went wide and her face colored prettily.

Slade grinned evilly. "A sleepless night last night? How so?" Putting his hands to his waist, he watched her color deepen and her mouth open and close in embarrassment. Until her gaze shifted just to his right, her eyes narrowed, and her attention stayed focused there. Slade turned, too.

Dudley and Pemberton stood side by side, looking like an advertisement for a circus sideshow, what with the disparity in their sizes. Dudley's orange and brown plaid suit next to Pemberton's black clothes and dirty napkin only intensified the effect. Slade cringed with Dudley at Hannah's sweetly sarcastic greeting to the senator's son. "Why, there he is—my husband's best man. So nice to see you on your feet and aware of your surroundings, Mr. Ames."

Mr. Ames turned bright red and belatedly yanked his top hat off. "Good day to you, Mrs. Garrett. May I say you look especially fetching in that watered silk?"

Slade rolled his eyes. "No, you may not, you fool." *You look especially fetching in that watered silk,* he mimicked in his head. His terse words garnered for him Hannah's renewed attention. *Her beautiful Madonna face glowed with an inner light all its own*—in Slade's suddenly poetic estimation.

"You shouldn't insult your friend, Mr. Garrett."

"I assure you, I've said worse to him—and only a moment ago on the front landing. Now, tell me about your note."

She twisted her fingers together and cut her gaze from him to the two men behind him, and then back to him. "Can we speak alone, please?"

"Certainly." His stomach tightened. But now that he knew this woman was safe, he could handle—and gladly—whatever might be awry in her world. He turned to the butler and his friend. "Pemberton, take Mr. Ames to the dining room and have Rowena fix him a plate. I trust Grandmother is still at table?"

Pemberton managed a stiff bow—with Dudley snaking a hand out to steady him—and then straightened up. "One doesn't trust the elder Mrs. Garrett to be anywhere, when she's out of one's sight." He turned to Dudley, again bowing dangerously. "This way, sir."

Dudley waved the butler ahead of him, following him like a giant, ungainly puppy. "What has Mrs. Edgars cooked up for the menu today, old boy?"

"Some sort of charred animal carcass, surrounded by the fruit of the land."

"Oh, bully! What rare luck—my favorite. I only hope it's not Esmerelda. And for dessert, we're having . . . ?"

The two wandered off down the hallway, leaving Slade and Hannah to stare after them. But Slade ended up staring at Hannah, as always. He took a deep breath. She was more intoxicating than any liquor. With her deep-dark and shiny hair piled high on her head in thick ringlets, her sweet, creamy neck was exposed and needed kissing. She turned then, catching him.

He immediately scowled, widening his stance and punctuating his feigned displeasure with her by crossing his arms over his chest. "Now, then, what is the meaning of all this? First you push me out of bed and tell me to go away—on only our second day of marriage. Highly irregular. But I nevertheless go away.

"Then, when I'm pleasantly engaged in occupying my time—again, at your urging—you send an urgent message with Rigby telling me to come home. Which I did—pell-mell and leaving Champion hitched at the club, I might add. Only to have you chastise me for being gone. So, what in the name of all that is holy is going on?"

"Are you quite finished?" She poked her bottom lip out, which only accentuated its sensual fullness.

"No, actually, I'm not." With his arms still crossed, Slade frowned down at her, surreptitiously clutching at his own coat's fabric to keep from grabbing her right here—in the foyer, in broad daylight—and having her on that damned table in the center of the room. One day, he would. "I find I have one more thing to say to you. Dudley's right. You look lovely in that watered silk. The fabric's turned your eyes a deep green that I find . . . arousing."

He watched her pinken. When she looked up at him, innocently provocative with her mouth open and her wide eyes glittering, he frowned fiercely, barely maintaining his stern pose. "Well, madam? I'm waiting."

He watched his wife make two attempts to speak, and fail. Immediately alarmed, Slade dropped his pose, lowering his arms to his sides in an attitude of readiness. When her expression clouded and her eyes teared, he unraveled, as surely as any ball of yarn in a kitten's clutches. He reached her in one step and held her by her arms. "For God's sake, what is it, Hannah?"

She put trembling hands to her mouth and sniffed. "Oh, Slade. I'm so glad you're here. It's just been awful." She took a deep shuddering breath, releasing it in a rush with her next words. "Olivia is back."

"Olivia is back?" Slade repeated stupidly. He looked askance at this emotionally overwrought woman in his arms. And admitted to himself that he had no idea how these lovely creatures worked.

He did know that he'd slay dragons for her. Fight armies single-handedly and unarmed, one hand tied behind his back and blindfolded, if she asked him to. He'd even figure out this lady's-maid dilemma for her . . . if he could begin to understand it. He shook his head, thinking that nothing in his previous experience in life had prepared him for Hannah Wilton Lawless . . . now Garrett. "But aren't you happy about that?"

She nodded vigorously, loosing a long chocolate curl to trail over her shoulder. "I was," she sobbed, turning a frowning mouth and quivering chin up to him. "But she's changed. She . . . she doesn't like me anymore and says nothing's wrong and she won't smile or chat on or race about the place and not even Esmerelda can get a rise out of her and she's so thin and she looks so sad and then I saw Rigby and he's been beaten by someone and is all sullen too and I just don't know what to make of it all.''

*Was that all? And all in one impressive breath, too.* Blinking, relieved to his toes, he told her, ''Rigby, that young cuss, got himself beat up getting his horse back from some street toughs. His pride is more bruised than his face.''

Slade relaxed. There was nothing wrong here that he couldn't fix for her. But even more importantly, instead of acting rashly on her own, instead of dashing off headlong into danger with that little peashooter of hers, she'd sent for him. Her husband. She'd placed her problems in his hands to be solved.

She wanted, even needed his help. To Slade, it meant she trusted him. Finally. He was trusted and, yes, loved. She'd already told him that. A chip of armor flaked away from his heart. A tiny door opened. This woman loved and trusted him.

''Well, I feel better about Rigby, at least. But what about Olivia?''

He started to smile, but the new-husband voice in his head warned him that would be a big mistake. So he became appropriately serious and head-of-the-household authoritative, striving to show that her concerns were serious and important to him. ''I'll get to the bottom of this for you, Hannah. Don't you worry.''

She firmed up her chin and shook her head at him. ''You don't understand. Something is very wrong. Very. I wrote Glory—''

''Glory?''

''My baby sister. I wrote Glory and Jacey a—''

''Oh, yes. Now I remember.''

Her voice rose impatiently. ''Quit interrupting me, Slade. This is important.'' To prove it, she looked all around them and then clutched at his sleeve, dragging him into the privacy of the small family salon and closing the door after them.

Slade's eyes popped open wide at the mountain of wrapped and unwrapped gifts claiming every surface in the room. He made a sweeping gesture with a pointed finger. ''All this came this morning?''

Hannah turned to him. Gone were the tears and the uncertainty. Back was his pistol-packing spitfire. "This and more. The formal parlor is full, too. I told you it's been loco here." Then she poked a finger at his chest, speaking in low conspirator's tones. "Now, listen to me about Olivia. I wrote my sisters a letter this morning and asked Olivia to post it. When she left to do that, I came downstairs to help Isabel with her plans for that dinner ball—"

"Aha! I knew it. You couldn't stop her, either, could you? And here you were ready to leave over it last night. Now you're helping her."

Her chin came up. "I just happen to think it makes sense today." That settled, she launched into her story again. "At any rate, I was in the sewing room with Isabel, working on the menu for the party, when I got a chill. So, with Olivia on an errand, and me not wanting poor Serafina or Rowena to walk up all those stairs . . . They're so old and their knees aren't what they used to be. Besides, fetching for me isn't really part of their duties. So I—"

*Why do women have to give all the details and the emotions involved and every person in the house's ailments and duties and whereabouts? Why don't they just spit it out? Oh, well, at least I can enjoy myself watching her talk.* So, with stance firm, arms crossed, Slade nodded at the appropriate moments and battered his will into forming an expression of rapt attention to her words and not her person. *If Hannah ever lied, he'd know it in a moment. Her face gave her away. She wore every emotion on the perfect oval of her sweet face.*

". . . when I heard Esmerelda outside and raising a fuss. Afraid she'd gotten into the flower beds again—she digs something terrible—or maybe had another rat, I went to look out the window. And what do you think I saw?"

*How come I haven't noticed before now that she has a tiny mole on the highest point of her right cheek, almost to her hairline?*

Hannah smacked his arm. "Slade! Are you listening to me?"

Slade jumped and focused on her. "Of course I am. Aren't I standing right here?"

She frowned out her vexation. "Then, answer me."

He blinked, realizing he had no clue how, and then made a sweeping survey of the room, detail by fine detail, as he desperately searched his memory for anything he recalled her saying. Finally, he looked at her and placed his newly knighted husbandhood on the line. "Esmerelda?"

Hannah laughed. Slade let his breath out. "Of course Esmerelda, silly. Didn't I just say she was in the gardens?" Then she turned serious and still. "But, Slade, she wasn't the only one."

Now she really did have his full attention. A creeping coldness clutched his belly. "Who else was out there, Hannah?"

Wide-eyed, fingers all but covering her mouth, she whispered, "Olivia."

Slade stared at her. At the silver and white wrapped packages. At the comfortably shabby damask sofa behind her. He stared as if he expected them to interpret this woman for him. He finally swung his gaze back to her. "But didn't you send her to post the letter to your sisters?"

Hannah nodded, darkly . . . deeply. "Now you see. I knew you would understand. That's why I sent for you and waited."

Great. Slade understood nothing. Absolutely nothing. Here she'd shown her newfound faith and trust in him, and he couldn't figure out what the hell she was talking about. Irked at himself, he frowned his eyebrows down over the bridge of his nose. "Hannah, I don't understand one blamed thing. Not one. What have you been talking about—since I got home?"

She slumped and rolled her eyes. "For evermore. Think, Slade. Olivia was in the gardens. Do you think she's going to post a letter in the pond? Or the summer cottage?"

He stared off blankly into space. Then, thinking he had her meaning, he looked back down at her and puffed up like an especially slow-witted student who finally has the right answer. "Ahh, you want me to berate her for not posting your letter. I'll tend to it right now."

Hannah screeched. Slade jumped, nearly recoiling when she gripped his arms and tried to shake him. But she succeeded only in shaking herself and getting more and more worked up. "Forget the letter! Forget it! When I saw her, she was worming her way back through *the iron fence*. I saw her squeeze through the bars and then watched until she ducked out of the hedges and came running back to the house. Slade, she'd been at Cloister Point."

Slowly turning to stone as her words sank in, Slade looked

right at her. And then through her. "Son of a *bitch*."

Hannah exhaled a ragged breath, kept her grip on his coat, and laid her forehead against his chest. "Finally. What are we going to do?"

The despairing note in her voice only intensified Slade's reaction. His temper reaching a quick fever-pitch, he gripped Hannah's arms, holding her back from him. "Where is she now?"

"I sent her—" The despair on Hannah's face suddenly bled into a wariness that rimmed her blue-green eyes in white. "No, Slade. You still don't understand."

Seething now, Slade gripped her tighter, roaring out, "Oh, I understand. Maybe more than you do. You're protecting her and putting both our lives in danger. Don't fight me on this, Hannah. Tell me! Where is she? If I have to find the little traitor myself, I'll tear her limb from limb, I swear to God."

"Traitor? No! Slade, you can't. She's not—"

Slade pulled her against him. "Where is she, for the last time?"

"I won't tell you. She can't be—"

"She can't be anything but a spy for the same people who've had half your family murdered. And you and I are next. I won't let that happen, do you hear me? I'll find her myself. And when I do . . ." Slade trailed his sentence off, intending the ominous silence that followed.

When Hannah began to whimper and shake her head, he set her away from him, pointing at her as she backed up to the damask sofa and nearly fell over a package at her heels. "Stay here."

Turning, he ripped open the door, held on to it, and looked back at her. "I mean it, Hannah. You put this in my hands, so now you let me deal with it."

With that he stepped across the threshold and jerked the door closed behind him.

Sick inside, close to screaming aloud in fear as Slade slammed the door behind him, Hannah clutched at the soft and sagging sofa cushions behind her. She'd unleashed a murderous rage in Slade. *He'll kill Olivia.*

That thought galvanized her into action. She jerked upright, knowing she had to stop him. But how? Being her father's daughter, she felt in her pocket until her hand closed over the familiar shape of her pocket pistol. No. Not him. She couldn't.

But still, she might be able to use it to get his attention. That decided, she scurried to the door and opened it. Balancing her need for stealth with her need for haste, she held her breath and listened. She heard Slade's booted steps thundering across the foyer. *Dear God.* She'd never catch him. *Dudley!* Hannah slipped out of the room, watched as Slade began taking the stairs two at a time. She then fled down the long hallway to the dining room.

The sounds of luncheon in progress, Isabel talking and Dudley laughing, met her ears before she turned the corner into the room and grabbed their startled attention. Isabel put a hand to her throat. Dudley came to his feet and rounded the table. Hannah's breathless momentum carried her to the table's edge. Dudley clutched at her arms. "Hannah, what's wrong?"

She grabbed his plaid sleeve and gasped out, "Help me. Slade's going to . . . kill Olivia. Upstairs. Her room. Hurry."

From across the table came Isabel's shocked cry of "Kill her? Dear Lord, what on earth for?"

Hannah ignored her, knowing she didn't dare waste time and breath on more words—or chance looking away from Dudley until she was sure he understood the urgency required. The large man stared at her for less than a second before his face hardened. "Stay here." He let go of her, loping from the room like an angry buffalo.

Both palms flat on the table, arms straight, head hanging between her shoulders, Hannah took several gulps of air. She focused all her senses on listening for the sound of Dudley's pounding feet on the stairs. At last, she heard him. *Please, God, let him be in time.* And as soon as she could get air into her lungs, she'd be right behind him. *Damn this corset. She should've left it in the hallway where Slade threw it.*

It was another moment before she realized that Isabel was at her side and patting her back. Hannah turned to her grandmother-in-law, and read the question in the older woman's eyes.

"Tell me what happened, Hannah."

Hannah shook her head. "Have to . . . stop him."

"Stop him from what? What has Olivia done?"

Hannah turned her back on the table, perching her bottom

against its edge. "Olivia was at Cloister Point. I saw her sneaking back through the fence."

Isabel never even blinked. Her face became a hard mask. "Then Slade must throw her off the property."

Hannah held the white-haired woman's steady gaze. When her breathing calmed more, she spoke her mind. "What if she's not guilty of anything?"

Isabel raised an eyebrow. "Your own word for her behavior was 'sneaking.' Now, obviously you don't think she went over there for tea, or you wouldn't have sent for Slade. Am I right?"

Contrition sending her gaze to her slippers, Hannah nodded.

"I'm afraid there's only one explanation, Hannah. And you know what it is—she's in collusion with Cyrus and Patience."

Hannah looked up at Isabel, putting a hand on the older woman's thin, satin-covered arm. "Couldn't there be another explanation?"

"I can't imagine what it could be."

Hannah lowered her hand to grip the table's edge. "I can't believe there's an underhanded bone in Olivia's body. If she has dealings with them, they're forcing her somehow."

"More like bribing her. That's their style."

Had Olivia betrayed her? "You honestly think Olivia would accept money to endanger my life?"

Isabel shrugged. "It's possible. Money does strange things to some people. You need look no further than next door for proof of that."

Hannah knew everything Isabel said was true. But she just couldn't believe it. Or accept that she might have to deal with Olivia too when retribution was dealt. "I hope you're wrong, Isabel." Hannah firmed her lips and shoved away from the table, heading for the room's entryway.

"Hannah?"

She stopped and turned back to Isabel, waiting. Isabel stood where she'd left her, her hands clasped under her bosom. She appeared very small, very old. "If we act harshly with Olivia and are wrong about her, at least you'll be alive. But I couldn't bear knowing you died because we were right—and yet did nothing. We did that before with Cyrus. And it cost you dearly."

Hannah held Isabel's gaze as she took her words to heart.

"Yes, it did. I understand your concern. But there just has to be another explanation."

Isabel put a hand down on the table beside her. "But there isn't. Olivia has betrayed you. Is not Slade's reaction the same as yours when you found your parents? And then, was it not a desire for revenge that brought you here?"

Stung by the truth, Hannah nodded at the older woman.

Isabel went on, in a softer tone. "We feel the same way about protecting you. My grandson may not realize it yet himself, but he loves you. As do I."

Fat, hot tears filled Hannah's eyes. She raised her head, trying to blink them back and maintain her shaky control. "I love you, too. But this goes beyond that. Guilty or not, I can't allow Slade to harm Olivia."

Isabel sighed. "I tell you, he won't harm the girl. But go, if you must."

"I must, Isabel. You didn't see his face or hear his words. I did." With that, Hannah slowly turned away. Once she was out of Isabel's sight, she took to her heels, certain the demons of hell were chasing her. Perhaps they were, and perhaps their names were Revenge.

Hannah clutched at her skirts and flew up the stairs. By the time she'd climbed almost to the third floor, her lungs burned and her legs wobbled. Gasping, holding on to the stairwell's wall with every step, she kept her sight on the landing ahead of her. The servants' quarters.

Gritting her teeth in determination, she triumphed over the last few stairs. Finally she stood on the landing. Clutching at her skirts, Hannah looked up and down the long hallway that stretched to either side of her. *Something's wrong.* She cocked her head like Esmerelda did when she heard a bird chirping. But Hannah heard nothing, save her own rasping attempts at breathing. Sweat trickled down her spine and between her breasts. There was a faint ringing in her ears. Other than that, the hallway was ominously quiet. Hannah fished in her pocket for her pistol and drew it out.

Hannah tried not to think about whom she intended to use her weapon on as she looked at door after door after door down each corridor. All of them the same, all of them closed. Did she have time to try them all? Indecision mounted while

Hannah chewed at her bottom lip, hoping for a sound. A bump against a wall. Anything to alert her to where they were.

Just then, a scream, as jagged as lightning on a summer night, tore through the hallway's silence.

# CHAPTER FOURTEEN

—

Hannah jerked toward the sound, hurrying her steps and tuning her hearing to the echoes of the cry. Another scream, a raw sound, stopped Hannah's feet in front of the third door on her left. Her heart hammering against her ribs, she took a deep breath and turned to face the door. Muffled male voices from inside the room competed with the ragged sobs and tearful wails of a young girl.

Tensing in anticipation of what she'd see, Hannah attacked the door, jerking it open and stepping across the threshold. Taking advantage of the surprised confusion her entrance spurred, she quickly leveled her gun in a steady aim.

"Don't shoot!" Dudley, closest to Hannah's gun and blocking the view of the others in the room, obligingly dropped to the floor, lying facedown.

"What the—?" Seated on a spindly-looking wooden chair, against the room's far wall, and in a straight line with Hannah's weapon, Slade went wide-eyed and jerked backward, conking his head against the wall behind him. Grimacing, cursing, clutching two-handed at his head, he reversed his movements to lean forward over his own legs. Then, as if talking to his boots, he croaked out, "Put that damned peashooter down before you hurt someone."

On the narrow bed, Olivia jerked over onto her back and gasped. She then renewed her wailing. "Don't kill me! I didn't want to do it! They made me!"

*They? Slade and Dudley?* Hannah kept her pistol aimed at Slade, but she looked now at Olivia. No blood. No bruises even. "Are you okay, Olivia?"

Still talking to his boots, Slade answered for the girl. "Hell, yes, she's okay. I talked with her and then found Jonathan in his room and sent him down to get Rigby for me. Didn't you pass the boy on the way up?"

"I don't know any Jonathan, and I passed no one."

Slade sat up. His eyes were reddened and watery from bumping his head. "Then obviously he was already off and running before you came blazing up here." He paused, looking from her face to her gun and back to her face. "I'm taking care of it, Hannah. Put that damned pistol away."

But as he stared at her, at her gun, and she didn't yield, his face hardened. "You still don't trust me the least little bit. I see that now. And to think I—" His voice trailed off as he shook his head at her, eyeing her as if she were a disgusting something he'd just found stuck to the bottom of his boot.

Dying inside from the look on her husband's face, Hannah felt the first twinges of guilt tug at her arms, making them feel heavy. She glanced over to Olivia, saw a wet, red face and stringy hair all mussed. But otherwise, she was fine, just like Slade said. She then looked down at Dudley, saw a fair impression of a bear rug on the bare floor. He would never hurt or force a mere girl like Olivia to do anything. Slowly she lowered her arms and her pistol as she looked back at Slade. And knew in her heart that it was too late.

Because his face was now an implacable mask of hidden emotions. He sat on the tiny chair as if it were a throne, his muscled legs spread, and his arms crossed over his chest. "You've made your bed, Hannah. And now I'm going to let you lie in it."

Hannah frowned at him. "What are you talking about?"

"You'll see soon enough. But tell me this, what'd you think I was doing?"

"You . . . you said you'd kill her. That's what I thought you were doing."

Olivia jerked around to stare at Slade and burst out crying again.

Over the girl's wails, he shouted, "For crying out loud, Olivia—cease and desist. No one's going to hurt you."

Olivia immediately calmed to loud gulps and ragged breaths, keeping her brown-eyed gaze on Slade.

Shaking his head, he looked at Hannah again. "You think

me capable of murdering a child? I spoke rashly, yes. But I never said I'd kill her. I admit to wanting to wring her little neck, but running up all those stairs has a way of making a man more open to discussion once he gets up here.'' He eyed her gun pointedly. ''Apparently, the climb doesn't have the same effect on a woman.''

Hannah didn't know what to say. She'd erred terribly in not trusting Slade. She knew that now. And there wasn't anything she could do or say to undo her actions. That was the worst part. She remained frozen in position as she stared at her husband. She watched as he shifted in his chair, raising a hand to probe gingerly at the back of his head.

Olivia's sobbing became hiccoughs about the same time Slade wearily nudged Dudley with his foot. ''Get up, Ames.''

''Does she still have the gun aimed at my heart?'' came his muffled voice.

Slade gave Hannah a penetrating look as he answered the still-prostrate man. ''No, my brave friend. It's pointing at the floor now—where you are.''

''Do tell? Then I want no part of it.'' Dudley came inelegantly to his feet and dusted himself off.

Hannah looked again to Slade and found his black eyes, like twin gun barrels, pinning her to the spot and accusing her. A guilty sadness crept through Hannah. Why hadn't she listened to Isabel? She started to say something, anything, to apologize to him, but Slade spoke first.

''Either shoot me or put that damned gun away.''

''No!'' Olivia sat up on her rumpled bed and stretched her arm out in an imploring gesture. ''Don't shoot him. Mr. Wilton-Humes threatened my Colette—my baby—if I wouldn't spy on you. He said he'd hurt her and my mum, if I didn't. But Mr. Garrett's going to help me. Oh, miss, please spare him.''

Hannah's eyes widened as Olivia spoke. Her first fleeting thought was she'd been right—Olivia hadn't betrayed her for money. She was being threatened. But more than that, Hannah focused on the girl's revelation. ''Your baby? Colette is your baby?''

The girl's face lengthened morosely as she nodded. Quicker than two blinks, the gun was pocketed and Hannah was sitting on the bed, hugging Olivia to her. "You're no more than a baby yourself."

"I turned sixteen last month, miss," Olivia blubbered, holding tightly to Hannah. "Don't let them hurt my baby and my mum!"

"We won't, we won't. I swear I hate Cyrus and Patience!" Hannah held the girl a moment more before holding the young mother away from her at arm's length. "How did this happen, Olivia—your being a mother at so young an age?"

Chin quivering, emotion-dampened hair stringing in her eyes, Olivia looked down at her hands knotted in her lap. "Colette's father is a sailor. Jack's his name. He told me he loved me and had such pretty words. And I wanted love very much. But he wouldn't marry me . . . when I told him. He said he was already married. He went back to sea, and I never saw him no more."

Hannah's heart went out to the girl. "So, you're all alone to raise her—just you and your . . . mother, did you say?"

"Yes, miss. Pa died years ago. And poor Mum's a cripple in her legs."

Hannah knew a moment of real terror. "Crippled? How does she manage when you're here, Olivia?"

The girl shook her head slowly. "Not too well. I worry something fierce, I do. They both need looking after."

Hannah turned an imploring face to a very quiet Slade. His mouth a straight line, his jaw squared, he looked a blend of compassion and anger. The same emotions Hannah felt—compassion for Olivia, anger at the sailor who'd seduced an innocent girl. Hannah lowered her head and rubbed dispiritedly at her brow. "What can we do to stop them, Slade?"

He broke his silence. "I told you, I'm taking care of it."

Hannah looked up at her husband, so near and yet so far. Could the chasm be bridged? Damn her rash behavior, her rushing in like a faithless fool! Her gaze glanced off the granite façade of Slade's accusing stare. She turned back to Olivia and smoothed the lady's maid's hair from her face. "How old is your baby, Olivia?"

"Nine months, miss."

"Nine months?" Openmouthed now, Hannah turned again to the men. "Do you know how old that makes her when—?"

Slade frowned his brows down over his nose, but Dudley

raised his hands, ticking off his points on his thick fingers. "Let me see. The baby's nine months old, and it takes nine months to have one, correct? And Olivia's just now sixteen. So. . . ." Using his pointing finger and the air in front of him, he did his ciphering. "Carry the one. Eighteen. All right, eighteen months. So assuming she got pregnant the first time she—"

Slade slapped the senator's son's hands down. "You're quite fond of that first-time scenario, aren't you?"

Highly offended at being slapped, Dudley poked his thick chest out and glared his affront at Slade, who with a quick nod of his head indicated the women's presence in the room. Dudley looked over at Hannah. She raised an eyebrow at him.

Dudley sketched a bow. "I apologize for my indelicacy, ladies." He then turned back to his friend and spoke softly. But not softly enough. "If you use the first time, it makes the math simpler. I'm thinking she was probably—"

"Shut up, Ames."

Now he bowed up like a bulldog. "Well, did not Hannah just now ask us how old—?"

"She didn't really want an answer, you dolt. Her point is that some men can be beneath scorn."

Apparently unconvinced, Dudley swung his big head back to Hannah. "Is that your point?"

Hannah, who'd listened to the two men with half an ear as she whispered comfort to Olivia, now focused on Dudley. "Yes, it is. The things I've seen in my life make me believe that a length of rope and a tall tree are too good for some men. If you think about it, I believe you'll find I'm right."

Thus challenged, Dudley again raised his hands—shooting Slade a look that dared him to slap him again—and prepared to tick off his points in favor of men. "Well, let's see. There's—No, no, I can see how we'd be the cause of that. Wait. Of course, we don't—No, we do that, too." He frowned, his brown eyes darting side to side as he thought long and hard. Then, his face brightened. "I have it. We—No, we don't do that. Although we should."

Dudley lowered his hands to his sides and turned to Slade. "I say, Garrett, she is right. This is appalling. Apparently, we men *are* beneath scorn, and when I think about it . . . we're at our worst with our women. Why didn't you tell me that we're such cads?"

Slade grimaced his disgust. "Shut up, Ames. I'm develop-ing more and more sympathy for your long-suffering mother."

"Mother?" Dudley stared blankly for a moment before turning to Hannah. "Tell me, could it be that we are beneath scorn with our mothers, too?"

Hannah exchanged a glance with Olivia, whose mouth worked around a threatening grin. Heartened by the sight, glad now for Slade's and Dudley's banter with its calming effect on Olivia, she turned to stare so very seriously at Dudley. "One question, sir. How'd you come to be in this world?"

"Why, my mother, of cour—Dear God." He again turned to his childhood friend. "Slade, do you have any idea how much I weighed at birth?" He turned to Hannah. "If you will excuse me, I must go apologize to my mother for being such an unthoughtful infant. And for an entire score of things since then."

Before Hannah could say a word, Slade jumped in. "Do rethink this, man. Apologize to your mother? You'll put the poor woman in her grave."

Ignoring him, Dudley began an animated pacing up and down the length of the narrow room, hitting his fist against his other palm as his face worked with his thoughts. Hannah sought Slade's gaze. He shrugged his shoulders and then they both marked Dudley's progress.

Suddenly, he stopped cold and spoke to no one in particular. "I'll turn over a new leaf. I'll apologize to Mother. Then I'll call on Miss Wannamaker, as Mother's been begging me to do. I believe the young lady thinks favorably of me. Why else would she smile and bat her pretty eyes every time I see her? We can marry. I'll settle down into a life of home and hearth. Why, I might even run for high public office, too." He stepped up to the room's door and stared quietly out into the hall. "Senator Dudley Ames," he intoned.

Hannah exchanged another look with Slade. At that mo-ment, Dudley bolted from the room and charged heavy-footed down the hallway. His footsteps could be heard clattering down the steps at record pace. Hannah and Olivia and Slade stared at the empty space where Dudley'd stood not five sec-onds ago.

"Well, Hannah, I hope you're proud of yourself."

Her heart thumping at his words, she turned to her husband. "For what?"

"For apparently straightening Dudley out in less than five minutes. His mother may light candles to you in church and erect a shrine in your honor. However, don't expect me to thank you. I just lost a good friend to respectability. But worse, if my gullible friend should run for high public office and—God forbid—win, my fellow citizens may elect to hang you. Or shoot you at sunrise."

Hannah sat up straighter on the bed, clutching at Olivia's hands as her lady's maid asked, "Why would they do that?"

Slade crossed his arms over his chest. "Why? Well, when Dudley and I were twelve years old, I kept him busy for weeks climbing trees and crawling through shrubs as he, armed with a liberal supply of salt, hopped around after birds. I had convinced him that if he could sprinkle the salt on a bird's tail, it couldn't fly away and he could pick it up. The bad news for Hannah is he's still convinced that it's true. And now this man wants to be our senator."

Olivia turned to Hannah. "Oh, miss. Don't worry. I'll hide you."

Three evenings later, Hannah wished Olivia could hide her. With her cloak wrapped around her, her black-feathered bonnet tied in a bow under her chin, her handbag looped over her arm, she stood in the open doorway of her bedroom, facing Slade in his room. His back to her, coldly silent, he shrugged into his chesterfield and reached for his top hat.

His words up in Olivia's room came back to haunt her. *You've made your bed, and now I'm going to let you lie in it.* And he had. He hadn't so much as approached her in the last three days. Hot tears pricked at the backs of her eyes as she silently waited for her husband.

Behind her, she heard Rigby and two stablehands grunting as they hefted her trunks and carried them down to the waiting dray. Hannah swallowed the thick emotion that clogged her throat. She'd be damned before she'd allow Slade to see her cry or hear her beg.

A lancet of nerves shocked her heart's rhythm when Slade turned abruptly to her, eyeing her as if she were no more to him than a chambermaid whose name he couldn't remember. "You're ready, then?"

*Please, Slade, I'm sorry I didn't trust you, that I didn't believe you. Don't send me away.* Hannah's chin came up. "I have been for hours. Days, even."

"I don't doubt it." He held her gaze with his black eyes, the set of his jaw, the thin line of his firmed mouth—all beloved by her, all withdrawn from her now. "Said your good-byes yet?"

"You don't need to remind me of my manners, but yes, I have." She saw again the solemn, tearful faces of the Garrett household staff when she'd told them she was leaving, going to stay at Slade's brownstone. She saw Isabel, that tiny little bird of a woman, chin aquiver, bearing erect and queenly through their parting ordeal.

A muscle twitched in his jaw. "Then there's nothing left to say."

*I love you. I'm sorry I failed you, that I didn't trust you.* "I suppose not." Hannah stared unblinking at him.

He contemplated her for a moment. Something in his sober expression begged her to stop him. To say something. Yet Hannah remained stubbornly, pridefully silent. When he spoke, she felt she was hearing him through a wall.

"You've wanted to be on your own and find your own answers since the day you got here. And I've done nothing but keep you hog-tied—your words—to me, so you couldn't. It's no wonder you don't trust me or believe me. Why should you? All you know—again, *your* words—is what I tell you. So, I want you to think of this . . . move as getting your freedom back, your chance to prove to yourself what the truth is. Without my interference."

"What makes you think you know what's best for me?" Hannah put her fisted hands to her hips. "Slade Garrett, you are eaten up with your own pomposity. I could almost applaud that lovely speech, if it weren't so simpleminded and didn't prove that you really don't know me at all. No one—not even you—keeps me hog-tied anywhere."

She huffed out a hot, angry breath. "If I wanted to leave, if I wanted to search for answers on my own and make my own way, neither you nor anyone else could stop me. I stayed here because I wanted to. Not because you made me. You couldn't, if you tried. But thanks for all your preaching about this being for my own good. Well, let me remind you—you're not my father. I have a father.''

*There. That felt good.* Until she remembered. She'd *had* a father, but no more. She closed her eyes tightly and brought her hands up to cover her mouth. *Oh, Papa, Mama, I've failed you and Jacey and Glory. I've lost sight of my mission here. I've gotten so tangled up in my emotions that I can't see what's right or wrong anymore. I'm so sorry.*

When she opened her eyes, Hannah found that Slade hadn't moved, most likely hadn't even looked away from her. And then, it hit her. She'd lost Mama and Papa, she'd let her sisters down, and now, she was losing him. Beyond despair, beyond hope, she took her last look at her husband. Never before had he stirred her senses as he did now. Never before had he looked this virile, this ruggedly carved and handsome. Or so distant.

The moment stretched out until he made an abrupt gesture for her to precede him to the hallway. Hannah's heart dashed itself against the jagged rocks of his aloofness. But wordlessly she walked through his room, so familiar and yet so foreign-feeling now. She stalked proudly by him, not stopping until she stood in the hallway where she jerked off her glove and worked furiously to get her wedding rings off her finger. They wouldn't budge.

Drawing her glove back on, she made the first independent decision of her new freedom—she'd send for a jeweler and have him come cut the blamed things off. And have them delivered to Mr. Slade Garrett. Wouldn't he be proud? Finished with that bit of drama, she looked up to see Slade slumped against the hallway wall. His head lowered, he twisted his top hat around and around in his hands. Frowning, Hannah bit at her lip, suddenly feeling not the least bit vengeful or triumphant. Had he seen her trying to wrench off his rings?

He looked up, eyeing her from under the sweep of his thick, black lashes. A momentary flash of vulnerability, of raw hurt, exposed his heart. He'd seen her. But then it was gone. In its place was the familiar Slade. The dark and dangerous Slade. His eyes accused her, his stance rejected her, his silence condemned her. *Damn him. Damn her.*

With Lawless pride being the only thing holding her spine rigid, Hannah spoke curtly. "I don't see a need for you to escort me into Boston. I'm sure Rigby can find his way to your brownstone."

"Your brownstone," he amended, pushing away from the wall. "I signed it over to you today."

Her heart flopped, making her blink, but she quickly recovered from the surprise. "That wasn't necessary. I won't be needing it long. Because following Isabel's entertainment, no matter the outcome, I'll be heading back home. I wouldn't even stay until then, but she made me promise."

That got his attention. A self-satisfied smirk edged her mouth, turning up the corners. He narrowed his eyes at her. "You're leaving—just like that? What about your revenge?"

Hannah took the first steps that would see her past him and out of his house. And out of his life. When she drew even with him, she looked up into his chiseled face. "What about yours?"

His black eyes bored into hers. "This *is* mine." He turned on his heel, left her there, and walked down the hall to the expanse of the central stairway.

Hannah's heart thudded. She waited for him to reach the top of the stairs before she called out, "You're just like your father."

He stopped as if he'd hit an invisible wall. For a long moment, he stood with his back to her, unmoving except for his broad shoulders, which he shrugged around in his coat, as if fighting for control. Then he turned around. Even across the distance, she could see, and feel, the feral gleam in his eyes. "And *you* are just like your mother."

A quiver fluttered at the bottom of Hannah's stomach. *Here was the fight she wanted.* Released by Isabel from her promise not to tell Slade about *that night* in their parents' lives, Hannah nearly crowed. Isabel'd told her to use all her guns to keep him. And now she would. "In my case, that's a compliment. In yours? An insult."

He gripped his top hat a mite too tight, Hannah noticed. She prayed for strength in the face of the coming storm that was Slade Garrett. Pacing back to her, he stopped only inches away and seemed to hover over her, like an impatient vulture. "Say that again. I dare you."

Hannah's throat dried up and closed. Her heart plummeted to her feet. But she never looked away. "I said . . . telling me I'm like my mother is a compliment. But telling you that you're like your father is an insult."

She expected him to yell and rage. In fact, she wanted him to do just that, knowing that when he did, he revealed so much more than he realized. But not this time. He spoke in a voice of deadly calm that came from the depths of hell. "What do you know of my father?"

"I know why my mother left Boston. That's what I know of your father."

"Tell me what you think you know."

Hannah shook her head. "I don't just think I know it, Slade. I was told by someone who was there."

"Tell me." His black eyes took on a deadly sheen.

Only short, shallow breaths could get in and out of Hannah's constricted throat. If she spoke up, her words could mean her life. If she said nothing, her silence could cost her the love of her life. What good was life without love? "Your father, in a drunken rage, attacked my mother in her own room, after forcing his way into Cloister Point. Only my grandfather's interference kept her from being raped."

A sudden dusky red claimed Slade's face. A vein pulsed at his temple. His body went rigid and then shivered with some inner struggle. One hoarse word found its way out of the angry slash of his mouth. "Liar."

In pure, instinctive reaction, Hannah reared back and slapped Slade's face. Hard enough to snap his head to the side. Hard enough to hurt her own hand. In gasping reaction to her own deed, she stumbled back two or three steps. Slowly shaking her head, she held her stinging hand to her heart and stared wide-eyed at her husband.

The thunderous clap of her transgression echoed in the hallway. For the longest moment, Slade kept his head turned to the side. Hannah watched her palm print on his cheek turn from white to a rosy pink to a deep red against his smooth skin. Then, tears blurred her vision. Through their distortion, she saw Slade turn his head, saw him stare unblinking at her, saw him open his mouth.

"Keep your gun on you at all times. You're going to need

it.'' With that, he turned and strode to the stairs, taking them slowly, confidently, one at a time.

He'd threatened her and was just going to walk away? Suddenly wanting him to feel a measure of the hurt that tore at her heart, Hannah called after him, ''Ask Isabel. She'll tell you I speak the truth.''

# CHAPTER FIFTEEN

———

"Do you have everything—the letter to my sisters and the note to pass to Mrs. Wells? Good. Now, you be careful. Put your hood up."

"I'll be fine, miss. I've been meeting Mrs. Wells at the market for five days now. And nothing has happened. Besides, Rigby's never far away. He's very good at being sneaky, you know."

Hannah smiled at the way Olivia's face, now a little fuller and pinker, turned red whenever she said that particular young man's name. "I'm sure he is. But I still worry. I know you have to be the one to pass along false information to my uncle, but I don't like it. You're just a child, and anything could happen."

"Child? I'm a mother, miss. And it pleases me to play false with Mrs. Wells. Let her think she's giving right and true notes about your comings and goings to Mr. Wilton-Humes. Let him think he has me where he wants me."

Hannah sighed. "You're right. Now, go on." When Olivia balked, Hannah made a shooing gesture with her hands. "I'll be fine. Aren't there armed men all about this place?"

Olivia smiled and nodded as she started for the door of Hannah's bedroom at the brownstone, but Hannah snapped her fingers at her next thought. "Wait. I nearly forgot."

She rushed over to the mahogany chest of drawers and opened the top drawer. Reaching in, she lifted out a tissue-wrapped package and spun around, going hurriedly back to Olivia. She shoved the package into the girl's hands. "Here.

Mrs. Garrett had Rigby stop yesterday at a little shop, so we could get this for Colette.''

Olivia stared in silence at the gay little package in her hands. When she raised her eyes, unshed tears filled them. ''I've never had a gift for Colette.''

A fierce sympathy tugged at Hannah's heart, but she said nothing as the young mother looked down again, smoothing a hand reverently over the paper, eliciting a soft crinkle from its crisp texture. A tear fell on her hand. She looked up and blinked. ''Thank you, miss. I'm most grateful.''

Hannah smiled and briskly played down her generosity. ''It's nothing. Neither one of us was very anxious to get to Mrs. Ames's. She thinks I'm a saint now that young Mr. Ames and Miss Wannamaker have announced their engagement. We were glad for the delaying stop.'' She then turned the girl toward the door. ''You take that and enjoy your afternoon with Colette and your mother.'' Her smile faded. ''How is your mother, Olivia?''

A gray cloud settled over the girl's face. ''I don't think she'll be with me much longer, miss.''

Hannah's hand went to her heart. ''I'm so sorry. I know what it's like to lose your mother.'' She then put her hand on the girl's sleeve. ''Perhaps I can come help you?''

Olivia shook her head, dislodging her hood. ''Oh, no, miss. That'd only make Mr. Wilton-Humes more suspicious than he already is about your being here and not at Woodbridge Pond. Besides, it's enough what Mr. Garrett's done for me and Mum.''

The name hung in the air between them. Hannah withdrew her hand to knot it with her other one. ''Mr. Garrett? What's he done?''

''He didn't tell you? Oh, I'm sorry, miss. I forgot.''

Her heart stinging, Hannah raised her head a notch. She hadn't seen or talked to Slade in five days. ''It's all right. It's not your fault. What did he do?''

An eagerness to tell replaced her hesitancy. ''For me pretending to be spying on you, he moved in the nicest couple upstairs from Mum—name of Hill—to look after her and Colette. And he's paying for everything. What's more, he put in two men across the hall to keep an eye out. So, everything looks normal, what with me working my regular hours.'' Olivia then sobered, speaking as if in defense of the man. "Mr. Garrett's a good man, miss."

Looking into Olivia's brown eyes, Hannah accepted the censure of the girl's last words. "Yes, he is. You'd better go now."

"Yes, miss." Olivia pulled her hood back up over her braids, tucked the gift into her pocket, and turned to leave the room. But she immediately spun back to Hannah and grabbed her in a fierce hug. "Thank you for the present. I love you," she whispered and then turned and ran out of the room.

Hannah stood where she was, fingernails digging into her palms. She bit at the inside of her cheek until she no longer felt like crying. One drop of excess emotion and she would crack, crumble, and collapse. Taking deep breath after deep breath, she finally squared her shoulders. She had to get out of this house. She was suffocating.

Perhaps a trip across the street to the Public Garden was what she needed. The flowers weren't in bloom and the trees were bare. But it didn't matter. The garden was outside, and that was all that mattered. Besides, no less than four of Slade's men would follow her. What could go wrong? Hannah set off for the hallway, realizing she'd better tell Hammonds. No sense having the disapproving butler sound an alarm at her absence.

Now there was an odd one, that Hammonds. He had the strange habit of staring at portraits when he was talking to her. On the first floor now, she went in search of the little man who'd reduced her, more than once, to staring at the same portrait he did when she spoke with him. Hannah walked into the parlor. No Hammonds. But feeling the tug of the outdoors, she went to the window and pulled the lace sheer aside. And smiled.

"There it is," she said softly, but still aloud, "the outdoors. Oops. There he is, too, across the street. Jones—my square, silent guard. What's he posing as today? Looks like . . . hmmm—a lazy man sitting on a park bench staring at this house. That's original. Wonder how he likes city life over Woodbridge Pond?"

"Did you say something, Mrs. Garrett?"

Crying out, Hannah spun around, nearly bringing the lace sheer with her. Hammonds was in the doorway, staring at the portrait on the far wall. Hannah put a hand to her thumping heart. "Yes. I mean, no. Um, Hammonds, I was looking for you."

He cut his gaze over to her. "You thought I was outside, madam?"

A scorching heat flamed up her cheeks. "No, of course not. I'll be going out and will need my cloak."

"Outside, madam?"

*Was that all he could say?* "Yes, Hammonds. Outside. Surely you know it—all the world that isn't inside?"

Nose in the air, arms stiffly at his sides, he addressed the portrait. "I'm not sure that Mr. Garrett will approve."

"Well, then, we just won't tell him, will we? My cloak, please."

"Yes, madam." He bowed to the portrait and left the room.

Hannah turned back to the window, again pulling the sheer aside. In a wistful mood, she watched the passing pageant of people going about their lives. Would hers ever be normal again? Facing away from the scene, she hugged her arms to herself. Her mouth frowned in self-pity. Married, alone, in a strange city, Mama and Papa dead, Glory and Jacey and Biddy so far away, her life in danger. And all she wanted was a walk in the fresh air. Funny, how life came down to moments.

Hammonds came back into the room with her lined and hooded cloak draped over his arm. "I've alerted the . . . gentlemen as to your intentions, madam. They're most concerned."

Gentlemen, indeed. Her keepers, he meant. Hannah put her fisted hands to her hips. "Are they? Well, they're also about to be most cold."

"Yes, madam."

Hannah held out her hand for her cloak. It remained empty because Hammonds kept his eyes on that dead person in the portrait. Sighing, she stomped over to the rigid man. Tugging her wrap away from him, she flung it around her shoulders as he bowed and left the room. Waiting a moment until she no longer heard his footsteps, Hannah bolted across the parlor. Maybe she could get out before her keepers had time to be ready.

A smile already forming at that thought, she rounded the corner. And stopped suddenly. And sighed. There stood Hammonds, his hand on the front door's heavy knob. And with him stood three tall, beefy, serious men, all coated and hatted. They stared wordlessly at her. Bottom lip poked out, Hannah silently walked through their parting ranks. Hammonds opened the door, bowing her out. She deigned to nod her head at him. Then, over her shoulder, she said, "Last one out is a damned Yankee."

She stepped onto the stoop and lifted her nose to the air. Glorious, cold, and fresh. And skipped down the ten or so steps of the front stoop to the sidewalk below. Turning around, she smiled at the straight-faced damned Yankees who ambled with brute confidence down the steps after her, their hands in their coat pockets. No doubt those pockets held guns. Well, so did hers.

Hannah turned back to the street, waiting at the curb for a lull in the traffic, so she could cross. Sensing she wasn't alone, she looked up and around her. One on her left. One on her right. One at her back. Like huge elms around a sapling. Just then, the men on her left and right boldly stepped into the street, stopping the carriages and wagons with no more than a raised hand.

Hannah's eyes widened at that sight, but not so much as they did when the man behind her stepped to her right, took her elbow, and escorted her safely across the street to the park. Slightly intimidated, she kept her gaze on his craggy, impassive face all the way over. And pronounced herself glad these men were on her side.

When the man let go of her and stepped back, Hannah blinked at him and his two cronies who flowed into the crowd around her, no more detectable than one blade of grass from another. Public Garden stretched before her. Here was freedom. She smiled at the trees, at the benches, at the Bostonians, at the dogs, at the horses, at the children. Her smile faded. She tugged at her bottom lip with her teeth and eyed a group of running, playing children.

Suddenly she straightened up, clamping her hands over her mouth one half-second ahead of a loud cry. She watched the children, heard their happy shrieks of laughter. A baby. What would Slade do if she told him . . . ?

\*   \*   \*

Patience Wilton-Humes gasped and sat forward in the carriage. Without looking away from the figure in Public Garden, she reached behind her, roughly grasping at Cyrus's sleeve. "Cyrus, look there! I believe it's Hannah. Way over there. See her? By those children. And she's alone."

She scooted over, giving her place to Cyrus. Perching on the edge of the narrow leather seat, he looked this way and that and then turned to his wife. "Are you sure? Because she wouldn't be alone. She has those damned men surrounding her everywhere she goes."

*Damned fool couldn't see his hand in front of his face.* "Of course I'm sure. Those idiot men are probably lurking close by. Now, move out of my way." She yanked at Cyrus's coat, roughly dislodging him. "Tell Hankins to pull over. I don't want to lose her. Mrs. Wells can just wait for us a bit longer. That stupid Olivia's probably not on time, anyway."

She grabbed his coat again, this time pulling him toward her. "Cyrus, this could be the chance we've been waiting for. A nice, public accident. Runaway horses and all. Just the thing. Now, hurry it up—get Hankins to stop."

When she pushed him back again, Cyrus scrambled to tap at the small trapdoor set in the roof. It opened immediately. He told their driver to pull over. Patience leaned forward to peer out the window. A squawk of glee escaped her when she spied her great-niece strolling through the bare gardens. Patience sat back, a smug smile lighting her face. The meddlesome chit would pay dearly for her accusations.

The carriage slowly worked its way out of traffic and stopped alongside the park. Patience folded her hands in her lap and glanced up to be sure the trapdoor was now closed. She then cocked her head at the expression on her husband's face. "Are you scared, Cyrus?"

Cyrus's Adam's apple bobbed up and down as he shook his head no. "It's not that. We just need to consider those men with her. Should we try to run Hannah over, they're bound to recognize our carriage."

Patience stared. *The man was pathetic.* She huffed out her breath, closed her eyes, and pinched the bridge of her nose with her gloved index finger and thumb. Opening her eyes again, she exhibited the quality of her name by patiently explaining, "Cyrus, Cyrus, Cyrus. *We* won't run over her. *We* will hire some ruffian to do it for us and tell him that if Hannah's guards interfere, they're to die right along with her.''

"They are? What about our man?"

"Jones?" Patience waved her hand in dismissal. "He'll have a care for his own skin. But if he's so unfortunate as to be in the way? Well, it would be just as well if he did meet his end with Hannah. Prices himself and his information very highly, he does.''

She picked at a loose thread on her sleeve. "If that damned Olivia weren't relaying false information to us, we'd have no need of Jones's services. But, oh-ho, that one—she'll pay dearly for her betrayal." Patience then dug through her handbag, coming up with three coins. "Here. This ought to be enough. These low-class beggars hold life cheaply enough."

Cyrus took the coins, greedily pocketing them. His face eager now, he whispered, "Let's have Hankins hire someone. That way no one can point a finger at us. He's the one I had tamper with Hamilton's carriage the day of their accident. If he'd do that for us, he'll do this, too."

Patience gave her husband a look that bordered on motherly pride. "Cyrus Wilton-Humes, just when I think you're a hopeless idiot, you come up with something brilliant." Then she put her finger to her chin in a thoughtful attitude. "Of course, we'll have to rid ourselves of Hankins afterward. The man knows far too much."

"Rid ourselves of Hankins? We can't do that, my dear."

Patience's beaky face hardened. She sighed out her irritation. "What now? An attack of morals, my husband?"

"Not at all, my wife. If we do away with Hankins, then we'd have to hire a new driver. Hankins may know too much, but he does keep his mouth shut. A new man might not."

Patience raised an eyebrow in admiration of Cyrus's devious intuition. "Sometimes you surprise me, Cyrus."

He met her look for look. "Yes. Don't I?" With that, he reached up and tapped again on the trapdoor. When it opened and Hankins's pocked and pointed face appeared in the small opening, Cyrus held the three coins up to him. "Hankins, I want you to take this money and pay some ruffian . . .''

Ensconced in Isabel's ancient carriage, Slade cursed. No one escaped his tirade. Not the slow-moving traffic around Public

Garden for boxing him in. Not Isabel and her entire staff of ancient domestics for their reproachful looks. Not Esmerelda for chewing up his boot—and his glove. Not Dudley for being respectable. Not Hannah for being . . . Hannah. And most of all, not himself for being on his way to his . . . her brownstone.

Now, what was it he'd come up with? Oh, yes, important papers. Damned important business papers. Locked in the desk. Well, it was enough to get him in the door. He looked out the carriage window at the smiling, strolling citizens and hordes of laughing children, imagining he could see his destination. He'd get there quicker by walking. He could cut across the pathways in a direct line, instead of being subjected to all this roundabout.

Walk. Yes. He reached up and tapped on the trapdoor. A moment later it opened and in peered Sedgewick, Isabel's balding, nodding, decrepit driver, pressed into service what with Rigby trailing Olivia. "Yes, Mr. Garrett?"

"Pull over, Sedgewick. I'm going to walk."

"Walk, sir?"

"Yes. One foot in front of the other. After you let me off, continue on to my . . . um, Mrs. Garrett's brownstone and wait for me there."

"Yes, sir." The trapdoor closed and the carriage moved painfully, slowly over to the curb nearest the green expanse of the lawns.

The second Sedgewick reined the bays to a stop, and being too impatient to wait for the old man to take ten minutes dismounting the driver's box and another ten minutes to shuffle around to the side to fumble with the latch, Slade opened the door himself and neatly hopped out.

He tapped on the carriage to get the stiffly rising old man's attention. "No need, Sedgewick. Stay where you are. No, over here, old boy. Yes. I know I'm already out. Go on, then. Have a cup of tea with Hammonds. And while you're at it, ask him why he talks to my ancestor's portrait instead of me, will you?"

The doddering little man nodded. Or maybe that was just his normal tremor. At any rate, he agreed. "Yes, sir." And took his seat again, handled the reins, and jiggled them over the well-behaved horses' backs.

His heart in his throat, Slade watched the carriage pull into the traffic. Good thing there were drivers more alert than Sedgewick who could rein and draw aside at the man's incautious, unyielding maneuvers as he . . . merged with the flow. Wincing in relief that there was no accident, Slade turned and set off, with a jaunty, long-legged stride, down the tree-lined, shrubbery-edged pathway.

Tipping his hat to the giggling, simpering ladies he passed, stopping for or dodging around playful children, and nodding his greeting to the men he knew, Slade suddenly wondered why he didn't walk more. The air was briskly cool and smelled of coming cold, but the wind was mercifully light. The sun's warmth felt good on his face. The exercise was invigorating. His fellow Bostonians were in good cheer. And Hannah was alone and coming toward him.

Slade stopped cold, his smile of well-being fading into a grim line. Hannah was alone and coming toward him? *What the devil!* Bolting off to one side of the crowded pathway, he put his hands to his waist. No, she wasn't just coming toward him. She was ambling along, not a care in the world, smiling as she watched a group of toddlers being tended by their nurses. She hadn't seen him yet. But in a few more steps she'd hear his heart pounding for her.

Jerking at that thought, Slade cut his gaze to points all around her slender, cloaked self. And relaxed. Temple, Hardy, and Cates were no more than ten steps from her, but may as well have been a continent away for all the apparent attention they paid her. Jones probably still lounged somewhere close to the brownstone to keep an eye out for skulkers. Slade smiled at his men's well-paid devotion and then frowned, telling himself his dour expression was for Hannah's selfish endangerment of her guards. No doubt she'd poked that lip out— and her gun, to get her way. Otherwise, these men knew better and had other orders.

Well, he'd take Miss to task right now over that very point. Because here she came. Excited by this legitimate reason to confront her, he also decided to teach her a lesson. So, staying to the side of the path, he caught his men's alert gazes. A nod from him toward the unsuspecting Hannah was sufficient.

Anticipating her surprised response when he reached out to grab her, a rare stomach-rippling giddiness seized Slade. When he realized he was grinning like a jackass and his pulse was wildly erratic, the closer she came, he insisted to himself that his symptoms had to do with the impending upbraiding he was going to give his errant wife.

Slade stepped onto the pathway and grabbed Hannah's arm. He yanked his wide-eyed, gasping wife around and pulled her into a leafy bower just off the walkway. Immediately, the three guards formed a loose, lounging semicircle in front of their boss and his lady, forestalling the notice of even the closest passerby to the woman-napping that had just occurred.

"Slade Franklin Garrett," the boss's lady cussed through gritted teeth, smacking him soundly on his arm with her fisted hand. "You scared me out of ten years' growth. What are you doing lurking about in the bushes?"

Every fiber of his being screamed at him to cover her in kisses, to never, ever again let her sweet little body get more than a foot from him. However, he remained aloof and dignified. Except for the belligerent set to his frowning mouth. "I don't lurk, madam."

Hannah wrenched her arm free of his grasp and set about straightening her cloak and hood. "Call it what you want—you were lurking. What're you doing here?"

"That is my question to you. What are you doing here—outside, in a public park, leaving yourself open to intrigue?"

Watching her pucker up her winsome face into a petulant frown, Slade called himself a besotted fool. He locked his knees before he could slip to a kneel, wrap his arms around her waist, and beg her forgiveness. In broad daylight, in Public Garden.

"What am I doing out here?" Jerking her thumb back over her shoulder, indicating the three men behind her, she sassed, "I'm airing out the Yankees."

"The—? You're what?" Slade bit the inside of his cheek until his eyes watered. Under no circumstances would he laugh at her antics.

"Walking the dogs. The boys were getting quarrelsome inside. Rex snatched King's toy, and the fight was on. Then that stinker Prince, the biggest one, piddled on the carpet." She sighed a long-suffering sound. "It was this or take the newspaper to 'em."

Slade raised his eyebrows at her words and then his gaze to the three silent, competent, seasoned men behind her. And broke his own vow. He burst out laughing. Just threw his head back, hands to his waist, and howled out his high emotion. *God, how he loved this woman.*

That unguarded revelation broke Slade's hilarity off in mid-guffaw. He jerked upright, quickly sobering. He sought Hannah's face, saw her sun-sparkled blue-green eyes and lopsided grin. And knew it was true. God, how he loved this woman. And he just didn't have the heart to be grim and forbidding with her right this moment.

So, he shook his head and wiped at his eyes, seeing now the curious, bemused stares of passing Bostonians. As well as the over-the-shoulder, concerned looks cast his way from Rex, King, and—no. Temple, Cates, and Hardy. Another rumbling jolt of laughter shook Slade. Would he ever be able to look at these men again without laughing?

He lowered his gaze to a very smug Hannah. Shaking his head at this irreverent, curly-haired, gun-toting wife of his, he wondered how he'd survived the last five days without her. And admitted that he hadn't—he'd simply existed. And in such a bearish mood that he was no longer welcome at Woodbridge Pond. Well, no more would he be without her.

Taking her arm, he turned her and set them back on the path, striding briskly along and feigning unconcern for her squawks of protest and her hurrying feet. He didn't have to look to know that her trio of guards were on their heels.

"What are you doing?"

He spared a glance down at his wife. "I'm taking you home."

"To Woodbridge Pond?"

"No." His heart flip-flopped at the hopeful note in her voice. "Back to your brownstone, madam."

"Oh." She sniffed, turned petulant. "I don't want to go. I like it out here."

"You're sounding very childish, my sweet."

"I'm not your sweet."

Slade glanced down at her, at her poked-out bottom lip. His own lips twitched in amusement. "Yes you are."

"Like hell I am."

Slade stopped so suddenly, the three guards were forced to keep on walking past them a pace or two before they could adjust. Slade narrowed his eyes at Hannah's mutinous expression. "I'll thank you not to hurl obscenities in public."

*Oh, no.* He knew he was done for before she ever opened her mouth. Why hadn't he listened to Isabel years ago and married some well-behaved, timid little Brahmin girl? No, he had to join his life with the most belligerent, outspoken, independent Westerner this side of the Mississippi.

Whose leering grin right now belonged on the face of one of Satan's minions. "Take your hand off me, Garrett. Or I'll change the weather with my language. And you know I can do it."

Thus dared, Slade gripped her other arm and turned her to face him. He then pointedly looked around him, enjoining her to do the same, forcing her to realize her stranger-crowded surroundings. Then he leaned over her, almost touching the tip of her nose with the tip of his. "Go ahead. I dare you."

Her blue-green eyes blinked. And crossed. He was too close, he knew, for her to properly focus, much less to drag in the air she'd need to bellow. Nevertheless, she surprised him by opening her mouth and flaring her nostrils, all preparatory to an outburst. Jumping into the breach, Slade promised, "If you do, I'll kiss you so soundly that you'll faint right here."

She stiffened, closing her mouth and whuffing her air out her nose.

Slade straightened up and let go of her. "That's more like it."

"Go to hell, Slade Garrett."

He smiled his triumph. She'd no more than whispered it. "Want me to save you a brimstone? I have a feeling I'll see you there, hellcat."

In less than a moment's time, Hannah's expression crumpled. She stared silently up at him with those big, beautiful eyes of hers as fat tears began to stream down her cheeks. People passing by looked their way and stopped, murmured, and commented to companions about this silently crying woman—in public. Desperately, Slade sought out his men's eyes. They backed off immediately. Intrigue and death were one thing. A woman's tears were another.

A sneaking suspicion assailed Slade. Was she really crying? His face contorting to one of cautious doubt, he leaned down just enough to be at her eye level. Her face was red. Her nose was running. Her shoulders heaved with her effort. She was really crying. Aware of the gathering crowd and their murmurs asking what was wrong, Slade thought it best if he hurried her away. Turning to the people massed around them, he smiled and assured, "Nothing's wrong. She's a new bride. Nerves, you know."

With sympathetic understanding, the people smiled and nudged each other, patted at the shoulder of a wife, turned to pass the word through the crowd. Relieved, Slade put his arm around Hannah's shoulder.

She elbowed him in the gut, doubling him over. Then, edging her way through the gasping crowd, she took off in a run down the pathway. All talking at once, the highly entertained crowd, which had parted for Hannah, now closed in gaping curiosity around Slade. And Hannah's guards.

The three Yankees shouldered their way to Slade, who was just then trying to twist his way to an erect posture. Blinking, gasping, he pointed after his wife. "Hannah. Go . . . after Hannah."

Like three hunting dogs catching the scent, the men jerked their heads in her direction. And melted back through the crowd. Some kindly person in the gathering took Slade by the arm, holding him up. Slade managed to nod thankfully at his Good Samaritan, a nattily dressed older man with graying mutton-chop whiskers and a stout woman on his right.

"That's quite a right hook your bride's nerves have there, son."

Able to breathe and talk at the same time now, Slade nodded. "You ought to see her nerves with a Smith and Wesson in her hand."

Amid much male laughter and female tsk-tsking, Slade elbowed his way free and took off, in a sideways, lurching gait. He found running easier if he pressed a hand against his contracted stomach muscles. Sighting on the damned Yankees, as Hannah called them, since she was too far ahead for him to see her, Slade limped along. No one challenged him for space on the path, having been cleared to the side by the spectacle of the four running figures who'd preceded him.

Rounding a curve, closer now to the street that edged the park, Slade caught sight of Hannah's billowing cloak. Her hood hung down her back. *What in the hell had he said to make her cry?* Cursing, he knew that in only a moment, she'd be across the street and in the house. His entire fortune said she'd lock it against him. Slade decided he couldn't let that happen.

His stitch gone, he straightened up, smoothing out his pace and picking up his speed. In the next moment, he saw her run through the opening in the wrought-iron fence that marked the park's boundaries. Right there, she jerked up short, whipping around as if someone had grabbed her cloak. Slade's heart skipped a beat. Then he saw her desperately tugging on her heavy garment. A grin spread over his lips. A spike on the fence held her firmly in place.

She'd better hope she got free before he got there, because if he had any strength left, he was going to turn her over his knee. Nearing her now, able to see her contorted, reddened face, and feeling Fate was holding her for him, Slade slowed down. He caught sight of the three winded Yankees doing the same thing.

*Damned woman could run like a greyhound.* Slade no more than thought it before his ears were assaulted by a clanging, clattering commotion out in the street. Looking to his left, he jerked to a stop, breathing hard, hands to his waist.

"Hallo! Beware! Runaway team! Runaway team! Save yourselves!" A whip lashed. Screams rent the air. Jangling livery mingled with the guttural snorting and stamping gallop of horses out of control. A huge, weathered-wood carryall careened crazily back and forth in the street. And the driver looked straight at Hannah as he whipped his animals into a frenzy.

For Slade, time slowed to a molasses trickle. *He means to kill Hannah.* Slade turned his head to her, saw her look directly into his eyes, open her mouth to a surprised O, and then give a fierce tug on her captured cloak. Slade put his hand out, began running, his heart and blood pounding out of proportion with his efforts, and cried, "Hannah, get back. Hannah!"

Hannah's cloak came free. Her momentum staggered her back into the street, her arms flailing, her eyes wide. Slade thought he heard her cry out his name. One of her damned Yankees made a plunging leap for her. And they both disappeared under the wheels of the wagon. Sickening thumps and screams split the air. Gasps and groans went up from the crowd. Some froze. Some covered their faces with their hands. Still others stood transfixed, jaws slackened, as the team hurtled down the street and around a bend.

"Hannah!" Slade screamed from the bottom of his heart. And all went black.

# CHAPTER SIXTEEN

—

"It happened so fast. There was nothing we could do."

"Poor thing. To be trampled like that."

"Never had a chance. Just fell right under their hooves."

Slade heard the voices, understood the words, but not their significance to him. He opened his eyes, blinked at the bright sun overhead, at the wavering, distorted faces bent over him, and his head lolled to the side. He swallowed and closed his eyes. *World spinning. Can't... remember. Got to get... Hannah.*

"Here now, make room. Mr. Garrett's coming around."

That was Hammonds's voice. Slade opened his eyes. He was lying on the ground, surrounded by a crowd of strangers. When hands reached under his shoulders to sit him up, Slade looked up to see Jones behind him. *What was going on? What had happened?* Other hands brushed him off, patted him consolingly. He turned his head, surprised that he could control it, and saw Mrs. Stanley on her knees beside him. Tears streamed down her face. *Why?*

"Get me up, Jones." *Was that his voice?* It must have been, because Jones again put his hands under Slade's shoulders, pulling him up to a wobbly stand. Slade leaned against the man until he could gain his equilibrium. Just as suddenly, he remembered it all. *The horses. Hannah. The screaming.* He turned to Jones. "Take me to Hannah."

As Jones nodded and put a steadying hand on Slade's arm, Mrs. Stanley broke into a fresh round of tears and mumbled about the poor, young missus and so much blood. Hammonds shushed her with a sharp noise and then stepped in front of the two men. "This way, sir. We carried her bod—her into the house. Follow me. I'll move these street types out of the way." With that, he went ahead, yelling and clearing a path.

Slade stared after the man. *Her body? Is that what he almost said?* With his mind shying away from that harsh truth, Slade simply followed in his butler's wake. Slade had Jones stop when they reached the street. Feeling stronger now, he pulled away from the silent guard, who immediately stepped back, his hands crossed in front of him. Slade looked down, and took in a deep breath through his pinched nostrils. He went down on one knee and bent over the man lying bloodied and broken in the street.

Cates. It was Cates. Slade put his hand on the man's chest and closed his eyes for a moment. The man died trying to protect Hannah. Opening his eyes, Slade turned to Jones, who hadn't moved, whose face was pale but immobile. "Get him out of the street."

Slade stood up as Jones and Temple stepped forward to do his bidding. Numb to the core, Slade watched them. If Cates—a big man—looked like this, what must Hannah look like? Right then, Slade knew his worst terror. He looked up at the brownstone landing, saw Mrs. Stanley already there, her sons Jacko and Edgar hanging on to her skirts.

He couldn't go in there. He couldn't face what he'd see. To see Hannah torn and broken, like a lifeless baby bird, would make him lose his mind. He'd lost family—both parents and his grandfather Herbert, and it had been awful. But this was Hannah, the only woman he would ever love. And he'd never told her.

Someone put a hand on Slade's shoulder. He looked down. It was Hammonds, looking fierce and protective. "Come on, sir. Let's get you inside."

Slade stared at the man, but didn't move. "I can't."

Hammonds pressed his lips together and gripped Slade around the waist. "Of course you can, sir. You must. For Hannah."

"For Hannah," Slade repeated. He put one foot in front of the other and before he knew it, Mrs. Stanley and her boys were moving out of his way and he was inside. He looked around. "Where is she?"

Mrs. Stanley closed the front door behind him and Hammonds, who still held on to his employer. Her lips quivering, she pointed to her right. "We put her in the parlor, sir. On the sofa."

Slade stared at Mrs. Stanley and then pulled away from Hammonds. "I want to be alone with her."

Mrs. Stanley and Hammonds nodded silently and turned away, shooing her boys ahead of them. In the silence following their departure, Slade heard the outside noises through the closed door. He heard the hallway clock marking time, time in a world without Hannah. Stiffening against the shudder that ripped through him, he turned woodenly toward the parlor and peered into it. Filtered light from the curtained windows shadowed the room's interior.

But not enough that he couldn't see the figure on the sofa. Hannah. So still. Like a painting. Her outflung arm hung limply off the cushions. Her head lolled against her shoulder. He took a deep breath and walked over to sit in a chair someone had already pulled up to her. He sat down and looked her over. Cuts, scrapes, bruises. Smeared and spattered blood on her face and hands and clothes. *Enough!*

Leaning forward, he gathered her to him as best he could and rested his forehead against her soft hair. She was still so warm. The dam broke and took Slade with it. Washed away into a dry valley of anguish, agonizing shudders shook him, an intense sickness and desolation pounded at his soul. He called her name, rocked her, held her, begged her not to leave him. Finally, he whispered, "I love you, Hannah."

"I love you, too, Slade."

Slade jerked upright, wiped at his eyes, and stared down at her. Her eyes were still closed. And she hadn't moved that he could tell. Was it then some cruel twist of his mind? Testing his mental faculties, he repeated, "I love you, Hannah."

Her eyelids fluttered, finally opening. Blue-green eyes, the color of his world, stared at him. "I love you, too."

"Mother of God!" Slade abruptly released her and jerked back, stumbling and overturning his chair as he tried to stand up. He ended up sitting on the floor, a tangled mishmash of limbs and chair and flowered upholstery. For several seconds he stared at her and blurted out, "I thought you were dead. Son of a bitch! You scared the hell out of me, Hannah."

Hannah frowned, blinked, and confirmed, "I'm not dead."

Slade stared at her for a moment. *She's not dead.* His heart soaring, the sun coming out again to warm his soul, he thought that maybe once he extricated himself from this chair, he just might kill her for scaring him like this. "But everyone acted as if you were. I didn't know what to think."

Hannah smiled and then grimaced with the effort of pulling herself up onto her elbow. "Yes you did. You thought that you loved me."

If that was her only concern, she couldn't be too seriously injured. Everything in Slade softened, warmed. He wanted to throw his head back and laugh and take her in his arms to swing her around and never let her go. But being the man that he was, he sat in his tangle, frowned at her, and sparred with her. "I said no such thing. You were hearing things."

She smiled and shook her head. "Admit it. You said it twice."

Slade smiled back. Had it meant his entire fortune was forfeit, he couldn't have looked away from her knowing eyes. The little dickens now had the upper hand. And she knew it.

Frozen in place in a ridiculous tableau, one leg wedged under the chair's arm and resting on the seat cushion, his other one pinned under the chair's weight, Slade drank in her bruised and bloodied but so thankfully alive self—and realized he was an inch away from blubbering like a baby. Determined he'd die before he'd do that again, he forced himself to grin. "I never said it."

"Slade, please put me down. I can walk. I don't want to greet our guests like this. I'm in my bedclothes. Just because you gave Olivia another afternoon off doesn't mean I can't dress myself. Now, put me down."

"Not on your life. And have you go headlong down these narrow stairs, kill yourself, and ruin Isabel's party? I think not. I'd never hear the end of it."

Having made her token protest, Hannah relaxed happily in her husband's arms. She stared up at his noble profile, at the shell of his ear—no less masculine than the rest of him. At the curl of his night-black hair over his collar. At his shadowed jaw. And pulled herself up to kiss his neck.

Clutching at her spasmodically, Slade made a guttural noise that seemed to stumble his feet. Turning his shoulder to the wall just in time to stave off a horrendous accident, he leaned against its bulk, bracing his feet against two successive stairs. He turned an indignant expression on his wife. "Are you trying to kill us?"

Hannah grinned wickedly. "You didn't like that?" Then she shrugged. "Fine. I won't do it again."

His black eyes gleamed. "It's only been two days since your injuries. And I've been without you for a week. Don't toy with me, Hannah."

Looking her husband square in the eye, she slowly tipped her tongue over her lips, moistening them. "Why? What will happen if I do?"

"Goddammit." In the blink of an eye, he had her on her slippered feet and thoroughly kissed. But held gingerly against him, in deference to her bruises and scrapes.

Hannah would have none of his hesitance. She pressed herself to him—from her lips to her breasts, from her hips to her toes. She reveled in the hard, muscled feel of him. Taking his cues from her, he wrapped his arms around her back, his hands fisted in her loose wrapper. His mouth sought and resought hers, hungrily claiming it. Aching for him with a hurt bordering on the emotional, Hannah ran her fingers through his hair, pulling his head down to hers.

"Ahem."

She didn't care if she never drew another breath again. Just let her faint away locked in Slade's passionate, groping embrace. His hand went to her breast, cupping it—

"I say, two Garretts. A-hem. Knock, knock."

A loud knocking on the wall pierced Hannah's glazed attention—apparently at the same moment it did Slade's. She broke off when he did, stared up in shock at him, and then, still held in his embrace, spun to look down the stairwell to the first floor. At a smirking Dudley Ames. At a wide-eyed young miss with cornflower-blue eyes and blond hair. And at an openmouthed Hammonds.

"See, darling?" Dudley cooed to the satin-draped girl held so close by his side. "I told you Mrs. Garrett was well enough to . . . receive callers."

A frisson of embarrassment separated Hannah from Slade, saw her hastily arranging her invalid's gown, and setting her hair to rights. For his part, Slade immediately turned his back on the assemblage and took several deep, blood-redistributing breaths. Knowing his problem wouldn't . . . subside for a moment or two, Hannah drew attention away from him by descending the stairs alone in slow, aching steps.

Dudley quickly met her on the steps and took her outstretched hand, assisting her down to the foyer. Pretending the heat on her cheeks couldn't possibly match Dudley's hair for redness, she greeted him formally. "Mr. Ames, so nice to see you again."

All matured and polished gentleman now, neatly groomed and dressed in subdued shades of gray and black, Dudley bowed over her hand. "The privilege is mine, madam. May I say how sorry I am for your accident, and how happy I am to see you up and around?" Straightening up, he presented the young lady. "Allow me to present my fiancée, Miss Constance Holmes Wannamaker."

Hannah turned to take the girl's tiny hand. And gasped at the lovely confection she was. Hannah knew only one other girl who was this wondrously petite and china-doll beautiful— her own sister, Glory. So this was Constance. And she loved Dudley. How wonderful. With so much to recommend her, she received a warm greeting from her hostess. "Oh, Miss Wannamaker, you are beautiful. And may I congratulate you on your engagement? I just couldn't be happier for you both."

Without warning, Slade tromped down the stairs, brushed by them all, grousing his way into the parlor. "I could be happier, if I had a drink. Hammonds, see to it, will you?" Hammonds bowed himself out of the foyer. Slade then smacked Dudley's thick, broad shoulder when he passed him. "Good timing, Ames. Thanks."

His new pose dropping, Dudley turned to follow Slade into the parlor. "For what? What'd I do? We were in the parlor and heard the awfulest thump. Thinking the worst, we came at a worried run to see what was the matter. How were we to know you were . . . you know, right there on the stairs?"

Hannah's hand froze in Constance's. Her eyes teared as her face heated up to a blazing furnace. What must this girl think? Constance giggled, putting her other hand to her pink lips. The diamond on her ring finger was the size of a plum. Hannah's eyes widened, but she fell in love with Constance when the girl spoke, earning for her blond self a lifelong friend.

"That's our dear Slade. But, all things considered, I think our visit had best be a short one, don't you, Hannah? Oh, dear—may I call you Hannah?"

Hannah bent forward enough to grab Constance to her in a fierce hug. "You may call me Hannah, if I may call you Constance."

"Oh, I insist. We're going to be such great friends. I have you to thank for so much."

Pulling back and taking Constance's hands in hers, Hannah smiled broadly. "No you don't. Dudley came to his conclusions all on his own."

Constance freed a hand to wave it at Hannah. "Oh, pooh!" She then lowered her voice to a whisper. "Don't let his mother hear you say that. She swears by you and would defend you to the death. As will I. I'd have died an old maid for want of Dudley's declaring himself, had you not straightened him out."

Hannah grinned hugely and leaned over to whisper in Constance's ear, "Now if only someone could straighten out Slade."

"Oh, la. From what Dudley tells me, you're more than equal to the task."

Their feminine heads together and their whispering laughter brought Slade to their sides. "Here now." He stepped between them, taking both Hannah and Constance by an elbow and towing them—slowly, for Hannah's aching sake—into the parlor. "There'll be none of that. Poor, besotted Dudley and I can't be winning in this female tête-à-tête."

From the parlor came Dudley's plaintive voice. "Besotted? Why am I the only one who's besotted?"

"Oh, shut up, Ames." Slade smiled down at Hannah and Constance.

A wealth of happiness for Slade's love welled up in Hannah as her tall and handsome husband handed Constance over to Dudley. Slade then made a great show of ensconcing her on the sofa, amid a pile of thick pillows, fluffing them around her, and pulling up a footstool to put under her slippered feet.

Breaking the heavy silence that bore witness to his loving ministrations was Dudley's voice. "Tell me again who's besotted, Garrett."

Continuing his fussing with Hannah's comfort, Slade turned

his head to look over his shoulder and spoke out the side of his mouth. "Shut up, Ames."

They all four shared a laugh born of young love and then hoorahed Hammonds into the room with his tray laden with tea and cakes. No liquor. Slade eyed the tray and then Hannah, winking at her. Stepping back out of the butler's way, he seated himself next to her, stretching his arm across the sofa's back. His long fingers trailed onto her shoulder, which he rubbed lightly. Hannah's heart basked in this moment of perfect contentment.

Hammonds set his burden on the low table between the two pleasantly silent couples and arranged the silver and china to his perfecting standards. He then straightened up and turned to his employer, looking him in the eye. "It's much too early for anything stronger, sir. Perhaps later." He then bowed and turned away, walking stiffly, starchily across the room.

Dudley risked serious neck injury by whipping around in his chair to watch Hammonds's retreating back. Slade grinned at Hannah, and they both grinned at the bemused, questioning look on Constance's face. The senator's heir apparent whipped back around, jerking his thumb over his shoulder and staring at Slade, openmouthed. "When—? What—?"

Slade made a who-knows gesture. "Two days ago. The day of Hannah's incident."

And that became the topic. Constance poured and served, in deference to Hannah's remaining stiffness. They all talked at once, stepping verbally over each other, trading conversational partners depending on who was looking at whom at the moment, and shared opinions and fears, until they had all the major points dissected and were down to particular details.

"Oh, Hannah, you could have been killed."

Hannah felt Slade tense next to her as she answered Constance. "And I would have been, had not . . . Cates—" She stopped and looked down at her tea cup. Slade squeezed her shoulder reassuringly. She sniffed and raised her head, going on. "Pushed me out of the way. He went under the wagon's wheels, but I fell backward onto the front steps and then toppled into the flower bed."

"You poor thing. And that brave, wonderful man!"

Hannah could only nod through her guilt. If only she hadn't insisted on going outside. Her boredom had cost a man his life. "Yes. He was. I crawled over to him, tried to help him, but it was too late. Then I sat up and saw his blood all over me. And fainted. Later, Slade found out that Cates had no family. We had him buried yesterday."

Slade jumped up, a study in agitation as he ran his hands through his hair and paced over to the window. Hands to his hips, he kept his back to the room and stared out at the street. Awkward silence commanded the three still seated. Constance busied herself with the tea. Dudley wolfed down three more cakes. Hannah watched Slade.

She knew the source of his turmoil—he insisted her accident was no accident. He said it was deliberate, and that he wasn't leaving her side until this thing was solved. And he hadn't for the past two days. He even slept with her, chastely holding her bruised body. During the day, sometimes, she'd look up and catch him staring at her, some naked emotion bared in his eyes.

Whether it was fear for her or guilt for putting her here in Boston proper, in harm's way, she couldn't say. Probably a little of both. Why else would he refuse to discuss his father and her mother, the last words said between them before she'd left Woodbridge Pond? If she tried to bring it up now, he'd brush her off, saying one fight at a time.

Realizing that she was succeeding only in jumbling her thoughts more, and that her silence was rude to her friends, Hannah forced her features into a smile and spoke of inanities. "Are you coming to Woodbridge Pond next week for Grandmother Garrett's gala fete?"

"Oh, yes!" Constance's exuberance matched Hannah's smile for being forced. "We can hardly wait. It should be such fun. Positively everyone is coming. Grandmother Garrett rarely entertains, but when she does—whew!"

Hannah nodded and smiled. It became quiet again. She cast around desperately for a topic, wishing with all her heart that Slade would come back over to her side.

Dudley beat Hannah to the next topic. "Constance and I have set a date for our wedding. It's to be next year—the thirteenth of June. We're looking forward to your and Slade's being in our wedding party."

Hannah's expression of friendly interest crumpled. "Next June? How nice." Only she wouldn't be here. She'd be back in No Man's Land. Despite not wanting to, she sought her husband's gaze. Sure enough, he'd turned from the window to show her that black-eyed, penetrating look that said *You're not leaving me.* A muscle twitched in his jaw. He solemnly swiveled back to the sights outside.

Hannah refocused on her guests. Who now looked extremely uncomfortable. Constance turned to Dudley, putting her tiny hand atop his thick, square one. "Perhaps we ought to go, Dudley. I'm sure Hannah's tired, and—"

"Son of a *bitch*! That's it!"

Hannah and Constance gasped. Dudley came to his feet. They all three turned to stare at the suddenly animated Slade. Long-legged strides brought him to the sofa, where he promptly sat down, pivoting to face Hannah. He took her hands in his, his posture mimicking one of a marriage proposal. She looked from his earnest face to Dudley's and Constance's blank expressions, and back to Slade. "What's 'it,' Slade?"

"Jones, Hannah. Jones. Think—where was he when you went outside two days ago?"

She shook her head and frowned. "Why, I don't recall. I think—"

"No, Hannah. Don't think. Know. Where was he?" He squeezed her hands harder, as if the added pressure would cause the memory to pop out. Abruptly he turned to Dudley. "Sit down. I want you to hear this, too."

Dudley sat. "What the devil is going on? Who's Jones?"

"One of Hannah's damned Yankees."

Hannah turned her head at that and caught the look that Constance and Dudley exchanged. They must think her and Slade insane. Constance leaned forward frowning. "Aren't we all damned Yankees? We do live in Massachusetts."

"Yes, but in this case we mean the men I hired to guard Hannah." Slade turned back to her. "Where was he?"

Hannah frowned, looking at Slade's hands holding hers in her lap. Then, it came to her. She sat up straight, inhaling sharply. "On the bench. The one just across the street."

"I knew it." Slade jumped up.

Dudley and Constance followed suit and hurried to the window, looking out as if they could see the scene from two days ago. "Why is that important?" Dudley asked, turning back to them.

Slade never broke eye contact with Hannah. "Because Hannah's accident, my friend, was no accident."

A moment of shocked silence preceded Dudley's serious question. "Are you saying it was Cyrus in that wagon?"

Slade shook his head at Hannah, even as he answered Dudley. "No. He wouldn't be that stupid. He'd pay someone." Now he turned to Dudley at the window. "But something's been bothering me for the past two days. I keep seeing the face of the driver. He was looking right at Hannah—and whipping those horses. Those horses were no more runaways than I am."

Constance gasped. The tiny blonde was clutching Dudley's sleeve. Her heart-shaped face frowned up. "Hannah, you mustn't be alone one minute."

Hannah looked up at Slade. "I haven't been. But Slade's life is in as much danger as mine."

"I know. Dudley's told me. I hope you don't mind."

Hannah solemnly shook her head. "No, of course not. You should know. Especially if you're going to visit us. Because anything can happen." She stopped to laugh and gesture at her own battered and bruised self. "And apparently has. I'd understand if you don't want—"

"Pooh!" Constance waved her shapely, doll-sized hand in the air. "I'm not the least bit afraid of Cyrus Wilton-Humes. But Patience? I have a bad feeling every time I'm around her. As if I'm in the presence of evil."

Hannah sat as still as she could, what with her heart fluttering. Hadn't she felt and thought the same thing, from the first moment she'd been in her great-aunt's presence?

Dudley stepped in. "I agree. But tell me about this Jones character. How is he relevant?"

Hannah looked up at Slade, who still stood beside her at the sofa. He turned to Dudley now. "Look out at the bench closest to the street. That was Jones's posted station, so he could watch the house. Hannah says he was there when she and her three Yankees went outside two days ago."

Dudley stared out the window and commented, "I'm with you so far."

"Good. Now see if you can answer any of these questions

for me. If he was there when she left, where was he when Hannah went running back by? Why didn't he stop her? If he was there, why didn't he help her when her cloak snagged on the fence—right next to his bench? And finally, if he was there—why wasn't *he* the one to pull her safely away, long before the horses and wagons got there, long before Cates got there?"

A cold chill swept over Hannah. It seemed to permeate the very air she breathed. The coldness crept into her bones, her soul. She looked at Slade and Dudley and Constance. Their still poses said they felt it, too. Dudley released the lace sheer curtain. His voice a ghost of a whisper, he intoned, "Because . . . he wasn't there."

"Exactly." Slade's one word cut the air like the chop of an axe. "Wherever he was, it wasn't far, because he was the one to help me up—"

"Help *you* up? What happened to you?"

Slade's face clouded up and then turned red. His chin came up one I-dare-you-to-laugh notch. "I passed out when I thought Hannah'd been run over."

Hannah bit so hard at her bottom lip that she feared she'd draw blood. She chanced a peek at Constance. Her moony-eyed expression and clasped hands showed she thought this the most romantic thing.

And Dudley? Well, Dudley'd just been handed a silver platter on which lay, in a bed of satin pillows and pure gold, The Upper Hand on his friend for the rest of their days. But he didn't laugh. He didn't tease. Instead, he adopted a serious pose, hands behind his back, mouth and eyes frowned up thoughtfully, as he nodded and paced the room in silence. Hannah rolled her eyes when Dudley approached Slade and wagged his sausage of a finger under his friend's nose. *Here comes bloodshed.*

"Tell me something, my brave fellow," he began, drawing the moment out. "I've always wondered this, but have never been able to ask, since in my experience, it's been the *ladies* who faint at the first sign of trouble. But the ladies, being too delicate to question, and your being the only *man* I've ever known who's fainted—now, you don't have to answer if the question is too much for your frail constitution—what's it feel like to have the vapors?"

Slade, Hannah, and Constance spoke together. "Shut up, Ames."

# CHAPTER SEVENTEEN

Alone in the parlor, having just seen Dudley and Constance out, Hannah stared out into the foyer at Slade, who stood in stark profile to her. With him now were Temple and Hardy. All three men's hard-jawed expressions spoke of serious matters being discussed. Slade's words drifted in to her. "Hardy, check on Olivia. And Temple, see how Jones spends his afternoon off."

Hannah watched the men nod and then turn to leave. Unexpectedly, a possessive streak tore through her. This tall, virile male was *hers*. Forever? Or only until she returned home? Instantly, home's image in her heart and mind was Woodbridge Pond, and not the ranch house out in No Man's Land. Hannah slumped. She couldn't leave here. And yet she had to.

She had blood kin in No Man's Land. She'd made promises to them. She couldn't leave her sisters and Biddy alone. No more than she could leave Slade. But she had to. She'd hurt him terribly by not trusting him. And she'd failed her family by getting so caught up with Slade that she'd forgotten her real reason for being here.

A sudden tenderness tore at her heart. Slade was so good to her, and he said he loved her. Hannah sighed. She didn't doubt that he did. But he deserved better than her. He deserved someone who could unquestioningly put herself in his hands, someone who wouldn't hurt him at every turn. Hannah feared she'd been too independent for too long ever to just give herself over so completely to a man. Even one she loved so much.

And that was why she had to leave him when all this was over. She wasn't what he needed.

With bittersweet tears poised to fall off the tips of her eyelashes, Hannah swiped at the moisture and focused on Slade, who was entering the parlor. Dear God, how was she going to leave him? But her concern for his troubled expression as he came to stand in front of her took precedence over her own pain. She vowed that for as long as she remained here, his wants and needs would come first. But not over her revenge. She couldn't allow that.

"Did you hear what I told Hardy and Temple?"

Hannah nodded up at him. "Yes. But I hate to think that Jones is guilty of anything but being momentarily distracted or sidetracked."

He frowned at her as if she were a puzzle he couldn't figure out. "First you defend Olivia, and now Jones. Why am I the only one you think the worst of right off?"

Hannah's insides jerked in guilty reaction. She deserved that. To her, his words were further proof of the deep hurt she'd dealt him. And more proof that she was not the woman for him. She opened and closed her mouth, trying to form words, but nothing would come. She stared helplessly up at him.

He ran a hand through his hair and then dismissed his own words with a wave of his hand. "I'm sorry I said that. It's just . . . everything. But I haven't forgotten you were right about Olivia. Maybe you're right about Jones, too. He's worked for me for five years with no hint of disloyalty."

Hannah nodded, forcing herself to speak. "I always felt safe with him around. But that Isabel bedeviled the life out of him."

Slade chuckled. "She'd bedevil the poor souls buried in the cemetery, given half a chance."

Desperately clinging to this lighter topic, Hannah laughed gingerly, holding her ribs. "You're an awful grandson."

"Ahh, you have been talking with Isabel, I see."

Their bantering grins bled to sobering countenances. His innocent but loaded reminder that yes, indeed, she had talked with Isabel—about his father and her mother—sent Hannah's gaze to her lap. She rearranged the folds of her cambric wrapper—her erstwhile wedding gown. Their outrageous, drunken wedding. Would there never be a moment between them when some ''ghost of truths past'' didn't plague their every conversation?

''What did you think of Constance?''

Hannah looked up. Slade's expression willed her to jump at this new subject. She did. It was perfect because to think of Constance and Dudley was to smile. ''I love her already. She's not at all what I thought she'd be.''

Slade laughed. ''I know. All the young bucks in Boston, myself included, were half in love with her ourselves. Imagine our surprise when she let it be known she favored Dudley Ames.''

Hannah's mouth dropped open. ''You and Constance were—?''

Raising his hand to stop her words, Slade shook his head. ''Nothing of the sort.'' Then he grinned like a pirate. ''Are you jealous?''

Clamping her jaw closed hard enough to make her teeth hurt, Hannah airily fussed around on her cushion and suddenly found his boots to be of enormous interest to her. She stared openly at them, pretending not to notice he was wearing them. Or that he was still laughing at her.

''Good friends that they are, I'm glad they're gone.'' Slade took the few steps that saw him stretched out on the sofa, his long legs crossed and his booted feet extending off the other end. He gingerly rested his head on Hannah's lap and folded his hands together on his abdomen.

Surprised that he felt comfortable enough with her to lie all over her, she made herself scold him . . . even as she ran her fingers through his black wavy hair. ''That's not a nice thing to say. Dudley and Constance are wonderful people.''

''I know. But I want to be alone with you.'' He tilted his head back until he looked into her eyes. ''Very alone.''

Suddenly shy, Hannah concentrated on her fingers already threaded through his hair. He reached up to her, tucking his thumb and index finger around her chin, forcing her gaze back to him. His dark eyes showed a stark hunger. ''Is that so bad?''

It was awful. The worst. She had to leave him. Every word of love only made her feel worse. But she shook her head. ''No. It's wonderful.''

Slade turned abruptly on his side to draw his arms around

her waist, bringing his cheek against her unbound breasts. "I'm so glad you think so. Because you practically took me against my will on the stairs not an hour ago."

"Against your will?" Despite her heavy emotions, Hannah laughed outright at him. And instantly paid for it when an arrow of pain lanced between her ribs, causing her to grimace and grab for the area.

Slade sat up, his hand on her arm. "What is it? Did I hurt you?"

She shook her head. "It wasn't you. I'm all right. Just take me upstairs. I feel the sudden need for a nap."

"Of course." He jumped up and gathered her in his arms.

Before he could lift her off the sofa, Hannah resolved that if her days with him were numbered, then she was going to enjoy every moment she had with him. And just maybe, she could take back something of him with her. Something that would arrive in nine months. So, with her hand on his cheek, she forced his gaze to meet hers. "I want to take a nap with you."

A riveting second ticked off the clock. Awareness flashed in the fathomless depths of Slade's black eyes. Hannah slanted her head, placing a melting kiss on his firm lips. She tipped her tongue into his mouth and felt him tense. Only then did she pull back from him and again look deep into his eyes.

A low, aching growl from deep in Slade's chest rumbled up to lodge in his throat. Hannah's eyes widened. He grinned archly, promising delights as yet unthought of. When she gasped, he lifted her easily and carried her out of the parlor.

Perhaps luckily for the other inhabitants of the brownstone, none of them encountered their employer as he carried his wife up the stairs and to his bedroom, kicking the door closed behind him.

Still without a word passing between them, he placed her on his bed. He kept his gaze on her and tugged his shirttail out of his pants. Watching him intently, Hannah sat up and worked on her own fastenings. She stripped off her wrapper when he peeled off his shirt. Together they tossed aside their garments.

Bare from the waist up, Slade sat on the edge of the bed to tug his boots off. Watching the rippling play of his muscles across his broad shoulders, in his powerful arms, over his hard-hewn belly as he worked at them, Hannah distractedly slipped her satin mules off her feet. They hit the carpet with muffled thunks. When he stood to face her, his feet apart, and began unfastening his black, close-fitting pants, Hannah forgot how to breathe.

His motions themselves, just the very moving of his long fingers over the buttoned closure as his black eyes bored into her soul, were too arousing to be borne. Or so she thought, until Slade began inching his pants down over his lean hips. Hannah swore her heart wasn't even beating. But there was a definite pulsing much lower down. A definite pulsing. Pushed to the edge of control, Hannah pulled herself up to her knees and quickly lifted her gown over her head.

She didn't even get it off before Slade's naked body was warmly, carefully wrapped around hers. A rasping gasp from low in her throat carried her back with him on the bed. When they landed, bouncing softly against the mattress, Hannah's hands were over her head, her gown gripped tightly in her fists. Straddling her full length, his rigidness trapped between them, Slade pulled the white gown out of her hands and threw it over the side of the bed.

"You won't be needing that," he promised, his voice low and husky.

Afire with need, Hannah parted her legs and bent her knees, readying herself for the promised pleasures that flared his nostrils and opened his mouth to slant over hers in a kiss that reached to her toes. And curled them achingly. When Slade broke his kiss to slide down on her, roughly rasping her tightly budded nipples with his body, his chest hair tickling her soft skin, she arched into him, digging her fingernails into his shoulders.

"Not yet, baby. You aren't even close to where I'm going to take you."

"Slade, please," she cried out, her mouth open, her breath already coming in gasps.

"No." He shook his head, allowing his nose to rub across the soft fullness of her breast. Then his mouth closed over her nipple. The hot, moist feel of his lips, coupled with his tongue's delicious circling and flicking of her nipple exploded stars behind Hannah's eyes.

She arched again, ignoring the aching of her bruises and

bumps. Using the heels of her palms to push against his shoulders, she urged him down to where she wanted him. But he insisted on going slowly, on softly kissing any bruise he came to, on laying his cheek against any injury done her body two days ago. Suddenly she realized he was speaking, that he kept repeating, "I'm sorry, Hannah. I'm so sorry."

Moved by his gentle care with her, Hannah raised her head, opening her mouth to—Gasp out loud and clutch at the quilted covers under her when Slade finally . . . oh, so *finally* slipped lower and raised her to his mouth. Hannah splintered, fragmented. He took her hungrily, as if she were an oasis in his desert. As if she were the elixir of life to his dying man. He no more than closed over her than the rippling shudders shook Hannah to her soul. Rhythmic pulsations spread out from her center to the farthest ends of her clutching, tearing fingernails.

And still Slade rode the wave of her desire, eliciting from her more and more and more. Until she lay glistening and spent, and whimpering for mercy. Only then did he raise himself back up over her, wetly kissing his way up her belly, stopping only to sip at the tiny cup of her navel before he sat lightly atop her, straddling her hips, his arousal jutting proudly between them. He arched over her, leaning until his fisted hands rested beside her head.

Hannah rolled her head as if just awakening. Fitfully, she swiped her damp and matted hair from her face, and inched her gaze along him. Her hands followed close behind, smoothing across his muscled thighs, up his lean hips, around his buttocks, over his tensed back, down under his arms and then around to his chest, flattening out to race through the crisp and curling hair that accentuated his blatant masculinity. His head hung forward limply with sensual pleasure and left Hannah breathless.

Her hands raced up to his neck, his jaw, his mouth. She feathered her fingers over his lips, allowing him to suckle and nip them for only a moment before she teasingly took them away. She then lovingly raked her nails down his rock-hard chest, dipping to . . . close over his arousal. An ancient sound, flung from the back of his throat, arched his back and jerked his head up. She wouldn't have been surprised right then to hear him howl like a wolf.

Instead, he jerked forward, pulling Hannah's hands away

from him. "Cruel wench," he whispered as he lowered himself on her, sliding full length to fit himself into the saddle of her hips.

Victorious, Hannah grinned like a wanton. Until Slade entered her, slowly sliding himself up, up, and up to his hilt, into her depths. She gasped and tossed her head. "Please."

"Now it's *please*. Wasn't that you only a moment ago playing the tease, my sweet?"

"Yes," she cried out, clutching at his shoulders, afraid she'd die if he didn't soon begin the rhythm that would ease the killing tension between her legs.

"Are you my sweet, Hannah?"

She opened her eyes, saw the shadowed line of his jaw, the prominent cheekbones, the proud, hawkish nose. His black eyes waited. "Yes, I'm your sweet." Her words were no more than a groan.

"You always were."

With that, he gathered her to him, his arms under her shoulder blades, and held her . . . gently at first . . . and stroked her desire evenly. But then the cadence changed, became demanding, unyielding, bruising. At the same moment, he took her mouth, refusing to relinquish it, so that her every breath was taken with him, so that his fire fed her body. So that her soul merged with his in a swirling dance that mimicked their physical coupling, and elevated them to a place where they truly became one.

Only then, with cries wrung from them both, did their release begin. Hannah's undulations clutched at Slade's manhood, pulling him greedily into her, locking around him, holding him there . . . until he gave her his entire being. His seed spilled into her on his last climactic thrust.

Slade collapsed heavily onto her, only to slide out of her and then off her in a sweat-soaked slick of overly warm bodies. His head popped up, and Hannah tried to laugh, but could only grimace and gasp. Slade stared at her for a second and then gave up, too, and lay half on her, half off. Spent, weak as kittens, the only sounds in the room for long minutes were those wrenching gulps they made trying to feed their starved lungs.

Then Slade popped up again. Hannah turned her head—the only thing she could. Slade braced himself on an elbow. "Are you . . . trying to . . . kill me?" he barely got out.

Hannah grinned and shook her head, pushing a clinging curl off her forehead. "I suspect I'd have to get into a long line to do that."

His eyebrows arched and he tried to laugh, but no sound would come out of his mouth. So he rolled his eyes and just flopped back onto the covers, facedown, an arm and a leg flung over Hannah.

After several minutes of staring numbly at the ceiling, Hannah realized her breathing had smoothed out. She listened. So had Slade's. His was now deep and even. She turned her head. The man was asleep. She shook her head and chuckled. Big, strong man. She turned on her side, thinking she'd show him—she'd wake him up and . . . and have her way with him again. She reached out to him—

And someone knocked on the door. Hannah froze. Then, Hammonds called through the door. "Mr. Garrett, sir? Are you in there?"

Hannah's eyes widened. If he opened that door—! She reached around behind her and shook Slade's shoulder. He mumbled, pulling away from her, and settled himself more fully into a comfortable position.

"Mr. Garrett?"

Desperate, Hannah pinched the fire out of Slade's buttock. He leapt up and off the bed, landing on his feet like a cat. With his hand rubbing his offended part, he came out spitting and cursing, "Gee-sus! What the hell—?" Eyebrows meeting over his nose, he finally sighted on Hannah. And belatedly picked up on her shushing, hushing signals. "What?"

She pointed to the door, mouthing, "Hammonds."

His frown deepened, but he did whisper. "You pinched the living sh—you pinched me because Hammonds is at the door? Hellfire, Hannah, we're married, and this is our house. It's okay if we have sex." He turned to the door, bellowing out, "What is it, Hammonds?"

"Sorry to bother you, Mr. Garrett . . . and, um, Mrs. Garrett, but . . ."

Hannah nearly passed out, so acute was her embarrassment. But Slade matter-of-factly snatched up his pants and jerked into them, again bellowing out, "Then why did you, man?"

"Because, sir, I'm afraid that Mrs. Isabel Garrett and"—

Slade's eyes widened as he jerked around to Hannah. She popped up on the bed, her lower jaw dropping almost to her chest—"and her entire household, sir—her *entire* household—await you in the parlor."

A frantic scratching and whining at the door confirmed the scope of the *entire* household. "Except for one. Esmerelda. Who is here with me. What shall I tell her, sir? Your grandmother, that is."

A grin of pure evil stole over Slade's face. His ears grew pointy and horns stuck out of his forehead. Or should have. Hannah shook her head at him. "Don't do it. Don't. Please!"

He opened his mouth—Hannah squealed and covered her mouth with her hand. Slade laughed out loud at her and then called out, "Tell Isabel and her entire household that Mrs. Garrett and I were just—"

As soon as the first words left his mouth, Hannah scrabbled up onto her knees and leaned over, crashing nakedly into him, her hand over his mouth at the last possible second. Stumbling backward, he grabbed at her, pulling her off the bed. Her momentum carried them to the thick-carpeted floor, Hannah atop her husband. Fierce giggling and masculine guffaws followed and were quickly squelched. They lay there, a tangle of hairy limbs and smooth limbs, a muscular body and a soft body, listening, waiting.

Hammonds, obviously also listening, finally cleared his throat. "I see. Well, then. Come, Esmerelda, we'll think of something on our own. I say, big doggy, did you like your carriage ride into town?" Esmerelda whuffed her answer as the two walked away, as witnessed by the fading footsteps and clicking of doggy toenails on the wood floor.

Hannah flung her tangled hair out of her face and over her shoulder, the better to see the man under her. "You dirty polecat! You were going to say we were—you know."

His black eyes snapping with humor, Slade put his hands to her bottom and caressed it lovingly. "No I wasn't. I was going to say we were taking a bath together."

Hannah screamed out her disbelief. "That's even worse!"

Slade grinned. "You want to, anyway?"

Hannah nodded eagerly.

\*   \*   \*

"Well, here you are at last. I just don't know about young people today. Do you always keep your guests waiting an hour—and then greet them in such casual attire?"

"I do apologize, Grandmother. But Hannah insisted on dressing. Not that she was undressed, just in her night clothes." Clad only in his boots, black pants—one leg tucked in the boots, one leg not—and white collarless shirt, Slade threaded his way through the Garrett-domestic-packed parlor to bend over Isabel and buss the rouge-reddened cheek she raised to him. "Didn't Hammonds tell you we were . . . ?"

His words trailed off to a pregnant silence. Isabel arched a taunting brow at her freshly scrubbed grandson and his damp hair. "Tell me you were what?"

She cut her gaze to the equally scrubbed and damp-of-hair Hannah. After taking in her wrongly buttoned blouse and twisted skirt, she repeated her question to the girl. "Well? Tell me you were what?"

Not getting any answer there, either, she sighted on both the red-faced children. And squelched the insane urge to leap up and hug them desperately, so happy was she for their obvious love for one another. "You have no idea what Hammonds told us, do you?"

She waved her hand at the couple. "Well, don't look to him for help. I had him take Esmerelda outside, lest she piddle on the carpet. I suppose the least you can do is produce a great-grandchild out of your bold afternoon shenanigans."

"Isabel!" Hannah's hands went to her reddening cheeks.

"What?" But she knew full well what. She'd spoken out again in front of the help. She turned to them now.

The tiny parlor overflowed into the foyer with the ancient domestics, all of them seated on hastily brought in chairs and sipping at tea and nibbling suspiciously at the cakes Mrs. Stanley offered. After the housekeeper passed by with her tray, a visiting maid or two ran her fingers over a table or window sill, looked at the evidence, weighed it with her neighbor, and judged the young master's help with a sniff.

Isabel shook her head and turned back to her granddaughter-in-law. "You've no reason to be so coy in front of them. They know how to make babies." She turned to the room at large. "Don't you?"

Some gray heads nodded, some bald heads continued looking around the room, some deaf ones poked at their neighbors, asking what she'd said. Pemberton stood, taking it upon himself to yell out the question, as if this were a town meeting and he was presenting the next issue on the agenda. "Mrs. Garrett asked if we know how to make babies."

A hand or two went up in the doddering crowd. When Pemberton made as if to call on one of them, Isabel cut him off. "Sit down, you old fool."

The old fool turned to her, shrugged, and edged himself into his chair, with Rowena's and Serafina's help. "As you wish, madam. But one may never get an answer, as matters stand now."

Rolling her eyes, Isabel turned to Slade and Hannah. "You sit down, too. This is a social call, not a command appearance. You're making me nervous." Her heart warming dangerously at the sight of these two precious people, Isabel nevertheless kept her expression imperious and forbidding as she waited for them to obey her. "That's more like it."

She watched approvingly as Slade put his arm around his wife's shoulders and gave her a smile full of awareness. Isabel noted Hannah's darting, loving glances his way. A gloating smile almost got away from her. They were in love. She wondered if they knew it yet.

"Well, Isabel, what brings"—Slade gestured to include everyone in the room—"you here today?"

Pemberton answered. "As I recall, four carriages and both broughams."

Isabel turned with Slade and Hannah to stare at the man. "Pemberton, just drink your tea and leave the conversation to me, please."

"Yes, madam." He took the cup and saucer handed him by Rowena, making a terrible clattering sound with the delicate china in his tremulous hands. Under his breath, he muttered, "One was asked what brought us here. One would think one could take the liberty of answering."

Isabel huffed out a long-suffering sigh as she turned to her host and hostess. "What brought me here—Pemberton's interpretation not withstanding—was my concern for your well-being. I believe you both ought to return posthaste to Woodbridge Pond."

She watched Slade and Hannah exchange a glance and a

smile. Her grandson turned to her. "Isabel, dearest, do you miss us?"

Isabel dearest puffed up to her full seated height. "Hardly. Barely noticed you were gone. However, I can't help but be concerned by this recent turn of events. Why, a man was killed and your wife almost was. And we all know that was no accident. That being the case, do you think it wise to spread your men so thinly by having a few here, some at my place, and even others at Olivia's mother's? It's too much. I say we pool our strengths and make our stand together at Woodbridge Pond."

Slade's smile turned soft, entreating. "Are you scared, sweetheart?"

Isabel nearly came to her feet. "I have no use for fraidy cats. However, I will point out that I now have on my shoulders the full responsibility for the upcoming celebration of your marriage. Now, is that fair, and me an old woman?"

Slade's black eyes sparkled. "Admit you miss us, admit you're afraid—for us, of course—and we'll consider coming back. Won't we, Hannah?"

Isabel's heart beat eagerly as she watched him turn to Hannah. That one raised her eyebrows and grinned, nodding. Ha! They wanted to come back. She'd make them squirm—but then she caught the serious, attentive expressions on her domestics' faces. Great Thanksgiving turkeys! They'd turn her out if she didn't have Slade and Hannah in tow when they left today.

Frowning up into her best irascible expression, she blurted out, "Oh, all right, then. Yes, I'm afraid—for you, of course. You're merely children. Can't take care of yourselves. And yes, I miss you. They miss you. We all miss you. Esmerelda spends her days moping about in your rooms, baying dreadfully because she can't find you. We can't stand the noise anymore. Either you come back with us, or we leave Esmerelda here with you."

As if conjured up, the front door flew open and in bounded Esmerelda, her leash dragging butlerless behind her. On her heels, a winded, gasping, clothes-awry Hammonds clutched at the door's knob and stumbled in. The mastiff ignored the commotion behind her as her ears perked up. Grinning hugely, she cavorted over to Hannah and Slade, circling their chairs and loudly barking out her happiness. Everyone in the room covered their ears and squalled out their protests.

Esmerelda finally took pity on them all and went to lay her great head on Hannah's lap. Laughing, Hannah rubbed and smoothed the dog's head, leaning over to hug her fiercely. That was when Hammonds made his way into the parlor, leaned his back against the wall, and sank to the floor in a spread-legged heap, his stiff collar springing open in punctuation.

With all heads turned to him, he managed to gasp out, "We . . . outran—not by my choice—your brougham, Mr. Garrett. That little . . . lady's maid and . . . and Rigby are outside. I think . . . something's wrong. They have a . . . a baby with them."

Within seconds the combined households were out on the walk and braving the cold air to gather at the brougham's door. Hannah put her shaking hands to her mouth as Slade leaned in with a soot-covered Rigby to help Olivia out. It was hard to say which one was crying more—Olivia or her baby.

When the girl's feet touched the ground, Hannah had them in the best hug she could manage while still allowing for the child. Smelling the acrid scent of smoke which clung to them, Hannah cried, "What happened, Olivia?"

The girl put her head on Hannah's shoulder and sobbed. Hands reached in to take the squalling child. Hannah glanced up, exchanged a look with Isabel, and helped her bundle the blanket-wrapped baby to the older woman's soft bosom. Isabel bounced and soothed the baby with low, chirping tones of grandmotherly sympathy. Every gray head and gnarled hand ringed her, vying with all the others to pet and coo at the chubby-fisted little girl. Esmerelda managed to nose her way in and sniff at the child's bottom.

Hannah turned her head to see Slade pull Rigby aside and begin questioning him. Then, two huge men, of the Hardy and Temple and Cates sort, climbed out of the brougham. Her eyes widened at the glimpse of strapped and holstered guns under their unbuttoned chesterfields. Both men bore signs on their faces of a recent fisticuffs session. They too joined Slade and Rigby.

Hannah's attention centered again on Olivia when she raised

her head, which jerked with the force of her gasping emotion. Ignoring the biting cold that seeped through her thin blouse, Hannah smoothed a hand over the girl's cheeks. Olivia swiped her hair out of her face. "There was a fire. And me mum's dead."

"A fire? Your mother? Oh, Olivia." Hannah hugged her to her again. "I am so sorry." A horrible thought swept through her, chilling her in places the cold couldn't reach. She pulled back and held the shaking girl out at arm's length. "How did your mother die, Olivia? Was it the fire? Or was it—?"

"Inside. Right now. Everyone, get inside. Go." Slade startled the assemblage. He, Rigby, and the two big, armed men spread out and began herding everyone to the front steps. Slade took Hannah's arm in a firm grip, allowing Rigby to pull Olivia away and keep her close to him. Both men turned the women in front of them, keeping their bodies between them and the crowded street and curious onlookers.

Slade spoke in a low voice. "This was no accident. And I was right about Jones—he double-crossed me. Bekins and Smith tell me they smelled smoke at the back of the old building and went to investigate. Jones set a fire to distract them." He leaned down to whisper in her ear. "The only reason Olivia and Colette are alive is because Rigby hit Jones from behind, stunning him long enough for them to run out the front way. That damned double-crosser killed the old couple I had helping Olivia's mother."

"Oh, Slade, not the Hills. Those poor, innocent people. We've got to stop them—and I mean Cyrus and Patience, as well as Jones." She looked over her shoulder at him. "Did Jones . . . kill Olivia's mother?"

Slade nodded grimly. "Yes. But Bekins and Smith caught him. Before he died, they wrung out of him that Cyrus was paying him for information. And then he paid him to do away with Olivia and the others."

"Dear God, where will it stop?" Hannah spat her words with as much vehemence as she could while still whispering.

At the front steps now and waiting for Isabel and her gray-haired entourage to tread up the stairs, Slade answered her. "It stops right here. There'll be no more killing. At least, not by them. We're going to do as Isabel said—make our stand at Woodbridge Pond."

An ugly frown marring his handsome features, Slade looked down at her. "I've been going about this all wrong. I've been sifting facts and looking for evidence, while Cyrus has been having people killed. I've been too civilized, and that's cost three more people their lives. No more. My eyes are opened now. From here on out, I favor the direct approach."

# CHAPTER EIGHTEEN

———

That evening at Woodbridge Pond, Slade wasn't the only one feeling guilty over the afternoon's deaths. Nor was he the only one who favored the direct approach.

Up in her room, Hannah got down on her knees and tugged out a hard-sided case from under the bed. She snapped open the clasps and then turned for the tenth time to look all around her. Still alone. Funny how being sneaky made a person edgy. She bent again to her task. Opening the case, she eyed the two Peacemakers, lifting them, hefting their weight and balance. Just out this year from Colt. Mama'd made a present of them to Papa on their anniversary.

Hannah could see him now. He'd given his old Colt to Jacey, and then had strapped these on and strutted around the place like a cocky rooster. She saw him practicing his quick draw and challenging everyone on the spread to a target-shooting match. Jacey'd been the only one fool enough to go up against him. There they were, father and daughter, squared up, facing the cans and bottles, going toe to toe with their weapons. Papa'd beat Jacey—just barely. Hannah firmed her quivering lips and chin. No time for memories.

She wiped at her eyes, quickly loaded the guns, and slipped them back in the case and under the bed, beside her pocket pistol and a rolled bundle that consisted of Rigby's pants, shirt, and hat. She'd have them back to him before he ever missed them.

Just as she pulled herself to her feet, the door opened and in stepped Slade. Hannah's heart skipped a beat at the sight of him. He was dressed for the outdoors, but he looked different somehow, as if his civilized mask were thinning. But there was something else, something she couldn't put her finger on. He stopped in the doorway, smiling, his hand on the knob. "I wondered where you were."

Hannah smiled, hoping she didn't look guilty. "I'm right here." Why was her voice so high? She cleared her throat. "Did you just get back?"

"Yeah." His expression sobered, making him look tired. "We talked to the police, told them what we know about the fire. But that's all. The rest is my business." A jaw muscle jumped. "I told Olivia we'd bury her mother tomorrow."

Hannah nodded her acknowledgment of that as she watched him remove his hat. Her eyes widened. That was it! His hat. That's what was different. A black Stetson. She was so used to seeing men wear them that she'd barely noticed before now that he didn't wear one. Well, now he did. Why? What did it mean?

When Slade raised a hand to run his fingers through his hair, his motion opened his coat, revealing a holstered pistol in a shoulder strap. He caught her gaze, his eyes reflecting that he knew she'd seen the gun. "Why aren't you downstairs with everyone else?"

Hannah shrugged. "I was. It just got too crowded. We now have two households trying to be one. Pemberton and Hammonds nearly got into a duel over who'd open the door when Mrs. Hardison called on Isabel. And Mrs. Edgars is not thrilled to have Mrs. Stanley in her kitchen. I had to separate them before supper ended up on the wall. And Isabel has been raging around all evening, complaining about the noise."

He grinned and chuckled. "Well, sorry I missed all that. But don't let Isabel fool you. That old girl's thrilled—all the kids and Esmerelda tearing around. When I came in, Jacko and Edgar had Colette—" Without warning, his smile fled. "What the hell's going on here? You're up here for another reason."

"No I'm not."

"Then, why don't I believe you?"

"I don't know."

"Dammit, Hannah."

"Dammit, Slade."

His black-eyed gaze assessed her. Hannah burned with a

sweaty, sneaky feeling. Then he nodded and changed the subject. "All right. You're not up to anything. Are you ready for dinner?"

"Yes."

"Good. Why don't you go on down?"

Completely aware of the bed pressing against the backs of her legs, Hannah raised her chin. "Will you go down with me?"

He crossed his arms over his chest. "Will you tell me why it's so important to you that I do?"

Great. She needed a really good reason. Or he was going to stay right here and tear this room apart until he found her out. "Because . . ." She had to stop when her honest heart pounded out its objection. She was getting ready to tell the biggest lie she'd ever told. Maybe not. It could be true and, right now, it couldn't be helped. She swallowed hard and started over. "Because I want you with me for my announcement."

Slade raised an eyebrow as he slapped his Stetson against his thigh. Again and again. For a long stretch, it was the only sound in the room. Just when Hannah thought she would snap, he spoke up. "What announcement?"

"That I . . . that we're . . . that I'm—"

"Yes, Hannah? That we're, that you're . . . what?"

"Going to have a baby." Hannah twisted her fingers together at her waist and stared at her husband.

The Stetson slipped unnoticed from his fingers. He stared at her as if she'd just said she was a lilac bush. "What did you just say?"

Hannah wasn't sure she could say it again. Because maybe God hadn't heard her the first time. She didn't want to compound her sin by confirming it for Him. But what choice did she have? "I said, we're going to have a baby."

"Me and you? We're going to have a baby?"

"No, you and Dudley. Of course, me and you."

"A baby—like Colette? That kind of baby?"

"That's the only kind of baby there is. Except for boy babies." Suddenly afraid the shock was too much for him, that she'd addled his brain, she looked askance at him. "Are you all right?"

He stared and nodded, stared and nodded. And then, as if

made of wood, bent over to retrieve his Stetson. He put it on his head, low over his eyes, looked at her again, and backed out of the room, closing the door after him.

Hannah eyed the closed door. *That went well.*

Just then, the door burst open, making Hannah jump a good foot. Slade tore into the room, flinging his Stetson high and peeling off his chesterfield, revealing two shoulder straps, two pistols. A jackass-eating-briars grin on his face, he grabbed her up and swung her around, laughing and whooping for all he was worth.

Hannah'd never felt so miserable for lying in her whole life. Or so she thought until he covered her face with kisses and then dragged her by the hand all the way down the hall, then remembered her delicate condition and picked her up—protesting at the top of her lungs—and carried her downstairs and blurted it out to everyone's astonishment and hand-clapping congratulations, and then they'd all toasted her and Slade at dinner. All of them—family and domestics alike and even Olivia—came down for the good news. That was when she felt the most miserable.

Seated in the dining room and still being toasted repeatedly made Hannah want to cry. Why had she said there was a baby, when there was no baby? And even if there was, she wouldn't want Slade to know because she was leaving. What was worse, she had no idea how a woman in her supposed condition acted. She was only two years old herself when Mama'd had Jacey. And even though she was four years old when Mama had Glory, the only thing she remembered was Papa'd come home that day from somewhere, and then he and Mama'd shown her and Jacey their new baby sister.

Oh, why hadn't she paid more attention when the few other women out in the territory were talking about babies? Then, she sighted on . . . her lady's maid. Why, she'd had Colette less than a year ago. She'd ask her, acting as if she were just wondering what to expect. But not now, not tonight. Because tonight, she had some unfinished business to attend to. Next door at Cloister Point.

Hannah didn't exhale until, in her stocking feet, she slipped out a back door and closed it softly behind her. The first miracle was that she hadn't encountered any Yankees on her way downstairs. The second one was she hadn't awakened Slade, who was suddenly so cooperative in light of her . . . delicate condition. He hadn't even insisted they sleep together when she feigned tiredness and said she wanted to turn in early—and alone.

In fact, he'd agreed readily, had even shooed Esmerelda, asking Isabel to close the mastiff in with her. And that was the third miracle. Esmerelda hadn't awakened to raise the alarm as Hannah'd tiptoed past Isabel's room.

Hannah sat now on the top step of the narrow landing, slipping on high-topped, lace-up boots—so ridiculously dainty in light of her masculine getup. A huge yawn escaped her, coming out a vaporish cloud in the cold night air. She'd darn near fallen asleep waiting for the household to turn in. But now, all was darkness. All was quiet.

Hannah tugged at the gunbelt strapped around her waist. And felt the cold metal of the two Peacemakers and her peashooter weighing her down. She tucked her braided hair up under Rigby's slouch hat and pulled it securely around her ears. Right now she would have killed for her split skirt and sheepskin coat. But no, Slade had seen to it that her wardrobe held only ladified clothes of no practical value. Hannah shifted around in the uncomfortable getup, settled her guns low on her hips. *Jacey, lend me some of your bravery, girl.*

With that, and holding up her baggy pants as if they were the finest of skirts, she tiptoed down the stairs to step onto the grass, avoiding the crunchy gravel. Crouching in stealth, and keeping an eye out for the posted guards, she crept along the white stone walls of the mansion.

Once she lost the building's protection, she skittered over to the shrubberied edges of the formal gardens and worked her way almost to the summer cabin. At a spot she deemed perfect, she got down on all fours and pushed her way between the entwined branches of two tall and precisely trimmed bushes. She then stood up and faced the narrowly spaced iron rods of the fence that separated Woodbridge Pond from Cloister Point.

Sweating despite the cold, she edged her arm and leg between two bars and tried to shove through. But no amount of grunting and straining or just plain wanting through seemed to matter. Her doggone breasts and backside held her prisoner on this side of the fence. Dammit. Now what?

Just then, the crunching of gravel behind her turned her head in that direction. She backed out from between the two bars and flattened herself on the hard ground. She then rolled until her back met the cold fence. Listening intently, her cheeks stinging from the bite of November, her nose running, she sniffed. And froze in place. But no one called out. No one challenged the noise, so loud to her in the quiet night air.

Wondering now if she'd even heard the gravelly sound, Hannah pulled herself up to her hands and knees and crawled forward a space, rising up to squat there for a better look. She lightly brushed her hands together as she looked around. Earlier she'd cursed the full moon for its revealing light, but now she was grateful for it. Or would be, if the someone who was also outside would show himself.

And he did. A streak of surprised terror shot through Hannah. She clasped her hands over her mouth, locking them there forcefully. Afraid the whites of her very rounded eyes would give her away, she closed them for a long second. When she next peeked out through the thick tangle of her hiding place, she saw him—a big man with a rifle held at the ready—walking slowly toward the back of the property. In a line with her. The man looked all around himself, even straight at her hiding place. Hannah went rigidly still, ignoring the cold sweat drizzling down between her breasts and over her pounding heart.

The man moved on. Hannah let out her held breath. She watched him until he rounded the path to the summer cabin. Listening another moment more, just to be sure he didn't double back, Hannah cocked her head, sure she'd just heard more male voices—she pushed branches aside to raise up some—coming from the cabin. Could be he was checking in with another guard. If so, and they were distracted with each other, then now was her chance—

Was that Slade's voice? She listened, heard his voice again. Yes. What was he doing out here—and what was he up to? As if in answer to her own questions, certain things fell into place in her mind. Such as his cooperative attitude this evening. And his agreeing with her that she should retire early and sleep alone. The man had wanted her out of the way and not aware of his absence. He was a fine one to talk about trust, out here sneaking around in the dark.

Perhaps he was just checking on the guards. No, she discarded that notion immediately. Why would he need to do that in the middle of the night and out in the cabin, as if their being here were a big secret? These damned Yankees trampling up the place had been the after-dinner conversation this evening with the entire household present. So, it was more than that. But what?

Hannah pulled aside a particularly sharp branch that poked at her cheek and figured she had the time to find out. Just then, something wet and cold pressed against the back of her neck. Startled beyond caution, she squawked and sprang forward froglike—right into the shrubs, entangling her arms and scratching her face.

Desperately fighting her way free, expecting at any moment to be hauled up or shot without a question being asked, she frantically tore away from the prickly shrub. Only to hit her back against an iron bar and plop bottom first onto the hard dirt. Stunned, her cheeks stinging from the fresh scratches, she sat there blinking. And stared up at Esmerelda with her ears pricked and her head tilted. Hannah didn't know whether to hug the dog or chunk a dirt clod at her.

"What are you doing out here, girl?" she whispered, and then came up with her own answer. *Oh, no. This is Esmerelda's last trip outdoors for the night. Which means someone will quickly miss her and come looking for her. Great.* Hannah scooted forward and shoved at the mastiff. "Go away. Shoo! Scat!"

The dog didn't budge. Defeated, Hannah sat back on her haunches. The pony-sized canine sat back on her haunches too and cocked her head to the other side. Hannah whimpered. "Go away, Esmerelda."

Esmerelda frowned. And didn't budge. Completely put out, Hannah warned in a level voice, "Don't make me shoot you, you big cow."

Esmerelda crouched forward and licked Hannah's face. Her tail-thumping beat the bushes soundly as she affectionately rubbed against Hannah. And knocked her hat off. "Dammit, Esmerelda, go away. You'll bark and give me away. Now, go on"—Hannah shoved ineffectually at the mastiff's shoulder—

"I'm not your playmate. I don't even like you. Now, scat."

Esmerelda folded into a pathetic heap, lying down sphinx-like. Her expression could only be called mournful. Hannah wilted, hugging the great head to her chest. "I didn't mean it. You know I love you. Now, go catch a rat! That's it—a rat. Look, Essie, a rat! Go get it, girl. Get the rat." Hannah looked around, found a good-sized stone and chunked it out onto the lawn.

Essie merely raised an eyebrow ... and stayed where she was. Hannah flopped limply on top of the dog. She could still be out here tomorrow at high noon trying to get Essie to go. "Fine. Go with me. But just be quiet, okay?"

Esmerelda whuffed ... very quietly ... and turned to bite at the seat of Hannah's pants. Hannah jerked herself off the dog's warm, furry body and scooted around until she found her hat. Tucking her braid up under it, she tugged it down firmly, and turned to her partner. "You ready?"

Esmerelda stood up, slobbering and panting, her dark, intelligent eyes shining in the moonlight. Hannah came to a crouch, bracing herself with her fingers tented on the ground. "Now, stay close to me. I can't get through the bars here, so we're—" She looked at her partner. "I'm talking to a dog."

She turned to work her way back through the prickly branches and out onto the lawn's boundary. Esmerelda stayed close behind. Except for the one time Hannah looked back to see her squatting and relieving herself. Once at the end of the long hedgerow, Hannah tested the bushy boundary and found it too tightly interwoven to allow her to slip through. She and Esmerelda were forced to turn to their left and follow the configuration around to the gravel path. Scooting to its edge, the mastiff on her heels, Hannah risked a peek around the corner.

And was struck by the black and silver picture laid out for her. The full moon cast its white light on the still waters of the pond. Light and shadow alternated through the bare branches of the towering elms, throwing long fingers up the cabin's walls and in through the windows. The ghostly claws, shifting with the wind, grasped at but couldn't capture the tall, muscular figures moving around inside the cabin.

As Hannah watched, holding on to Esmerelda's collar with stiff, cold fingers, she saw Slade light a candle and then unfold a large square of paper. A map, perhaps. The men with him gathered around to stare at it and nod as Slade spoke and ran his finger over various parts of it. But a map of what? Woodbridge Pond? Or Cloister Point?

Frowning now, Hannah picked out details. Slade was dressed in dark clothes, like the other men. Like them, he was also heavily armed. And wore an expression of righteous intent. She looked at some of the other faces. Why, they all had that same expression—grim, determined. As sure as she was standing here, they were planning some sort of clandestine mission. And her husband, the father of her possible child, was obviously going to go right along with them. *The direct approach.*

The phrase took on a concrete meaning now. Slade meant to confront his enemies. Tonight. Personally. He could be killed. Hannah decided she couldn't allow that. Cyrus and Patience were her family, her enemies. If anyone was going to put himself—herself—in peril, it would be her. After all, she was already out here and on her way over there. She wasn't waiting for Isabel's entertainment to confront the Wilton-Humeses. No, tonight was the night. And it all came down to her.

Hannah took deep breath after deep breath, trying to buoy up her courage. She'd promised her sisters to exact revenge for Mama and Papa and then to come home, and she would. She'd promised Slade to get the hell out of Boston and never let him see her face again once this was over, and she would. It would break her heart, but she would go.

There it was, the reason for her hesitations up to this point. Slade wouldn't be in her life once she dealt with Cyrus and Patience. Hannah stared through the window at the man she loved. Now she understood. He was the reason she hadn't acted yet—because once she did, there would be nothing keeping her from leaving for No Man's Land.

Instantly, she saw her sisters' faces before her. She should kick herself for thinking only of herself all these weeks. She should be thinking of them. She should be thinking of their blood oath. She should be thinking of the people who'd died at Cyrus and Patience's hands. Hannah firmed up her mouth and her courage. She had to act, and then move on with her life.

She backed around the corner of the hedges, dragging Esmerelda with her. Once they were on the secure side of the hedge, the dog looked up at her, as if to ask *What now?* Staring at her, Hannah put her finger to her mouth, biting thoughtfully at the nail. The direct approach. She raised her head and saw the roofline of Cloister Point. She focused on her partner. "Let's go."

Just then, Esmerelda's name was called in the wind. Hannah froze, as did the mastiff. They exchanged a look and then turned to the source. Hammonds stood on the back landing, in a long nightshirt and with a blanket around his shoulders, calling out for the dog to come. Hannah raised an eyebrow at Esmerelda. She raised an eyebrow at Hannah, who drawled, "Well, pardner, it's your call."

Esmerelda perked up her ears when Hannah spoke. Then she drooped her head and her tail. Immediately, she padded off, sticking to the long shadows, only to disappear through the hedges by the iron fence. A moment later she poked her head back through, as if to say *You coming or not?*

Hammonds again called for the dog. This time his voice sounded a little closer. Hannah knew it was now or never. Crouching, she skittered to the hedge and, keeping her arms up protectively around her face, pushed her way through to the iron fence. Only to see Esmerelda already on Wilton-Humes property, her large head turned back to peer at Hannah.

How in the world did that huge dog get through these narrowly spaced rods? Hannah gripped them, tugging on them, testing them. None of them was loose. Then she tried again—inching, worming, squirming, groping. Nothing. Just like before, she couldn't get through. Which was strange because there Esmerelda stood. Hannah knew she was bigger than Olivia, but she wasn't as big as the mastiff.

Frustrated, she looked again to Esmerelda. The bright moonlight revealed her padding back to the fence. Hannah reached through the bar to her partner, thinking she was coming to her. But the mastiff veered off to Hannah's left. Maybe . . . Hannah poked and edged her way through the bushes, staying on all fours. And nearly fell into her answer. She jerked up short and then reached a hand out to pat at the shadowed depression in front of her.

Yes! Essie had dug a huge hole right under the fence. The

sides were worn smooth from long use. And rooted grass edged the perimeter. Apparently, Esmerelda had enjoyed the grounds of both properties for quite some time. Bless her. Hannah went headfirst, belly down into the hole, kicking and scrambling with her booted feet until she was on the other side. Pushing up to her feet, she brushed herself off, checked to be sure she still had both of her guns, and hugged Esmerelda to her. "Good dog."

Esmerelda grinned hugely, wriggling her entire body as she wagged her tail, finally woofing out her agreement.

"Esmerelda, is that you over there? Get over here. Bad girl!"

Hannah spun around. Hammonds's voice placed him mere feet away on the other side of the hedges. She looked back to Esmerelda—and found her gone. Where—? There—loping toward the mansion at Cloister Point. Taking her cue from the mastiff, Hannah tore out after her.

Slade rolled up his map of Woodbridge Pond's grounds. "That should cover it. I've staggered the shifts, so we're not vulnerable at any one time. Just be alert and investigate anything out of the ordinary. Temple, Hardy, Bekins, and myself will take this next outside shift. The rest of you get some sleep. Be back here at seven in the morning. And let's hope everything stays this quiet."

The men nodded and turned, heading for the cabin's door. Just then, they all heard "Esmerelda! Is that you over there? Get over here. Bad girl!" And stopped. Metal clicked as rifles were cocked.

Slade held up a hand. "It's okay. That's Hammonds—my butler from my brownstone. He's calling for the mastiff." The men relaxed, letting out held breath, releasing the catches on their weapons. Slade grinned, satisfied with their alertness. "Go on to your posts or your beds. I'll see to Hammonds."

The men nodded, muttered, and began filing out. Slade snuffed out the candle. Suddenly, his shoulders bowed under the weight of his guilt. He'd promised Olivia only last week that if she'd cooperate, he'd keep her mother and baby safe. And look what had happened. Damn Cyrus and Patience! Never again would he let them get the upper hand on him. They'd have to kill him to get to anyone in his house.

Immediately, Hannah's sweet face and that thick tangle of chocolate-colored hair popped into his mind's eye. She was carrying his child. His child. He blanched with knee-weakening fear when he realized that Cyrus could just as easily have sent Jones after Hannah—or Isabel—as he had Mrs. O'Toole and the Hills.

When a jolt of cold wind snapped Slade out of his thoughts, he stepped outside, closing the door behind him. His men's booted feet crunched the gravel, and their low voices carried on the wind. They burned as much as he did over Jones's defection. They felt they had something to prove because of the one bad apple in their midst. One bad apple bought off with money. But one bad apple killed off by his own. There was a certain justice in that.

Slade heard Hammonds speaking with Bekins. Sounded pretty irritated with Essie. A grin came to his lips. Who wasn't at some point in the day?

And what a hell of a day it had been. Thank God it was almost over. Glancing off to his right, catching the moon's reflection on the pond, Slade strode to its edge. In the still water, he imagined he saw a reflection of Olivia's brown eyes. He'd pay until the day he died every time he looked into those eyes. That was his burden, and he accepted it. He could shoulder it.

But he knew he wouldn't survive the loss of Isabel or Hannah to those thieving murderers next door. Having to harbor his loved ones this close to them made his nights sleepless, even though they were well guarded. Slade felt a pain in his chest, a pain born of his murderously fierce love for all the lives in his care. He'd let them all down. But never again. He'd die first.

"Mr. Garrett, sir? Are you back here?"

Slade jumped. He hadn't even heard Hammonds approach. Some sentry he was. "Right here, Hammonds."

Facing the darkened cabin, Hammonds whipped around, his hand going to his heart. "You startled me, sir."

Slade smiled, hearing Hannah's voice saying those same words. "I do that to a lot of people. Is Esmerelda giving you the chase?"

"I'm afraid she is. Forgive me, sir, but she's such a spoiled beast."

"Aptly put." Slade looked the man up and down. Under a blanket, he wore a nightshirt that came to his knees. And knobby knees they were. "Where did you last see her?"

"Well, it is dark and I might be seeing shadows, but I could swear she was on that first rise there beyond the fence."

Slade went on the alert. "Beyond the fence? You mean Cloister Point?"

"Yes, sir. I told that Bekins person a moment ago, and he looked all about. But he didn't see her."

Bekins was sharp-eyed, so if he didn't see something the size of Esmerelda, then Hammonds probably was mistaken. Still, his mood being the suspicious one it was, Slade stared at the fence, mentally measuring Essie's breadth against the spacing of the iron bars. She couldn't squeeze between them. He started to dismiss Hammonds's story, but his mind made the next logical leap for him. She may not be able to squeeze between the bars, but she could dig under them. *Son of a bitch.*

All right, so what did he have? The dog was on Wilton-Humes property. Maybe she'd run off before Bekins went to investigate. And, if she had a hole dug, she'd come back the same way—when she was damned good and ready. Slade turned to his man. "She's probably hiding from you. Go on to bed. I'll keep an eye out for her."

"As you wish." Hammonds turned away, but then turned back. "One more thing, Mr. Garrett. I could swear Esmerelda wasn't alone."

# CHAPTER NINETEEN

———

"She wasn't alone? Someone was with Esmerelda?" Fear spiked through Slade's guts.

"Well, perhaps not *with* her, sir. But this someone did take off after the dog. As if he were following her."

Suddenly, standing there in the bright moonlight, Slade was certain Hammonds wasn't seeing things. Too much detail for him to be wrong. And what had he just told his men? Investigate everything. Slade looked over to the next property and applied suspicious logic to the circumstances.

If Esmerelda was running ahead of this someone, then she hadn't been chasing him off Woodbridge Pond. That was good. But it also meant that someone here had escaped the notice of any and all his sentries and was now at Cloister Point. Now, who would be bounding after Esmerelda at this hour? Olivia? No, he'd certainly proved himself an ass there once. Then who? Everyone else was too old. Except for— Slade inhaled sharply. "Hammonds, what did this someone look like?"

Hammonds shook his head. "Why, I don't know. I gained only a fleeting impression, sir. I could be completely wrong, but—"

"You're not wrong. All our lives could be at stake, Hammonds. Now, think. What did this someone look like?"

"Um, er—a boy! That's it, sir. A slender young man. In dark clothes. Running very fast, sir. Very fast. Like a greyhound."

Slade settled his hands at his waist, thinking. *Like a greyhound.* Why did that sound familiar? Then he realized he'd said it. But who had he said it about? *Son of a bitch. Hannah.* Slade felt the life force drain right out of him. He bent forward, putting his hands on his knees.

"I say, sir, are you all right?"

Slade looked up at Hammonds. "I may never be all right again." He then straightened up.

Hammonds remained silent, as if he knew Slade needed to think this through. But all Slade could think was *It's her.* In a man's clothes. Who else would be so bold? He'd kill her. He'd go get her, make sure she was unharmed, and then he would kill her. She was Isabel all over again—you couldn't trust her ever to be where she said she would be. Or where you told her to stay.

Another thought leapt to the forefront of Slade's feverishly working brain. "What are you doing out here looking for Esmerelda? I told Isabel to keep her in her room."

Hammonds resettled the blanket around his shoulders and clutched at it with both hands. "Indeed, you did. But Mrs. Garrett had other plans."

Certain his hair stood on end under his Stetson, Slade pulled himself up to his full height. "What the hell did you just say?"

Hammonds took two giant steps back. "I said Mrs. Garrett had other plans—"

"For the evening. I heard you. What other plans?"

Hammonds assumed his butler pose, managing to look imperious, even in his nightshirt and with his knobby knees. "I assure you, sir, that the lady of the house does not consult me as to her plans."

*Had the entire household absconded the minute he stepped outside?* Was his word not law in his own home? Slade turned his head to sight on Cloister Point. Apparently not. Because if Hannah Wilton Lawless Garrett and Isabel Winifred Cummings Garrett were not this minute at Cloister Point, then he was a stripe-assed zebra. He looked back at his butler. "Son of a *bitch.*"

Hammonds breathed in through his nose, enough to puff his chest out. "I *beg* your pardon!"

But Slade heard the man's protest on the run. He had to get there in time. He just had to. His heart pumping as fast as his legs, he sped toward the hedges that fronted the iron bars. Had to get to Hannah. Had to get to Isabel. He scratched and shoved his way through the shrubs, only to have his footing give way in knee-twisting suddenness. Cursing and clutching at the iron fence, Slade scrambled for even footing.

"Hammonds," Slade called over his shoulder. "Go find Bekins. Tell him I'm going to Cloister Point and that I said I can handle this. Tell him to stay at his post and keep the other men at theirs. This could be a trap or a distraction. If it is, I don't want Woodbridge Pond exposed. You got all that?"

"Yes, sir. I'm on my way. You can count on me."

*Well, that's one, then.* As Hammonds sped off, Slade, still clutching at two iron bars, looked down over his shoulder. Just as he'd suspected. A hole. A big hole. Big enough for Esmerelda. Big enough for Hannah. But not for him.

He'd kill them, that's all there was to it. Gritting his teeth, he faced his immediate enemy. The fence. How best to get around it—or over it? He knew, from childhood years of looking up at it, that each bar was topped with a spear-shaped tip. If he tried to go over the top, one slip of his hand or foot and he would be impaled. In frustrated rage, he shook the fence, but succeeded only in rattling his own teeth.

Breathing hard, Slade tried to jiggle individual bars within his reach, checking for a possible loose one. Just one. That's all he needed. *Who the hell were the Wilton-Humeses trying to keep out, anyway?* But he knew—his father. His drunken, enraged father, bent on forcing himself on a defenseless girl.

Was he his father's son? He saw himself threatening Hannah at Cloister Point—in her mother's room. And thought of the depth of his love for her now. How would he behave if she rejected him? Would he react any less violently?

Slade's head slumped against the cold iron bars of reality. His breath clouded in front of his face. If he could forgive his father, it would be because he now understood what it meant to love. And possibly to lose. Raising his head, he looked across the grounds to the Cloister Point mansion. This fence, erected to keep his father out, wouldn't keep him out. Because the difference between him and his father was that he wasn't trying to hurt but to save.

Using his righteous anger to fuel his body, he crouched down like a mountain cat and filled his lungs with icy air. With a mighty effort, he vaulted up and up. Gripping the top horizontal railing between two spearheads, and swinging his legs over, he was on Wilton-Humes soil in one smooth leap. Resettling his Stetson and his pistols, he loped off toward the lighted room at the back of the mansion.

As he ran, each step echoed with but one thought—*I'll kill them, I'll kill them.* And he didn't know exactly who he meant—Cyrus and Patience, or Hannah and Isabel. Maybe all four of them. Slade ignored his burning lungs, his labored breathing, his cramping legs. To slow down now could mean their deaths. Later he could be tired. But not now. Had to reach Hannah.

His eyes watering, his cheeks stinging with cold, Slade slowed only when he neared the mansion itself. The light from within spilled like a waterfall onto the lawn outside. Slade knew whom he'd see when he looked in. Hannah, Isabel, Cyrus, and Patience. He feared only what they'd be doing. Fighting in a pitched battle? Lying in pools of blood?

He swiped a hand under his nose and sucked in air through his open mouth. His first instinct was to kick open the French doors and burst into the room, guns blazing. And maybe get them all killed since he didn't know the situation inside. He gritted his teeth in frustration. *Dammit!* Only that afternoon he'd cursed his own slowness to action, his tendency to think through every possibility, to weigh every option, before making a move.

And now, when it came right down to life or death, he had to rely on those same traits. The very ones of his which had seen no less than eight people dead in the past three months. How then could he save, in the next few moments, the two people he loved most in the world?

Images of Isabel and Hannah popped into his head. Immediately, a surge of pure instinct, pure emotion, welled up in him. *Hell, yes, he could. Look out, Cyrus, you son of a bitch, I'm coming for you.* Borrowing on every primitive instinct in his soul, Slade curled a lip and went into a crouching run alongside the white stone wall of Cloister Point, right up to the window. His back braced against the wall, he edged to his left, closer and closer to the French doors.

So far, no thumping and bumping or yells and hoarse cries assailed his ears. Only night sounds, the wind in the trees, the hooting of an owl. So, either he was in time or he was too late. Either way, Cyrus Wilton-Humes would die tonight.

Slade reached for his twin pistols in their harness straps. His cold fingers fumbled slightly as he drew them out. Cocking each one, he held them up and ready. Pushing his hat to the back of his head, he peeked around the stone corner to look inside.

*Tea. Isabel's having tea with Cyrus and Patience. She's having tea.* Stunned into forgetting himself, Slade stepped into plain view and froze. Guns raised, he stood framed in the rectangular, many-paned glass of the closed doors. Just then, Isabel, the only one of the threesome who sat facing the doors, glanced up and saw him. She jerked back in her chair, her eyes went completely round, and she threw her teacup and saucer to the carpet. Cyrus and Patience jumped up. Now was his chance. Slade reached for the outside latch.

And someone caught him sideways in a full body blow. His Stetson and guns somersaulted with him down the wooded and sloped ground. He rolled and cursed and clutched at the earth . . . grabbed at a low branch . . . scratched for a handhold . . . dug for a toehold. And realized that whoever'd hit him was following him down. Finally, he lay at rest, on his back, in a depression at the slope's end. Stunned, blinking, he lay there, trying to digest what had just happened. *Hannah. Isabel. He had to get to them.*

Slade came straight up, only to be knocked back onto the bone-jarringly hard ground. His attacker pressed into him, lying on his chest. Beyond enraged, past murderous, Slade gritted his teeth and curled his hands around the man's . . . *furry neck? What the hell?* He felt further. Esmerelda! Slade pitched over onto his side, dislodging the mastiff at the same time he grabbed for her collar, scrambled to his feet, and kept a firm hand on her, lest she run off again. His voice no more than a hiss, he scolded, "What are you doing over here?"

Esmerelda woofed, jumping at him and nearly succeeding in knocking him to his knees. *Damned dog was strong as an ox.* Slade kept a death-grip on her collar and got right in her face. "Essie, you big horse, this is no time to play."

Essie sounded a low growl in her chest, the first one Slade had ever heard from her. Surprised, he pulled back, and then realized she was trying to look back the way she'd come. She then set up a wrenching, twisting fight. Slade's grip on her slipped. The mastiff took off in a mad tear, clambering effortlessly up the slope. Slade caught intermittent sight of her as she ran into and out of the moonlight. She finally disappeared around the back of the mansion. Could it be that Hannah was in that direction? Or was he just plain nuts for thinking the dog understood what was at stake here?

Only one way to find out. Slade quickly climbed up the hill after her. He peeked again into the parlor. Patience still had her back to him. Cyrus wasn't in his chair. And that damned Isabel was sitting there, all composed and again sipping tea as if she were the Queen of England.

He waited until she next looked up and then caught her gaze. This time she remained cool and collected, never giving a thing away. Slade gestured, trying to signal *What's going on?* Isabel made as if to smooth her hair but then stabbed her finger off to her right. Frowning, Slade stretched and craned, doing his level best to see what she meant. No good. Whoever or whatever she wanted him to see was blocked by the room's corners and his restricted angle.

He then heard a hoarse cry. From inside the mansion. From inside the room where Isabel and Cyrus and Patience were. No—from where Patience and Isabel were. *Where the hell was Cyrus?* Tensing, straightening up, Slade narrowed his eyes, listening. The low cry sounded again. A mewling, feminine sound. Slade looked directly at his grandmother, and saw the wrenching fear in her eyes. Then, it came to him—another person was still missing from this little tableau. Hannah.

Slade cast his gaze to the building's corner. Esmerelda'd gone that way. And Isabel pointed that way. Suddenly sure he had no time to look for his guns—as if he could find them in the tangled undergrowth of shrubs and trees all about, Slade slipped away from the doors and slouched around to the back of the mansion. Aha. A long, narrow window with a view into the room.

And outside with him stood Esmerelda, staring into it with an intensity that was almost human. Gone from her was all sign of playfulness. Gone was the puppy. In its place was a full-grown and deadly hunter, every muscle tensed, every sense honed. Sighting on Slade, she backed off a step, stared accusingly up at him—as if to say *What took you so long?*

A chill that had nothing to do with the deepening cold of

the night slipped over Slade's skin. He hated like hell all this delay, all this skulking around outside. He wanted to be inside and dealing with that bastard Cyrus and Patience for the last time. Slade moved until he could see into the room.

What he was looking at suddenly registered. Bile rose to a gorge at the back of his throat. He clutched at the cold stones of Cloister Point to keep from staggering to his knees. He couldn't blink. He couldn't breathe. He couldn't move. Nor could he save both Isabel *and* Hannah. He'd have to choose.

Bound to a chair in front of a narrow window and across the room from Isabel, Hannah tested the ropes that cut into her wrists. But even those slight movements brought her wincing pain from the lump on her head. That damned Cyrus. Who'd taught him how to hog-tie a critter? Thinking of critters, Hannah realized she no longer heard Esmerelda at her back. Had she perhaps gone home? Maybe she'd be seen coming from here and would raise suspicions about the goings-on here.

And what goings-on they were. Hannah again saw herself shooing Esmerelda once she entered Cloister Point through the tall window in Cyrus's office. She'd no more than put both feet inside when the door opened and in walked her great-uncle. He'd been as startled as she was. And had proven to be a lot stronger than he looked. In the ensuing struggle, he'd hit her over the head with a paperweight. And that was the last she remembered until she'd come to and found herself hog-tied to this spindly old chair.

Hannah rocked her weight, feeling the chair's loose joints give some. Interesting. Frowning from the throb in her head, she tipped her tongue over her split and swollen lip. The slightly metallic taste of blood slid down her throat when she swallowed. She looked up when Cyrus approached her. And figured she had nothing left to lose. "Kill me if you want. You won't get away with it. Slade will come after you."

Stopping in front of her, Cyrus tucked one of her Peace-makers into his waistband. And then slapped her face, snapping her head to the right. "I told you to shut up, Lawless bitch!"

Despite the shooting pain in her jaw, and the ringing in her ears, Hannah raised her head, sighting on Isabel when she heard the older woman's gasp and her coldly threatening voice. "Leave her be, you monster. My grandson will tear you limb from limb when he gets here."

Cyrus rounded on her. "I have every right to—"

"You have no rights. None," Isabel raged, effectively shutting him up. She then turned on Patience, who sat facing her—and who aimed the other Peacemaker at her heart. "As for you, Patience Wilton-Humes, you either use that peashooter or put it away. Don't think for a moment you can frighten me with a gun." She calmly, with steady hands, lifted her teacup and saucer.

A smug smile cragged Patience's face. "Oh? Try getting up, my dear. See how far you get. I think it would be especially fitting to kill you with one of Hannah's own guns." She looked over at her husband. "Cyrus, why are you letting her talk to me like that? What sort of husband are you?"

Hannah, still numb and blinking, nevertheless watched with a degree of satisfaction as Cyrus's face reddened. He strode stiff-legged to the empty chair next to his wife and sat, leaning forward to glare a threat at Isabel. When he spoke, his voice was the whining snarl of a coward with a gun. "You keep a civil tongue in your head. And I have every right to deal with her"—he pointed at Hannah—"as I see fit. I caught her red-handed in my office, trying to rob me. My own brother's child—breaking into my home."

"I'll not listen to this drivel."

"You will listen!" Cyrus screeched, sending spittle flying. "Patience and I, out of the goodness of our hearts, intended to show you our evidence of your grandson's guilt in all these murders, so you'd understand and could protect yourself from him. You could be next, Isabel—for your money. He'd do anything for money—even marry Hannah, a woman he hates, to keep her money."

"No! You're lying!" Hannah jerked about in the chair and tore at her bonds, wanting to scratch her great-uncle's eyes out. And hoping to shake the chair apart so she could get to the peashooter in her pants pocket.

Cyrus sniggered evilly at Hannah. "You think I'm lying? Oh, it was him. Not us. We killed no one. Slade had Catherine killed, you know."

Hannah exploded with a rage that nearly toppled her chair.

A hoarse yell tore from her throat. "Don't you ever speak my mother's name."

"Slade killed no one. That is absolutely preposterous," came Isabel's outraged cry.

"Is it? You know this—all without seeing our evidence? I find that very interesting. Hannah's at risk, too. Slade's using her until she no longer serves his purpose. And then he'll rid himself of her, just as he has the others. Patience and I are next, you see. He had Hannah make her public accusations right here in our own home. As a result, Patience and I are cut off from all help, shut out of society. Ruined. No one will receive us.

"And we're practically penniless—because of my grandmother's misplaced loyalty to Catherine and to Slade. Again, Slade. Always Slade. We must rid ourselves of him—you and me and Patience. He'll kill you for your money, too, Isabel. You must forgive the late hour, but we had to see you tonight—alone. To warn you."

Isabel sat as still as an oil painting, her teacup suspended halfway between the saucer and her lips. "You're quite mad, Cyrus. Insane."

An oily grin exposed his crooked teeth. "Am I? Or am I just clever? Either way, that makes me quite dangerous, doesn't it? So, if I were you, I'd sip my tea while we await the arrival of young Mr. Garrett."

"No." Isabel thumped her cup and saucer on the low table in front of her.

"Pick it up," Patience warned. "Pick it up, or I'll shoot your precious granddaughter-in-law." She hefted the Peacemaker with both hands and waved it at Hannah.

Isabel glared at the white-haired woman and snatched up her cup and saucer. "What makes you think Slade will show up? He's asleep. He has no idea that I'm even here, much less that Hannah might be. Because, following your own instructions in your note, I told no one of my destination. And my carriage still awaits me out front, so—"

Cyrus's cackling cut off Isabel's words. "Are you sure your carriage awaits you? What if I told you I sent that old fool driver of yours—Sedgewick, isn't it?—back to Woodbridge Pond with a note to Slade? A note that said he'd best show up in thirty minutes or have your blood on his head. And as for Hannah? Well, she's simply a bonus, a surprise, if you will.''

Even as Isabel's eyes rounded and she gasped and threw her teacup and saucer onto the carpet, all Hannah could think was *Slade's walking into a trap*. She worked furiously at her ropes, chafing and burning the skin over her wrists. Were the ropes loosening, or was it just her wishing it to be so?

When the tea spattered and stained the carpet, Cyrus and Patience jumped up, calling for Mrs. Wells, who popped in so quickly that she had to have been listening at the door. Hannah narrowed her eyes at the smirking snotty-old-ass as she cleaned up Isabel's spill, poured her another cup, and exited the room as if she owned the place. Hannah's gaze followed her until she closed the door behind her hefty self. Hateful hag. She'd get her comeuppance.

Hannah snapped her attention back to Cyrus as he again approached her. ''Feeling a strong urge to hit a woman again, Uncle?''

''Not at the moment.'' He fairly minced over to her. ''Don't think I don't see you over here, trying to work the ropes loose. Let's see if they're still tight enough.'' He went behind her and gave a savage yank to the big knot that secured her wrists.

Hannah grunted with the pain, but bit back a groan. Some primal instinct warned her not to show fear or weakness to this creature. He was of the sort to jump on her like a badger and tear her apart if she did. When he began yanking on the ropes around her booted ankles, Hannah looked to Isabel.

And frowned. Isabel now stared intently out the French doors behind Patience. Mindful of not alerting her captors, Hannah cut her gaze to the doors. Her angle was too sharp to see anything. It was probably just Esmerelda out there. Hannah looked back to Isabel, only to see her patting her hair . . . and poking her finger out, as if pointing at . . . *Me? She's pointing at me? Why?* Why would Isabel gesture like that at Esmerelda? Well, the answer was—she wouldn't. The dog would have no clue what she meant.

Then suddenly Hannah knew. *Slade's out there.* Her heart pounded against her rib cage, against the crisscrossing ropes over her chest. When Cyrus stepped in front of her and tested the ropes binding her torso, Hannah smoothed her features into a poker face. But inside she crowed, *Prepare to die, Cyrus*

*Wilton-Humes, because my avenging angel has arrived.*

When Cyrus knelt in front of her to yank on the ropes securing her booted feet to the chair, Hannah shot Isabel a look, trying to let her know she knew Slade was out there. That formidable lady dipped her eyelids in a slow blink of acknowledgment. Hope surged through Hannah. Because if Slade remained true to form, he'd come heavily armed and he'd have a host of men with him.

And when she and Isabel were freed? Well, that was up to Cyrus and Patience. If they were still alive after the next few moments. But Hannah knew what her preference was. Given one clean shot, and then another, she'd kill them both.

When Cyrus straightened up in front of Hannah, he glanced up, peered out the window behind her, and screeched in terror as he backed up.

Patience came to her feet, waving her Peacemaker wildly. "What is it, you fool? Are you frightened of a tied-up girl?"

"There's a wild animal at our window!" He drew Hannah's Peacemaker from his waistband.

Hannah frowned, thinking, *Wolf? Slade? No—Esmerelda!* "No!" Hannah's cry tore from her at the same time Cyrus fired wildly, narrowly missing Hannah's head, but shattering the glass behind her. A high-pitched animal yelp of pain signaled the beginning of the end. *The bastard shot Esmerelda.* Hannah pitched about in her chair, enough to actually move it, and screamed out in her anger. Cyrus shoved at her shoulder as he pushed past her to look out the broken window.

Using the momentum he'd given her, Hannah purposely pitched the chair to the floor. She hit the carpet with a painful thud, head and shoulder first, and heard a splintering sound. Of wood? Or of bone? A split second's assessment of her body told her that, flipped over like a turtle though she may be, nothing was broken on her. A grunt of hallelujah escaped her as she struggled to further weaken the chair's structure and just maybe free herself.

Fighting her own pitched battle, she belatedly became aware of the sounds of other struggles in the room. More shattering glass. Frightened screeching. The blunt impact of body against body. Grunts, cries, blows, thumps. And an opening door. On edge now, Hannah jerked her head back as best she could. To her mounting horror, she saw Isabel—that grande dame and

Garrett matriarch—locked in a death grip with Patience as they both fought for Hannah's gun. Into Hannah's line of vision flew Mrs. Wells—at a dead run and with a large vase upraised over her head.

Hannah screamed out, "Isabel! Behind you!"

A gun roared, freezing Isabel and Patience in each other's grip. Her own heart bleeding in fear, Hannah watched the two women stare at each other, waited the interminable, heart-stopping seconds with them for one of them to fall, mortally wounded. But neither one did.

Had the gun simply misfired in their struggle? Then, Hannah heard the thump. Isabel and Patience pushed away from each other and jerked around. Hannah wrestled her chair until she'd scooted herself around enough to see.

Mrs. Wells lay facedown on the floor. The vase rolled ineffectually across the carpet, stopping when it hit the sofa at Isabel's back.

In the benumbed silence that followed, Hannah realized something else. The shot had come from behind her. *Surely Cyrus hadn't shot Mrs. Wells just before she crashed the vase down on Isabel's head?* The same thing apparently occurred to Isabel and Patience because they spun to the shattered window. Try as she might, Hannah couldn't wrench her chair enough to see who'd shot Mrs. Wells, but what she heard made her want to cry.

"Drop the gun, Patience. One false move, and I'll shoot Cyrus."

*Slade!*

Hannah wilted in a crying slump of relief and joy. Her movement freed her tied hands from her chair's broken slat. But freeing herself didn't matter now, because Slade was here and everything would be fine. In another moment, his men would come bursting in and the nightmare that had begun out in No Man's Land would finally end.

"Shoot Cyrus? You? I hardly think so. He's bungled events so badly that he doesn't deserve to live, much less share all the money with me. So, allow me to save you the effort, Mr. Garrett."

Hannah's head snapped up. Surely she hadn't heard that right. Surely—

Cyrus screeched. "No, Patience! Don't! I beg you—"

Another shot rang out.

"Jesus Christ! You shot him."

Hannah froze at Slade's incredulous words. She jerked mightily in reaction, forcing her legs out straight, an action that splintered the chair. Her mind registered that she was free of the chair but still tied up. She kicked and rolled over as best she could to face the window.

With one of her Peacemakers held loosely in one hand, Slade held on to a bloodied and slumping Cyrus with his other. Hannah's great-uncle, his eyes open and staring at his wife, clutched at his chest as he flowed with his blood to the floor. Transfixed, Slade stared at the body.

Hannah's mind registered another sound—the metallic click that signaled a round being chambered. *Dear God, no.* Time slowed. And everything happened at once. Wasting no breath or reaction time on calling out, Hannah tore at the ropes that bound her wrists. She kept her gaze riveted on Patience, saw the hateful woman swing her weapon to align it with Slade's chest.

Hannah then saw Isabel react, saw her outstretched arms as she jumped at her enemy. Screaming in her head, Hannah wrenched her arms apart in a superhuman effort and came up with her hands free. From her position on the floor, realizing the crying gasps she heard were her own, she ripped her Smith & Wesson .32 out of her pocket, cocked, aimed, and fired— at the same time both of her Peacemakers, the one in Patience's hands and the one in Slade's hand, belched their fire and death.

In the unearthly quiet and calm that followed the loud reports, people fell to the floor. Patience. Isabel. Hannah flipped over. Slade. "No!" was the one wrenching scream that ripped her asunder. "No!"

*Had she then lost everyone? Slade, Isabel, Esmerelda. Mama and Papa.* Hannah repocketed her gun, sat up, and attacked the ropes around her ankles. Her fingernails were torn and bloody by the time she freed herself.

"No, Slade. No. Oh, please, God, no," she whimpered as she scrambled in a crawl toward her husband's prone, face-down body, mere feet from Cyrus. With Slade's face turned toward her, she could see that his mouth slacked open. His eyes were half-closed, and his face was an ashen gray.

Intent on her husband, and crawling over Cyrus, paying him no more attention than if he'd been a log, Hannah sucked in a shocked breath. A hand grasped her ankle. Before she could do more than absorb the fact that it had to be Cyrus, she heard a gun being cocked behind her.

Her heart set up a pounding, even as her mouth dried and a hot nervy feeling snaked over her. She felt the weight of her weapon in her pocket. Timing would be everything. She inched her hand toward her pocket.

"Did you think I'd die that easily?" Cyrus's voice sounded weak and bubbly. "They're all dead now. Except you." He stopped to wheeze and cough. "And when you are, the money will be all mine."

While he was talking, Hannah slipped her hand into her pocket, closing her fingers around the pistol's comforting steel form. Knowing he'd fire when he'd said his piece, Hannah ripped the pistol out of her pocket and jerked her leg. Wrenched off-target, Cyrus fired wide to Hannah's left.

Hannah heard him cocking the Peacemaker again. She jerked over on her back and saw him, bloodied and near death's door, but nevertheless using both hands to level the gun at her again. Vengeful hatred burst forth in Hannah as she raised her arm and took aim at Cyrus's openmouthed face.

She looked deep into his eyes. She wanted to be sure he knew and understood. "The only thing that's all yours, you murdering bastard, is a free trip to hell. This is for J. C. and Catherine Lawless."

Cyrus snarled out one word. "Bitch." And steadied his aim.

Cold to the core, Hannah squeezed the trigger, centering a bullet right in the middle of his forehead. Cyrus jerked backward and then toppled over. Dead. Hannah sat up, staring at the gun in her hand as if she'd never seen it before. Turning, she pitched it out the broken window. It was done. Vengeance was hers and her sisters'. It was a hollow feeling.

With her mind shrouded in a sanity-saving cloud, Hannah crawled to her husband. Stopping by his unmoving side, she crouched in a kneel and stared at him, her hands over her nose and mouth. She couldn't touch him. Her arms refused her brain's order to turn him over. Just as her legs refused the order to get up and go check on Isabel. She would, she promised, but right now she had to . . . had to see to her husband.

So, breathing raggedly, her heart thump-bumping painfully against her chest wall, she stared transfixed at the blood oozing from an unseen wound in his head. Her gaze lowered to the small pool of red that stained the carpet, that forced her horrified yet fixated attention to its deadly pattern. Watching Slade's lifeblood flow from him, Hannah felt nothing, heard nothing, did nothing. Time, unnoticed by the living or the dead, ticked by.

She closed her eyes, hoping against hope that when she opened them, Slade would be alive. She opened her eyes. She stared at the unmoving body before her. With no conscious forethought, she slowly dragged out her shirt's tail. Leaning over, suddenly galvanized, she scrubbed savagely at the blood on the carpet and pleaded with it. "No. Stop it. He's not dead. He won't be dead if you'll just stop. Why won't you stop?"

The cloud lifted. A wrenching sob tore its way up from the bottom of her soul, giving her the strength to lift his shoulders, turn him over, and slide her legs under him so she could cradle his head. She doubled herself over him, putting her cheek to his forehead, still so warm. Rocking him, holding him close, she cried, "No, no, no. I love you. Don't leave me, Slade. I love you."

With a dizzying suddenness, she jerked upright and stared at him, feeling a deep anger invade her heart. She thumped his unmoving shoulder. "Do you hear me, damn you? Don't you die! Don't you *dare*. I will never forgive you." Realizing what she was doing, she sounded a cry of sorrowful despair and doubled herself over him again.

"Hannah? Is that you?"

# CHAPTER TWENTY

The feeble cry brought Hannah's head up. She turned to look toward the sofa. The voice was Isabel's. Relieved beyond measure for this one blessing, but still numb from her grief, Hannah scooted out from under her husband. And froze. Blood. Everywhere. On her hands. Her clothes. *Just like Mama and Papa.* Hannah shook her head. *No. No more blood. Please.*

"Hannah? Are you . . . unharmed? Can you . . . help me . . . get this horrid . . . old bitch . . . off me?"

Standing at the cliff edge of sanity, Hannah laughed at Isabel's words and her angry grunts of effort. One word of sympathy, one word of pity from Isabel probably would have sent Hannah leaping over that precipice into madness. As it was, though, the older woman's feistiness set Hannah's feet in motion. And away from the edge. "I'm coming, Isabel. Hold on."

After no more than three steps in Isabel's direction, Hannah was staggered and spun when someone ran past her, hitting her legs, knocking her sideways. An involuntary cry escaped her as she whirled away from the passing body's momentum. Spreading her arms and legs to steady herself, stumbling to the sofa, Hannah clutched its upholstered spine with one hand and slipped her other hand into her pocket. Empty. No gun. Then she remembered—she'd thrown it out the window.

Forgetting about guns, forgetting about her own bruised and dizzy self, refusing to lose anyone else dear to her, Hannah grimaced in hatred as she whipped around and flung herself— to a standing halt. Her eyes flew open wide as she put her hands to her mouth. Then, joyfully, tearfully, she went to Isabel—and helped Esmerelda pull Patience's dead weight off her mistress.

Once their joint mission was accomplished, Hannah assisted Isabel in sitting up. She then beamed at the mastiff, noting the wound that grazed the dog's powerful shoulder, noting the matted blood in the tan fur, and the intelligent intensity in the dog's brown eyes. "Poor Essie," she whispered, her throat clogged with emotion. "Were you out there hurting and licking your wound all this time?"

Esmerelda inclined her head regally. Hannah's hand went to her heart in recognition of the mastiff's newfound majesty. Until the dog pricked her ears up, flopped her slobbering mouth open in a wide grin, and lolled her tongue out to the side.

That sight burst Hannah into real tears. Isabel clutched at her sleeve. Hannah dragged her other sleeve across her eyes and focused on the woman. The grande dame's white hair was as rumpled as her clothing and her mood. "Stupid old woman, thinking she can shoot my grandson. Hannah, dear, where is Slade?"

Hannah couldn't answer her. Not with words. Her chin quivered, her eyelids blinked rapidly, and she looked down, shaking her head.

Isabel became deathly quiet. She reached out a trembling hand and ran her fingers through the drying blood that coated Hannah's shirt. She wiped it on her own skirt and then put her blue-veined, wrinkled hand up to Hannah's cheek, pulling back a hand covered with the same red. "This isn't . . . this isn't"—she felt of her own fingers, smoothing them together in tiny circles—"yours?"

Hannah shook her head no.

"Oh, dear God." Isabel's voice held a death-knell quality to it.

Esmerelda nosed Hannah's shoulder and whined. Hannah clutched at the huge dog, hugging her fiercely, burying her face in the warm fur. For once in her life, Esmerelda sat still for such familiarity, even licking at and nosing Hannah's shoulder.

"Slade!" Isabel suddenly cried out.

Hannah heard her, but couldn't seem to raise her head to comfort his grandmother. She heard too Esmerelda's tail thumping on the carpet. Then, strong hands clasped her arms and turned her, sobbing and crying, to hold her against a warm chest. Hannah took a gasping, lurching breath and clung to this new comfort, this new and broad and masculine-scented chest . . . that was very familiar . . . in feel and texture . . . and breadth.

Hannah jerked back, opening her eyes, and very nearly lost consciousness, so great was her shock. "Slade." The word was a whisper. A wondrous, disbelieving, thank-you-God whisper. "Slade," she repeated, just above a whisper. "Slade." This time, aloud. She raised a trembling hand to touch the cheek of the only man in the entire world she would ever love. "Oh, Slade. You're not dead?"

He chuckled—the most beautiful sound in the whole world—and shook his bleeding head. "No. But if you'd like to try, the line is shorter now."

The swirling crowd, glittering in their finery, moved as if one body to the music that swelled and violined throughout Woodbridge Pond a little over a week later. Their Brahmin bellies full of the wonderful bounty of Isabel's repast, the toasts to the somewhat subdued newlyweds drunk, the horror and scandal behind them, Boston's best danced and laughed and flirted and gossiped.

Off in one corner of the large ballroom stood the honorees and their two best friends.

"Oh, come now, Slade. You can't just stop at the point where you're still at Cloister Point and have just let Hannah know you're alive. Isabel and her gray-haired staff have kept everyone away. So you must tell all. Now, I know you're both lying to make yourselves look good, but what happened next?"

Hannah, tucked against Slade's side, his arm possessively around her waist, laughed when he did and then took up the tale herself. "All right, Dudley. Just then, just as Slade held me in his arms and asked me if I'd like a chance at shooting him, in burst every single one of his men—armed to the teeth, and totally unneeded at that point."

"Oh, Hannah, you're so brave. I would have been absolutely rigid with fear. I've never even lifted a gun."

Hannah smiled at Constance's widened blue eyes and then

turned her face up to Slade's. "I was frightened," she answered, warming at his wink. She looked back at Constance and Dudley. "Out West, it's know how to shoot, or die. Still, I couldn't believe how lucky we'd been. Patience's aim was knocked off by Isabel, and Slade was only grazed and knocked unconscious."

"Like Esmerelda," Dudley supplied.

Hannah nodded at him, feeling Slade's warm, possessive hand through the thin fabric of her teal-blue velvet ballgown. She almost giggled at the memory of him upstairs earlier with her and again tossing her corset out into the hallway, telling her she didn't need the damned thing. All her bustles had quickly followed.

"Now, tell me, old man," Dudley addressed Slade, "how did all this sort out? Who did what to whom? And why?"

Hannah lowered her gaze to her hands. The chandelier's lights caught her diamond and flashed blinding sparkles over them all. She never had remembered to send for a jeweler to cut the darned ring off. And she never would—not even after she left Boston. Not even after she left Slade. Afraid her sadness would translate to tears she didn't want to explain, Hannah forced herself to listen to Slade's answers to Dudley's question.

". . . and then it turns up in Patience's room—the evidence we've needed all along. Temple found it tucked under her pillow when we searched the house. That woman actually kept a detailed journal of every act of hers and Cyrus's. Unbelievable. She wrote everything down—and worded it so that guilt was deflected to me. If you read that thing, you'd swear I killed Hamilton, Evelyn, Ardis, and Catherine. Not to mention the Hills—that couple I had taking care of Olivia's mother and baby—and Olivia's mother. And apparently I paid to have Hannah and Cates run over by the wagon."

A sudden dizziness threatened to send Hannah to the floor. The cloying scents in the close, crowded room roiled her stomach. But so had everything else for the past several days. Suddenly she felt hot and nauseous. And just as suddenly she felt sorry for having finally told Slade she wasn't really carrying his child. Because she was. But he'd never let her leave if he even suspected the truth. And so, another lie. Still, she tugged at Slade's sleeve, capturing his attention. "Slade, I've got to get some air and sit down."

Instantly, he had her elbow and nodded to indicate their concerned friends should follow them. Hannah allowed Slade to thread them through the congratulatory crowd, make their apologies, and then lead the foursome down the long hall to the music room. Hannah gratefully lay back on the fainting couch, thanked Constance for fanning her, and listened to the sound of Slade's steady footsteps as he strode to the window, opening it to allow cool air in.

Constance hovered over Hannah. "Oh, dear, I'm afraid this ball is taxing your strength. And so soon after everything you've been through." She turned to smack at Dudley's arm. "And you with all your questions."

"What did I do?" Dudley's injured expression, as he rubbed his arm, brought a smile to Hannah's face.

"I'm fine, Constance, really. And I don't mind talking about events." She struggled to sit up. "Really, I—"

"Lie back down." Slade deposited two chairs on the hard-wood floor and clamped a hand on her bare shoulder, holding her prone. "And stay there." He turned to Dudley. "Ames, you and Constance sit here."

Dudley turned to his fiancée, whispering as loudly as possible. "Bossy old devil, isn't he?"

Hannah put a hand over her mouth to stifle a threatening giggle. Constance did the same thing. Slade frowned mightily as he pushed Hannah's skirt aside to sit at her feet. He turned to her, his hand familiarly on her velvet-covered calf. "Better?"

She nodded, not trusting herself to speak without bursting out laughing. Slade narrowed his eyes at her and then turned to Dudley. "Back to the story. Now, where were we?"

Dudley slid Constance, chair and all, up against his side and put his arm around her shoulders. "You were telling me how the Wilton-Humeses had everyone killed, including—beg your pardon, Hannah—J. C. and Catherine Lawless."

Hannah's mirth fled her heart. Slade sought her gaze. She nodded almost imperceptibly. He considered her a moment and then turned to his best friend. "Hannah thinks they didn't kill her father. Just her mother."

Dudley's brown eyes widened. "The hell you say! Forgive

my bluntness, Hannah, but didn't you find him lying dead atop
your mother?''

Hannah shut her eyes against the memory and felt Slade
take her hand. Opening her eyes, she sent a grateful smile to
her husband and then turned to Dudley. "Yes, I did. But Patience's own words in her journal reveal that my father was
not to be killed. She even noted that she'd told her assassins
that if they killed him, she'd not pay them at all.''

Constance's slim, elegant hand, with the plum-sized diamond adorning her finger, went to her mouth. "Oh, surely he
wasn't to be spared out of any affection she might have borne
him?''

· Hannah shook her head. "Hardly. She and Cyrus had a
twofold plan in killing my mother. One, she would be elimi-
nated as an heir to Ardis's fortune. And two, they knew that
killing Mama would lure Papa here. When he arrived, they
were going to set up a confrontation between Papa and Slade.
Based on Slade's''—Hannah cut her gaze to him and then
away—''hatred of him, they felt sure that wouldn't be too hard
to do. They were counting on Papa naming Slade as Mama's
killer before he shot him. In that event, any suspicion would
be off my aunt and uncle. And with Slade dead and Mama
dead, the money would be Cyrus's alone.''

Dudley and Constance sat as still as death and stared
blankly ahead. Dudley roused himself to say, "Absolutely diabolical, as well as brilliant, I'm sorry to say. But tell me this,
Hannah, what steps had they taken to ensure that your father
would believe Slade here was responsible?''

"Nothing more than a half-burned scrap of Wilton-Humes
letterhead with my name on it.'' All heads turned to Slade
when he answered for Hannah.

Dudley repeated his judgment. "Diabolical.''

"As always,'' Slade quipped. "There's more that's possibly
related, but I'll let Hannah tell you.''

When they turned to her, Hannah thought first about what
she knew before she spoke. "A tiny portrait of Great-
Grandmother Ardis, a replica of one hanging at Cloister Point,
is possibly missing from home. Seeing the original portrait
jogged my memory, so I wrote my sisters asking them to see
if it's there or not. I'm betting it's not.'' Her grim certainty
settled on her features.

Constance frowned in thought. "And if it's not, what does that mean?"

"It means whoever has it is also responsible. And is still alive and out there somewhere. I'll find them. Wherever they are. This isn't over." She cut her gaze over to Slade's black eyes and the grim line of his mouth. They'd fought about this very point. But she was going. She was.

Constance recaptured Hannah's attention when she sat back and huffed out her breath. "Then you don't believe that the men who killed your mother took that portrait?"

Hannah shrugged. "They could have. But I doubt it, based on their orders from Patience. If they killed Papa, they got nothing. So if they'd had to kill him, they would have taken every valuable they could carry as their payment. But the only thing missing—if indeed it is—is that portrait. So, I'm beginning to think Cyrus's hired guns killed Mama and took off, before Papa came home. And then someone else, for some other reason, killed him."

Over the gasps of their friends, Slade jumped in. "It makes sense. But the only thing we can't figure is why Cyrus's assassins, having done their deed, never returned for their payment."

"How's that? The assassins never came back?" Dudley burst in.

Slade met his gaze. "Never made it back, never got paid. And that's according to Patience in her journal. She made a notation that it was just as well because she didn't have the money to pay them and Hannah was already here with me. Two birds with one stone, as the saying goes."

Constance shook her elegantly coiffed blond head. "Amazing. Didn't I tell you that Patience was the one who frightened me the most? And she even shot her own husband. Hard to believe."

The ensuing silence was broken when Dudley slapped his big hands down on his knees. "Enough unpleasantness." He turned to Hannah, a tentative smile on his lips. "Well, then, Hannah, I suppose you and Slade here still have to produce that heir so you and your sisters can inherit."

Constance smacked Dudley's arm and made a cautionary noise. Hannah flinched. And did so again when she caught the look on her husband's face.

Undaunted, Dudley turned to Slade. "By my calculations, Cloister Point is now yours, old sock. So, I'd like to propose a sale. Constance and I have been discussing buying it from you, perhaps put some happy memories in the old place. Wouldn't we make bully neighbors? And of course, my first act will be to tear down that fence, so your children and ours can be constant nuisances at both places."

Hannah could only frown at the wonderfully cheerful Dudley. She looked at Slade, who looked away from her, sighting on the harp across the room. Hannah looked at it, too, remembering his words comparing her to it.

But still, Dudley awaited an answer. And one didn't appear to be forthcoming from her husband. So, she forced a smile and answered him, striving not to give away any of the undercurrents between her and Slade. "I think you and Constance would make lovely neighbors for Woodbridge Pond. I'm sure there's some legal something or other you have to do, but . . . we'd be proud for you to live there."

Constance squeezed Dudley's large hand and then clapped her own tiny ones together. "This is the best of all endings. That hateful Patience and Cyrus are gone, you've found love, Dudley and I've found love, and best of all, you and your sisters are safe now."

Hannah looked from Constance's open and beaming face to Slade's closed one. He answered before she could. "Sorry, but you're wrong—about several things, but mostly about Hannah and her sisters being safe. Remember those trackers I told you about—the ones following the Lawless girls?"

Dudley ran a hamlike hand through his red hair. "Don't tell me—Cyrus and Patience didn't send them out?"

"Exactly. There's absolutely no mention of them in her journal. So, as meticulously as she entered every other detail, we have to assume she and Cyrus had nothing to do with them. I have some information on the trackers trickling in, but not enough to name their employers." He looked at Hannah as he finished. "You may be right. It's more than likely that someone besides the Wilton-Humeses either killed your father or had him killed."

Before Hannah could react, Constance humphed out her opinion in a pretty pout. "Well, I certainly hope that some lovely Western gunslinger shoots their guts out, whoever they are.''

Eyebrows raised like distress flags, Dudley pulled back from the china-doll darling by his side. ''I've never seen this violent side of you, my dear.''

She lowered her lids coyly and batted her thick fringe of dark-blond eyelashes at him. ''There are a lot of sides of me you've never seen, my big lovely boy.''

Dudley grabbed for her hand, held it to his heart, and then melted into a besotted liquid form at her feet. All that was left of him was his formal attire. Or so it seemed.

Hannah had an amused expression for the lovebirds, but only a shy, fleeting one for her husband. With her leaving in two days, and with Slade not liking it one bit, the strain between them was nearly overwhelming. And they still had to tell Isabel after her party. She deserved this night, at least. So Hannah sat lost in her predicament, so close and yet so far away from her husband. How would she get through the next two days?

She nearly gasped when Slade slid his hand up her calf to her knee—under her skirt. He spoke in that low, husky tone of his that told her exactly what he was thinking. ''Have you no sweet words or pretty smiles for me, my love?''

Hannah had the hardest time meeting his gaze. ''I wasn't sure you—I mean, we shouldn't—We—''

His hand clutched her knee. ''We love each other. We're married. What aren't you sure about?''

Hannah's heart hurt just looking at Slade's imploring and ruggedly handsome face. ''I'm not sure that . . . being together would make things better.''

Slade's face contorted into a mask of barely leashed emotion. ''How could they be any worse, Hannah?'' His voice was a rough, ragged sound.

Hannah looked down at her lap. Slade withdrew his hand and leaned back against the wall. He closed his eyes and shook his head. Had they been alone, Hannah would have burst into tears. Or would have grabbed him to her. Or perhaps she would have done neither.

Couldn't he understand that she had a blood oath to fulfill? She'd vowed to make the guilty ones pay. And she'd done that—but only partially, as it turned out. No, this was far from over. Now she wanted the actual shooters—Papa's and Mama's. And Slade knew himself that Jacey and Glory were still in danger. She couldn't just sit here all safe and secure in Boston, as he wanted her to do.

But beyond that, she'd already admitted that Slade deserved better than her. He deserved a woman who trusted him and wouldn't lie to him. Tears now pricked at Hannah's eyes. She did trust him. Completely. But she was still lying to him. Oh, she'd made such a muck of her life—and of his. Taking in a deep breath, she admitted that he could never find another woman who loved him as much as she did. It wasn't possible. And that was the most horrible part. Leaving his love.

But at least she would have his child, a beautiful part of him for her own. Hannah rested her gaze on her husband's determined jaw and knew a moment of terror. God forbid he should ever find out her treachery on that score. She slipped her hand down her gown to rest atop her womb. Their child. Hers and Slade's. She looked at its father, at the handsome, chiseled profile she'd see in her mind every day of her life. She loved him with every fiber of her being. She always would. But she wasn't what he deserved.

Those pricking tears now filled her eyes. Why was life so cruel? When Slade, still leaned back against the wall, rotated his head to look at her, Hannah rapidly blinked back her tears and tried to smile at him. But her quivering chin wouldn't permit it.

Slade smiled as if in sympathy and took her hand. He began pulling her to him. "Hannah, I know you're going. And I know I can't stop you. But I need you . . . now and forever. If I can't have you forever, then give me now, give me tonight. And I'll let you go without a fight. I swear it. Your life, your freedom, are your own."

They were the most achingly beautiful words he'd ever said to her. And they broke her heart. Still, she allowed him to tug her against his chest. She wrapped her arms around his neck. Into his ear, she whispered. "Love me, Slade. Love me."

Later that night, or closer to the next morning, Hannah lay spent, satiated, naked, and curled up against Slade's side. Her head nestled in the crook of his shoulder. His cheek rested atop her head, his arm around her back, his hand on her hip.

Hannah knew she'd never feel another such moment of supreme contentment as this one. Because she'd leave for home in two days—no, it was tomorrow already. She'd leave in one day on an early morning train.

Slade's powerful chest rose and fell under her hand, his breathing telling her that he too was awake. She shifted to look up at his square-jawed profile. He was such a good man, a noble man. And he loved her. Hannah almost groaned. She was lower than a snake's belly in a ditch for not telling him of their child. No matter what else might be between them, he had a right to know that. Hannah lowered her gaze from his jaw and made small circles with his chest hair and her fingertip. "Slade, there's something I—"

"Hannah, I want you to—"

They spoke at the same time. And both laughed.

"You first," Hannah prompted.

Slade took a deep breath. "All right. I want you to know that I don't blame you for leaving."

Hannah frowned at his brown, flat nipple. Never raising her head to look at his face, she swallowed back sudden tears and had to clear her throat before she could answer him. "You don't blame me? What does that mean?"

"Well, we Garretts—except for Isabel—are a sorry lot."

Now Hannah raised her head to stare at her husband. "I won't listen to you talk like that. You're not a sorry lot."

Calm, a level expression on his face, he shook his head. "I'm not feeling sorry for myself, Hannah. I'm being truthful. I've been lying here thinking of the one reason you should stay and all the reasons you need to go. And the truth is— you need to go."

"I do?" Her voice was no more than a whisper of emotion.

He nodded. "Yes, you do. I keep seeing myself threatening you, grabbing at you and handling you in a rough manner, and practically locking you away in my two homes." He looked to a far-off point and shook his head. "I even tried to use you as a pawn in my own twisted notion of revenge. I'm a sick bastard."

Hannah blinked back tears. "Don't say that, Slade. You're not."

He finally looked at her, self-honesty blazing in his black eyes. "Yes I am. You know what my revenge was to be,

Hannah? Marry you, seduce you into loving me, and then discard you, thereby destroying you. Like my mother was by my father. Admirable family trait.'' He shook his head. ''We Garrett men are hell on our women. I talked to Isabel after you left—no, after I *made* you leave here—for my brownstone. She told me the same thing that she'd told you about my father . . . and your mother.''

He firmed his mouth to a straight line. ''You're better off leaving. And, after thinking about it, I'm . . . glad there's really no child. Because I don't know what kind of father I'd be. My own wasn't much of one, so God knows what I'm capable of. But along those lines—your leaving, that is—I've spoken with my attorneys this past week.''

Hannah stared at him for the longest time, feeling her guts churn and her heart break. He refused to meet her eyes, so she scooted across him to lay her head down over his tom-tomming heartbeat. ''Do you want a divorce?''

Under her ear, Hannah felt his heart lurch into a skipping beat. ''God, no. And I don't want to hear any protests, either, but I've settled property, stock, and a sum of money on you, the exact sum Ardis left your mother. You may not be able to inherit because we produced no heir, but my money I can do with as I please. I know you didn't come here for money, and you keep saying you don't want it, but you have to take it, Hannah. For your sisters, if not for yourself.''

Hannah forced her breath out slowly through her nostrils. She—a lying, mistrustful woman—did not deserve this kind of unselfish love. And yet a part of her wanted him to convince her to stay. ''Tell me your reason why I should stay.''

He shifted about, dislodging her to his side again as he stretched his long, muscular legs and hugged her to him for the briefest of seconds. ''It doesn't matter now. Besides, it's not enough of a reason. Apparently.''

''It's not apparent to me.'' Hannah raised her head again to look at him.

He flicked his gaze to her face and then looked away. Wrapping her long hair around his hand, he smoothed the silky mitt up and down her back. He finally looked down at her and smiled. ''Well, it is to me. Otherwise, your trunks wouldn't be packed, and you wouldn't have a train ticket home. So it doesn't matter what my reason is, Hannah. Besides, you're right—you need to get home to your sisters.''

Agreeing with him but certain she'd lost everything that would ever be important to her, Hannah frowned and laid her head down again on his shoulder.

''Hannah?''

''Yes?''·

''What was it you started to say to me? You said there was something I should know.''

She squeezed her eyes shut as tightly as she could. ''Nothing. It was nothing.'' She remained quiet for several minutes. As did Slade. Not a sound stirred in all of Woodbridge Pond to distract her from her sad thoughts of leaving. Then, feeling the inevitable closing in around her, feeling the darkness of the room invading her heart, Hannah pulled herself up and over him. She smoothed a hand across his cheek. ''Slade, will you love me again?''

His chest heaved and jerked mightily, as his stomach muscles rippled. Alarmed, Hannah gripped him tightly as he tugged her head down to rest against his neck and shoulder. If she didn't know better, she would swear he was crying.

''Again and always, Hannah,'' came his choked reply.

# CHAPTER TWENTY-ONE

—

"Do you have everything?"

"Yes, Isabel, I do. I've checked. You've checked. Olivia's checked. Rowena and Serafina have checked. I haven't left anything." *Except my heart.*

"Well, if you're sure."

Hannah hugged her grandmother-in-law to her, holding her for the longest time. Tears squeezed out from under her tightly closed eyelids. "I love you," she whispered.

Isabel held Hannah in her embrace as her ample bosom shook, but then she abruptly pulled back and dabbed at her reddened eyes with a balled-up hanky. All business now, she spun Hannah around to the wide central steps that would take her downstairs, past all the combined Garrett household domestics, through the front door, and out of their lives.

"Go on with you. You don't want to miss your train. The infernal contraptions wait for no one—even if we do own them."

Hannah nodded and tried to smile. But her lips wouldn't stop quivering long enough to hold an expression. "I'll miss you, Isabel. I love you."

Isabel burst into tears, burying her lined and puckered, highly rouged little face in her hanky. She made a gesture for Hannah to leave as she spoke through her hanky's folds. "Go now, or I'll never let you leave. Go. I love you."

Hannah stood still, staring at her. Towering emotion threatened to send her to her knees. She locked them, determined to get through the next few moments with a modicum of dignity. Just then, Esmerelda drooped out of Hannah's bedroom.

The mastiff's ears and tail almost dragged the ground. She nosed under Hannah's hand and then plodded to the top of the stairs, turning back to peer solemnly at Hannah.

With fat tears rolling down her cheeks, Hannah clutched at her handbag, and took the first steps that would lead her away from everyone she loved at Woodbridge Pond. "Come on, then. Let's do this," she told Essie softly.

With that, the unlikely pair proceeded down the polished-wood stairway, their footfalls and pawfalls echoing hollowly with each step. Hannah wished with all her might that she could look away from the sight at the bottom of the stairs, but there was nowhere else to look. Wasn't it bad enough that they were all there, every last one of the domestics, all with their heads turned up to her, all with their sad gazes and their snifflings meant for her?

But even worse were Dudley and Constance by the open front doors. Hannah's gaze flicked to Slade, behind them. So, he'd come after all. He stood with his hand on the knob, holding the door open, waiting for her to leave. Making it easy for her to leave.

Then, so be it. After the night of the ball, he'd stayed away, at his brownstone. Until this moment, she hadn't even been sure he'd be here this morning. Looking him up and down, she noted he looked like hell. He needed to shave. His hair was unkempt. His clothes weren't even the immaculate style she was used to from him. But it was his eyes. They were bloodshot and red-rimmed, as if he'd been sleepless. Or on a heavy drinking spree. But right now, no matter the cause, those eyes bored into her soul.

Hannah looked away from him as she stopped in front of Rowena and Serafina. The ancient twins each clutched the hand Hannah offered them. The old maids stared at her, their individual double chins quivering. But they said nothing. Neither did Hannah. She then moved down the line to each elderly chambermaid, each ancient kitchenmaid, stopping, saying her good-byes, squeezing hands, having hers squeezed. Mrs. Edgars, the hefty, gregarious cook, held her white apron up to her face and cried loudly. Hannah smiled and patted her shoulder. Mrs. Edgars wailed anew and aloud.

Then Hannah and Esmerelda came to Hammonds. All stiff starch and spit and polish, he bowed formally. Hannah's stomach muscles clenched as she bit down hard on the inside of her cheek. Hammonds straightened up, keeping his gaze at a point just beyond her. "Madam, it has been my distinct pleasure to serve you. I wish you the best of—" He choked off his words, raised his chin, and went on. "I wish you the best of everything."

"Thank you, Hammonds. You've been wonderful." No one else but Hammonds could have heard her, so low did she speak. She moved to Pemberton. And her heart melted into a sloppy pool of emotionalism. The sweet, white-wispy-haired and bent-over little man took her hand in both of his knobby-knuckled ones. His rheumy, watered-blue eyes blinked up at her. "One thinks one will miss you most fiercely, Mrs. Garrett."

Hannah nodded. "One thinks one will miss you, too, Pemberton. You keep Miss Isabel corralled, you hear?"

He pulled her toward him the slightest bit. "Could one perhaps leave a length of rope toward that end?"

Hannah chuckled and pulled him to her for a hug. "I love you," she whispered. And thought he whispered it back to her. Then, she stepped over to face Mrs. Stanley and her sons, Jacko and Edgar. The two little boys, about eight and ten years old, stood solemnly to either side of their mother. When the housekeeper curtsied to Hannah, they bowed. "Mrs. Garrett, ma'am. You've been a joy."

"As have you, Mrs. Stanley." Hannah smiled at her and ruffled the boys' heads, telling them, "You be good boys and help your mother." They mumbled out their opinions of that, but nodded nevertheless.

Then, Hannah faced Olivia. Just behind her, with his hand possessively on her shoulder, was Rigby. In Olivia's arms was Colette, the only happy, chortling one in the crowd. Olivia bobbed a curtsy and blinked back a wealth of tears. "I wish I was going with you, miss. We all do."

Hannah nodded and held out a finger for the baby to grab. Colette clutched at it and promptly tried to stick it in her mouth. Hannah chuckled with Rigby and then spoke with Olivia. "I wish you could, too. But it's best you stay here with Rigby. Where I'm going is no place for a baby."

*What about your own?* Hannah swallowed the lump in her throat. She then turned to Rigby, pulling her finger from Colette's grasp to shake his hand warmly when he stuck his out to her. "Rigby, I couldn't be happier for you and Olivia. Take good care of them. They mean an awful lot to me."

"Yes, ma'am. They mean an awful lot to me, too." Rigby squeezed Olivia's shoulder as she turned her smiling face up to him. The loving sight was almost more than Hannah could stand. These two had a bright future together. Unlike her and Slade.

Hannah stepped over to Constance and threw herself into the blond girl's open arms. They cried and sniffed and moaned until Dudley's heavy hand tugged on Hannah's arm. She looked up at the big man. Unabashed by the tears that stood in his eyes, he pulled her gruffly to his chest and patted the life out of her. "We love you, Hannah—more than you'll ever know. You've changed everyone here for the better. But especially me. Godspeed."

Hannah drew back, holding both his hands. "Thank you, Dudley. But I didn't change you." She pulled a hand loose and patted the center of his chest. "You always had it—right here, future Senator Ames."

Dudley pulled himself up to his considerable height and beamed as Constance clutched at his elbow and laid her curls against his huge arm. Hannah smiled at them through her pain. She couldn't move. She couldn't turn . . . not to *him*. But she didn't have to, not right away. Because Esmerelda nosed her hand again. Hannah knelt down and gathered the dog's massive head to her and hugged her tightly. Finally, she stood up. "Esmerelda, you're a caution. And I love you."

Esmerelda sadly waggled her drooping tail, looked Hannah right in the eye, and then turned, padding up the stairs to take her place beside Isabel, who stood with a hand on the railing and her other to her heart. Hannah faced them all, raised her hand in a half wave, half salute, and turned to Slade. She had no idea what to expect from this man—her husband.

Into the silence marred only by vagrant sniffles and quiet sobs, Slade straightened up to his full, heart-wrenching magnificence. His black eyes were unblinking. His sensuous mouth was unsmiling. He could have been carved from granite.

Hannah glanced past him and saw the waiting carriage outside. Sedgewick proudly sat on the driver's box, looking her way. Behind the brougham was the young stablehand, Jonathan, at the reins of the carryall, which was loaded with her belongings. She looked back to Slade.

A muscle ticked in his jaw. "We'd better go. You don't want to miss your train."

Perched on a tufted, overstuffed seat, set in an alcove of the plush, private railcar, Hannah sat alone, silently staring out at the Boston skyline. The city was wreathed in November's late-autumn tones. Trees stood denuded of foliage. The sky threatened a leaden gray. Even the people at the station seemed downcast, seemed to walk with heads bent down against the wind. Hannah took a deep, shuddering breath against the wind.

When was this darned train going to leave? They should have pulled out long ago. Hannah felt sure this was a test, someone was giving her a last chance to change her mind. But she couldn't. As much as she wanted to, she couldn't. All she could think of, all she dared think of, were Jacey and Glory and Biddy. She'd promised them to come home. They were in danger, and they didn't even know. They needed her.

*And Slade doesn't? What about your baby? What about you? What do you need?* "Stop it," Hannah gritted out.

The train lurched. Hannah grasped at the seat's edges. The whistle blew. Steam rolled back in vaporish clouds. People hugged, kissed, and hurried to embark. Finally. She was leaving Boston, just as she'd arrived—alone. No, not alone. Hannah's hand went to her womb. *I love you, little baby.*

Not able to face Boston passing swiftly by her window, Hannah turned to look at her stunning accommodations, at the rich woods and elegant furniture. She finally rested her gaze on the upholstered and empty seat across from her. Slade had insisted she ride in style. She was after all a Garrett and now part owner of the rail line, he'd said.

She shook her head. What did it matter? Private car. First class. Coach. In with the luggage. It didn't matter. She was too numb to enjoy the luxury. Would've been too numb to notice the crowded public cars, the jostling, the loud talking, the smells. Too numb.

The train lurched again and then rolled smoothly on its tracks. Slowly and smoothly. Almost involuntarily, Hannah looked out the window. Not one familiar face to see her off.

Not one. Slade had merely taken her hand to help her out of the carriage, had allowed her a moment to say her good-byes to Sedgewick and Johnny, and then had scooted her here to this very car. He'd stood there in the doorway a moment and—

She looked now to the doorway at the end of the car, hoping against hope that he'd—No. The door remained closed, impassive.

Well, he'd stood there, filling the doorway, had stared long and hard at her, shook his head, said, "You're even more stubborn and prideful than I am," and turned and walked away. Just turned and walked away. *What the devil did he mean by more stubborn and prideful than him? In what way?* A drop of moisture splatted onto Hannah's hand. She looked down at it, saw her folded hands through a blur. And realized she was crying.

"Oh, stop it, you big baby," she admonished herself aloud as she dug through her handbag, pushed aside her peashooter, and finally found her hanky. She pulled it out and wiped her tears. It was the same hanky, without the burned letter in it, that had put her on a train less than two months ago. She balled it up in her hands, seeing again Slade wordlessly handing it to her in the carriage on the way to the depot.

Hannah looked again out the window, saw the city pass by, saw the pasturelands and the countryside begin. "Good-bye," she whispered.

The door to her car slid open. Hannah jerked toward the sound and peered hopefully around the alcove's wall. And slumped. Her own private, nice attendant stood in the doorway. He was smiling, albeit somewhat hesitantly. A middle-aged, ruddy-faced Irishman who'd introduced himself earlier as O'Malley, he now ducked his head respectfully. "Beggin' yer pardon, Mrs. Garrett. But I'm afraid there's a wee bit of a problem with your ticket."

Hannah frowned. "My ticket? I didn't think I needed one. Didn't my . . . husband take care of everything?"

He nodded vigorously. "Of a certainty, he did just that, yer ladyship. Of a certainty. But I'm afraid we're a mite more crowded than first expected. I'm needin' ta ask you if you'd mind sharin' yer ride—just to the next stop this afternoon—with a few good people?"

Hannah frowned. The last thing she wanted, in her present mood, was company. Then she thought again. Perhaps the one thing she needed was company. And it was only for a few hours. She focused on O'Malley's cheerful face. And smiled. "Certainly. Show them in."

He ducked his head and grinned, showing big, slightly yellowed teeth. "I'll certainly go and get them and then do just that, yer ladyship. And it's right nice of you to allow these folks yer car."

Hannah sighed at the man's gushings. "Well, you're nice to say so, O'Malley."

He smiled again and stepped back outside, closing the door behind him. He had to go get them? He'd acted as if the people were right behind him. Hannah shrugged and turned to look out the window again. She sincerely hoped these people were friendly sorts, And not loud, obnoxious talkers who'd make her want to shoot them before their ride was up.

The private car's door slid open. Hannah turned at the sound and leaned over to see around the alcove. Well, there was O'Malley. And—*No*. Hannah gasped, her hands flying to cover her mouth. She suddenly realized she was standing. "Esmerelda! What in the world—?"

Esmerelda bayed and bounded to Hannah, jumping up to put her feet on Hannah's shoulders, the better to knock her back onto the upholstered seat and slurp her face. Hannah closed her eyes in self-defense, and laughed and screeched as she batted at the dog. "Stop it! How did you get here, you big goose?"

"One believes she came in the second brougham, madam. Is that right, Hammonds? Or was it in one of the other carriages?"

Hannah started at the voice and opened her eyes, shoving Esmerelda down. What she saw sagged her jaw open as far as surprise could carry it.

Flanked by the entire and combined Garrett household staffs of broadly grinning domestics, Hammonds gave Pemberton's question serious thought. Or appeared to. "Hmmm, I believe it was in the last carriage." He turned to Rigby. "Or, young man, did you have her in the carryall?"

Rigby looked at Olivia, who shrugged her shoulders. He then turned to Hammonds. "I think she rode with Mrs. Garrett." He turned around, looking through the now-parting crowd. "Wait. I'll ask her."

Isabel fussed and shoved her way through, until she stood in front of Hannah and irritatedly straightened her clothes all around. "Damned people wouldn't get out of my way. Now, what's the question?"

"Miss Hannah asked how did Esmerelda get here," Rowena and Serafina said together, sounding as if they'd rehearsed it that way.

"Oh, that's easy." Then Isabel eyed Hannah. "Close your mouth before you catch a fly, girl. Just because my grandson is fool enough to let you leave doesn't mean we are."

She then snapped her fingers for Esmerelda to come to her. Which the dog didn't. "Minds like the rest of them." She finally looked again at the stunned, unblinking Hannah. "I believe she came in the brougham with Mr. Ames, Miss Wannamaker, and that stubborn grandson of mine. Let me ask them."

Isabel turned to face her employees. And they parted as if at a predetermined signal. Constance and Dudley swooped through the gauntlet of servants, smiling and yelling, "Surprise!"

Hannah finally remembered how to work her muscles. Screeching in a purely feminine wail of joy, she jumped up and grabbed Constance to her and then Dudley and then Isabel and then Olivia and Colette and then Pemberton and then Slade and then Hammonds and then—*Slade?*

Hannah backed two steps down the line. And there stood that damned Slade Franklin Garrett, grinning like a jackass eating briars. He put his hands up defensively when Hannah's hands went to her waist. "Don't blame me. You try to deal with all these people."

Everyone in the car laughed . . . nervously. But Hannah could only stare at her husband. And drink her fill of him. "What in the world are you doing here?"

Slade shrugged, ran a hand through his thick, black hair. "They came to see you off."

Hannah narrowed her eyes at him. "I already said my goodbyes to them. I asked you what are *you* doing here?"

The private car got deathly quiet. Hannah cut her gaze to individual faces in the crowd. A few dared grin at her. She squelched those happy faces with an upward tilt of her Lawless chin. And then burst out laughing. "Oh, God, it's so good to see you. I love you all."

She opened her arms, trying to encompass all of them, and got hugged silly by the entire assemblage. That done, everyone stood around watching Hannah and Slade standing around watching each other. Dudley, Constance, and Isabel, who clutched at Esmerelda's collar, finally took charge.

Dudley's booming voice, as much as his herding gestures, moved everyone to the far end of the private car. "Come on now. Over here. There's food and drink for everyone. Let's leave the lovebirds to themselves. Come on now."

In only a moment, Hannah was alone with Slade. As alone as two people could be with twenty others in their presence. Slade took Hannah's hand and led her back to the alcove seat that she'd occupied only moments ago. He sat next to her. Hannah could do nothing but beam at this man.

Slade smoothed a curl back from her face. "Did you miss us?"

Hannah chuckled. "I haven't even shot at you yet."

Slade raised an eyebrow at her and Hannah caved in, launching herself at him, throwing her arms around his neck. "Of course I missed you." Her voice was muffled as she spoke into his wonderfully masculine-scented neck. "I was sitting here crying and feeling sorry for myself." Just as suddenly, she pulled back from him to hit at his rock-hard chest. "You're terrible. Letting me think—"

His finger at her lips cut off her words. "Shh. I told the truth—this wasn't my idea. It was last-minute, and it was theirs." He pointed at the crowd gathered around the refreshments.

Hannah sobered some, drew back from him and looked down at her lap. "You didn't want to come?"

He tucked a finger under her chin to raise her eyes to meet his. "Yes, I wanted to come. Hell, I never left the train. What I meant was, it wasn't my idea for all of *them* to come, too. We've been in the next car arguing about how far they can ride with us before I make them get off and go home."

"But they said that Esmerelda rode with you in the—"

He shook his head and laughed. "That was just their way of shoving me into your view. I'm the big surprise for you."

Hannah smacked at him again. "You certainly are." Then, she grew shy, bit at her bottom lip. "What . . . what did you mean about arguing with them about how far they can ride with . . . us?''

Slade grinned and moved across to sit in the upholstered seat facing hers. He crossed his arms over his chest. ''Just that. They're crazy if they think I'm going to let them go all the way to No Man's Land with us.''

Hot moisture pricked at the backs of Hannah's eyes. She blinked and took a heated breath. ''With us?''

''Us. Me and you.''

''Me and you?''

Slade shook his head and chuckled. ''Has carrying our child sapped your mental faculties, Hannah?''

Hannah's eyes rounded in shock. The father of her child sobered some, ducking his chin and raising an eyebrow until he looked absolutely dangerous. ''Uh-huh. Our child. You weren't going to tell me, were you?''

Hannah tried a smile, but guilt wouldn't allow her to hold it. ''I didn't know for sure when I first told you I was expecting. In fact, I lied. But I did know I was, when I told you I wasn't, because I knew you wouldn't let me leave if I was, and then I tried to tell you I really was, but you said you were glad I wasn't, and then . . .'' Hannah frowned. ''Where was I?''

''I have no idea.'' He kept a grave expression on his face. ''I'm just glad you are. I said I was glad you weren't, because I thought you didn't want to be with me and have my child.'' He stopped and frowned. ''Hell, now you have me doing it. At any rate, the sickness, the dizziness, no appetite. I could tell.''

Hannah raised an eyebrow at him. And he caved in. ''All right, dammit. Olivia and Isabel and Mrs. Stanley told me you were.''

Hannah snapped around in her seat to stare at the named women, all of whom were engaged in spoiling Colette. They knew? She hadn't even told them she was. She twisted back around to her husband. ''*When* did they tell you?''

Looking mighty sheepish, he scratched at his temple. ''Just now. When they all arrived here.''

Hannah laughed. ''You had no idea?''

He shrugged and managed to look petulant. ''How was I supposed to know? I thought you were sick and tired from . . . from last week at Cloister Point. I've never been around''—

he waved his hand in her general direction—"women in your condition."

Endearing as his answer was, Hannah's next thought sobered her. "Then are you here for me only because I'm carrying your heir?"

Slade cocked his head at her, looking as serious as a hanging judge. "No. I'm here because this train was carrying you away from me. I'd already made up my mind to follow you out West—whether you wanted me to or not—before they ever arrived."

Hannah fought the smile that wanted to lay claim to her mouth. "Whether or not I wanted you to? You told me to leave."

"Yes, I did. You have to go—I agree. What kind of man would I be if I tried to keep you here when you need to see to your family? But I also know there's still a fight to come out in No Man's Land. I would like to be by your side when you face it. But unless and until you allow me to help you, that fight is yours alone."

He shook his head. "The truth is, I couldn't *keep* you from going, not because I don't love you, Hannah, but because I have no right to stop you. You deserve better than me. As I told you the other night, I meant to use you, to hurt you for my own revenge. I'm hoping you can forgive me—"

"There's nothing to forgive. I'm the one who came here intending to kill you, remember? If you can forgive that, then I can certainly—"

"You had every right to think me guilty, Hannah. Every right. But it's all over now. It's in the past. What's important now, and to our future, is . . . Well, dammit, if it's what you want, I love you enough to let you go, to keep you safe from me."

"It's not what I want. Because I feel safe only when I'm with you," Hannah said just above a whisper.

His black-eyed gaze softened dangerously. Slade looked down at his lap and then up at her again. "What about trust, Hannah? You have to trust me. And not lie to me. Ever again. I want us to be together. But I don't know how to get there."

Hannah breathed in slowly, deeply, and felt her heart thumping hopefully. They were so close, but one wrong word could shatter their fragile negotiations. Being careful with her words, she said, "Slade, all those things you said two nights ago, about Garrett men and not knowing what you're capable of, and—''

He waved away her concerns. ''I've spent two days pacing the floor and not sleeping or eating. But I've gotten it all straightened out now.'' His tense expression leaned him forward in his seat. His black eyes shone with crystal-clear truth. ''Hannah, I'm not my father. I'm stronger than him. And unlike him, I love my wife. I have the woman I love.'' He stopped and seemed to think about that. ''Don't I?''

Hannah's soul warmed up as she smiled at her husband. But there was more she had to say. ''I've changed, too. I do trust you. I have faith in you. How could I not after everything you've done for me? But more than that, Slade, I want so much to have someone to sometimes take charge for me—and of me. I'm so tired of being the oldest, of being alone with my decisions, of trying to decide what's best for everyone around me, of—''

Slade grinned at her. ''You want me to take care of you? Is that what you're trying to say?''

''It would be a relief if you would.'' Then, Hannah bit at her bottom lip and blinked back her tears. ''Do you think me a silly goose of a woman for that?''

Slade's eyebrows went up. ''Hardly. You're the bravest, strongest, most capable woman I've ever met. The only thing that exceeds my respect for you—and that hair-trigger gun hand of yours—is my love for you, Hannah. Do you love me?''

''I do. With all my heart. And I want you in my life and at my side. I do.''

''Then say it.''

Hannah huffed out her breath, as if exasperated with him. ''I love you with all my heart. And soul. And body. There. Are you happy?''

Slade grinned broadly at her, showing off his white and even teeth. ''I am. Because I never want to be on the bad side of a woman named Lawless who packs a peashooter and two Peacemakers. Not that she'll ever have any trouble from me. Especially since she's a better shot than I am.''

Hannah grinned as widely as her lips would allow. ''Is she now?''

Slade quirked a wounded expression and put a hand to his heart. ''It pains me to admit it, but yes she is.''

That settled, Hannah spoke of her next concern, her next hope. "Are you really going all the way home with me?"

"Yes, ma'am. My luggage is already stowed with yours. Why do you think I put you up in a private car? I'm not going to share you with anyone after the first stop this afternoon. We'll put all these good folks onto the next train back to Boston."

Hannah lifted her chin and turned a playful attitude on him. "And what if I didn't really want you with me after all? What would you have done then?"

He rubbed thoughtfully at his chin as he looked up and away from her. Then he lowered his head and gave her that black-eyed gaze that sizzled her skin. "I seem to recall once telling you that if you tried to leave, you'd have to drag my bed with you because you'd be tied to it."

"Your bed's not here."

He smiled . . . sort of. "That's true. But my heart's here. You're dragging it around now, but you just don't know it."

"I know it, Slade. It's safe with me."

"Good." He surprised her with a sudden shyness as he cut his gaze away from her and took several breaths. When he finally looked at her, he became all brisk business, even to spreading his arms to rest them over the back of his seat. "Well, that's settled—thank God. And I'm willing to bet that by the time we get to No Man's Land, we'll even have worked out where we're going to live."

Hannah hadn't thought about that. Not in the last few minutes. She opened her mouth to speak, but Slade leaned forward again. This time, he took her hands in his and held them gently. "Hannah, you're my wife. I made a few solemn, if drunken, promises to you when we married, but I remember them all. Mostly I promised to love you from that day forward. But I lied. I've loved you from the first minute I saw you. And I will always love you."

He spoke with such simple elegance and sincerity that Hannah's heart and soul were warmed in places that hadn't been warm since she'd found Mama and Papa dead. That thought sobered her some. "I don't know what we'll face when we get home, Slade."

"I know," he said softly, his love for her shining in his eyes. "But we'll face it together, Hannah. I promise you that."

HERE'S AN EXCERPT FROM *JACEY'S RECKLESS HEART*— THE NEXT EXCITING INSTALLMENT OF *THE LAWLESS WOMEN* SAGA:

Glory nodded and swiped at her eyes. "I know all that. But, Jacey, first Mama and Papa are . . . murdered. And then Hannah leaves for Boston. And now you're going to Tucson. What am I supposed to do?"

For a long moment, Jacey stared levelly at her sister. "I don't know, Glory. You're a grown woman now. You tell me what you're supposed to do."

Glory's pouting doll-face only made Jacey more impatient. Mama'd babied the nineteen-year-old girl until she couldn't do a thing for herself. That perfect little form, her auburn hair, her wide green eyes, and her helpless pose always got her what she wanted. Well, not now. Times were different. Mama and Papa were gone. Glory'd just have to get tough to survive. Starting now. "Glory, I don't mean to hurt your feelings. But I'm leaving tomorrow, and I have plans to make. I don't have time to stand here holding your hand."

When Glory's pouting frown only deepened, Jacey took a deep breath and let it out slowly. Shaking her head, feeling her heavy black braid swing with her movement, she fought for calm. "Try to understand. I *have* to do this. It's killing me to sit here, Glory. I should've gone to Boston with Hannah. She's all alone with those murdering Wilton-Humeses." Jacey pounded her fist into her other palm. "Those rich, uppity snakes-in-the-grass. Mama's own family. And to have her and Papa killed. And what do I do about it? I sit here like a clucking hen on a nest. Well, I can't do it anymore. I'll go crazy."

Glory's tears dried instantly. Her face darkened with . . . could it be? . . . anger. "I'd rather you go crazy here than go get yourself killed over a missing keepsake and a piece of spur. That's all you really have, Jacey. A piece of silver spur and a sliver of wood-frame from Great-Grandmother Ardis's portrait. With nothing more than that, you're going to race off to Tucson?"

Astonished at Glory's tirade, Jacey could almost smile at this first sign of gumption from the family's youngest. But she didn't dare. Not in this instance. So, with slow, measured steps, her booted feet scuffing across the wood floor, she advanced on Glory. "You're danged right I am. This piece of spur"—she held up the spike-like rowel she'd just strung through the silver chain around her neck—"is an exact match with Papa's. And I should know. Which one of us three girls spent the most time listening to his stories of his outlaw days? Who's held and admired his silver spurs maybe a thousand times? Me, Glory."

She paused to allow that to sink in before going on. "And now this broken-off rowel turns up here. In our house. It's not off Papa's. I've got his up in my room. So it's got to belong to someone else in the Lawless gang. And where are those men still? In Tucson. So, that's where I'm headed."

Again, she paused, staring at Glory. "The same son-of-a-gun who left his spur calling-card also took that portrait. You know he did. We—you and me, not ten minutes ago—searched Mama's room and didn't find it. And where were you when I tripped over that rug by the fireplace and came up with these things tangled together? Wasn't that you standing next to me? So, how'd they get there, Glory? Was there a fight? If so, who was in it, and why? All I've got is questions. You got any answers?"

Glory's chin came up a notch. "No, I don't. But what does it all prove? Please—just once, Jacey—*think* before you go off half-cocked. Read Hannah's letter again. It's just a passing notion that makes her even mention Mama's keepsake. She's not asking you to look for clues. All she wrote was she saw the original portrait at Cloister Point. And it started her thinking . . . where was Mama's copy?"

With her last words, Glory's face darkened. She spun around, fisting her hands at her sides. Her voice choked with emotion. "For God's sake, Jacey, Hannah was only curious. Nothing more. Why can't you let it go?"

"Let it go?" Jacey stalked over to her sister and spun her around. "I cannot believe we read the same letter. Don't you get it, Glory? The portrait is *gone*. And it's the *only* thing missing from . . . that day. Why is that, do you suppose? I'll tell you why—because someone from the old gang came here and stole that keepsake. The spur proves who it was. Trust me, this is no coincidence. It happened *the same day,* Glory. It had to have, because we were gone only that one night.''

Jacey searched Glory's eyes for understanding. ''Aren't you the least bit curious about *why*? I know I am. I've got to go to Tucson—to find out the why of it. And mark my words, I'll get my keepsake back and make some sorry old outlaw pay with his life for ever taking it in the first place.''

Glory's frown creased her brow. ''I understand how you feel, Jacey. I do. No one knows better than me what that little oil painting meant to Mama. And I know what it means to you. I do remember her saying that when she died, she wanted you to have it. But you can't—''

''I can't what? Get back what's rightfully mine? That little oil painting, as you call it, is of the only Wilton-Humes that Mama gave a fig about. And she wanted me to have it, Glory. Me.'' Jacey swallowed around the sudden constriction in her throat. ''She said I have Ardis's spunk. Her fire. Mama loved that old woman, and I reminded her of her.''

Jacey's face worked with the depth of her emotion. When she could safely speak again, she went on. ''But now, she and Papa have been taken from us. There's not a blamed thing I can do to bring them back, but I can sure as shooting get back her keepsake. And I will. It's mine now. So whoever took it, stole it from me.'' Her chest rising and falling in the deep, even breaths of firm conviction, Jacey awaited her sister's response.

For long moments, Glory stared at her. Then, without a word, she stepped around Jacey, who turned to watch her go. Head erect, her bearing queenly, Glory walked across the big comfortable room that retained the memory of the Lawless girls' childhood laughter and tears. When she reached the stairs and put her foot on the first riser, when she laid her hand on the railing, she finally turned to face Jacey.

''You *are* trying to bring Mama and Papa back, Jacey. That's what this is all about, even if you won't admit it. But I know you—you're still going to try. Once you set your mind to something, no one and nothing—not God, and not reasoning—can stop you. So, go. And don't worry about me or Biddy or the ranch. Like you said, I have to grow up.''

Tears stood again in Glory's eyes, and then spilled unheeded down her steadily pinkening cheeks. "But don't expect me to see you off tomorrow. Don't expect me to wave as you ride off to what could be *your* death, and not some sorry old outlaw's." She glared for a moment and then added, "I, for one, have had enough of death."

With that, she ascended the stairs. Jacey watched her all the way up, but not once did Glory hesitate or look back. When she was out of sight, when her footfalls no longer echoed upstairs in the hallway, when Jacey heard a door close, she looked down at her hand, at her older sister's now-crumpled letter. Dry-eyed, she lifted her gaze to the impassive stairway, set against the great room's far wall.

She relaxed her fist. Hannah's letter fluttered to the floor. Jacey then clasped the jagged piece of spur on her chain. She gripped it so tightly that its edges cut into her palm.

*JACEY'S RECKLESS HEART*— COMING IN NOVEMBER FROM ST. MARTIN'S PAPERBACKS!